FORTRESS
of
AMBROSE

BOOKS BY J. ELLE

House of Marionne Trilogy

House of Marionne
Shadows of Perl
Fortress of Ambrose

Wings of Ebony Duology

Wings of Ebony
Ashes of Gold

The Little Mermaid

Against the Tide

Park Row Magic Academy Series

A Taste of Magic
A Whisper of Curses

FORTRESS of AMBROSE

HOUSE OF MARIONNE
BOOK THREE

J. ELLE

PENGUIN MICHAEL JOSEPH

UK | USA | Canada | Ireland | Australia
India | New Zealand | South Africa

Penguin Michael Joseph is part of the Penguin Random House group of companies
whose addresses can be found at global.penguinrandomhouse.com

Penguin Random House UK,
One Embassy Gardens, 8 Viaduct Gardens, London SW11 7BW

penguin.co.uk

First published in the United States of America by Razorbill,
an imprint of Penguin Random House LLC 2025
First published in Great Britain by Penguin Michael Joseph 2025
001

Copyright © J. Elle, 2025
Map copyright © Virginia Allyn, 2025
Art on pages 493–99 adapted from Adobe Stock

The moral right of the author has been asserted

Penguin Random House values and supports copyright.
Copyright fuels creativity, encourages diverse voices, promotes freedom
of expression and supports a vibrant culture. Thank you for purchasing
an authorized edition of this book and for respecting intellectual property
laws by not reproducing, scanning or distributing any part of it by any
means without permission. You are supporting authors and enabling
Penguin Random House to continue to publish books for everyone.
No part of this book may be used or reproduced in any manner for the
purpose of training artificial intelligence technologies or systems. In accordance
with Article 4(3) of the DSM Directive 2019/790, Penguin Random House
expressly reserves this work from the text and data mining exception.

Design by Alex Campbell
Text set in Adobe Garamond Pro
Printed and bound in Great Britain by Clays Ltd, Elcograf S.p.A.

The authorized representative in the EEA is Penguin Random House Ireland,
Morrison Chambers, 32 Nassau Street, Dublin D02 YH68

A CIP catalogue record for this book is available from the British Library

HARDBACK ISBN: 978–0–241–68155–8
TRADE PAPERBACK ISBN: 978–0–241–68156–5

Penguin Random House is committed to a sustainable future
for our business, our readers and our planet. This book is made from
Forest Stewardship Council® certified paper.

*For my first writer friend,
Jessica*

A Note from the Author

The fictional settings and events in *Fortress of Ambrose* are inspired by various parts of the world. None is intended as a faithful representation of any one event, culture, or people at any point in history.

HOUSE OF AMBROSE
SPECIALTIES OFFERED

ANATOMER
Transfigurer of anatomy
Discovery: Can alter the
appearance of others

AUDIOR
Transfigurer of sound
Discovery: Still researching

SHIFTER
Transfigurer of matter
Discovery: Still researching

RETENTOR
Remover of magic
Discovery (in progress):
Repair of broken magic

CULTIVATOR
Transferer of knowledge
Discovery: Removal and storage
of parts of transferred magic for
short periods of time

DRAGUN
By invitation only

HOUSE OF ORALIA
SPECIALTIES OFFERED
by cohort

SENSARUS

EMOTER
Revealer of emotion

SENSASHIFTER
Transferer of emotional energy

CEREBVIS

AUDIOR
Transfigurer of sound

CULTIVATOR
Transferer of knowledge

CORPOREAL

ANATOMER
Transfigurer of anatomy

CORPOSHIFTER
Transferer of physical energy

DRAGUN
By invitation only

HOUSE OF PERL

SPECIALTIES OFFERED

ANATOMER — *Transfigurer of anatomy*   **AUDIOR** — *Transfigurer of sound*   **SHIFTER** — *Transfigurer of matter*

RETENTOR — *Remover of magic*   **CULTIVATOR** — *Transferer of knowledge*

DRAGUN — *By invitation only*

KNOWN SPECIALTIES

TRACER   **MEMENTAUR**

PERL DISTINCTIONS OF VIRTUE

DISCRETION   **VALOR**   **HONOR**

SACRIFICE   **LOYALTY**   **DUTY**

HOUSE OF MARIONNE
SPECIALTIES OFFERED

ANATOMER   **AUDIOR**   **SHIFTER**

Transfigurer of anatomy   *Transfigurer of sound*   *Transfigurer of matter*

RETENTOR   **CULTIVATOR**

Remover of magic   *Transferer of knowledge*

DRAGUN

By invitation only

Officium est honor volentis.

NORE'S COTTAGE
TEMPLE
MORTUARRI
OBSERVATORY
DISCOVERY WING
COURTYARD
NAUGH
ICE GARDEN

THE DRAGUNHEAD

The Dragunhead tightened his grip on the phone, wishing it were the caller's throat. After months of scheming to fix the mess the Order had made, his initial plans had failed. The Sphere's magic was *living* inside a human body. This was his last chance.

It was time to shift focus.

When the caller stopped talking to take a breath, the Dragunhead grabbed the silence in a choke hold. "At this news, I have to explore *all* options." He waited.

"You do realize the position this puts me in, right?" the voice asked, and he resisted the urge to end the call. Minions weren't useful when they rattled off nonsensical questions masquerading as intellect.

"You say that as if I have no heart," the Dragunhead said. "It complicates things for the both of us. But we must remember what's most important." He swished the untouched glass of amber liquid. *"Ad summum bonum."*

The line was silent. He could feel the tenuous hold he had on a very delicate situation. This was why before now he'd always worked alone. But the world was a glass ball, teetering on the edge of a cliff. And to rebuild it, he had to first shatter it beyond repair. For that, he needed help.

"Have I steered you wrong yet?" the Dragunhead asked.

"You have not."

"Well, then. Be scarce and wait for further instruction. We will need to shift locations." He hung up, and when he spun in his chair, his frail secretary stood in the doorway, looming like a flamingo out of season.

"Maei, no interruptions. You know the rules."

"Y-yes, sir." She fidgeted. "I only thought I overheard that we might be moving . . ."

He bit back a groan. She was a faithful helper. He could tell her to pick at the scab on her elbow and she'd do it until it bled. He stretched his arms behind his head, considering the worry written in her brow. Her mind was racing, he knew, cycling through a dozen questions about where they would be moving, when, and why. None of which he could honestly answer without causing her much anxiety. Maei was loyal with a penchant for doing the right thing. She was an ideal employee but an awful partner for what lay ahead.

He picked up a cup on his desk and slammed it down, breaking the glass.

Maei gasped, rushing to his aid with a cloth for his bleeding fingers. He watched her mind turn as she glanced from the wound, unnaturally dark blood blooming from it, to him and back to the wound, before swallowing hard and hustling to bandage him up.

"Maei, bring me my ornamental dagger, without its case."

She blinked several times. "The silver one with a gem-encrusted handle?"

"That's the one." She was special. She was a great help, but what he needed now, she couldn't give.

He would make it painless. And permanent.

She smoothed her skirts and hurried off to retrieve it. He drank the amber liquid in his glass before refilling his and pouring another, one for her this time. He met her at her desk.

"Sir, I wondered—"

"Drink up." He handed her the glass and she brought it to her lips, draining it quickly. She blew out a breath.

"Is everything alright?" She handed him the blade. Maei's chest rose and fell like a hummingbird's wings. *She knows.*

"I am sorry, Maei. Truly." He would prefer to free her rather than force her to compromise her morality. Death was a kindness. A mercy. A gift.

She trembled when he pointed the blade at her. "May the Sovereign, Sage, and Wielder judge me fairly," she muttered tearfully.

He kissed her on the forehead and ran the blade through her.

"*Yaque*," she cried before collapsing.

He stared at her as if he'd seen a ghost. He skimmed her desk as her body hit the ground, but her files had all been tidied up. Then he pulled at a dreadful feeling asleep deep in his bones. His body shuddered as the magic awakened inside him, like a bear disturbed from hibernation. The magic felt strange moving through him, not hot or cold but heavy, like a boulder that had been in place for generations.

He rolled Maei onto her back to expose her chest. He felt for a heartbeat and exhaled when there wasn't one. His hand hovered until the glow of her soul pulsed beneath his palm.

Magic rose up in him, and at the next flash, he tore the light from her corpse.

PART ONE

ONE

Jordan

Cold eats away at my bones as I search for Lady Ruby.

The Sphere's magic sludges through me, wrapping around my spine as I move my hand to my heart, which has been wounded in both the literal and figurative senses. The urge to sleep in a sunlit field of fresh jasmine and never wake up pulls at me. But the magic brings a face to mind, with dazzling brown eyes that glitter with defiance. My heart twinges with longing.

"Quell." Her name slips from my lips like a song. A wish.

I should be with her. That was the plan.

Not here, in Washington, DC, hunting down a notorious Trader who *might* be able to help me contain the magic festering inside me. My ribs begin to pulse with pain. But Quell is the Headmistress of House of Marionne now. If I lose the Sphere's magic—Quell dies.

Saving her is what matters most.

After everything I've done, I must. I try to blink her memory away and focus on the bleeding skyline of dilapidated buildings before me. The Sixth Ward's lively retail district and vibrant nightlife of east DC used to pulse with the city's heartbeat. But the few buildings still standing are boarded up and tagged with angry slashes of paint: distorted House sigils and elaborately detailed suns.

The silence reeks of death. I move carefully through the slick streets, past torn-down streetlights, busted-out windows, and the singed metal hulls of what used to be cars. The stench of rotting flesh stings my nostrils, stopping me dead in my tracks. Three bodies are tied to a storefront.

Blood for blood is written across them in bright yellow paint.

The few windows of the shop that haven't been broken are painted with the same number over and over: *1822*. The year the first House was founded by the Upper Cabinet. Also the year Misa, the ancient magic city, fell and most of the residents were burned in their beds.

My throat thickens. But it's the suns branded onto the corpses' eyelids that make bile lurch in my gut. An old ritual of Darkbearers, meant to light a path to the afterlife; an act of mercy, they called it.

"Deaus misereateur."

My hand moves from my throbbing side to the scar inches below my heart, where the Sphere's magic disappeared inside me several weeks earlier. The gash has spread into a meaty, purpling bruise across my chest and down my left side beneath my heart. Every day the flesh there thins, hanging like draped fabric over my ribs.

Toushana-bound Darkbearers . . .

On the loose . . .

Guilt threatens to choke me as my head swivels. *There was no one here to stop them.* My side throbs and I grit my teeth. I can't save Quell if the Sphere's vessel—*me*—is rotting from the inside out. *I need to be healed.* Then I need the magic out of me and into something safe. I tighten my fist and keep walking, staying out of sight, skimming for some indication of where the infamous Lady Ruby could be.

There are stories of a legendary Retentor stone with healing properties powerful enough to mend any severe magical wound. The hero always saved the day, rescuing his love from peril and curing whatever ill magic befell them with this elusive stone. Lore always has a seed of truth. Lady Ruby will know if the stone's real.

She's a Trader who's been on the brotherhood's wanted list for years. The rarer the item, the harder it is to procure, the higher the chance Ruby's tried to get her hands on it or knows how to. But she never meets for a trade in the same place twice. I couldn't even find a consistent description of her. It's taken me all these weeks just to suss out a whiff of where she *might* be. Tonight she's supposed to be meeting up for a trade here.

I skirt a fleur-de-lis drawn across the sidewalk in a red that is not paint and walk quicker, the Sphere's cold magic inside me stirring.

Clack. Clack. Clack.

My heart stutters at footsteps echoing mine.

I turn. But there is only darkness behind me.

I continue walking.

Clack. Clack. Clack. My jaw ticks. I despise games. Slipping into the shadow of the streetlights beneath an awning of a building, I listen for the direction of my follower, summoning my Dragun senses. A stir of hot magic rustles inside me like a reed tugged by the wind. Heat blossoms in my chest, pushing the Sphere's toushana aside. My senses sharpen for the first time in a long time.

The world comes alive in a symphony of sounds. The footsteps have stopped, but I can hear breathing that isn't my own. My bones tremor, the Sphere's magic pulsing inside me with its own heartbeat.

A sudden pain shoots up my spine, a thousand icy needles scrape my insides. The Sphere's warm magic retreats as the sounds and sights begin to dull.

The breathing quiets.

I ease out a shaky breath. *I am broken.*

Dueling magics, proper and dark, have lived inside me, constantly at war with one another. The warm thrum of my own magic is gone. I can't feel it at all. When I reach for magic, the Sphere's magic answers, weighty, like wearing shoes filled with lead.

After the fight at the Sphere, as the dregs of the Sphere's magic finished siphoning into me, I lay there, unable to move. When I reopened my eyes, I was somewhere else, all alone and in excruciating pain. I thought I was dead. But by the fourth day of waking up with life in my limbs,

I dragged myself up, determined to form some sort of plan. Quell and Abby were supposed to meet me at the Tavern near Chateau Soleil. But I couldn't be near them in this condition, this unsure about what the Sphere's magic inside me was doing. I refuse to accidentally hurt anyone, but especially them. Especially Quell. My eavesdropping from one northeastern Tavern to the next led me here.

Someone crosses the street up ahead before disappearing between the buildings. Fear seizes my chest. I touch the cured paint and notice it's peeling in several places. Whoever destroyed this neighborhood did it some time ago.

I hold on to the feeling of magic inside me as I close in on a girl in slick pants, a flowy teal shirt, and a silver diadem arced over her head.

Too young to be Ruby.

She dashes down the alleyway, and I catch up to her, grabbing her by the wrist. Cold snakes through my bones to my fingertips, ready to strike.

"Let me go!" She tugs against my hold. The girl's a living work of art. Her face has been painted like a canvas. Strokes of every color coil and twist around one another across her olive skin. Icy rouge on her cheeks, earthy tones slope beneath her eyes. Sharp, bright pink paints her lips. Gems adorn her thick brows, trailing around her face and neck, disappearing into her clothes.

"An Emoter." Prodigiously skilled painters who use colors to reveal emotion. My grip on her slips and she rounds her wrist, freeing herself before clamping her hold on me. She cocks her head, and surveys my chest with curiosity, not malice. I'm not sure if it's the suddenness of her touch or the way it only makes me miss Quell more, but I don't immediately resist.

"What's your name?" I ask as she shows me her palms, which have turned blue.

"I'll tell you my name if you tell me what makes you so sad."

I shift on my feet. She's far too young but maybe . . . "Ruby?"

Recognition glints in her eyes as she scopes the surroundings, looking for the Trader. My instincts were right. But she knows her.

"You're meeting her tonight," I say.

"The temperature is dropping. Can you feel it?" As she smooths her palms against her pants, the color of her palms returns to her olive skin tone.

"I'm Harmony, Secundus, fourth of my blood, Emoter candidate, sensor type. Oralia."

"I'm—"

"I know who you are." She gazes around again. Shadows begin to shift. The darkness thickens. "Look, if I were you—"

Silver protrudes from her throat and the sentence finishes with a gurgle. Her body hits the ground with a thud. Her attacker lunges for me, a fresh blade slashing in my direction, when several things happen at once.

TWO

Quell

Silence hangs in the air around me like a guillotine. I'm still cold from the cloak I used to travel to the Sixth Ward in DC. My heart rams in my chest as I skim the darkness, looking for Jordan. But there isn't a person in sight. Only moonlight washing the ground in light, telling secrets the darkness was supposed to hide.

The last time I saw Jordan, he was surrounded by Draguns and I was riding away on a horse with Yagrin at the reins. He was supposed to meet back up with Abby and me at a Tavern. We needed to hatch a plan to deal with the Dragunhead and Beaulah trying to steal the Sphere's magic—everyone's magic, *my* magic!

But he never showed.

And worse, Yagrin and Nore agreed to find the piece of the ancestral House of Ambrose Scroll that promised immortality, so if the Sphere's magic is lost and the Headmistresses die, Jordan could use it to save my life. But there's no word from either of them. My mother's remains at House of Perl, Beaulah trying to use me to steal the Sphere's magic, House of Duncan showing up to fight House of Marionne, my grandmother dying . . . It all still haunts my dreams.

But it's the whispered rumors about what Jordan might have done that congeals my blood more than any memory.

I move faster down the streets, careful to skirt the streetlights. I've heard that magic is dying out, the Order is fracturing as Marked turn on one another, that House of Marionne didn't hold a funeral for my grandmother. I've also heard rumors the Dragun brotherhood has disbanded and Beaulah's niece, Adola, is recruiting ex-brotherhood to their side. Darker rumors suggest Jordan tried to steal the magic, and it *killed* . . .

A lump rises in my throat as I hug around myself, searching these battered city streets. When I intercepted a deal among a seedy group of Traders two days ago, I overheard that the Dragunheart would be in the Sixth Ward of DC tonight. It could be bad gossip, but I am taking my chances.

The boy who first saw in me what I couldn't see in myself *is alive*. I know it in my bones. I just have to find him.

If the Sphere's really broken, if the Order's really fallen apart, we will face its destruction, and whatever it means, together. Like we faced Beaulah at the Sphere, her Draguns at the inn in Aronya. Together we are unbeatable. Together we are free.

My feet are lead, doubt trying to outweigh my hope as I read messages painted across what's left of the buildings in this ransacked neighborhood. There's no sign of Jordan anywhere.

Toushana moves in my chest, and I try to focus on the chill to grow its intensity to bring some comfort to my shaky hands. It's been weeks since I felt my magic burn intensely. I assumed it was exhausted from how I used it, harder than I ever have—consumed with rage—trying to break the Sphere. Before realizing Beaulah was using me and no amount of fury would take away the feeling of not having my mom. My physical bruises have healed at least, thanks to Abby, and I'm lucky my travel cloak got me here.

I hustle along the sidewalk, searching for some sign of life on the streets, and my shoes slide against something slick, a fleur-de-lis—my House sigil—painted on the ground in angry strokes of fresh blood.

As my grandmother died, she urged me to find Nore, to work with her. For what, I'm not sure.

But I'm done taking orders.

I haven't given much thought to the Chateau or my old maezres. Abby and I have kept our heads down the last several weeks, glancing only at the occasional headline. I look around and feel sick. The neighborhood's retail shops are hulls of carnage. Hollow high-rises with shattered windows loom like soulless monsters. The world is blurring at its seams, bleeding two realities together that should never touch. *This isn't my mess.* I tighten my fists. I need to know that my magic, and Jordan, will be okay. I was Beaulah's puppet, I won't be anyone else's, even for a good cause. That is not freedom.

I cross the street, where a critter scurries away from a body, looking for some sign of Jordan. The boy who set out to take my life, but gave everything to save it in the end. I run harder, searching, listening, nails digging into my palms, until I hear a commotion, and follow the sounds around a building.

A hooded figure holds Jordan from behind, edging a dagger to his throat.

My heart knocks in my chest. I'm flooded with memories of the last time we were together. He'd finally opened up to me about the scars of his past, about how trapped he's felt his entire life by the Order, how in my eyes is where he finds courage to fight for freedom.

And I betrayed him.

I snatched the Dragunheart pendant right from under his nose.

And yet he chased me down and fought off the Draguns trying to kill me. When Beaulah tried to coerce me to break the Sphere, it was Jordan who reminded me of who I am. Finding him feels like finding a piece of me that's been missing: a home.

That's being ransacked.

Jordan wrestles the blade from him and shoves it backward into the attacker's side. The assailant groans, keeling over. But Jordan holds his body against himself as a shield, spinning to block another strike from someone lurking in the shadows. Voices sound somewhere. The feeling of being watched sticks to my skin, and my world dizzies as another hurtles past me, my eyes too slow to translate the darkness.

Jordan howls in pain as a blade disappears into his shoulder.

One attacker shoves another. "*No* hurting him!" He reaches for silver restraints, and it shakes me back to the present. I pull at the bite of chill in my veins, determined to intervene.

But then Jordan's body begins to bleed shadows. Dark magic engulfs the alleyway. And it's the most comforting sight I've seen in a long time.

Until the others bleed shadows, too.

I blink, watching the magic come from *inside* them. All.

The way only those bound to dark magic, like me, can do.

The darkness around us deepens. Shadows swallow the fight, despite the dagger stuck in his shoulder.

At the same time, my toushana finally answers my call, seeping through my hands in a thrilling chill that jolts me into the nearest attacker. I wrap my toushana-bleeding hands around his face. He howls, clawing at my grip. I shove him with all my might against the brick, and he collapses. Jordan makes short work of the others, wielding darkness, piling up bodies on the ground.

He spots me and turns pale as he holds the last attacker's body, silver buried in their chest as he checks some kind of mark on the back of their neck.

"Quell."

"Jordan, I—"

He throws the body down, skims their pockets, takes their weapons, and sprints away.

THREE

Nore

The tattoo shop doors were coated in yew leaf stickers and neon paint. Nore had always pictured her first trip to an Ambrose tattoo parlor under very different circumstances. Before stepping inside, she gazed around for the dead, her grip tight on her bag strap.

The Pact her House had with their ancestors haunted her day and night. It gave Ambrose the ability to push the bounds of magic. In exchange the House Headmistress gave the dead her heart. They channeled its magic to cling to life. But Nore didn't have magic. Her heart in their glass box would be the death of her.

She had to find the full Immortality Scroll before her time was up.

She held in a breath, searching the skies outside, but they were clear. When she stepped inside, the place reeked of sour peckle smoke, but the three tattooists at their chairs didn't seem to notice.

"The wait's about an hour," the tattoo artist farthest from the door said. Brown hair rippled down her back. The sides of her shaved head were branded with a gate of tally marks. Nore pulled her thick red hair over her shoulder, her sleeves down and collar closed. She had zero markings. And if anyone figured out who she was, she didn't want to give them any excuse to look at her sideways.

A handful of seats were occupied. She'd discovered half the Scroll almost two months ago, digging up her inaugural Headmistress's grave, when the Sphere broke. Her brother, Ellery, tried to steal it, but the scuffle ripped the half Scroll in two. She needed the missing half.

Or when her brother went through with his threat to kill their mother, Headship of House of Ambrose would pass to her.

Nore sat and watched the door, waiting for the person she was looking for to walk through. He was the key to finding the rest of the Scroll. She was sure of it.

When it opened and the tall, dapper Dublin Kyn walked in, her nails bit into the underside of her thigh. He got the same greeting and strode over and sat two seats down from her. She sat up, trying to look casual, flipping through art samples. But she couldn't tear her eyes away from Dublin, whose swept-back reddish-brown hair and lightly stubbled beard only punctuated his cavalier aura. He wore one of those shirts that didn't look like it had top buttons, showing a sliver of chest. His brightly colored suit fit him with a precision that meant it could only be tailored.

She watched him with a hand gripped on her seat. For someone who'd built a reputation for methodically skirting the Order's control over his life, she'd expected someone more . . . discreet.

Dublin was one of her House's most infamous graduates. He was offered his top internship choice after Third Rite but publicly announced he was going to take a sabbatical year to visit the Order's most mystical locations instead. A slap in the Council of Mothers' face. At first, the Council tried to stop Kyn from making a mockery of the rules. But everything they could hold over him—status in the Order, membership in a House, camaraderie, access to Marked venues, wealth—he didn't actually care about. Escaping the Order sounded impossible, but somehow this man had done it. Questions scraped at her skull as he settled into his chair, unbothered.

He'd spent weeks in the Sahara; winter in Mali; months, one headline said, in a tiny village in the Paro valley of Bhutan. He was famously quoted saying, "I want to tour places so remote, not a living soul would dare follow me there." Unmarked headlines had Dublin's name everywhere, heralding his travels to the most gravity-defying, difficult places in the world to reach. He published excerpts from his journals that had detailed depictions of everywhere he traveled and all he explored. Proof he'd seen it with his own two eyes. He used magic to build the life *he* wanted, gloating for all the glory the Unmarked world had to offer. He returned to the Council after two years of travels with a journal chronicling all he'd seen and said that after seeing *all* magic had to offer, he was bored with it. Then he rescinded his membership in the Order himself.

If anyone alive had tried to hunt down the missing piece of the Scroll, Dublin Kyn had.

And Nore'd bet he'd written about it in his legendary travel journal.

One of the tattooists' chairs emptied. A client with a fresh cherry blossom tree snaking around their arm slung their bag over their shoulder and eased in Dublin's direction.

"I don't mean to be weird," they said. "But, um, are you Dublin Kyn?"

He flipped his hair back, foot propped up on his knee. "I am." He felt around for something to write with. "And you are?"

They fanned themself. "Could I have your autograph?"

Nore grimaced as they raised their shirt and had Dublin sign across their ribs, then professed they were never bathing that part of their body again. Another couple of waiting patrons hopped up courageously as well. He signed whatever they asked and suggested taking a few pictures before the shop settled again. Nore caught herself staring and jerked her chin away. Dublin grinned as he pulled a brown leather journal with a brass clasp around it from his satchel. Nore's heart skipped a beat. She leaned forward in her seat, trying for a glimpse of the pages.

"Is there something you'd like me to sign?" he asked.

Nore hesitated, chewing on how she could get close to someone like him, who lathered in attention. He didn't even bother to look anyone in the eye who approached him. And the way he kept flipping his damn hair.

Yagrin had long hair, and he never flipped it. He was too serious to flip his hair. But he'd rake his hands through it when he felt pensive. Sometimes he'd ask her to play in it, raking lines down his scalp. It relaxed him like nothing else. Of course, he had no idea Nore knew any of that. Because he had no idea the girl he was in love with, the girl he thought was dead—*Red*—was also Nore. She slumped in her seat, more irritated than sad at her predicament. She made sure to appear indifferent to Dublin, awaiting her answer.

She would deny him the one thing he wanted—her interest.

That would lure him in so she could get a better look at that journal.

"My body parts are just fine without your endorsement, but thanks."

He closed his journal and smiled, drawn to her numbness of his ego. Sarcasm rarely failed her. Dublin flipped his hair again and she tossed him the hair tie on her arm.

"Seems like you need it."

He rotated in his seat to look right at her. "You're funny."

"You're . . . good at signing things."

"Do you know who I am?"

"I'm sure you would love to tell me."

Again, he smirked. "It's said the view from the top of the Kenetican mountains will make anyone cry."

She'd heard. Her brother had taken her hiking twice. It was pretty, but not her idea of recreation. If Dublin was intrigued by her wit, she definitely wasn't going to give him the satisfaction of the punch line.

"From the peaks of the Kenetican, the clouds condense on your face, forming what looks like tears. Only one human has ever actually been there before."

"You do know who I am, *or* you hike."

"Both."

"But you said you didn't know—" His mouth bowed as he remembered what she'd actually said. "Clever." He extended a hand. "I'm Dublin. It's nice to meet you." When she let his hand go, he held on to hers and quirked a brow. Nore held up three fingers, then knotted them. One for each yew leaf of the sigil of their House.

"What other hobbies do you have?" He sat back in his seat with a sugary grin.

"I enjoy painting. I've dabbled in oils. I enjoy fire made with my hands, really anything with my hands. I used to—" The truth formed a lump in her throat. "Have a farm."

"The more simply we live, the wiser and happier we are. The layers we add are full of complications."

"So much complication."

"It's odd to meet someone . . ." He grasped at the air. This was an Order-approved tattoo shop, though still open to Unmarked. Discretion was paramount. "Who has such a fresh way of seeing things."

Oh gosh, is he flirting? She fought the urge to vomit.

"What do you make of the extreme *weather* we've been having? *Everyone* is talking about it." *The Sphere shattering, I mean.*

"I don't worry about the *weather*. I try to act as if the weather doesn't exist at all."

"What if a storm is coming, Mr. Kyn?"

"I suppose I'll have to find a really good umbrella. And it's Dublin."

"There was just a *huge* storm, actually, Dublin."

"So glad I was out of the country for it."

There were so many things she wanted to ask him, such as how he got away from the Order. And what it cost him. How he created a new life without changing his name. Or living in hiding. He jotted something down in his journal on the page he'd held before. As he wrote, he tucked his bottom lip, pausing to tap his jaw a few times.

"You're up." The tattoo artist gestured at her. "My gun is sparking." She tucked away her tools, sliding them into metal drawers before tidying up her workspace. "Let's move to the back room."

"Would you care to join me?" Nore stood, hoping she'd played her cards right with Dublin.

He slapped his journal closed and tucked it under his arm. He watched her eye it, then said, "I would hate to impose."

"It's a lot less crowded back there," the artist said, and Nore made a point not to look her way. "I can probably work you in faster."

"Sure," Dublin said. "Why not?"

The back room was elaborately decorated with Ambrose paraphernalia. The artist ducked out to get her things and Nore took it all in. Framed clippings from *Debs Daily* commissioning this location. Another with a ribbon cutting. A poster for an upcoming Audior concert.

Beside the shop owner in one picture was someone Nore recognized, with cropped bangs, a severe expression, and gray hair. *Mother, decades younger.* Nore's jaw locked.

Dublin set his satchel in a chair before walking the length of the room with hands clasped behind his back.

"Reliving the glory days?" she asked him.

"Just observing. I meant what I said about the weather."

"Mm-hmm."

"Truly, I'm not lying. I have nothing to hide."

Her chest squeezed. *A life I dream of.* "Surely you've found *some* discoveries satisfying. The Immortality Scroll is quite impressive as far as magical accomplishments go." Her heart hammered.

"Eh."

She slid to the edge of her chair. "Is that indifference?"

"Ambrosers have tried to find that Scroll for generations. I looked, too. Learned all kinds of things about the places where it's hidden. But death is what makes living life so thrilling. I don't need an endless one."

His satchel with the journal inside still sat on a nearby chair. "What brought you here today?"

"I just returned from Croatia. I get a new tattoo to commemorate a trip. Call it a tradition from my House that stuck, I suppose."

He might live on his own terms, but he was Ambrose-bred. *How is such a thing even possible?* Their world couldn't give him the fame he craved. So he found it elsewhere. Loyal to himself, like everyone else in the Order.

"Ready?" the tattoo artist asked when she returned.

"Oh!" Nore hadn't *actually* planned to get a tattoo. "Dublin, why don't you go?"

"Ladies first. I insist."

Nore hesitated. Dublin's brow furrowed.

She climbed into the chair.

"Tally mark? How many?"

If she was going to get a permanent mark, it wasn't going to be anything her House made her. She agreed with Dublin on that. Instead it would be something that meant a lot to her.

"Can you do hemlock flowers in the shape of a heart?"

The tattooist nodded, and Nore adjusted her clothes to expose her hip. She didn't want to answer questions about what it meant. Dublin jotted something in his journal before setting it back on the chair.

"Why poison?" he asked.

Her heart pounded in its cage as a flood of frustration reddened her cheeks. "You defy possibilities. But in my experience some are finite. For me, love is an impossibility. And this is a reminder of that."

"You only grow more intriguing," Dublin said, as the artist started the drawing. "You're very brilliant. A deep thinker."

"I'm aware."

He took more notes.

"You've been writing in that thing since you arrived."

"Not *writing*. Revising, tweaking, making minor adjustments."

"Still, it's rude." She held out her hand and her pulse thrummed. He handed the journal to her. She looked at what he was sketching. He'd crammed a drawing of her in a tiny space between all kinds of dated notes. *Several* were about travel. Her grip on the journal tightened. Next to the sketch he'd written then erased a word. He took the journal back and thumbed through the well-worn pages before returning it to his satchel. "Not much room left these days."

He said a few more things but something struck her.

Had he said *places* when he was talking about looking for the Scroll? As in, not one.

"I take it everywhere. There are certain first impressions I don't want to forget. You're a rare find," he said, just as the tattooist finished.

She stared at the sprawling buds carving red lines through her irritated pale skin. Her heart twinged. She let the tattooist bandage it before readjusting her clothes. Dublin moved into the chair. He took off his shirt, and the artist began a drawing on his clavicle. As he stared at the ceiling, Nore moved closer to his satchel.

"Your Unmarked accolades are endless," she said. "How well rounded are you in the Marked world?"

"Try me."

To keep him distracted as she snooped, Nore questioned him about every manner of magical anatomy that she could think of. When she ran out of those questions, she asked him to name every discovered enhancer stone in alphabetical order. Only once did the tattoo artist glance at her as she traded the journal in his satchel for a book she'd brought with her.

The tattooist finished. A small pair of dragon wings ornamented his clavicle like a pendant. He sat up, adjusting his clothes.

"Oh, look at the time," he said, grabbing his bag strap and roping it over his shoulder. "I'm only visiting for a few days. But I'd like to see you again. Are you free tonight?"

"I might be," she lied. Anything to keep him from growing suspicious as she hooked her own bag, with his journal hidden inside, onto her arm.

"Meet me at Le Blanc on East Third at seven." He stood, dusted off his clothes, and moved toward the door.

Nore smiled, willing herself to blush.

"Hope to see you then, miss?" He scrubbed a palm down his face. "I can't believe I don't know your name."

She froze. She told herself she wasn't hiding anymore.

"Delia. Which reminds me, did you do all of your traveling alone?" *Who else knows what he discovered about the Scrolls? A friend? A lover?*

"I have instant friends everywhere I go." He grabbed the knob. "I'm never alone."

"Funny, to me that sounds very lonely."

He laughed as he pulled the door open. "Well, perhaps you could be the first one. See you tonight, Delia." He tipped his head and left. Nore collapsed against the wall.

The tattooist exhaled, too. "I never want to do that again." She held out her hand, and Nore filled it with a few gems she'd brought from Dlaminaugh.

"Thank you, seriously, so much."

"Sure. Give my love to your brother."

There was that sick feeling again. Everyone loved her brother, Ellery. The brother who wanted to kill her to take Headship of their House. The brother who was out there somewhere, plotting to find her.

"Sure thing." Nore dashed out the shop's back-alley door toward a waiting Yagrin.

FOUR

Yagrin

Nore strutted toward Yagrin with a satisfied smirk, hand clutched around something. She was smart. Long red hair. Soft-spoken but with angry eyes. When she focused intensely on something, she'd chew her bottom lip so hard it was often swollen on the right side.

"Well?" he asked. "Did you find out if he's ever looked for the Scroll?"

The Immortality Scroll outlined the steps to achieve a one-use sort of magic for an endless life. *Even* for someone who had already died. Her brother had a piece of the Scroll. They needed to steal it back. Jordan wanted him to assemble the Scroll pieces to be ready to save Quell's life if it came down to it. But the other half was still somewhere. And that seemed easier to focus on finding first.

Yagrin was going to find the pieces of the Scroll, alright.

And steal them for himself.

Red will live again.

Jordan was doing just fine with the world of magic on his shoulders, he bet. It was just like him to take the Sphere's power *literally* into his own hands. Yagrin didn't care about magic or the world. He just wanted Red back. If it meant stealing from his brother, so be it. Jordan Wexton would be *just* fine. It was Yagrin who lived at the bottom of the barrel. No more.

But he and Nore had been searching for weeks and turned up nothing. Nore agreed to help in exchange for kidnapping her mother from

Ellery once the Scroll was in hand. The bargain had surprised Yagrin. She didn't seem close with her mother. Over the last several weeks, she hadn't mentioned her more than once, and when she did, her tone was rife with disgust.

Yagrin wasn't sure stalking Dublin Kyn was the best idea either. But Nore drafted a chart to explain the statistical likelihood that someone of Dublin's reputation and experience would have at least researched where the missing piece of the Scroll could be. All the endless research Nore'd done on Order territories and geography, the deep dive into archival maps in Unmarked history in case it was hiding in plain sight, had gone nowhere.

Yagrin didn't need research. He worked on instinct. A person's actions revealed their truest desires, not their words. And it was clear to him that Nore was desperate to find the lost Scroll half. Almost too desperate . . . Either she feared what Jordan would do if she failed to keep her end of the bargain or she had ulterior motives. He cleared his throat.

But so did he.

They would be on the same team until they weren't anymore.

Nore's smile widened as she drew out the anticipation, and it ground his annoyance. Another reason he preferred to work alone.

"Out with it," he demanded, reaching for what appeared to be a book in her hand. "What is it?"

"Stole it right from under his nose."

He tried to take it from her, but she didn't let go, raising a single brow.

"Can I, er, see it, please?"

She released it. *Intellectus secat acutissimum* was inscribed on its leather-bound cover.

"The personal discoveries of Dublin Kyn. How?"

She went on to tell him about how she made a deal with the tattooist to help her get them alone when the sky suddenly darkened. Nore grew pale, looking over her shoulder.

"Not here," she said, taking the book and walking off at a quick stride. "Can you cloak?"

"Magic's been funny since the Sphere broke. You have any transport powder?" he asked.

"I—um, no, I don't. All out." She hurried, leaving him there, and he had to hustle to keep up when she stopped several blocks away to find a discreet spot.

Lit-Tea-Rally was a quaint used-bookstore teahouse. Yagrin opened the door and stepped aside to let her through. A line stretched from the counter in a room full of books, bistro tables, and cozy chairs. But she skirted the crowd and stared out the shop window.

"What is it?"

"Nothing."

His jaw set at the lie. Running around with an heir in the Order, what had become of him? When the sky began to brighten, Nore blew out a sharp breath and held her stomach.

"Would you like a lemon poppy-seed muffin? I read the heir of House Ambrose likes lemon."

"You've *read* about me?"

"I've read about all the heirs, their families, their histories. It is part of Perl's House studies."

Nore hugged around herself. "I'm fine." She skipped the line and traipsed through towering bookshelves to the back of the store near the historical section. He followed. She slid into a seat at a small table, and though the chair beside her was open, he sat across from her.

Yagrin knew he was selfish, but he wasn't a monster. So he'd done his best to keep his distance to avoid giving her the wrong impression while they worked together. The nights she spent researching, he'd rest. Then they'd switch. When they ate, they'd take turns, never opening an opportunity for conversation. This girl would hate him by the end of their time together—because the minute they got their hands on that final Scroll piece, he was done helping her.

And he wasn't sorry for it. Since when had anyone ever given consideration to what he wanted? His father's shadow loomed, the sting of his "love" still hot on Yagrin's cheeks so many years later. His aunt had left her mark, too, in bruises and canine bite marks all over his body. He had been broken, beaten, and bred to be an assassin errand-boy for House of Perl. He was resigned, at first, to do what he was told and steal in-between moments to live his life with Red.

That would be enough, he had told himself. Until the Order killed her.

But if Red could live... He forced down the lump in his throat. Maybe revenge wasn't the only thing worth his life's devotion. For once, he was putting himself first.

Nore reached for the journal. "You're going to have to get closer."

He hesitated but moved to the chair beside her. The smell of her assaulted him. Rubbery and plastic, with an undertone of florals. "You smell like . . . paint?"

Her face flushed.

"Didn't take Ambrosers for the creative type."

"I'm not your typical Ambroser."

Yagrin's lip twitched. A pair sauntered by, flipping through a stack of books. When the coast was clear, she pulled out the journal and set it on the table and they both reached to unlatch the strap at the same time, fingers brushing.

She snatched hers back. He did, too.

"Go on," he said. With a twist, the brass hook opened for her, and his heart skipped a beat. For once, thoughts of the Sphere bleeding out weren't swarming in his head. Instead he could see a nest of dark red hair shrouding a face bright with laughter. He could hear her laugh deep in his soul. A laugh that set his heart on fire. A laugh that once comforted like a hug but now haunted him like a ghost. In the Unmarked world, she wasn't consumed with anyone or anything, other than what brought her happiness. She lived wild and free.

And she died because of me.

Yagrin tightened his fist as Nore opened the journal. She flipped pages, noting the dates on each one. The pages weren't long entries as he expected, more of a smattering of one-liners. Some pages had sketches with a word or phrase next to it. And a date. Everything had a date.

He found a page with a sketch of a girl with large eyes. Next to it was the word *conundrum*. And today's date. Nore peered over to see what he was looking at, her fiery hair grazing his arm. It sent tingles through him. It wasn't the same shade as Red's, and Nore didn't look anything like her, really. But the touch was enough to send shock waves through him as he stood on the precipice of possibility that he could see Red again. Nore pulled her hair over her shoulder. He cleared his throat.

"That one is from the tattoo shop," she said. "He drew it while we were talking." She turned the page and gasped. *Scroll research*. Nore's mouth pushed sideways. Yagrin put some distance between them and blinked, staring at the words. The letters had been traced several times.

A simple title, in minuscule handwriting, inconspicuously placed at the bottom corner of the page. Like an afterthought. There were comments on the weather. Some doodles of a rose garden. The next several pages were mostly missing. Black and jagged as if they'd been burned out.

"There's something here."

Yagrin watched Nore trace a constellation drawn on the page. Each of its four corners connected to a sketch: Flowers. A wolf's head. A book. And a drama mask. Her tongue poked her cheek.

"There's some connection between the Houses and the Scroll. This means something."

"Does it, or is he just an amateur artist?"

She slammed it shut. "We have to get him to tell us what it means."

"Did he say where he was going?"

"He did when he asked me to dinner."

Yagrin didn't know what he was expecting her to say, but that wasn't it. So be it. "Where is the dinner and what time? I'll make him."

"You're going to hurt him." There was a lilt of surprise in her tone.

"He's going to tell us what we want to know."

"You don't strike me as a violent person. There has to be another way."

"I could care less what a little heiress thinks of me." He pulled out and flipped the Dragun coin in his pocket. Just because they'd been working together for weeks didn't mean she knew him.

Last Season, she was a name on a page, an invisible heir to a House he couldn't give two shits about. Oh, there were all kinds of rumors about the heir to House of Ambrose and her overprotective mother. Some said she was sickly. Others thought she was conceited so she separated herself from everyone. There were other *strange* rumors, like her mother had possessed her magically. And it went horribly wrong, which forced her to keep to herself. But House of Ambrose was a place for the magic obsessed. It was the *last* place or people he ever thought about.

Nore's lips pursed and a challenge glinted in her gray stare. But she only turned and gestured for him to follow.

Dublin hadn't wandered far.

They found him interrogating a host outside a restaurant. He was exactly as the media described him: neat, long hair, warm tan skin that oozed with *ask me where I've been*, and a tone that dripped with condescension.

Nore folded her arms. "I don't think he should see me."

"Stay. You will alarm him."

As if on cue, Dublin turned and gaped at Nore.

"You!" He strode toward them, glaring at her with a dark expression. Something sharp flashed, hidden in his hand.

Yagrin reached a protective arm backward. The hostess yelped, pulling out her phone.

"Look, we'll return the book." Yagrin had expected him to be furious, but *this* he didn't expect. "We just have a few questions."

Dublin's gaze darted to the bag on Nore's arm. "I should have recognized you." An ambitious gleam shined in Dublin's eyes. "You have any idea of the value on a vial of your blood?" He swiped at Nore and the silver tip of a knife poked from his fist. She cried out, holding her arm. Yagrin urged her back.

A guy like Dublin didn't need money. Yagrin dodged as the blade swiped past again.

"Maybe we can make a barter," he said.

"Yagrin!"

But he held up a hand. He knew what he was doing. "Tell us what the sketches mean on the constellation. Somehow it's connected to the Scroll. And we'll give you a sample of her blood. You can gloat in all the glory you want. Just say she got away." No one would touch Nore's blood. They had to send the message to her brother that *they* had the upper hand.

"Your brother would accept that excuse?" Dublin asked her. "For some useless details about each of the Houses."

What a piece of work her brother is. To put a hit out on his own sister. When Yagrin turned to look at Dublin again, he prepared to lunge.

"Perls are all liars."

Muscle memory took over, his Dragun senses awakening. He shoved Dublin in the chest, knocking him backward. Then he gripped his throat, closing his fingers tight against the windpipe. The blade hit the ground and he kicked it away.

The hostess's eyes grew as she watched, filming.

"Handle her," he said to Nore.

The air was crisp, trees still. He broke out in a cold sweat. But he held tighter, waiting for the cold toushana to answer. Nore hadn't moved.

"*Nore*, the host. Her phone."

No toushana zipped through the air to aid him. Dublin clawed at his grip. He felt his hold slipping. He needed her magic. "Whatever you've got, Nore. I need it."

"Help!" Nore screamed. "He's deranged, *please*!" Nore staggered into the hostess stand, *hard*, and it tumbled over. Menus, the hostess's purse, and all manner of things spilled out onto the sidewalk. *What on earth is she doing?* Magic, he meant—magic, for Sovereign's sake! When the hostess bent over to gather her things, Nore slipped the thinnest blade from her sleeve. But before Yagrin could see what she did with it, Dublin pulled free.

He shot them one last hateful glance, snatched the bag with his journal Nore had dropped, and scowled before rushing into street traffic, disappearing. Yagrin grabbed Nore, who was dislodging her blade from the hostess's hand, and dashed down an alleyway.

They came to a stop once Yagrin could feel his head throbbing harder than his feet on the cement. His lungs burned. He couldn't remember the last time he literally ran from a consequence.

His magic didn't answer. A chill slid up his spine. The Sphere's magic lived inside Jordan now. Was his brother okay? He paced and noticed Nore still catching her breath.

"Are you alright?"

She used the hem of her skirt to wipe the blood off her arm, staring in the direction Dublin had gone.

"You said I didn't seem like a violent person."

"You don't," she said. "I never said I wasn't."

He was speechless.

"Besides, she'll be fine. And—" She dangled the girl's phone.

He collapsed against the brick wall in the alley, replaying everything that just happened. Something irked him. "Why would your brother want your blood?"

She was sweating. "It is probably some way he's trying to steal Headship."

Yagrin raked a hand through his hair, trying to make sense of how things got so out of hand. "I asked you to help. You didn't even try to use magic quietly."

She fidgeted, refusing to look him in the eye.

He stepped closer.

Her hand tightened around her blade.

FIVE

Quell

As Jordan darts away, and before I have a moment to wonder why, someone grabs me from behind. I shove an elbow backward and pull at the cold weight of my toushana. But my magic sputters out in whiffs of darkness and only from one hand.

So I opt for a threat.

"You can let me go, or I will burn your eyes out of their sockets."

They release me and take off. Jordan is already across the intersection and down a block, running with a limp. I chase after him.

"Slow down," I yell when I'm close enough to shout. "Jordan, please wait!"

He stops suddenly, and I do, too. His skin has a sickly pallor. Where he was sharp and edged before, now he is hollow.

"Stay back." The knot at his throat bobs. "You more than anyone need to be far away from me."

As if I could stay away now that I've found him. I step toward him. He moves back, raising his hands. Darkness bleeds from him and a cloud of toushana surrounds him in a rush that I envy. It is so strong. And it's coming from *within* his body. He's not calling it *to* him.

"I mean it, Quell. Get away." He sways.

Shadows siphon back inside him, not vanishing in the distance as his toushana once did. It is hiding *inside* him like mine does. I rush to his side.

"What's happened?" I reach for him and he winces, protecting his torso with an elbow. I pull his shirt up and gasp. His body is badly bruised, and his ribs are partly decayed.

"Jordan," I gasp.

"It's the Sphere's magic," he says. "All I could salvage. The rest is gone. This is all we have left." He stares off, haunted. "There was nowhere safer."

Tears sting my eyes as I glare at the wound slowly killing him.

Everyone I love dies.

After all we fought through, Beaulah's Draguns, freeing myself from grief, Jordan pulling the Order's claws out of his skin. Didn't we just touch freedom? Now fate would rip it out of my hands. I shove the tears off my cheeks. Cold thrashes in my chest with a comforting sharpness.

"I won't stand for this. *I refuse.*"

Jordan shakes his head. "*I* will fix this," he says. "The Sphere's magic is still tied to the Headmistress's lives. If it is lost, you die." He swallows.

I run my fingers across his purpled skin. The flesh is tender. *Why is this happening? I need to talk to Abby and Nore.* "This has to come out of you. And soon."

"It's more than your life, Quell, it's all magic. For your toushana to survive, for any magic to survive, I have to keep the magic inside me alive."

"It's killing you!"

Jordan moves the hair out of my face, pushing it behind my shoulder before he traces my cheek slowly. Then my jaw, even slower. His touch is like a blanket when it's cold out. I curl into him, laying my head on his chest. He winces and I hesitate.

"It's okay," he insists.

My head fits perfectly under his chin and I listen to the thrum of his heart, synced in melody with mine. A song trying to compose itself.

"I will fix this," he says.

"*We* will fix this."

"It's not safe, both strands of magic in me are unpredictable. They don't . . ." He huffs, exasperated. "Answer when I want. They're strong when I need them to be subtle, weak when I need to be forceful. And the toushana seems to be the fiercest. I've never felt more out of control in my entire life. There are moments I worry—" He gazes off with a wild look in his eye. "Never mind."

"You always say magic doesn't serve us. We serve magic. Well, you're its vessel now."

"I don't want to be its vessel. I just want it safe. But I can feel it attaching to me. It might be too late."

"We still have to try."

He opens my palm and kisses the soft flesh of my hand. "You being here, holding you like this, feels like . . ." His eyes water. He looks away. But I pull his face back to mine, and he says, "It feels like the sun shining after a long rain. Like a meadow of wildflowers just in bloom."

I rise on my toes and meet his lips. My eyes close, rimmed with tears. For all it has cost to get us here. For all it's going to cost to keep us here. He parts his mouth, his tongue exploring, and our bodies melt into one another. He holds on to me tightly and it feels like it did the last time we were this close. Like hope isn't a dream. And our future hasn't already been decided for us. He kisses me deeper and I let myself taste his love, believing all it promises. That it won't ever leave me like everyone else I've loved has. That a life in hiding with toushana isn't all my mother's death will amount to. That the girl who should be dead by now will fly, one day.

Jordan's hold tightens around me, closing the sliver of distance between our bodies. He breaks the kiss, pressing his forehead to mine as his thumb strokes my lips.

"I dream that this could be us forever."

"I am yours, Jordan."

He tries but fails to bite the smile away from his lips. "Say that again."

"I'm yours." I pull us apart and set my hand back on his chest where the bruise is the worst. "And *you* are *mine*. *We* fix this. Which includes dealing with those people after you. Who—"

His jaw ticks. "Darkbearers. The way toushana moved back there, I just knew."

My mind races, remembering that Beaulah tried her hardest to make me into a Darkbearer, a toushana-bound magic wielder who weaponized Dysiis's teaching to terrorize and pillage to feed their own power. Even though they are not all monsters, Beaulah was trying to control me, and I almost fell for it.

"They want the Sphere's magic," he says, his gaze moving beyond me.

"You hold all of magic's future inside you. Of course they do." Suddenly, magic shudders in my chest. The sharp cold twists painfully. Toushana rushes through me like a live wire, bubbling beneath my skin. It stings.

He shoves me away. "Did you feel that?"

Everything burns. I stumble backward, when I notice toushana bleeding from him again. But when he closes his fist to call the magic back, it doesn't stop, shadows billowing from him like smoke. The burning tugs beneath my skin, growing sharper, as if my magic is being pulled from my body. To *his*. I try to go to him, but he puts more distance between us.

"*Away*, please!"

The pain is so strong my head rings. Then slowly, as his shadows settle, seeping back into him, the searing feeling of magic settling in my body curls around my bones. "*What* was that?"

"The trace. It's confusing the magic."

"I don't understand," I say, inspecting the parts of my skin where the hot sensation was the worst.

"Like calls to like." His skin is clammy. "Because of the trace between us, the magic in me is a part of the magic in you. It is pulling your magic to mine like a magnet."

That's how it felt. Like my magic was going to rip itself out of my skin.

"Because we're bonded, there's a bridge between us that magic doesn't have to work very hard to cross. And I can't seem to stop it. *I tried.*" He widens the distance between us and shakes his head. "You have to stay away, Quell."

His words hit me like a hammer to glass, like the wings I just dared to spread have been clipped. But if his magic pulls at mine and he can't stop it, he is right. Until we can get the Sphere's magic out of him or better control it, touching is a risk.

He stuffs his hands in his pockets. "I need this out of me."

"Then we keep a distance. But we still do this together. I know a place where you can be healed. Please, Jordan, come with me."

SIX

Jordan

Quell's eyes glitter with a hope I cannot give her. The Sphere's magic is hurting me, and now it can hurt Quell.

"I can't come with you. I'm sorry." If I can find more whispers of Lady Ruby, I can use my connections, if I must, to get into places. My stomach begins to twist at the reprehensible abuse of duty, until I remember the coppery smell of my own blood and the Dragunhead's face as he stabbed me. The leader of the brotherhood—one of the highest-ranking officials in the Order, the man I trusted to shape me into the next Dragunhead—tried to kill me. His second-in-command.

Screw them all. They can burn.

But *magic. Quell's life.* That is worth all I have left.

"We need to get you to a Healer," she says.

"I'm not putting you in danger."

"Jordan, you are so stubborn!" Her mouth tightens in that way it does when she is really frustrated. It is probably meant to show me she's serious, but I smile. The cutest dimple appears in her cheek. I bite my lip, resisting the urge to kiss her there.

I wish I could pretend the last half hour never happened. But the radiating cold rippling through my body is a reminder I can't forget. The longing to hold her intensifies, to bask in her warmth and let it chase away the chill.

"I'm going to figure this out."

"Not without me."

"Shouldn't you be worried about House of Marionne? You're Headmistress now, Quell."

She flinches.

"What are you going to do about that?"

"I don't know. I haven't thought about it, to be honest." The fire in her dims.

"Life is about more than protecting the people you care about," I say. "It's also about embracing what you're going to do. And who you're going to be. Your family legacy." I think of her grandmother. Darragh Marionne was many things I did not like, but she had redeemable qualities. And sacrificing her life to save Quell's proves it. Quell would just *not* honor her grandmother's memory? But every sobering thought dies at my lips at the look in Quell's eyes.

When she closes and reopens them, I know I've pushed too hard.

"I'm sorry." I burn with a desire to touch her, to take away the pain of my words. But I hook my hands instead.

"Jordan, nothing is guaranteed in life. I've learned that these last few months. And right now, all I can think about is that the two things I love most in the entire world are at risk: my magic and *you*."

My chest warms, sending a flush up my neck. *She loves me.* I'll never tire of hearing it. I can't go to her, but I can hold her words and tuck them safely away.

She crosses her arms. "Run from me for the rest of this miserable half existence you're limping around with now or *let me help you*."

She isn't fighting for control or to manipulate me like every other person who weaponized that word. My father, my aunt Beaulah Perl, even my first love—Yaniselle.

"I love you, too." The words ricochet through my chest. How is my life worth anything, how could *I* be worth anything, if I don't give everything to save this girl? Even if it means folding to her demands now.

"There's a Trader by the name of Lady Ruby who knows how to procure anything." I explain how my plan to meet her tonight failed.

Quell glances at my side, now covered with my shirt. "That takes time you don't have. We need to get you to someone who can help now." She tries to close our distance, but I hold up a hand, fighting the urge to be near her and smother her with promises of how this will soon be behind us, how we will both come out the other side of this just fine. But magic thrashes inside me and I bind my lips. Until I'm sure, those promises feel reckless.

"We have to get to a safe house," she says. "They are discreet and well connected. If Darkbearers are looking for you, they'd *never* look there."

My heart ticks faster. Safe houses are full of descendants from Misa who escaped the Sorting Years. They are filled with dark magic and descendants of the deadliest Marked to exist. I made a living hunting safe houses. Now I'm supposed to just march into one and ask for help?

"I know of one," she goes on. "They've moved locations. But they had to have a Healer. There was a pregnant girl there. The person in charge is named Knox."

My chin hits my chest. I recall Knox's bright blue eyes and how her stare penetrated deep into my heart. "I put her in the Shadow Cells for working with the financier, Audubon."

"You did what? No! You have to break her out of Headquarters."

"Quell, everyone's out for themselves." I gesture at the devastation. "The Dragunhead hasn't been seen anywhere. I don't know what we'd be walking into."

"The last time I wanted to expose the Order, you didn't listen to me."

Shame burns hot in my chest. At her Cotillion she was convinced that the Order wasn't what it appeared to be. That it was full of snakes and all the honorable things it professes to stand for are lies. But that was before I was willing to see. Before I was ready.

My heart yearns for her; it envies her strength. I concede, unable to walk away from the determined kindness in her eyes. One I don't deserve but desperately need.

"It's a plan, then," she says. "We get Knox, then link up with her safe house crew." Quell turns. Deadly magic claws its way over my ribs up into my chest. I can feel more flesh withering away, but I tighten my coat around myself and follow the girl I'm not worthy of.

I will save her, even if it's the death of me.

SEVEN

Nore

Nore's bones rattled with panic. She wasn't sure why she grabbed the blade. She didn't want to fight with Yagrin. She didn't want this at all.

Yagrin's eyes swirled with suspicion. But she knew he was always more frustrated than angry.

"If you've lied about your intentions—"

"Yagrin! Stop." Her cheeks flushed. She lowered her arm. "I would never hurt you."

Yagrin's expression cinched, his eyes narrowing.

"Ellery has our mother imprisoned for all I know. If I could rescue her from him myself, I would have done it. I need your help. And I'm helping you in exchange."

"Then what was that back there? I asked you to help. I meant *magic*." The lines of his face deepened.

She could practically hear the wheels of his mind turning, questioning whether she was trustworthy, assessing whether he'd have to kill her. She tucked the blade away. "I got scared. Okay? I'm sorry."

He glared.

"Stop looking at me that way. I had a *moment*. Am I *allowed* a moment?"

A war wrestled in her chest. Nore wanted to tell him the truth, that she was Red. She wanted to believe that he would forgive her for lying and making up an entire existence. That his love for Red—*for her*—would outweigh any betrayal.

Telling him the truth was futile. Yagrin's favorite hobby was holding grudges! And he had one against the Order in a death grip. He would never forgive her if he knew. He'd never believe her feelings for him were ever real.

He wet his bottom lip before tucking it. Her neck heated. She knew what was coming.

"You're lying to me."

Nore put on her best incredulous tone. "I've done nothing but help you!" Her voice cracked. And it made her feel naked.

She dated him as Red for months. She should be able to lie to him better. But as Red, it was different. She didn't look like herself. She could make up new mannerisms. Red chewed her nails. Nore didn't. She'd started the disgusting habit to create distance between her and her persona. Red was sassy and didn't care what people thought. Nore was terrified people would see deeply into her. She wanted to be more like Red. She wasn't exactly the mousy daughter she was under her mother's care. But she wasn't the person she wanted to be either. She was some mixed version of two people—brave one moment, a coward the next. Sure of herself until someone stared at her too long. She clenched her fists but bit her tongue.

She couldn't shatter his heart or her own *a second time*.

She forced the lump in her throat down and exhaled. She had to sell this act better than she ever had. He could never find out. Ever.

"We're wasting time," she said. "I'm sorry I didn't think to try magic. Next time, I'll be there."

Yagrin hadn't moved. His dark amber eyes tore into her as he said, "Show me your magic now."

She stopped breathing.

He folded his arms.

"I was trained as a Cultivator. And we don't have any rings."

"That's what you're forced to study. Your natural magic is something else."

Shit. He's read about me. Nore couldn't keep straight the lies her mother kept feeding the *Daily*. She couldn't remember what she'd told them she liked to do magically. All she remembered was that heirs were Cultivators and they used rings to augment magic in others. She opened her mouth, but words wouldn't come out.

"You don't have magic." His gaze widened.

The truth shook her in the best way. It was actually refreshing to hear it spoken aloud. One less lie between them. She hooked her hands together and stood taller, picturing Red.

"And so what if I don't?" She tried her best to look cavalier. Truth was, she didn't care that she didn't have magic. But it was nauseating for people to know. Protocol meant he should kill her now because Unmarked, the non-magical, couldn't look upon magic and live.

She knew Yagrin. Revenge kept his heart beating. This new Yagrin was someone else entirely. She watched his hand. It didn't move, just as she'd thought. He could never hurt her physically. Not when he could do much more damage with the truth.

"Since you're not going to kill me, should we go?"

"You've been playing the whole Order?" His mouth bowed. He exhaled in wonder. "How'd you even pull that off? Your mother must be in on it? Or your brother."

"It's been my entire life's practice to hide it."

"You lie so *well*." The awe in his expression darkened. "You fit right in with the rest of the Order. Corrupt and dishonest."

The world bled red. "You can take your opinion of me making sure I'm not *killed* and shove it up your ass."

"The mouse has a voice."

She balled her fists.

"Let's get on with this business. We need that Scroll for my brother."

He was so bad at lying to her. She could always tell. This time his hand fiddled with his pocket. He could be grumpy and bitter, but Yagrin's heart was made of mush. He cared deeply, and that's why he hated the Order and everything it touched. She longed to go to him. To wrap her arms around him and tell him he didn't need the Scroll. She was right there! Instead she stood watching as he stewed. She tried to look like her heart wasn't ramming in her chest.

His mouth pulled sideways, and he laughed.

"What's funny?"

"Nothing." His hand pulled at his pocket harder.

"And you say I lie well."

"Look, I don't trust you. I can tell something about you is off. You're terrible at pretending."

She bit down the urge to guffaw. How wrong he was.

"But I don't care what your story is or what you're after. Just keep your word," he said. "Find the Scroll, and we're good."

He dared judge her?

"Keep yours—once we find it, rescue my mother. And you have nothing to worry about." As long as her mother was alive, Nore would never inherit Headship. And with the Scroll in *Nore's* hands, her mother could live *forever*.

The dead would kill Nore if they realized that her heart had no magic! That she *couldn't* fulfill the Pact. A shiver raced down her spine. Her magicless heart would *never* be shoved in the ancestors' glass box, as had been done to her mother. If Yagrin tried to outsmart her before rescuing Isla Ambrose, Nore would just use the Scroll herself.

Either way, Nore would *live*.

She refused to apologize for doing what was needed to stay alive. Everyone was loyal to themselves. She was no worse than the rest. That was why loving Yagrin in any pure way was utterly impossible. They were both liars.

The Order wouldn't own her life anymore. Then she could find another farm somewhere and make a life of her own. A place where she would wall herself in with trees. Picturing her future homestead tugged at her chest with a sharpness that felt more like pain than relief.

Her greatest hope was that at this new home, she'd *finally* be able to forget about Yagrin.

EIGHT

Yagrin

Yagrin wasn't sure how to read Nore. She stood there in the alleyway, her eyes sparkling with mischief. He could smell the dishonesty on her even though he wasn't sure where to pin it. *She's been living a lie her entire life.* The girl had no magic. He blinked, really seeing her for the first time. And it stunned him.

"The journal is long gone," he said, trying to move on, reminded they'd made no progress. If he'd known she didn't have magic, he wouldn't have put them in that situation. "We'll have to think of something else."

Nore shook her head. She reached into the back of her dress and pulled out the leather journal.

"How did you—"

"I wasn't taking any chances. The one in my bag was a fake. I swapped it quickly with one I found at the hostess booth. He ran off with *Sixty Clever Uses for Saffron.*"

Yagrin burst out laughing. She was really something.

"Still, we don't know what the sketches mean. And there was that weird thing he said at the tattoo shop. Maybe I misheard." She tapped her lip. A bicyclist zoomed past and Yagrin hardly saw him coming. The day had dimmed, with no glimpse of sunlight between the buildings.

"Let's get moving," he told her. They walked back toward the main road in the direction of the place where they'd been staying—a room at a hotel unaffiliated with his father's. He had to be careful. It was a long walk, a dozen blocks at least, and they did most of it in silence to a backdrop of the buzzing city streets. He watched her. It wasn't often someone got one over on him like that. The not having magic *and* the decoy journal. It was a bit impressive. He chuckled under his breath.

"What are you laughing at?" She cut him a glance that could kill.

"Nothing, really."

"Because I can't think of anything that's funny. People are after my *blood*." She bit down on her already swollen lip. "We've been at this for weeks and the one idea I had ran off thanks to you attacking him."

He wouldn't take the bait. Arguing wouldn't get them anywhere. And he was too distracted, captivated, even, that she'd made it to the ripe age of—

"How old are you?"

Her brow furrowed. She sighed, exasperated. "Here I thought the last few blocks you were drumming ideas about how to find the other half of the Scroll, when you're clearly replaying your favorite comedy routine in your head and pondering my age." She rubbed her temples.

"It was just a question. And I'm fully on task. You're the liar here." He winced. Maybe he shouldn't have said that. After all, he told his fair share of lies.

She stopped.

"That came out wrong. I didn't mean it as an insult. To be honest—"

"I don't care what you think of me, Yagrin Richard Wexton the First. In case I didn't make that clear the first time."

Hearing his full name felt like a punch in the chest. "How do you know my middle name?"

She started walking again, this time faster. He had to jog a little to keep up.

"When it comes to research, I assure you that I have you beat." There was a spark of challenge in her eye. As if she dared him to question her. He smirked.

"Well, you've warmed up."

She exhaled a long, dragging sigh as they entered the hotel at Washington Avenue. She watched every corner of the busy lobby with her arms tight around her. Ellery putting a bounty on her blood had shaken her up. He'd abandoned his recent engagement, apparently to focus on apprehending her. Inside the elevator, Yagrin watched as she pulled out her perfect ponytail and flipped her hair forward, then back, before scooping it up into a messy bun.

The cut on her arm was still bleeding, so Nore cleaned it as soon as they entered their room. There were two beds, as requested. She kicked off her shoes and fell onto one of them, trying to be mindful of the cut. He caught himself tracing her features.

"Nore, if having the truth out there made you feel better, I'm glad you've told me."

Her chin slid over her shoulder at him. "Sure."

"We have Dublin's journal. We now know Ellery's on the offense. *And* you seem to have relaxed a bit." He kicked aside the shoe she left in the middle of the floor to avoid tripping over it. "Now I know not to put you in a situation where you have to use magic. I almost think we'll work together better now that I know."

Her lips pursed. "You mean that?"

"I do. It makes sense, doesn't it?"

"I mean, yes, it does."

"Alright. So I won't throw it in your face anymore. And you can stop worrying about pretending with me."

She pulled the covers over her. "Fine."

He grabbed the journal and sat beside her on the bed, flipping through the scorched pages. "What weird thing did he say at the shop?"

"I was just thinking about it." She rolled onto her side to face him, her fingers lost in the edges of her red hair. Her skin looked so soft. The room was a little warm, and the walk was long, so her cheeks were flushed. She had the biggest eyes, a shade of gray that reminded him of fog-hugged mountains. There was a dark depth to them. When he realized he'd leaned toward her, he shifted to put more distance between them and tried to focus on the words she was saying.

"Dublin said he'd looked for the Scroll and learned about the *places* where it's hidden," she said. "He spoke of places as if there was more than one."

"Right, the half you and your brother have."

"He wasn't talking about our House. He lived there while he studied. This seemed like multiple places that he traveled *to* . . ." She folded her legs up against her.

"He did say something weird when I tried to make a deal with him." Yagrin hadn't thought much of it then, but it *was* odd how he'd mentioned multiple Houses.

"*Each* of the Houses, right? I thought it was weird, too." She grabbed the book, looking at the sketches again, and he stared, not at the pages, but at her. It was a shame that her position would corrupt her eventually, if she wasn't already fully corrupted.

"No way!" She shot up and flipped through the journal, stopping three times to skim a page.

"What?"

"When Caera Ambrose discovered immortality, her greatest fear was that someone would discover it."

"And?"

"Do you think the Uppers just *let* her keep a secret to something so powerful?"

His heart hiccupped. "No, they'd want to keep it as secret as possible."

"Exactly. They'd want it protected. Hard to find. And with checks and balances in place."

Yagrin could feel her brain buzzing. She showed him the page in Dublin's journal just before the scorched ones. Travel notes from his Scroll search.

"He noted the unseasonably warm weather in a cliffside palace built of flowers," she explained. "It doesn't say where it was, but there's only one place described as a palace of flowers."

Yagrin's heart thudded with knowing.

"Begonia Terrace," they said at the same time.

"Next, his notes mention monstrous mosquitos beside a curious garden, where he attended a tea party," she went on. "What garden could be more curious than one with black roses?"

Chateau Soleil. Yagrin pulled the journal toward him and read on. Dublin also noted an oily stench that pervaded the third and final place he visited that summer. It was the first place he'd seen a chandelier made of bone. House of Perl.

"The Scroll is not in two pieces." Her grin was wide. "It's in multiple pieces, one in each House."

Goose bumps ran up his arms. He looked at the journal again.

"What other reason would Dublin, who's seen all the Order has to offer and these great wonders in the world, visit each of the four Houses *during* the time when he was searching for the Scroll?"

"You're right." Ellery and Nore shared the Ambrose piece. There was a piece at House of Marionne, Oralia, and . . . He felt sick at the thought of going back to Hartsboro. "We should start with House of Marionne. It's safest, since Quell is Headmistress now."

"Is she there?"

"Last I heard, she went to try to find my brother. But regardless, with her mother dead, she is technically in charge. We should be safely received." This plan could actually work.

She hugged the journal, still smiling. She was damn clever.

"Your brain must weigh a thousand pounds," he said.

She guffawed. It felt odd and nice both at the same time. Until her smile melted to dread as she gaped at the window.

"They're back," she muttered at darker, thicker storm clouds forming outside. "We have to go. *Now!*"

PART TWO

NINE

Quell

The Wexton MidCenter Hotel, where Dragun Headquarters is located, is plastered in yellow caution tape.

My magic answered weakly, but Jordan was able to cloak. The early-morning Chicago air is icier than my toushana, whipping around us as we approach the tall glass doors. The last time I was here, Jordan had intercepted me as I tried to kill Beaulah and convinced me to partner with him. He brought me here to get the Dragunhead's permission. It's hard to believe that was only months ago.

He smooths the condensation off the windows before cupping his hands to them. "There's no one here."

We share a glance. He slides the tape aside and pulls at the sliding doors. They don't budge.

"Have you seen any of the brotherhood?" I ask.

"No, but I've heard things." His jaw works. "If the rumors are true, the protocol if the Dragunhead is incapacitated or, in this case, has vanished, is to promote me, the Dragunheart. But the rumors about what I've done are far worse. My best guess is with no clear leader, the Draguns fled, too. Some may stick together in small flocks. But with no governing, who's to stop them from doing whatever they want with toushana?"

"You talk about them like they're Darkbearers."

"A Darkbearer is bound to toushana. A Dragun just borrows toushana from the Sphere's magic. The only real difference between them is a code of honor. Without the brotherhood, that's gone. Toushana is enticing, even for those of us trained to use it."

"I'm not so sure it's that cut-and-dry." I peer through the window. The place looks like it's been ransacked, with overturned furniture and the art on the walls in pieces on the floor. "Would Draguns come back for people in the Cells who were going to die anyway?"

"Protocol is to establish a new spot and sanitize this place." He gazes inside again. "Whatever is happening isn't protocol."

"Get me in there. If Knox is gone, maybe there are clues to where she went."

He tugs the doors harder.

"Use toushana."

He tenses.

"If you won't, I will." I am about to nudge him aside when he flattens his palms, and a weak whiff of black unfurls in his grip, much fainter than before.

"Back," he says.

"You're scared of it. It works best when you trust it."

"Quell, it's more complicated than that. This is the *Sphere's* magic. More toushana than you've ever touched. Even if I wanted to, I can't give in to that much power at once." He flinches, and the magic in his hands grows. "Something's happening," he says.

I watch closely, imagining commanding *that* much toushana. "What does it feel like?"

"Like my flesh is wrapped around an iceberg." More black seeps from him. "And somehow it burns like holding the sun in my bare hands. When it flows through me, I don't feel it. I don't feel anything." Shadows shift the air around us. "I cease to exist completely and the world is—" The growing fog billows to the ground.

I reach for his wrist to push his hand onto the locked hotel doors but stop myself, remembering the risk of getting too close. We share a glance. Something burns in him that has nothing to do with magic.

"To the door," I tell him. His magic slinks along the ground. Magic tugs in my chest toward him, and I put more distance between us. His magic eases closer to the hotel's glass, blackening every inch of the pavement it touches, subduing everything in its path. *So much power in one body. No wonder it's killing him.*

I glance at the spot where his wound hides beneath his shirt. "Does it hurt? What do you feel?"

"Darkness. Everything is unfeeling darkness." When the shadows connect with the glass doors, they shatter. A shrill alarm rings.

He stares as if he's seen a ghost. "I didn't want to *break in*."

"You directed the Sphere's toushana *with* control."

Sirens wail in the distance, and I urge us inside. Jordan presses his talon key against the elevator button, and the doors open to take us down. His head rests backward, his stare dead ahead.

"What happens when you use the Sphere's *proper* magic?"

"I don't know, it's been so long since I've tried."

The elevator doors open to Dragun Headquarters, and my heart stammers at the scene in front of me. What was a pristine lobby looks like a war zone. The Brotherhood's sleek marble walls are scorched and cracked in several places. The glass partitions, which used to house cubicles where Jordan's desk was, have been destroyed. The floor is an ocean of glass confetti.

"Who would do this?" I ask, then the answer hits me. *With the state of the world, who wouldn't?*

The Order leadership is corrupt but not complex. Four Headmistresses rule their Houses like dictators as long as they honor the Three Rites, Rules for Cotillion, and Internship. Most other matters are handled by the Dragunhead, not as their superior but as their equal. One transcontinental Order, five in power over it all.

And now one is dead. I swallow hard.

One was caught red-handed trying to *rob* the Sphere.

Another is a prisoner to her own son.

And the fourth is keeping her head down.

To make matters worse, the one protective force in charge of maintaining order and discipline has disbanded. Their leader has vanished.

"Literally everyone has a reason to be angry."

"Things are out of hand," he says. "In a way, I've done this."

"Not our problem." I rush over to the reception area. Behind a sleek wide desk are large office doors engraved with a crest bearing the sigils of each House. But the horror behind the desk stops me dead in my tracks. A body. Or the shell of one. A hollow suit of skin lies in the chair like a deflated balloon.

Jordan mutters under his breath, moving closer. My toushana bristles, tremoring, urging me backward, far away from whatever twisted magic this is.

"What happened to her?" I ask, but he is frozen in shock. "I'm sorry. You liked her, if I remember."

Jordan doesn't respond. He's pulling open her desk drawers, which are all empty. Too clean. Then he tugs on a bottom drawer that won't open. As he skims for a key, I pull on the thread of cold still buzzing in my veins, and to my relief a puff of toushana drips from my hands. It's open in seconds.

Jordan pulls out a stack of photographs, all taken from the same vantage point, standing over a body at its feet. He flips through photos of the dead at various locations, with closed eyes and suns branded on their eyelids. Darkbearer attacks.

"She was looking into their return," he says.

"But why hide evidence Darkbearers were on the rise?" This is the place where people investigate magical crime.

"I'm not sure." Before he can take us another moment off track, I step into his path.

"The Shadow Cells. Knox. Police will come through those doors any moment, and there are all kinds of things here we don't want to have to explain. We *have* to go. *Now.*"

We rush toward the stairs to the lowest level of the building, underground, and my gut is in my throat. A cold seeps over my body so biting my bones shiver when we reach the basement floor. I fidget nervously, but my heart slows at the steep drop in temperature as the Shadow Cells come into view.

We walk the long aisle of cells sealed with a writhing veil of mist in place of a door. The curious vapor turns and twists like a curtain of smoke. I touch it carefully.

Blood drains from my limbs, and the bones in my hand throb. A scream bites my lips as I try to stretch my fingers, but I've lost all sense of feeling in them. My hand dangles from my wrist, unable to move.

Jordan reaches for me before closing his hand into a fist. *"Quell, no—"*

I rub my hand as blood rushes back to it, and I can flex it again. "What kind of magic is that?"

"It's a way we've manipulated toushana to paralyze and repel. Stick with me." He stops at a cell and flips out a fire dagger from his waist. Flames erupt from it before he slashes the veil in half to reveal a familiar woman in a metal chair.

"Knox!" I rush inside. Her cell is piled with trays of food covered in bugs and a nearly empty water trough leaking water across the floor. The last time I saw her, she'd found out Yagrin and I were lying to her about who we were and why we were at her safe house. She and Willam made Yagrin leave for the betrayal. I chose to leave as well to find my mom, but it still felt like saying goodbye to people who could have been like a family.

"Quell?" She blinks in the sudden light flooding her cell. "Is that really you?" She pulls me over with a tight tug at my wrist, studying me closely before a smile bows her lips. "It's so good to see you again."

"You're okay."

"I have seen worse days. It's actually been quiet the last several weeks."

The brotherhood just left them here to die. My stomach turns. I search my pockets for some morsel of food or *something* but realize I have nothing.

"We have to get you out of here."

"Mm, not so sure that's in my best interest." Knox turns her attention to Jordan, who is hovering near the door. "Mr. Wexton, am I correct that you've finally accepted your fate?"

"We need your help." Jordan tucks his dagger away. "We can talk about my fate later." The strain in his voice rattles my pulse. "You have to come with us."

"Please," I add.

She moves closer to Jordan and grabs a fistful of his shirt before he can resist. He swallows hard, and I can't tell if it's irritation or fear. Her chilly blue stare roves his chest.

"You foolish boy! *What have you done?*" She looks at me. "You went along with this?"

"There was no other choice." I explain the chaos that happened at Dlaminaugh months ago. But the concern carved around Knox's eyes doesn't change. "I didn't expect you to care what happens to magic."

"I don't care about magic. I care about what the threat of its loss will make people *do*."

Jordan's gaze hits the ground. "It's carnage out there."

Knox exhales sharply. "If one person can steal all of magic, anyone will think they can. The world is after you, boy. You better *run*."

"We have a plan," I say. "Show her."

Jordan lifts his shirt, showing her the wound. She inhales sharply but doesn't flinch.

"We want to have a safe house Healer heal it. After that we plan to get the magic *out* of him and into something else."

"I couldn't let Beaulah win," Jordan says.

"We came here because there is no one else I trust more," I say.

A clang somewhere on the floor above us shatters the silence.

"Will you come?" Jordan asks. *"Please."*

She gazes between us and sighs. "We should get moving."

Jordan grabs the handles of Knox's chair and rolls her quickly toward the elevator. We rush inside and up.

Still haunted by what we saw earlier, I whisper, "*What* happened to Maei?"

He tightens his mouth.

"Stop protecting me," I tell him. "We're a team."

When the doors open to the lobby, he says, "Her soul's been ripped from her body. She was an Ambroser. They've advanced magic somehow to allow them to roam postmortem in spectral bodies, the academic texts say. I've read they look like shadows to the untrained eye. Whoever killed Maei killed her body *and* her soul so that she can't come back as one of their ancestors. So that whatever she knows is gone forever."

I gasp. "How do you kill someone's *soul*?"

"No idea."

"Who could do that kind of magic?" I ask.

"Someone playing a game we are still learning the rules to."

TEN

Jordan

The L train whooshes by underground. Knox urges me to push her faster, but I can't stop glancing over my shoulder. Being out here like this, exposed, with the world's magic inside me, isn't my idea of being discreet.

"Hurry, we'll miss it," she says.

But we aren't proceeding toward the platform where the next train will halt. We hurry beneath the glowing signs for the blue line. Quell hasn't said much since leaving Headquarters. Since I told her about Maei's body, her expression hasn't changed from a pinched glower. Would Nore know what this means? We cross the platform, and the train we want comes to a screeching halt.

I turn to Knox. "Where exactly—"

Quell's scent assaults me when she presses in beside me as the car fills. I forget what I was going to say. Her warm brown gaze is riddled with worry, still unsettled by what we saw at Headquarters. I adjust where I'm standing to put plenty of distance between us. Her lashes dip with disappointment before she looks away. *I'm sorry*, I want to say. Knox points at a sign for O'Hare airport as the doors close.

When we reach the last stop, we get off in a flood of passengers rushing to catch their flights. A person lingers a bit too long on my periphery. As Knox leads us down the platform, toward the airport's check-in, the figure follows. I usher us along faster but catch a glimpse of his face; stringy, long dark hair; and a gangly frame. *That face.* His dark glasses and bulky coat make the rest of him hard to see. We cut a sharp left toward the bathrooms before security, and I look back. But he's gone. *He looked like . . .*

"What is Abby doing? Is she still dating that sorry excuse for a Dragun, whatever his name is?" I ask.

"Mynick," Quell says. "And no. She's still at the Tavern, waiting for me to write. We loitered long enough to convince the owners to let her do the costume design for one of their shows. She's living her wildest Vestiser dream, healing career and her parents be damned."

"Good for her." At least someone is squeezing happiness out of this sour world.

Inside the women's restroom, we get a few weird glances. But when it empties, I lock us inside.

"The last stall." Knox pulls off her necklace and holds it tight in her fist. "I'll hold the stone. When I grab the stall door, everyone needs a hand on me. When we step inside, we'll arrive at our destination."

"Wait." I stop her, eyeing the blue stone pendant in her hand. Transport powder is how Marked travel if they're privileged enough to have access to a supply. Draguns use toushana to travel by cloak. But this? "I've never seen magic like this before."

"You have."

I lean closer and see granules glow beneath its glassy surface. *Sun Dust.* "A cloak veil?"

"Astute. Cloaking magic has been tethered to the bathroom stall door with tracer magic. When the veil or key touches where the cloak has been placed, the stall door summons toushana. You step through and it works like any cloak would, taking you where you need to go."

"Cloaking magic is proprietary information."

"You still think the world is that black-and-white, Mr. Wexton?"

I don't know how the world works anymore. This cloak veil is one more piece of a re-forming puzzle I've never seen before.

"You knew this?" I ask Quell.

"Your brother and I traveled by regular cloak."

"This is—" I stare at the pendant in disbelief. It wasn't taken from Knox when she was captured because it looks like some kind of jewelry. But it's a magic more sophisticated than I've ever seen, and it was right under the Order's nose. "Brilliant."

"A network of thousands of safe houses has existed for generations," Knox goes on. "We're in hiding, not inept. Every major airport in the world has a cloak veil. We are well coordinated, well funded, and invisible, Mr. Wexton." She gestures at the bathroom. "Shall we?"

We enter the bathroom stall, my pulse rattling.

"To," Knox says, "Monsieur Audubon."

The grand estate where the financier lives is ornate and sprawling, like a petite Order House in a gated community. The travel cloak sets us in a wedge of shrubbery beside the pool. As we pull ourselves out of it and find the gravel path, my irritation bristles. The last time I saw this man, he got away from me as I tried to corner him handing off money to Knox for a new safe house.

He is an untouchable Unmarked, well connected. He isn't *in* the Order, but he knows enough to be dangerous. The Dragunhead issued execution orders on him multiple times, but they were always quickly recalled.

"The deal you blew up last fall was going to secure us a new safe house because our location became compromised." Knox looks at Quell, who shuffles on her feet. "But since I was captured, I have no idea where my partner relocated us. Audubon will."

"I don't like this," I whisper to Quell as we follow Knox up the gardening path.

"Knox knows what she's doing."

"It's not her I'm worried about. Audubon is an opportunist. He's made a living on disloyalty. I usually try to kill this man when I see him. And we're going to walk in here and trust him?"

"You're walking in on Knox's credibility. Start acting like you see in you what she sees in you."

I follow at a reluctant pace up a stone ramp and to the grand doors. A melodious bell brings the butler to the door. He greets us stoically and shows us to the library. When half an hour has passed and only refreshments have arrived, I stand and pace.

"Jordan, what do you fear?" It's Knox. My stomach twists at the intensity in her stare.

So many things. "Losing everything." I lace my hands together, resisting the urge to look at Quell. "Because I trusted the wrong people."

"I won't lie to you," she goes on. "Part of the reason I am helping you is because I trust Quell. I also have seen your heart, and there is good in there somewhere. But there is a war inside you, and the final battle hasn't yet been decided."

Her words skid up my spine like ice. I rub my hands so hard together my skin is red when the sound of footsteps clacking on the polished floors turns me in my chair.

"Knox." Audubon greets her with a kiss a bit too close to her mouth. And for the first time, she smiles. He's a man of small stature with warm brown skin, a thick head of white hair, and a mouth that's crooked. He snaps for his butler. "Bring them some brunch bites." He studies Quell from head to toe with a lecherous expression. The cold inside me leaps, and I force my feet to stay in place. We need this man's help. I should not rip his eyes from their sockets.

"The very last person I thought I'd see here." Audubon traces his jaw, giving me a curt nod. He extends a platter of hand-rolled cigars. "But these are grave times, full of surprises."

I don't take the peckle. Knox does, and so does Quell, to be polite I imagine. I try to at least say, *Good to see you again,* but the words won't come. I force a tight smile that feels more like a grimace.

"You look well, considering the rumors," he says to me.

"Never felt better." I cross my arms, watching his movements.

"Are they true? Do you possess the Sphere's magic?"

"You don't ask questions you don't already know the answer to."

His crooked mouth twists into a smile.

"I'm glad to see you're alright," he says, turning to Knox with steepled hands. "Let's get into it. What's on the table today?"

"Nothing, officially," she says. "I need to know where Willam is."

He smooths his pants, and Quell's foot begins tapping. "The network of safe houses is evolving, finding common interests in surprising places."

Audubon doesn't even look my way. "Should we speak privately?" he asks Knox, but I'm tired of wasting time. I know how to bait an opportunist.

"Safe houses don't need to be in the shadows if the Order is falling apart, I get it. New alliances are being formed. But we see an opportunity for you, as the money cleaner, *if* you help us."

Audubon sets down his cigar. "I am *really* beginning to understand the appeal of this guy." He crosses his legs. "But not all causes are profitable, even if they pay well."

"Cowards hide behind riddles."

"You are highly sought after, Mr. Wexton. So sure, I could help you all and magic and everyone. Or I could help *me*."

Knox's stare widens in shock. "Lennox, please. Willam's location. That's all I'm asking."

"Life is a game of Russian roulette, Knoxy, you know this. I make my bets with the best information I have. And this one has *so many bidders*."

"Don't do this. After all we've been through, we're as good as family."

He shrugs. "Times are changing."

She frowns. Ice pricks my chest, the Sphere's magic rising up in me, burning a degree colder every second I stare at Audubon. Quell's foot taps faster beside me, and I can feel the fear rippling in her chest.

"New clients are emerging," Audubon says. "And they all have one thing in common—they want *this guy*." He taps my knee, and I consider how good it would feel to snap his finger in half. Black seeps out of my pores, spreading across the floor in a fine mist. Audubon's poker face is unreadable. Quell grabs my arm, and her touch stills me like an anchor. When she realizes what she's done, she snatches her hand away.

"Everyone out," she says. "I want to speak with Audubon privately."

ELEVEN

Nore

Nore could feel the lurking dead gaining on her and Yagrin as the gates of Chateau Soleil came into focus. She kept looking back. And each time, Yagrin eyed her warily. Others only saw the dead as oddly placed shadows or looming dark clouds unless their eyes were trained.

"We're almost there. Relax," he said, as if he could tell she was a knot.

When their feet found the paved path to the gates of Chateau Soleil, the dead stopped. She rushed to the iron wall around the estate, with Yagrin on her heels. She expected them to continue their pursuit, but the dead lingered at the edge of Darragh Marionne's property.

"What is it?" Yagrin asked, gazing up at the trees to try to make sense of the shadows.

"Do you know how we get in?" she asked, ignoring his confusion. The more she told him about the dead, the closer she got to the truth of *why* she was so willing to help find the Scroll. She didn't need him putting any dots together.

She studied the perimeter of the estate. The Chateau was nothing like she remembered. The gate spindles were taller than she recalled and overgrown with thorny black roses. Right up on the gate, she could hardly see the mansion behind it. She gave it a nudge, and the world darkened more, like a storm cloud had moved in.

More dead had arrived. She could feel stares on her skin.

They circled like hungry sharks, but they still didn't move past the estate property line. The dead might have found a way to leave the Ambrose grounds, but they couldn't cross onto another House's property. She tried to exhale, but the knot in her shoulders cinched. Who knew what her brother was doing, how he was able to stretch magic to influence their ancestors? How had he gotten them to leave Dlaminaugh in the first place?

"Nore?" Yagrin gazed right past them. "Are you alright?"

"Just worried we won't get inside." She tugged on the knotted vines around the gate.

The thicket of roses shifted.

"Watch out," Yagrin said with an outstretched arm.

Her body felt rigid, then it ached, at the warmth of his arm against her. She stepped aside, creating a generous distance between them. It was difficult enough to keep her memories at bay *without* him so close. Dark magic coiled in his hands, and her heart skipped a beat. She'd never seen him actually do magic before. And she'd only ever seen a small drip of the magic from her fingertip twice—once when her mother poisoned her and the next time when she accidentally disintegrated her gloves at Darragh Marionne's tea party. Toushana sprang up in the air from his palm like a snake charmed by a song.

"Never been around a Dragun before, I see."

She straightened. "Ambrose doesn't put out many Draguns. The few we have on security are kept on the perimeter of the grounds. Any protection we need, the ancestors provide."

Shapeless shadowed bodies shifted restlessly on her periphery, and her pulse picked up.

Yagrin eyed their general direction warily before raising a brow at her. "Spoken like someone who really loathes their house." The branches swallowing the iron gates grew at the brush of dark magic. Their spiked stems slithered around the iron, thickening, tightening. Dark flowers deepened their blossoming, and new sprouts appeared. The gate grew harder to see as the plants took over it. Yagrin scowled. Nore kept an eye on the hovering dead, watching them as if they were on the other side of a glass that wouldn't shatter.

A voice cut through the brush.

"Closer, so I can see you clearly." The voice was familiar. Like Darragh Marionne's but with a higher pitch and a rolled *r*.

"Closer*rrr*."

Yagrin approached, and a warning stuck in Nore's throat. Darragh was dead. These were her black roses. She was superstitious about them. Goose bumps rose on Nore's skin. But the voice? *Audior magic.*

Yagrin reached for the gate.

"Wait!" But before he heard her, the roses coiled around his wrist. The thorns had him bound to the iron within moments.

"Do something," he forced out, trying but failing to fend off vines now wrapping themselves around his chest.

Nore scrambled, trying to remember all she could about the roses. Darragh was the only person she knew who held to the old wives' tales about them. Nore pulled at the dregs of her memory. She'd studied up on them in order to harvest a few for the bouquet she left for Darragh in apology at the end of last Season. Cutting them was no easy feat.

Death.

The roses were supposed to attract death and allow whatever living souls were close a chance to get away. They could not be damaged by magic. They were territorial and took over any other plant nearby. They were aggressive. Competitive. *He has to appear defeated.*

"Yagrin, prick yourself. Draw blood."

He watched her with a wild expression, sweat slick on his brow. He worked the dagger from his pocket and nicked his arm. Red pooled at the seam of his skin. *It will work.* The writhing roses encircled his limb near the cut, then stilled.

Yagrin panted. "Now what?"

She dashed to him, snatching the tiny blade from her sleeve and slicing him free. His clothes were riddled with rips and red skin underneath. She smoothed her thumb over the long cut, where blood drenched his sleeve. He sucked in a breath at her touch.

"I'll be alright."

"I'm sorry, I didn't mean to grab you like that. I couldn't think of another way."

"Don't apologize to me. Don't ever apologize to me." He wrapped a rip of his shirt around his arm.

"It needs pressure." She gestured to take his arm in her hands. He met her eyes, and she could see the battle behind them. The curiosity he had about her, the way he enjoyed her company, the way she made him laugh. Her hand hung there, waiting, until he gave her his arm. She held it against her body, savoring the warmth of him against her.

"How do we get in there now?" he asked.

She tried to answer but realized since she'd taken his arm, she stopped breathing. Tears welled in her eyes. Her chin slid over her shoulder to hide them as she applied more pressure to his wound.

"I can help." A voice came from the other side of the gate. "Down the far end," it said. "There's a break in the foliage."

Nore was rigid, looking for the trick of the roses again. But the blur of a body moved beyond the gate. There was an actual person talking to them this time.

"Who's there?"

"There isn't much time. We must get back inside. This way!" The voice trailed away from the main gate and into the landscaping surrounding the estate. Yagrin pulled his arm from her grip, and Nore felt it like a tug in her chest. She'd missed holding him. Touching him.

When the sound of footsteps over crunching leaves stopped, so did they. A hand stuck out between the gates where the shrubbery was thinnest. Through the bars she could see an older woman with gray hair, dressed in all black. Over her face was a mourning cloth embroidered with a fleur-de-lis.

"I'm Maezre Dexler." Her voice was dry. "You are Nore Ambrose, and this is our former Ward's brother, I assume."

Yagrin's brow knitted.

"The rumors in the *Daily* are true, then," she went on. "About the chaos that's happened at your House with the Sphere, Miss Ambrose. The late Headmistress sent a message, heralding your bravery. You're wanted everywhere, you know?"

Nore blinked. She was a fugitive? They were a team of fugitives. People who knew her *name* knew what she'd done!

"Quell sent you?"

Nore opened her mouth, but Yagrin set a hand on her arm. She fought the urge to move closer to him. To lay her hand on top of his. Instead she froze and savored the feel of him again. The gentleness, his comfort. His willingness to trust her. It all was more than her own mother had given her.

"*Yes*, she did," Yagrin said. "Your Headmistress requires you to help us locate a particular item here on your grounds."

Nore bit away a mischievous smile at the well-placed lie. It was more of a stretch of the truth. And judging by Dexler's softened expression, it was working. They made a good team.

A colorless stone glowed on her ring as Dexler pulled a brush out of her pocket. She rubbed the round Retentor stone in circular motions against the gate, and the magic sealing the gate vanished. Then she swapped her ring for a beaming purple-jeweled one before shifting the gate's spindles to a thin, bendy material. She parted them like strings.

"Please, come."

Yagrin stepped through first. Then Nore. Something sharp grazed her skin as she slipped between the branches, and a cut appeared on her arm. Once they were both on the other side of the gate, Dexler shifted the gate to its rigid state and pulled back the black sheer draped over her face.

"We can get that mended for you inside."

Nore covered the wound, watching Dexler closely. Her brother had friends everywhere.

"It's fine."

"As you wish." Dexler's wrinkly skin was pale, and dark circles rimmed her eyes. She held her hand to her heart. "We'd hoped the intrusion was our new Headmistress. But at least she sent someone." She took a big breath.

"What's wrong?" Nore asked, unsure how to read her nervousness.

"There were bold claims at Quell's Cotillion about the late Headmistress—that she had a tether on every graduate of the House. The truth has a way of coming to the light. When she died, the tether broke, flooding us with missing memories." She cupped her mouth. "I never knew. Then the news of the Sphere breaking reached us. A few members tried to burn the house down while we were sleeping weeks ago, trying to steal artifacts, books, anything rich in ancient magic that could strengthen their hold on the magic we have left. A lot of the staff has fled. I and a dozen others are living barricaded in session rooms." Her nostrils flared as her eyes brimmed with tears. "This great House has fallen."

The sky had cleared when they passed through the gate, the dead gone. Nore exhaled sharply as they crossed the overgrown grounds. Once-sculpted plants had lost their form. A fountain was as dry as bones. But it was an unruly garden of black roses like the ones outside the estate that caught Nore's eye. A thicket of thorns grew outside the fence, the thorny stems coiling and twisting over one another high in the air, forming a dome over the garden. On the gate, a metal chain with a gold lock dangled against the nest.

Nore had picked roses in there a Season ago. There was no lock. There was no wall of roses. Only neat rows of scentless blooms. Everything was overgrown, but the garden was incongruously so. Nore stopped.

"It transformed to that mess when she died," Dexler said as they entered the house.

Inside the halls of Chateau Soleil, there wasn't a sound.

Massive ornate hallways glittered with lights and scorched walls. Dexler strode with purpose, so fast Nore had to nearly run to keep up with her.

"How is your brother?" she asked. Yagrin's jaw tightened at the question. An answer stuck in Nore's throat. Her arm had stopped bleeding.

Ellery was congenial, befriending everyone he met. *And* he was engaged to the social darling of their House—Elena Hargrove. There were few who would refuse his company. "He is doing okay, I hope," she went on. "He was always such a nice boy. One hears things, you know?"

Nore let the unanswered question drown in the hurry of their footsteps. Dexler didn't press, thankfully, showing them various areas of the house where the fires had gotten out of control. There were blackened, crumbling walls and soot all over the floors.

Yagrin strode along behind them, and each time she looked back he was being very careful where he put his steps, studying everything. "What have you been doing here all this time?"

"Surviving. The serving staff is mostly all here, but we're trying to conserve what we have on hand. I was the only maezre who spoke up and stuck up for Quell. I insisted we wait. But I'm at a standstill without any express instructions," Dexler went on. "Now that you're here, maybe we could figure out what to do about keeping the House running. There are members with questions, some have written requesting to come here to seek safety. But we aren't sure who has ill intentions. And Darragh's protection magic on the outer gates doesn't keep members of this House out."

The lines of Yagrin's face deepened.

"Magic is working inconsistently. We've managed to use some simple Shifting magic, when we can, to disguise where we're hiding." She approached a wall crumbled into rubble and smoothed her hand with the purple ring over the pile. Nothing happened.

"See what I mean?" She huffed. "We'll try another way."

Nore didn't even have magic, and she knew this *wasn't good.*

Dexler led them through the grand halls and past grand ballroom doors that hung from their hinges. Above them chandeliers swayed lopsided from the grandiose gold ceiling. "There is so much history that must be protected." She grabbed Nore's wrist tightly. "Perhaps since you're an envoy, you could help."

Nore peeled herself away. "It's terrible what's happened here. I'm very sorry."

"I don't mean to pressure." Dexler kept walking. "I'm just no Headmistress . . ."

Neither am I. Nore didn't have magic—how could she possibly help? And every second they delayed or got off task, her brother could be getting closer to her. Quell was in a much better position to help. For now, Nore had to focus on saving her own life. Because no one else was.

Nore let Yagrin catch up to her and whispered, "We can't get wrapped up in this. We need the Scroll piece and to get out of here."

Yagrin smiled darkly. "I couldn't agree more."

"Tonight, when they're asleep, we can look around." Nore studied the slopes in his sharp cheeks. She couldn't tell if he was amused or perplexed, but his gaze stayed on her as he considered her suggestion. It made her bones feel weak.

Finally he said, "It's a plan."

Nore exhaled. "We start with the late Headmistress's private quarters."

He nodded. "Maezre, we are tired from traveling," he said. "Could we talk in the morning?"

Dexler's shoulders sagged. "Of course." She led them into a dim corridor to a pile of debris. This time the stone on her ring glowed as she moved her hands around the rocks in a massaging motion. They shifted aside. She stepped through the pile to the wall behind it, beckoning them to follow. As they navigated the bowels of the estate, Nore walked closer to Yagrin. Her stomach wriggled as she rehashed their plan. She wasn't sure if it was being back in a House or their plotting, but she felt closer to him. Like old times, but better because she wasn't in disguise.

"You know, you're even more clever than I realized."

She dipped her chin.

"And you wear whatever you're feeling all over your face."

"I do not."

"Relax. I meant it as a compliment. Your candor is refreshing. When I pay close attention, you're *not* as convincing at lying as I'd initially thought. I despise liars."

Dexler led them deeper into the estate, where there was little to no damage. But Nore only had eyes for Yagrin. The truth would devastate him. She let the distance between them stretch, shaking off any tinge of longing she felt. There was no world in which Yagrin could ever love the real her.

TWELVE

Yagrin

Nore was a conundrum. Clever and rebellious. Did she love the Order, or did she not? It didn't sound like she knew how she felt about her House. But he liked the way she thought. Living all these years without magic, not good enough by their standards but refusing to let it define her. He knew a thing or two about the Order making you feel like you weren't good enough. It was admirable. More than that, it was enviable.

When Dexler gave them a session room to themselves, Nore hardly spoke. She paced for a while, and he watched her, imagining her mind analyzing every statistical likelihood that something could go wrong. What would happen if they were caught? If Dexler found out their motives weren't pure? Her frustration carved lines beneath her fiery red hairline, and it reminded him of beachcombing at sunset.

Once she stopped pacing, she sat at a desk and laid her head onto her folded arms. The sounds in the passageways had died down completely, and Yagrin was convinced the others were asleep.

"Nore?"

Her chest rose and fell gently. Her face was buried in a nest of silky hair. He almost felt bad for concealing his true intentions with the Scroll. Almost.

"Nore?"

She didn't move, peacefully asleep. Watching her knotted his insides, confusing everything. His hand reached to move her hair behind her so he could see her face better. Her pink lips were smooshed against her flattened arm, and a dribble of drool ran down her cheek. He laughed. She blinked slowly.

"Yagrin," she muttered. "I'm *so sorry!*" She blinked again, more lucid, then shot up from her seat. "What are you doing, standing over me?" Her hair was still wild, her words saturated with sleep. It reminded him of a dead girl he once knew who was wildly free. For a reason he couldn't put into words, he reached toward Nore's sleep-deranged expression and smoothed away the drool from her chin. "It's time to get up, Buttercup."

She batted his hand away, blushing, and hurried to the door.

His insides twisted. What was he thinking? His missing one person couldn't make him reckless with another. For so long Red was dead, which meant the feeling being with her gave him was also dead. The way Red looked at him, without harsh, angry words, without disdain, with pure trust in who he was, he could never see again. Her laugh made him feel alive like nothing else. Her love was the only thing that outshined the burn for vengeance.

But now life had been breathed into Red's memory in the form of hope. Hope that he could see her again and hold her. He wasn't sure exactly how the Scroll worked, but he knew it was his only chance. Death was otherwise final. The Scroll was his only shot at having some kind of happiness in his life. His heart belonged to Red or no one. He couldn't let the clever Ambrose girl confuse that. She might be a bad liar, but she was an heir. And people in the Order were eventually all the same. He tightened his hand into a fist and followed Nore out the door.

Nore navigated the halls of Chateau Soleil too well.

"How long has it been since you've been here?" he asked.

"Months. Before Quell's Cotillion." She moved along the second-floor landing's balustrade, heading for the stairs to the third floor.

He stuck to her heels, and once they reached the landing, Nore rushed down the hall, past dozens of doors and sweeping views of the estate. The sun was setting, its golden light slicing the hallway into pieces.

"It's there." She dashed to the very end of the hall and a pair of double doors. She twisted the scorched brass handle. The door didn't budge. She shook it vigorously, but still the door held. With balled fists, she spun on her heel and fumed.

"Let me try," he said, opening his hands to summon the cold magic that hung in the air. Toushana gathered and snapped to his hands quickly, but as it pooled, it barely formed a wisp of darkness. Nore watched, arms crossed. His heart beat faster. He held still, focusing on the strength of his will, and called to the darkness more firmly this time. But the hazy dark magic wouldn't quite come together.

"And *my* magic isn't reliable?"

His stomach knotted. He tugged harder, and—thank the Sovereign—the dark mist in the air shifted, and a rush of toushana siphoned to his fingers. He smoothed the dark magic along the wood, but it only blackened more. Her eyes narrowed with focus, a thoughtful crease forming between her brows. She stepped closer to the wall, and he noticed the way she got this look in her eye when her mind was maneuvering. Like she was calculating several mathematical equations all at once.

"What?" she asked, looking over at him.

"I didn't say anything."

"You're smiling."

Am I? He turned as heat rushed up his neck. When he looked at her again, she was inspecting the wall paneling beside the door. She walked down the length of Darragh Marionne's private quarters and placed her hand on the wall again.

"What is it?" he asked.

"The doors are protected. Toushana isn't going to get you in." She knocked on the wall, and it rang back hollow.

"You want me to go through the wall? Just burn a hole right through it? As we try to, I don't know, be *discreet*?"

"You're scared of getting caught?" Nore set her hands on her hips. "I thought you wanted to get out of here without ruffling feathers."

"I don't care how we get out of here. I just want that Scroll." Fire burned in her gray eyes. They were the kind of gray that only existed on rainy days or in a storm. Where the shade changed depending on how long he looked. She could be fearless. In fact, the only time he'd seen her look remotely afraid was when dark clouds rolled in nearby.

"Do you care about this place or something?" She quirked a brow.

"I care about one thing. The Scroll."

"Well, then, get to it." She took a few steps backward as he approached.

"Out of the way." He drew on the magic, still hovering in the air, and thin rivulets of black dripped from his hands. He ran toushana across the wall, and the paneling began to peel like molting skin. He kicked the damaged wall in and found himself in Darragh Marionne's bathroom. He held out his hand to help Nore through the wall. She eyed it warily and didn't take it. But she stepped inside, beaming.

Darragh Marionne's bathroom was stark white and utterly spotless. A bouquet of wilted flowers sat on her vanity. Nore hurried out of the bathroom, and he followed her into a grand bedroom with a generous sitting area. He spotted a row of drawers beneath a bookshelf and tugged on each. Inside were small luggage items. Nore pulled through shelves, knocking books on the floor, overturning whatever she found. Her fingers grazed jewelry laid out on the counter. She took a piece and stuck it in her pocket.

The heir, a petty thief? He chuckled.

"Maybe she has a proper office." He pushed open the double doors to the room, and it opened up to a sitting room with prim, proper furniture and a fireplace. There were leather-bound books and delicate vases everywhere. Gold-inlaid maps lined the floral-papered walls. Even Darragh Marionne's curtains sparkled with a glamour and elegance that he'd never seen at Hartsboro.

"There!"

Across the room was a writing desk. He rummaged through the open drawers and tried his magic on a locked one. It wouldn't budge.

"It's not here," Nore said.

"How are you sure?"

Nore pulled a diamond necklace with chunky stones from her pocket. "This is the Fon't Le Mai. And Darragh just left it *out* on her table."

"The phone le what?"

Her mouth puckered to stifle a laugh, but her cheeks rose and he grinned. She handed him the necklace. Their fingertips brushed, and Nore flinched. "This piece was the first replica made of the Regent."

Yagrin's brow quirked.

"A one-hundred-forty-carat brilliant-cut diamond owned by the French Crown. Nita Nobu, ancestor of *this* House, snuck into a party to get a look at it. She ended up getting in a world of trouble and sprouting the Order's first diadem. But she did get a look at the necklace, used Shifter magic to make a replica, and sold it. That was the Order's first source of wealth. A few generations later, one of her successors shifted *another* replica as a trophy keepsake. This is pure history. And it was just out on a desk."

He turned the sparkly jewel in his hands. From what his brother had mentioned during his years as Ward, Darragh was a woman who trusted few. Someone so incredibly full of pride wouldn't hide things in their personal space. Nore was right: Something from another House, of only legendary value, wouldn't be *hidden* here.

"Has that massive brain of yours figured out where it actually could be?" He handed her the necklace back, careful to not brush her skin this time. She watched his methodical movement, and their eyes met. The air in the room seemed to rise several degrees as they stood there, frozen, watching the closeness of their hands. Yagrin's throat was dry.

Suddenly, a whoosh ripped the air, prickling his Dragun senses. Yagrin snatched Nore out of the way, pulling her against him just as metal zipped past her face. She gasped.

"*Excuse* me!" Dexler spat. The maezre held another dagger raised high. Behind her were a half dozen glaring House members. "Put down the Le Mai and step away!"

Yagrin moved backward, pushing Nore behind him. But her nails dug into his arm.

She elbowed him aside. "I am so sick and tired of people trying to kill me!"

"*Nore.*" He lowered his voice but kept it firm. "Don't be rash. Too much is on the line."

"I ought to lock you up!"

"Careful with the threats, old woman." He pulled on darkness, and though it churned weakly in his grip, Dexler swallowed hard. He didn't want to hurt her, but he would if she moved that blade an inch closer to either one of them.

"You parade in here pretending to be on our side!"

"I am doing what Quell asked," Nore said. Yagrin's ears pricked at the subtle twist of truth. Jordan wanted to save Quell's life with the Scroll; that's presumably why they were here. Yagrin had built the deception; she was just driving the nail into the hole. If it took the heat off them in this moment, he couldn't blame her for it. She marched up to Dexler. "Excuse us for not telling you every single detail. But I'll have you know what we're looking for here could save lives." She set the necklace down. "I was going to give this to Quell."

Dexler lowered the blade an inch. Yagrin held on to his feeble magic.

"We're looking for—"

"Careful," he warned, recognizing that truth was about to slip from her lips.

Nore's menacing glare was fixed on Dexler. "You can help us, or we can roll the dice to see whose magic is going to win."

Dexler fidgeted.

Yagrin held tighter to his magic, hoping Nore knew what she was doing.

"We're looking for a piece of a very important historical Scroll," she said. "One that was entrusted to you by my House generations ago."

Dexler lowered the blade before shooing the others outside. "A member in the Headmistress bloodline has finally arrived to collect. You should have told me. We have the piece." She ran her hand along the edge of one of the framed maps on Darragh's wall, the lavender stone on her finger glowing. The glass front of the map vanished, and she reached through the gaping hole where it had been into a hidden safe behind the portrait. Inside was a tear of old paper. She handed Nore the brittle parchment.

Nore clutched her chest as she studied it, feeling the paper, turning it on both sides.

"Well?" Yagrin said.

"It's it." She nodded, biting the smile at her lips.

Yagrin tried his hardest but couldn't help but smile, too. "Well done," he said under his breath. His heart thundered in the best way. As long as she kept her word to him, and he kept his head clear about her, they would make a good team.

"Don't doubt me, Yagrin," she said. "I'm playing to win."

That she was. It both inspired and unsettled him.

THIRTEEN

Quell

The address from Audubon takes us to a winding cement drive in the middle of nowhere. Jordan surveys the surroundings before pushing the stable gate open. Knox leads us inside. High noon sun beats down overhead, and by the time we spot an actual house, I'm dripping with sweat. The boarded-up shack is a ranch-style one-story with a dilapidated roof and a horse stable and barn behind it.

The address matches the rusted numbers beside the door. Knox stops several feet from it, and I do, too. Jordan starts to approach, but I urge him away.

"Stand here, beside me." I point to the windows with their curtains pulled. "They're watching."

Nothing happens for some time. But Knox doesn't move, so neither do I. Finally, the door opens, and out steps Willam, all nearly seven feet of him, in worn jeans and a plaid shirt buttoned all the way to his neck.

"Willam!" I start toward him but realize his eyes are narrowed beneath his wide-brim hat. He hangs a shotgun, barrels open, across his forearm, slipping a bullet into each hole.

"Willam, it's Knox. I've gotten her out." I clear my throat and give Jordan a warning glance to not even look his way. But Willam's hard glare doesn't leave Knox. If he doesn't let us in, if we don't get access to their Healers, if this doesn't work, Jordan is out of options. The Sphere's toushana is out of options. *I* am out of options. "Willam—"

"*Hush, girl,*" Knox says, sitting taller in her chair. "She is telling the truth. They got me out of the Cells." She moves toward him.

Willam snaps the shotgun closed and points the barrel at her head. Then mine. Then Jordan's. When the gun is back on Knox's face, I notice the windows on the front of the house have jutted open and gun barrels are pointed at each of us.

"Willam, follow protocol," Knox says.

He flinches, and I've never seen the tall, stoic giant look so mean. "Where were you for the last equinox?" he asks her.

"I was with you in the kitchen after one of the twins had just broken their ankle." Knox leans toward the gun barrel.

The knot at Willam's throat bobs.

"We spent the whole night icing it down and trying to calm the hounds," she says. "When the sun rose, we realized the hounds weren't yelling because they were worried about the twins."

He lowers the gun.

"They were hollering because a nasty badger had gotten ahold of one of the puppies."

He swipes at his red eyes and folds over her in a hug.

"I'm sorry," she says.

He hugs her tighter, and Jordan stuffs his hands in his pockets, looking away.

"What did they do to you?" Willam inspects her.

"I'm fine."

He glares at Jordan, who sticks out his hand. "I'm Jordan Wexton, thirteenth—"

"We can explain everything," I say. "Inside."

"He's not coming in, Quell," Willam says, eyes pinned on Jordan, who has taken his hand back.

"Let him in. Put him in the safe room," Knox says. "The way we'd do any visitors."

"Respectfully, in your absence, this safe house is run by me now," he tells Knox before turning to Jordan. "Your kind aren't welcome here."

"This is ridiculous," Jordan says. "I'm no longer your enemy. I *brought* you Knox. That has to count for something."

"You're also the soulless monster who captured her."

Jordan's nostrils flare.

"There is only so much I can do," Knox says to me, and my heart sinks. "I've been out too long." She heads inside, and with her goes any hope I had of this going smoothly.

"You *must* listen. Jordan has absorbed the entire Sphere's magic. It's inside him. *My* magic. Everyone's! But it's killing him. We have to get it out."

"Is your memory that short, girl? I don't care about the Order, the brotherhood's prize pony, or *magic*. I care about the people between the walls of that house. You can come in. But he stays out."

"Sir—" Jordan starts.

Willam raises his gun.

"Shut up, Jordan," I say. "Please, we have nowhere else we can go. You can't just leave us out here to die. The magic is killing him. Isn't this a place where people—"

"It's not personal, Quell."

"It *is* personal!"

"I'm sorry, Willam," Jordan says.

"You were doing your job; I'm doing mine." He turns his back on us and disappears inside with Knox.

I march toward the stables at the back of the property. "Come on." When we're alone and out of sight, I tell Jordan, "They have no reason to let you in."

"I understand that. But I loathe the Order just as much as they do now. Our interests align."

"To know so much, you know so very little about some things. Jordan, you could never hate the Order as much as they do. Look around."

He walks the rest of the way in silence. We reach the barn, where two horses graze.

"You have to show them who you are. Tell them about what happened to you at Hartsboro."

He's silent.

"People learn a lot about a person by their battle scars."

"And you're so sure about these people because?"

"Because I've lived with them. They are caring people. But very protective because they *have to be*."

"And if you're wrong?"

"I'm not wrong, Jordan. Not about this. *This* I know." He has to *prove* he is not for the Order anymore. He has to *prove* that he will do whatever he can to help *everyone*. "This is what loving me means."

Jordan stares at me so intently it makes the leaves outside stop rustling. It quiets the chirps of birds and brightens the light streaming through the barn's windows. This isn't how I wanted this to go, for him to have to recut his wounds to prove he's worth taking a chance on. I have a fistful of my clothes when Jordan steps toward me. The air between us buzzes, and my gaze falls to the spot below his chest, where his shirt hangs oddly because of the rotting flesh. His gaze follows mine.

"You're asking me to bare my soul to people I hardly know. I've seen horrid things in houses like these, Quell."

"Jordan, I'm right about this. I would not risk this."

"Your magic?"

"Your *life*. I will do everything I can to change Willam's mind, but you have to be *all in*." Without touching me, his hand follows the curve of my cheekbone, as if there is an invisible barrier between us. His distant hand trails down the slope of my jaw. I close my eyes, imagining the warmth of his touch. Longing for the way it feels. When I open my eyes, he has crossed the barn and settled on a wooden bench beside a heap of hay.

"Can I at least get a pillow?"

I ENTER THE back of the house through a mudroom with bare shelves and squeaky-clean floors. Willam has to understand holding the world together means Jordan's life is the priority. Inside, four are gathered around Knox.

Rein, who had a hugely swollen belly last I saw, hands a bundle wrapped in blankets to her, and the tiniest little face emerges from its folds. The twins, who have grown so much in the last few months, sit on the carpet, fishing out various rocks to show Knox. Kedd watches from the doorframe with a grin. Willam gestures for me to join them, offering me a drink.

"It's good to see you back." His sloped posture and sideways smile have returned.

"It's good to be back. This is the most home I've had anywhere. I only wish—" My chin hits my chest. *When they offered me a place among them, I insisted on leaving to find my mother. And she's gone.* I turned my back on them. But I had to. "I needed answers. And I got them."

"There's some peace in that, I know," he says.

The words that come to mind send a quake through my chest.

"Where are the others?" I ask, realizing there's no noise coming from other rooms or the kitchen, where they would typically be finishing lunch. Knox and Willam cared for over a dozen at least in the safe house we were in before.

"Gone."

"I don't understand."

"We were dwindling every day at one point, waking up to more cold beds. I'm not sure where they're going or why. I just hope they're safe. It does not sound kind out there." There's a heaviness in Willam's voice that sounds a lot like grief.

With so much uncertainty in the world and no organized brotherhood, some probably see an opportunity to strike out on their own and see what the big, scary world outside is all about.

"You did the best you could for them while you had them."

"Where is he?"

Jordan. "In the barn."

"He has to go by curfew."

"I need to talk to you about him."

"Knox!" Dimara dashes toward her. I haven't seen her since she learned of Yagrin's betrayal and that the safe house was being relocated because of it. She had been furious with me, yelling across the dinner table.

"You're back," she says to me. "Who said she could come back?"

Kedd, still hovering in the doorway, folds his meaty arms and shrugs. The twins shrug as well.

"Knox brought her home," Rein says, fixing her blouse. "Please don't upset things."

"*I'm* the one at risk of upsetting things?"

She doesn't even know about Jordan yet.

"Dimara." It's Knox who speaks this time. "Willam tells me that you're getting quite good at that pirouette you've been working on."

Her bright eyes shine when she throws her arms overhead and demonstrates.

"It really is good," I say, trying to broker some peace. Dimara ignores me, and I consider it a win, leaving the living room to find Willam. He's in the kitchen, brooding beside a bay window that overlooks a sprawling lawn and, in the distance, the barn.

"I am grateful you were able to get Knox back to us."

"I know."

"But bringing him here does give me deep concern for your and Knox's judgment."

"I know." That is only fair. "There is so much that has happened. You don't understand. The world is a disaster, to put it lightly."

He pulls open a cupboard that's sparsely filled with nonperishables, moving them aside before pushing the wall along the back of the cabinet. It springs open. Inside the hidden compartment are piles of folded newspapers. He hands me one. Then another. I flip through the issues of *Debs Daily* from the last several weeks. Some with headlines I've seen. Others I haven't.

THE FUTURE OF MAGIC UNCERTAIN

HEADMISTRESS DARRAGH MARIONNE AWAITS JUDGMENT

**CORRUPTION ABOUNDS IN THE
BROTHERHOOD—HEAD OR HEART**

BEGONIA TERRACE TAKEN OFF THE MARKET, UNSOLD

**ELLERY AMBROSE & ELENA HARGROVE
NUPTIALS ON THE ROCKS?**

FIVE TIPS FOR EVADING A DARKBEARER

DARRAGH EARLISE MARIONNE, OBITUARY

MAGIC MISSING, VIGILANTES ON THE RUN

I flip to the last article and read. The report pins the rumors about the Sphere's destruction on Jordan and the Dragunhead. Then it mentions that I, the heir to House of Ambrose, *and* "someone else" may know of his whereabouts. My heart knocks into my ribs. Without the brotherhood to pursue justice, the article encourages Marked citizens to be on the lookout. Sun tracking classes are being offered to track down Jordan. The words on the page blur at the rapid ram of my heart. *I have to tell Jordan about this.*

"Fortunately sun tracking is not easy or fast to learn," I say. Yagrin was the only one in his class expertly skilled at it.

"Probably because it requires patience." Willam chuckles. "News travels fast. And ambition even faster." Willam doesn't want anything to do with Jordan. He's a moving target. I chew my lip, realizing I hadn't considered that before coming here. I'm surprised he let me in here at all. Still, we are out of options to heal Jordan without his help. Then it hits me. Willam being on edge. The safe house being so empty.

I know exactly how to persuade him. I can give him something they have never had—a say.

"I understand helping us is a risk. But when has a safe house ever had the chance to shape the Order?"

Willam's forehead creases.

"What if the Order could look different? What if the Houses could look different?"

"Spoken like the heir to a great ancestral House."

"Don't be mistaken. I have no interest in running Marionne. I haven't even been back to Chateau Soleil."

"You're saying you don't have plans for House of Marionne?"

I shift uncomfortably at the legacy I never asked to carry put on my shoulders. The weight of being responsible for so many others is suffocating. I can hardly keep myself alive. I'm not here to talk about a responsibility I did not want. A ship I didn't ask to captain.

"What do *you want* to happen with the Order?"

He paces the length of the room before pointing to a paragraph in one of the articles detailing vicious attacks like the Sixth Ward in DC, on other Unmarked neighborhoods in San Francisco, Chicago, and New York City.

More Darkbearer attacks.

I swallow. The Darkbearers' existence is *why* the brotherhood formed forever ago.

"Everyone's out for themselves. Why shouldn't we be?"

"Jordan's different. Check your rumor sources, he absorbed the Sphere's magic to keep Beaulah Perl from getting it. Willam, he needs a Healer to look at him *soon*. Or there won't be any Order left to build because magic will be gone. This is an opportunity like no other. You *have to* be able to see that."

I've never cared about the Order before. I'm not sure I care about it now. But Willam needs to be convinced. My mother's face flutters to mind, blanketing the conversation in a sudden wave of grief. She is all I cared about. Her, my toushana, and Jordan. She slipped through my fingers. And now the rest is trying to.

"If you don't trust him, bet on me."

"I'll say this, the safe houses are hungry for change, Quell." He glances over his shoulder at the swinging door separating us from the living room where the others are. "Who could stop us from creating *our own* Houses?" He straightens his collar. A tattoo peeks from his top button, hardly visible, with pointed rays or something over where his scar used to be. It must be some kind of new sigil.

"You've started your own allegiance?"

"Us and three other safe houses. So far." And here I thought I could inspire vision as a way to regain his trust. He already has vision. He needs help executing. I'm speechless, proud of them fighting for a place in the magical world to come. And terrified—because Houses breed power. And power breeds monsters.

"I want to know more. If these are to be magical Houses, you'll need help."

"Later." He leans forward. "I want to tell Knox my own way, in my own time. I'm asking you to be discreet."

"Fine. But you *will* help me get a Healer for Jordan."

He doesn't speak for several moments. "I'll think about it and give you an answer this evening."

He doesn't fully trust me. But it's a start.

FOURTEEN

Jordan

The world is falling apart, and I'm hiding in a barn. Coming here might have been a mistake.

The stench of this place makes me dizzy. I walk the length of the metal building, past a dozen stalls. And in the last one there is a broody mare. Black and sleek with eyes the color of the ocean at night. A Fresian. *It's been years.* The horse stares.

Yags and I were boys when we did the circuit. He jumped, and I failed miserably at dressage. My father insisted a man could keep even the unruliest horse in hand. Yags said something at the time that got him backhanded. I broke my arm after a bad fall, trying to show Father I could do just as he expected. That I could be the son he wanted. That was the last time I rode as a boy.

I spit on the ground and turn my back to the horse. She whinnies, but I keep walking until the sound grows distant. There is no sign of Quell. I clench my fist. Then pound it into the wall.

It blackens under my touch.

Toushana moves through me swifter than instinct.

I glare at my hands and assault the wall again. But the faint toushana bleeding from them dissolves. So I beat my fists raw. Remembering how toushana bled out of me suddenly, hurting Quell. *I'll never hold her again.* I reach for the feel of warmth blustering around inside me, looking for the magic I was born with. But the thread of heat that livens in my body is heavier and stronger than anything I've ever felt.

The magic that made me who I am is gone.

My heart turns like a stone in my chest. Then it thrums as a grainy sensation races underneath my skin, buzzing through me, gathering near my heart, then spreading to my limbs as the Sphere's proper magic answers fiercely. With my eyes closed, I focus on the sounds in the air. The gentle sensation of Audior magic, reminiscent of how my own magic used to feel, grows hotter until the hum of magic burns my ears.

Faint whinnies morph into the soft crash of rushing waves. I release the magic, and the scalding feeling that has spread to my face begins to cool. But I smile at the Sphere's proper magic answering at first call. Maybe I'm not completely done for.

My side aches where the flesh has begun to waste away. Despite it, I pull at the jolt of magic again, wondering if I can use the Sphere's magic to do the kinds of magic I used to have. It answers. I urge the earthy feeling up through my chest and into my head, holding my breath, until I feel like an inflated balloon. My lips lose feeling first. Then the Anatomer magic sends a rush of heat across my cheeks, and they numb.

My hands find my face, following the curve of my shifting cheekbones, then my hairline. The pain in my body intensifies. Despite the loss, this is the most I've felt like myself in months. I tighten my fist and dig harder for the parts of myself that feel familiar. My eyes shift farther apart and thin as my Anatomer magic takes over. When I've transformed, I exhale.

When the numbness fades, I collapse against the barn wall, half-worried using magic is making things worse and half-relieved I can still reach proper magic, despite the toushana feeling so much stronger.

An idea strikes me, and it twists like a dagger in my gut. I was an Audior, an Anatomer, and a Shifter. *But with the Sphere's magic, could I do any magic?* I peel myself off the wall. Retentor magic requires an imbued stone, which I don't have. But I could try the other one: Cultivating. Cultivators augment magic in others, using rings with stones full of magic.

I shouldn't need rings. The magic is inside me. I am the stone. I stare again at my hands, blinking.

Cultivators grow magic in others.

Retentors remove magic.

Is there some way to combine them to get this magic inside me out and into something else? Is reverse-Cultivating a possibility? I bite my lip, my mind racing. I would have to be able to do both kinds of magic first.

"Jordan?" Quell appears between the barn doors like a dream, holding a sandwich wrapped in a napkin. Her forehead wrinkles in the way it does when she's stressed.

"Are you okay?" I ask.

"I'm fine." She hands me the food, and I set it aside. The lull of my heart has slowed to a steady beat, but the ache from using magic hasn't.

Quell holds her own heart, feeling the tracer bond we share, where we feel each other's deepest emotions. "You're clearly not."

"Are they going to get a Healer?" I ask.

"I'm still working on that." With a tentative hand, she reaches to push my hair out of my face.

I dodge her touch.

"Your lips have no color, and you're covered in sweat."

Her words unfurl something hot in my chest that's not magic, and I almost wish I'd let her touch me just then. To feel something other than pain. "You're looking at my lips?"

Her chuckle doesn't melt her annoyance.

I sigh. "I am frustrated with the way things are between us. And how helpless I feel. I'm alright now. What else happened in there?" It is written all over her face.

"Willam mentioned some things that have me thinking."

"Like?" I follow her, allured by the notes of honey and jasmine in the air but more concerned about how hard she is pulling at the thread of her clothes.

"There are more Darkbearer attacks in other cities, Unmarked neighborhoods."

I scowl. *More death, more destruction by magic, means more fear of magic.* This is my duty to fix. I glare at where the Dragunheart pendant used to hang against my chest.

"But . . ." She stops. So do I, careful to keep a pace between us. She tangles her long brown coils around her fingers. When she finally meets my eyes, hers are all worry.

"What happens with magic and the Order is sort of up to—"

"Me." I shift on my feet. The Order has always dictated who can use magic and who cannot. It wields access to magical training, like a bargaining chip. Sign over your soul to us, and the world is yours. The Order gives power to some and rips it from others. But the worst part is that it destroys people in the process. Whatever I do with this magic, I won't let it be weaponized like it was.

"Us," she says.

"You've never cared about the Order before."

"I'm realizing I need to care."

Need. Not want.

"Who better to decide how this all should look than someone with your past and my present? You have lived in the ugliest parts of the Order at Hartsboro. I am in the world but not seduced by its glamour anymore. We could work with the people *here*, who've been forced to the margins. Three valuable perspectives."

The warmth drains from my body, the toushana inside me writhing. "You, me, and . . . Willam?"

"The safe houses."

Now I'm pacing. Each step feels heavier than the one before it. My hands are slick with sweat. I want to reassure her, but I can't. When I absorbed the Sphere's magic into my body as a last resort, it was because deep down I don't trust anyone else to handle magic's future.

"Quell, we can't pretend that just because you met a few nice people in safe houses, they're all that way. I've seen things that would give you nightmares." *Willam is one of hundreds, maybe thousands.*

"What Knox has lived through would give *you* nightmares." Her burgeoning frustration burns in my chest. I don't like this divide between us. I can't hold her, stroke her hair, assure her that I am in this, *with* her and *for* her. Whatever it takes.

"We need to take things one step at a time. My wound healed first. The Sphere's magic out of me. Then we rebuild."

"Agreed." Her voice is softer, and it settles my pulse. "I did allude to the idea with Willam already, trying to get him to help us."

"You did not." Cold lurches in my chest. I stagger, it hits me so sharply. "And *what* did he say?"

"He said he had to think about it."

"We should have talked about this first."

"There was no time. It just occurred to me. And it feels right." She is getting worked up again. Hasn't he caused her enough heartache for a lifetime? I plop down beside a bale of hay. It takes a moment to situate my body in a way that doesn't exacerbate the pain pinching my side. Quell grabs my bag from the ground and joins me, keeping an arm's length of space between us. She digs around inside my satchel with a mischievous smirk and grins when she pulls out a bag of candy.

"Thief!"

I swipe at her with minimal effort, not willing to actually chance touching her. Her eyes are wild with mirth, and it lights up the darkest part of me convinced this won't work. Then she rips the candy open, tosses me a few green ones, and tips one end of the bag into her mouth. The curve of her lips assaults me with memories of being near her. Touching her. I look away.

"Where do you see yourself after all this is behind us?"

"Wherever you are."

She pushes the rest of the candy bag my way. "Promise me." I can feel her sadness. "I don't have anyone else." Her lips tighten as she fights to hold back tears. Grief has a mind of its own.

"Do you want to talk about her? Your mom."

"Just promise me."

"I'm here." My fingers crawl to the bag of candy. I grab it. She doesn't let go of her end. "But you have yourself, too. You have to be enough for yourself." *Beaulah showed me that's a hole no one else can fill.*

"I still want you."

"You have all of me."

"And yet I feel so far from you." She hovers her hand over mine. I don't move, daring to believe a stolen moment could be okay. When she brushes her fingertips across my knuckles, it sets my soul on fire. Her touch is a promise. I savor it as I pull away.

"When this is all behind us, we will lie on the beach in the shallow waves until our fingers prune." Not hiding or running.

"It sounds like a dream."

"I will make it real. It's the least I could do to deserve you."

She wrinkles her nose. "You deserve all the happiness, freedom, and love in the world without having to earn it, Jordan."

My jaw hardens. I take the candy bag and finish eating the rest. Quell doesn't understand. She can't. With all I've done as a Dragun, the horrible things Beaulah made me do, the people I've hurt, the bodies I've racked up, I deserve nothing. Certainly not her. We sit for a long time in silence. So long, Quell dozes, and I watch her sleep, attuned to the slow cadence of her heart.

Then a gunshot wakes her up.

FIFTEEN

Yagrin

The train into the city took a corner too fast, and Nore bumped into Yagrin. He steadied her as she toppled, with a firm hand at her hip. She blushed, and he pretended not to notice. She was full of questions about how he planned to get inside Hartsboro. And he hadn't worked up the courage to tell her that was *not* where they were going next. If she knew his reasoning, she wouldn't agree. And on *this* he was not negotiable. So he avoided the conversation altogether and endured the nausea swimming inside him.

When the train stopped, they hopped off right at Central Street Books, the library in downtown Boston. The biggest library in the area, one he'd visited numerous times for Dragun meetings. Nore watched every direction suspiciously. She gazed up at the clouds. Whatever she was wary of faded at the clear blue sky, and her cautiousness was replaced with foot-tapping frustration when she read a nearby sign.

"Hartsboro is hours from here." She adjusted her shoulder strap as the train zipped off.

He shushed her, walking faster toward the doors. She didn't follow.

"Yagrin."

"Come on, I have a plan." He didn't turn back. He didn't dare look at her disappointed face. He hated liars. It made him feel sick that at times he had to be one.

"Yagrin!"

He stopped. Others did, too.

"*Why* are we at a library?"

"I thought you liked books, come on!" He tried to usher her along, but the more he pushed, the more she stiffened. She was more stubborn than Muddy, Red's mule. He was an ass. Nore was an ass and a half when she wanted her way. It had been three days since they left Chateau Soleil. The last two nights they slept in one of his father's hotels, and they'd changed rooms three times because she wanted one close to a fire exit. Then the next one smelled. The third room only had one bed. They both decided to ask for another room after that one.

"I *knew* you were up to something!" She'd caught him sending a written message to his House a couple of nights ago. She assumed it was preparation for their arrival. She was wrong. "All your secret conversations, writing letters, sneaking out. Yes, I know. I saw it. I'm clever, remember? You're—"

"Yes?" He braced for the insult. He'd heard them all.

"*Lying*," she shoved between her teeth, noticing people now watching, remembering they were in public. "I'm not going another place with you if you don't tell me the truth."

A couple shuffling their children stared at them. It was midday. The streets were full of lunch patrons and remotely-employed booklovers, apparently. The Order was nowhere and everywhere.

"Take my arm," he said under his breath, nodding at another onlooker, who was swiping their phone while staring. "I'll explain."

Nore's lips were thin, but she roped her arm around his.

"Now smile at me like everything's alright."

"You're pushing it!"

"Darling, I know you didn't plan on a trip to the library, but please. You know I can't resist a good book," he said, an octave louder than an outside voice.

Nore gazed around nervously, pulling her sweater tighter over her shoulders as she realized how many people were watching them argue on a public street. "Next time, just tell me, *darling*, so that I remember to eat first and am not *starving*." She smiled tightly, and he led them past the onlookers, up the library steps, and through its glass doors.

She ripped her arm away from him the moment they were inside.

"You said we were going to your"—she looked around—"*home*."

The mere suggestion made him queasy.

She leaned closer, and the smell of her ignited Yagrin's senses. Tiny bumps raced across his arms. "There are four pieces of the scroll, one in each House. Ambrose is split between Ell and me. Marionne's, we have. Hartsboro should be next easiest to get because it's your home."

He wasn't ever setting foot on his home estate again. And he had no interest in discussing why with her. Or with anyone. Red hadn't even known. His life in the Order was the one piece of himself he had never shared with her. The only part of him she didn't truly know. And in a way, it felt like because of that, Red never really knew him at all.

He was a terrible person.

He wasn't sure what to expect when Red returned from the dead, but he dreamed of them seeing each other again every night. Would she remember him? Would she be some shell of a person? He'd have to research the Scroll's magic carefully before using it. If she did remember everything, he'd explain who he really was, what the Order was, and hope that bringing her back to life made him forgivable.

"That place is my House," he told Nore. "Not my home."

She crossed her arms. "You're scared to go back there."

He smoothed his clothes. Thankfully, their whispered conversation was the least concern of the passing library's patrons.

"But you don't want to talk about why." She wouldn't relent.

"*Stop* analyzing me." He skimmed the sign for an escalator and marched in that direction.

"*Stop* withholding information, and I wouldn't have to."

He froze. She had a point. He wasn't giving her the benefit of the doubt or making it easier for her, to be honest.

"You were too trusting with the crew at Marionne," he said. "But I realize what it got us—another piece of the Scroll."

"I've inspired you."

"Something like that." The truth was, she had. And it hadn't occurred to him until he saw where trusting Dexler with the truth got them. He'd been bred not to trust people, by a woman who was an expert on the topic. Suspicion was in his DNA. "I thought maybe trusting a little more could help." Hartsboro was a nightmare he longed to forget. If this worked, he would never have to go back there.

"I know you're hesitant about people, Yagrin. You spend most of your time alone."

His brows dented. "How the hell do you know how I spend my time?"

"That's how you come a-across," she stammered. "Is what I meant." Her eyes darted from his. "You mentioned how much you despise your House when we first met. Which means they did something to you that you can't forgive. Trust issues come from somewhere." She covered her tracks well, seasoning her slip with some truth. But her nerves couldn't be covered no matter how smooth her tone. What was the heiress hiding? Something. Now he was sure. It shouldn't surprise him. She was an heir, after all.

It didn't matter. Only the Scroll mattered.

"We are meeting my cousin. I'll give her instructions, and she is going to get what we need. Then to Oralia. And finally—"

"We face my brother." The color drained from her face when she spoke of Ellery. "What do you know about your cousin? I've heard horrible things about your family."

"What you've heard probably doesn't hold a candle to reality. I trusted you back there with Dexler. Trust me now."

"People only get one chance to show me who they really are. If she betrays us or fumbles this somehow, our partnership is done."

"That won't happen. My cousin is different." *I hope. Time with Beaulah wears on a person.* He hadn't seen his cousin since he last visited Hartsboro, before Red was killed. But he'd written insisting he needed to see her about an urgent House matter. He left Nore there, perusing books, to go meet Adola with his heart in his throat.

He found his cousin dressed in black, head covered with a raincoat hood. She leaned over a parted book, dark hair tied in a braid dangling over her shoulder. He joined her in the row. She sucked in a breath as he passed.

"We can't be seen together," she said.

He cleared his throat and pulled a book off the shelves, careful to keep his back to her.

"You—" She started, when an elder woman poked her head into the row. Her finger traced spines, and Yagrin stood there unmoving, not daring to look his cousin's way. Adola swapped out her book for another and turned a few pages until they were alone again.

"You're alive," she said. There was a lilt of surprise between her words. And something else. *Caution?*

"It seems I've disappointed our aunt in that, too."

She inhaled. Adola was always the obedient stand-in daughter to their domineering aunt. She wasn't exactly shy, but she wasn't outspoken either. How had she done living under Beaulah for those years after he'd left? Jordan made it sound like she'd done alright and found her confidence. But her nerves here, with him, made his heart hiccup.

Adola is trustworthy.

But she is also . . . an heir.

Both directions in the library were clear. Trusting her felt much less risky than showing up at Hartsboro. When he was sure they were alone, he said, "I'm glad you're alright."

She didn't respond.

"You *are* alright, aren't you?"

"As much as I can be, considering."

"I'm sorry I couldn't make it to your Trial. Or Cotillion. I don't—"

"I know, Yags. I know. It's alright. How's Jordan?"

"Haven't seen the bastard in some time."

"I've heard things, Yagrin." Her whisper shook. "*Impossible* things."

"I wish I had better news."

She let out a breath. "What will happen to magic? Does he have a plan?"

"*We.*"

"You're actually working together?"

He shifted at all the questions. Hadn't he called *her* here? She exited the row. Her chin over her shoulder urged him to follow. There was no joy in her turned-down lips, no hope in her make-up-streaked eyes. He followed her to the next row of books. For a few minutes they perused, until Nore appeared.

The book fell from Adola's hands as she gaped at her.

"What are *you* doing here?"

Nore gazed between them. "I hope you know what you're doing," she said to him before leaving them there. When she was out of sight, Adola replaced her book on the shelf and hustled toward the exit.

"Wait, please." He rushed after her.

She walked faster.

"Excuse me, miss," he said, far too loud on purpose. Heads swiveled in their direction. Adola huffed and pulled him hard by the sleeve into a shadowed corner. Window light cascaded over hard lines etched into her face. It had only been three years since he lived in the same prison with his cousin, and she'd aged so much in such a short time.

She squeezed his wrist. "You're working with a 'Roser now? Are you out of your mind?"

"I know what I'm doing. She's smart as a whip and hates her House. The perfect ally."

"So she says."

His nerves churned. "Look, I need your help."

"I'm not helping her."

"You're helping *me*." It felt good to be honest with someone. "I wouldn't ask if it wasn't critically important. I need you to find something at Hartsboro. It's a piece of old parchment from House of Ambrose that we were given stewardship of—"

She covered her gasp.

"What?"

"A scroll."

Ice slid down Yagrin's spine. "How did you know that?"

"Ellery Ambrose and his fiancée visited recently. They spoke with Mother privately two days ago. The girl left hours after they arrived. Then she brought me to greet him. As I was leaving, I overheard him saying Mother'd been entrusted with something from his House."

"Do you know for sure it was the Scroll?"

"I don't. But the next morning he left with a square of old parchment. I used the corridors between the walls and watched him pack it in his things."

Yagrin's heart leapt. Beaulah didn't just hand over things of value. Even if she'd written off the Scroll as legend, she wouldn't pass up the opportunity to have power over someone who devoutly believed in it. "Why'd she give it to him?"

"I don't know. But I do know that halfway through dinner, Mother sent the dogs out of her quarters, to their kennel. And she and Ellery dined until well past midnight."

His neck broke out in sweat.

"I have to go, Yagrin. Don't call for me again."

"Ado—"

"Stay away, alright?" Her stare deadened. "Stay far away. Mother's sick. I've been moved into position. It's not official yet, but it will be soon. She's *ravenous* for blood. I have to commit, you understand?" Her grip tightened, and a glint in her eye he'd never seen before sank his heart like a stone in a river.

"Goodbye, cousin."

Her hood fell when she turned to leave, exposing the bone behind her ear, where there was a tiny mark: the cracked column for House of Perl.

But this sigil was wrapped in a vine of thorny roses.

She turned and caught him staring. "All that was broken by Mother's reign will bloom again under mine." She hurried off.

SIXTEEN

Nore

The sky darkened outside the library as Nore stood near its doors looking for Yagrin. Adola exited without a glance in her direction. Nore followed her out, at a distance. But despite her suspicions, the girl walked alone down the street for several blocks before disappearing around a corner. The sidewalk filled with people carrying umbrellas, but not a drop of rain fell from the sky. And it wouldn't because this wasn't bad weather. The dead were coming.

Yagrin.

Just as she thought his name, he burst through the doors of the library. She waved him over.

"Hurry."

They rushed down the steps, when the sight of dark, shadowed figures curdled her blood. Yagrin froze beside her.

"What? What is it?"

But she was speechless as darkness billowed above her, separating from itself like storm clouds being ripped apart. Her ancestors descended like an army from the sky, shards of black slamming into the street like roadblocks. She'd never seen so many before.

Is Ellery doing this? Getting more of them to come after me?

Yagrin tugged at her sleeve, but his words were drowned by a car crashing into a shadow of nothing. The vehicle's front was crushed on impact.

The dead didn't move as people rushed to pull the driver out. Cars swerved around the accident. Screams tore at her ears. Shattered glass covered the asphalt, and shadows drew a message in the wreckage.

SOON

"There are so many more of them," she said.

"Who?"

She couldn't keep this secret anymore. Not when they were so good at finding them. She blew out a sharp breath and explained how some ancestors were able to die in their natural bodies but allow their souls to roam as spectral spirits around the estate, tethered to life.

She didn't mention the Pact. Or the glass box, where the Headmistress's heart was kept. She didn't want to give him any reason to be suspicious of her helping him.

"Why are they looking for *you*?" he asked.

When her mother died, it would be her turn to honor the Pact by putting her heart in the glass box.

When the dead realize it is magicless . . .

That I can't fulfill the Pact . . .

I am dead.

It'll be quick and painless, like falling asleep. I'll bring you back immediately, I swear. Her brother's words as they stood over the grave still felt like a sword through her chest. He wanted her to let him kill her so he could then murder their mother. Headship would pass to him, and he promised to bring her back with the Scroll. When she refused him, he turned on her.

Fear thickened Nore's throat. *Will it hurt to die?* Her eyes stung. But she clenched her fist. She had no intention of finding out anytime soon.

But she couldn't tell Yagrin any of this. He already suspected her of being dishonest. Giving him any clue she had a motive to steal the Scroll for herself would ruin everything.

"What is it?" he pressed as emergency response wailed in the distance.

"I"—she patted her pockets—"thought I left something. But I have it." She bit her lip. The throng of dead still hadn't moved, voids of darkness with the loose shape of a person were scattered eerily on the street like soldiers standing sentry. "I hope that person in that car is okay." She turned and rushed off.

Yagrin stuck with her pace. She led him around a corner, then another, but the storm streamed behind them. She couldn't outrun the dead. She clawed at her skin, wishing she could peel it off as she picked up to a run. When they crossed an intersection, Yagrin threw his hand in the air, and a driver came to a swerving stop. He opened the door and they slid inside.

"Where to?"

"Park Hot—"

"Logan International!" They needed to get to Begonia Terrace, home to House of Oralia. "Our flight, remember?"

Yagrin's brows dented, but he sat back in his seat. "I'd almost forgotten."

The car zoomed off, but the dead followed. At least the car was moving faster. They'd said *soon*. Was her mother dying? Nore's nails carved moons into her arms. They would get inside the huge airport and hopefully lose the ancestors that way. The dead didn't cross thresholds that weren't their own. She tried to sit back, but her grip dug into the driver's leather.

"Did your cousin say yes?" she asked.

Yagrin's posture sagged. She braced herself, unsure how much more bad news she could take at the moment. Everything was going wrong.

"Your brother was with my aunt."

Nore's nails sank deeper in the seat.

"We're too late. He got what we needed from her."

"No." Her eyes burned with tears. Ellery, too, had figured out that there was a piece of the Scroll in each House. He already had half of the Ambrose piece. Now he had another. Suddenly their progress at Chateau Soleil felt like nothing. They were tied. Which meant she and Yagrin were behind.

They rode in silence the rest of the way. She had more questions, but she wanted to get down to specifics, and speaking in code was only infuriating her further.

Once they were at the airport, Yagrin tried to shift their tickets out of a scrap of paper, but the paper only rippled, his magic malfunctioning. *Everything truly is falling apart.*

They hustled to the counter to buy tickets the old-fashioned way. She presented her identification, but when the counter attendant grabbed it, Nore couldn't let go. All this, the dead showing up at the library, traveling with her real name, her brother being ahead of them, set her teeth on edge.

"Ma'am, is there a problem?"

Nore released her ID. "No, sorry. Here you go."

Once they were through security, waiting for the plane, she noticed the sky outside wasn't as dim. Maybe they'd managed to lose them. Yet her shoulders wouldn't uncinch.

"What else did your cousin say? Any rumors about my mother's health?" She had to be alive, the more Nore thought about it.

Nore's brother wouldn't let that happen. If he was going to steal Headship, he had to have Nore in place before their mother died. So that her heart could be handed over to the ancestors right away. Had he sent the ancestors to *capture* her? They never got too close, but their presence was enough to make her flee.

"I didn't get into that with her," Yagrin said.

"Well, I need you to *get into that*. Getting my mother from my brother is the second half of our agreement, unless you've forgotten."

"I've forgotten nothing, alright?" Yagrin smoothed his pants with his hands. "Look, all I know is that your brother practically skipped out of my home. Adola doesn't trust you or any Ambroser."

Nore huffed, frustrated.

"We were going to face him eventually. I'd hoped when we did we would have more of an upper hand. But nothing's changed. We're doing fine."

Her stomach twisted. How was she going to out-clever the most brilliant magical person she knew? Her jaw ticked. She'd avoided thinking about it, but the time was growing close.

"Do you know if he's on his way to Begonia Terrace as well?"

"We're about to find out."

"I don't like this."

"No kidding."

"Have you been there before? Do you have a relationship with Headmistress Oralia?"

"I don't. You've met Drew, I'm sure."

"I have, but barely." At the tea in Darragh Marionne's rose garden, Drew and Adola had played a trick on Quell with a saltshaker. It was lighthearted, but it had made Nore uncomfortable. She didn't know or trust either of them.

"You're going to have to get us into her good graces," she said.

"Do I strike you as someone who does well with people's good graces?"

A strangled laugh escaped her.

"Somehow it's going to be alright," he said, turning to look at her.

"How do you know?"

"Because we have you."

She waited for a smirk. But Yagrin's deadpan expression did something to her insides. It felt like the pressure of a warm, tight hug. She scooted closer to him and leaned on their shared armrest. His body was stiff against her, but he didn't move. She was too nervous about everything else to smile, but it felt nice.

Maybe she could win him over *as herself* after all.

SEVENTEEN

Quell

Willam holds his shotgun on the front porch of the safe house as Rein and Kedd hold a girl with dark hair, dressed in the color of blood. As Jordan and I get closer, I recognize her.

"Yaniselle?" Jordan says.

"Your ex is here?!" Her hands are tied behind her back, and the barrel of Willam's gun is pressed to her head. Jordan walks faster. The last time I saw her was at the Sphere, standing beside Beaulah, filled with rage at Charlie's death.

"How did you find this place?" Willam demands.

"I sun tracked Jordan." She slides a Dragun coin with a cracked column from her back pocket.

"This is why I don't want him here." Willam slips a finger onto the trigger. Guilt cinches in my chest.

"She's *lying*," Jordan says. "She doesn't know the first thing about sun tracking." Jordan approaches, and Willam turns the gun on him. The barrel of the weapon swivels back in Yani's direction. A hard line etches between her brows as Willam nudges her with the gun up onto her feet.

"The truth, Yani," Jordan says.

She looks between both of them.

"Jordan, it's *me*."

"Precisely."

Her nostrils flare. "I did come for Jordan," she spits. "That part wasn't a lie. I've been kicked out of Hartsboro, and I didn't know where to go. I visited one of the brotherhood's contacts to ask about a safe place. He told me I'd find a friendly face at this location. I took it to mean I'd find you."

Audubon. "That snake."

"Jordan, you know how Mother is. Please, let me stay." She jerks against Kedd and Rein's grip.

"He has no say here." Willam's jaw works. Knox exits the house.

"I can't vouch for her, Willam," I say.

Jordan's lips thin, and it fills me with confusion. He can't feel sorry for her. He can't care one bit what happens to her.

"If you have a way to lock her up, I believe she could be telling the truth," he says.

"I didn't ask what you thought." Willam does not take his eyes off Yani. He raises the gun again, and Jordan steps forward.

"*What* are you doing?" I say under my breath to Jordan.

"You're trying to keep everyone safe here," he says to Willam. "One of your allies just handed off your location. Questioning her more about Audubon and what else is going on out there could be useful."

Willam turns the gun back on Jordan. "Maybe I wasn't clear."

Jordan swallows.

"Knox, what do you see?" Willam asks.

"We need her alive," Jordan whispers when he returns to my side.

"*Why?*" I burn with irritation. Yani stiffens as Knox moves around her before focusing on her heart.

Yani struggles against her restraints. "What kind of magic is this?"

"Her heart is dark," Knox says. "But it is broken. I don't mind the boy's suggestion."

"Take her to the basement," Willam orders. "Seal her in. She's watched on a twenty-four. Fed on the twelves. The only reason she's going inside is for information. Draguns, former or current, are not welcome here."

Willam, Knox, and the others follow as Yani is led in.

Jordan exhales, and I see red. "You still love that trash?"

"Don't be ridiculous."

Before Willam crosses the threshold, he says, "Jordan, there will be dinner shortly. Take some for yourself and to Yani. Question her thoroughly. I expect to hear everything you find."

"Does this mean he can stay?" I ask.

"For dinner." He and the others are inside as we trail behind them.

"You're having *dinner* with your ex. That's fantastic."

He smirks. "I think you might be cutest when you're mad."

Jordan and Yani have known each other since they were young. They grew up together, bonded by the trauma of being raised at Hartsboro. It's not lost on me that she knew him in a way I never can.

"Quell, this is our chance to get more insight into Beaulah's plans. We can't forget she was working with the Dragunhead when the Sphere broke. Not to mention the Darkbearer attacks feel too coordinated to be random. We need to know who all we're up against, what they're planning, and how close they are to finding us. Don't let trifle thoughts like jealousy divide us."

My skin heats. How stupid I must look, acting jealous. That is not me. I won't be that person. "I hope you know what you're doing. Because that girl still wants you." If he thinks she's innocent, he's naive.

He steps so close to me that when I breathe, the air is only him. Sandalwood and earth. Something sweet underneath, like vanilla or cashmere.

"I don't care what she wants."

A pang runs through me—a need to lean closer to him, to suffocate the space between us. To feel the promise of his words in an embrace.

"She is nothing to me anymore. I'm yours. Only yours. As far as I see, there was no one before you. There will be no one after."

The tenderness in his expression warms the coldest parts of my heart.

"I don't trust her. And we don't have the full truth about why she came here. But I can handle Yani."

My chest uncinches a little, and when Jordan unclasps his hands, I suck in a breath, thinking he might allow us a moment of something closer than this. But his hands slide into his pockets, and my fingers move to my chest. Despite what he says, he is nervous.

"Be on guard and in control in her presence."

Towering over me, he hinges at the neck, bringing his mouth a breath away from mine. His nerves settle. Golden light from the setting sun catches in his unruly strands of hair. He's so close, my lips part. I've stopped breathing.

"Self-control happens to be something I'm very good at." His breath on my lips sends a rush of heat all over my body. I lean toward him, daring him to kiss me. But he puts distance between us and heads to the door. I can't decide if I'm annoyed or impressed.

EIGHTEEN

Jordan

Yani is expecting me when I descend the basement stairs.

The room is sparsely furnished but clean. There's a bed, a full bathroom, and a small table with two stools. Yani cleans a scrape on her arm. She wears dark red pants with a red corset over a sheer long-sleeved top, which is torn at the shoulder. Her diadem sparkles, gunmetal silver with bright blue gems. It's the only part of her that doesn't look haggard. I set the change of clothes Knox gave me for her and a plate of dinner on the table.

"Are you alright?" I ask.

"Sometimes it feels like you've forgotten who I am."

Beaulah trained her to wear masks well. But ironically, it was being with Yani that forced me to learn how to see through them.

"I hope you weren't too shaken up."

She rolls her eyes, but she's as unconvincing as she was the night I stepped in to save her life. I was sixteen. She and some Perl peers dragged me out to attend one of Charlie's raids. When she tried to single-handedly apprehend a dangerous target, he almost choked her to death right there in the middle of a nightclub. I stepped in, and Charlie showed up. The target let her go, but the moment moved on as if Yani wasn't just gasping for air. Charlie didn't even address it. But I did. Even then, Yani didn't flinch. She was "fine." It wasn't until she snuck into my room that night and curled up next to me that I really saw through her.

"I know who you are better than you do sometimes," I say.

She laughs. "You still flatter yourself, I see." She moves from the stool to the edge of the table. "You think these safe house freaks are going to kill me?"

"Depends. Are you ready to be honest about why you're here?"

"Mother made me leave. It's true." There is an earnestness that gleams in her eyes. But she fiddles with a silver buckle on her corset.

"I remember when we first met," I say. "Everything with you is a strategy."

"You're still not over that kiss?" She grinned, a real smile that hugs her eyes.

"You walked up to me at my birthday party and *kissed me*! I was fifteen, surrounded by all my friends. And then you didn't say a word to me for a year."

"You loved it."

It was the only thing I thought about for the next year. A girl *kissed* me. And not just any girl, but the one everyone whispered about being so pretty. Did that mean she liked me? She didn't talk to me after that. Did that mean I was a bad kisser? Back then my head spun every time I thought of it.

"It was an angle," I say. "You admitted as much when we . . ."

"Broke up."

The two syllables crack in my head like thunder, taking me back to that vicious fight we had. A year after the kiss, I'd worked up the courage to approach her and ask her to the Tidwell. We danced all night. I was sixteen, recklessly confident, well mannered. She was into Jordan with the big ego. Gone was the insecure boy she'd made blush at his birthday party.

By the end of the ball, I dropped her off and told her I wanted to kiss her again. Just one kiss could last me another year, I told myself. She gave me permission and spent the night with me. The next morning I smelled like her. We only saw each other a few times a year. It felt like

I was dangling from a string. She was the cat, I was the toy, no matter how hard I tried to maintain the upper hand. She insisted we shouldn't get too attached, and yet all I could think of when she was gone was her. She never asked me for loyalty and shamed the idea, never reciprocating when I said I loved her. But back then, no matter who I was with, it was Yani I imagined.

"I don't know if I'd call it a breakup, because it wasn't really a relationship."

She admitted that at my fifteenth birthday party Beaulah had told her to get close to me. She knew I'd be Ward one day in House of Marionne, and she wanted eyes on me to make sure that my loyalties hadn't wavered.

Yani was dead to me then.

And I've never looked back.

"Sixteen-year-old Jordan wouldn't have said that."

My cheeks heat, images of her I should not remember flashing in my mind. She hops off the table, moving toward me, and Quell's warning plays on repeat in my mind.

"Come on, Jay. We were fun, weren't we?"

"I don't look back on us with the fondness you do."

She throws down a cotton swab dirtied with blood. "How could you say that? It was me breaking your heart that turned it to steel." Her chin rises. "I wear it like a badge of honor."

"So what is your angle this time? Coming here. What badges are you auditioning for now?"

She steeples her hands.

"The truth."

Her expression shifts, the mischievous purse of her lips melting into a deadpan stare. Her gaze drifts past me. She turns her back to me, pulling at the stack of clothes I set down. She yanks the ratty string at her back, and the bow from her corset comes undone.

"The truth is, Beaulah believes you still have feelings for me." She wiggles in her top, loosening it before reaching inside the corset, pulling at the bone of it. Out comes a small blade. It clangs on the floor. "She says a first love doesn't just go away." Yani pulls at the next bone in her corset. Another blade. When she's done, there are half a dozen razor-sharp daggers on the table.

"She sent me here to sway you to my side and bring you *and magic* back to her." The shapeless corset falls to the floor, and she pulls the sheer top off. "And to kill anyone who gets in my way."

"And you have no intentions to obey?"

"Not this time. She didn't do right by Charlie, doing experiments to bind him to toushana, letting him die like that. I can't get past it. I said what I had to to get out of there." She holds out her arms. "There. I have nothing else to hide." She turns in a circle before snatching the dress from the table. There is a mark on her back: a cracked column wrapped in a vine of roses. She tosses the dress overhead before plopping on a stool and dragging her dinner over to her.

"I've never seen a mark like that before."

She hunches over her plate, shoveling food. "Yeah. And?"

"Does it mean anything?"

"It means everything." Metal scrapes her plate. "It's the mark of the future. Adola's mark."

A shiver runs up my arms, and it sends my heart knocking into my ribs. Adola, making a move for her own independence. Could House of Perl be an ally? Or was this another layer to Yani's master manipulation? "What do you know?"

"Just that I picked the right side. That's all."

I watch her eat in silence, finishing every crumb on her plate.

"How long did it take to find us?"

"Audubon wasn't exactly eager to help. He made me . . ." She grimaces. "Entertain him before giving up the address."

"You should have stabbed his eyes out."

"I carved them out of his skull." She takes another big bite.

I smile, and cold licks my insides, the Sphere's dark magic stirring. "Good." A beat passes.

"She picked me first, you know? For her little experiment. Putting toushana in a person. But after the first session, I told her no." She sits taller. She may lie to my aunt, but standing up to her? I'm not sure I buy it. However, if she believes I'm starting to trust her, that will only loosen her tongue.

"Do you know anything about the Dragunhead's whereabouts?"

"I've heard things. But I couldn't tell you what's true. He hasn't been at Hartsboro. Beaulah's done with him, or he with her. That's all I know." She pushes her plate away. "I also hear the darkness could eclipse the sun soon." She smiles darkly.

Darkbearers rising up, taking over. Impossible. Before the brotherhood crumbled, our raids of safe houses turned up many descendants of Darkbearers and some *actual* practicing Darkbearers: the target with the red ball cap at Yaäuper Rea; Stryker, the boy my aunt kidnapped. How many more is Beaulah protecting? The Sixth Ward comes to mind. And the other neighborhoods ransacked by dark magic that Quell mentioned.

If this is true, Darkbearers would have to be organizing somehow, somewhere.

I grind my teeth at the guilt twisting in my chest. I should be out there, using the power I *do* have to stop this carnage.

"Scared silent?" She mocks me.

"Magic is in *my* hands. I fear nothing." I block her view of my ribs.

"What side do you think your pretty little do-gooder will end up on if it gets ugly?"

"You assume you know the side she's on now."

Yani throws her head back in laughter. I've gotten all out of her that I can for now.

"I can't make you any promises about what Willam is going to do with you. These people don't like me much either. Be honest for once. See where that gets you." I gather her daggers to take them with me. I owe her nothing. But every person against Beaulah—if she's honest—is an arrow in our quiver.

"I can help you and Quell if you give me a chance," she says. "What is your plan with the Sphere's magic?"

I start up the stairs.

"You and Quell will never work, you know."

I climb faster.

"She's too caring, and you're rotten on the inside."

"Wouldn't you love that to be true."

"You being rotten? I couldn't care less."

"I meant Quell and me."

I know I'm rotten on the inside.

When I reach the ground floor, I secure the locks on the basement door, where Willam is waiting. I tell him everything Yani admitted about Audubon and Beaulah's real intentions for sending her here, and give him her weapons. I leave out my cousin Adola's alleged mark.

"Do you trust her?" he asks.

"Not for a second. Do you trust me a bit more now?"

"If I did, I wouldn't tell you." He indicates the den nearby, where Knox and Quell are sitting, waiting. He's made his decision about whether I can stay. Quell and I meet eyes as I sit down beside her. Her expression doesn't look promising.

NINETEEN

Quell

Willam pulls the doors to the den closed. He and Knox have to understand everything depends on keeping magic safe. Jordan sits beside me on a love seat. The distance between us rattles my already-frayed nerves. Recklessly, I cross the bridge with my arm, running my fingertips across the cushion for a brief graze of his skin. His magic doesn't disturb mine instantly. A fleeting moment of comfort *has* to be okay. But he shakes his head and doesn't come closer.

Knox and Willam are across a coffee table from us with untouched drinks. Willam's fingers drum on the table, and I can feel their thump in my chest. He isn't going to let Jordan stay.

"I think it would be helpful to get a better understanding of what you want, Quell," Knox says, jumping right in.

"What *I* want?"

Jordan doesn't look at me, and somehow that makes it easier to answer.

"I want my magic intact."

"Are you only concerned for yourself in all this?" she asks.

After all I've been through, don't I deserve to focus on me? Why is it my job to fix everyone's burdens? "If I say yes, then what?"

"I just don't believe Rhea's daughter—" Willam starts.

Jordan's grip tightens on the seat.

"*Leave* my mother out of this," I say.

"Tell *us* what you want." Jordan folds his arms. "What do you picture the Order looking like, if you had a say?"

"To be clear, the offer was that we *would* have a say if we helped you." Willam's finger stabs the table.

"That's not an answer to my question," Jordan retorts, and I shift in my seat. *This is going sideways.*

"Clarity is important," Willam says.

"It was just an idea I threw out," I say.

"Which is my choice to refuse or accept," Willam says. "And I am still chewing on it all."

"She can't offer things that are not hers to give," Jordan says.

I glare at Jordan. The tension in the room is sharper than a knife. Knox whispers something to Willam.

"We are no longer willing to be hunted," Willam says.

"That's a brotherhood decision," Jordan says.

"Aren't you the face of the brotherhood?" Knox says.

"Hardly," Jordan says.

"Regardless"—Willam leans forward—"we expect this new version of the Order will grant safe houses the right to form our own Houses."

"I don't see why you being allowed to have official Houses is our concern at all," I say. "Jordan, we don't care. Tell them we don't care what they do." I smile tightly. We need some kind of support, and right now they're the only ones open to helping us.

"I don't care what you do," Jordan says. "Or Knox. Or the others here. But I can't give you a blanket pass for anyone in a safe house. That goes against everything I believe is right."

Willam slaps the table. "I guess we have our answer!"

"No, hear me out," he goes on. "There are dangerous people in safe houses. You can't deny that. People who make a sport of hurting others. For centuries, Darkbearer descendants have hidden in safe houses. And now, some of them are resurfacing, committing crimes like their predecessors. The Sixth Ward. The others in the papers."

Willam glares. Knox purses her lips.

"He's saying we trust you," I say. "But we can't trust everyone because we trust you." I try to sit straighter and realize my hand is cemented to the edge of the coffee table.

Jordan goes on. "The Dragunhead *is* out there somewhere. He tried to kill me. I *know* my aunt is plotting to turn this chaos in her favor somehow. I can only do so much with the Order when its old leaders are still in power."

He isn't wrong. The Houses have been silent. Only Isla Ambrose issued a formal statement after the Sphere was destroyed. The front page headline heralded her House for their "deep commitment and pioneering intellect" as they study up on new uses of magic that could be helpful in finding the guilty culprit or aiding in restoring magic to a safe location.

"I'll need time to act on any of this *after* I'm healed."

"You possess *all* of magic—you can do whatever you want whenever you want," Willam says.

"That's not leadership. Which is precisely why I am in charge and you are not."

The tension in the room grates. This bargaining isn't working. Willam doesn't trust me. And he isn't going to start trusting Jordan if he doesn't fully trust me, because I brought Jordan here and am vouching for him. The only way to prove I'm trustworthy is to put something on the line. I shoot up from my seat. "*Look*—the way magic exists isn't equitable or fair. I spent most of my life on the run. You've been forced to live the same way. Saving dark magic is a shift from the way things have been done. It's a change in a good direction for both of us. Can we all agree on that?"

Heads nod around the table.

"Bringing Jordan here was a risk. If Yani could follow us, others could." A question burns in Jordan's eyes, but I ignore it. I know what I have to do. "We need to get everyone here behind the walls of an estate with more protections in place. It's more secure."

Knox sits up, her eyes widening.

"You're saying, relocate to . . ."

"Chateau Soleil. Kedd, Rein, the twins, you all are welcome at House of Marionne." *It's technically my House.* Willam's jaw dangles open. Jordan stares, stoic, but I can feel his anger burning in my heart.

"You would take us there, breaking how many rules?"

"Didn't you just say we make the rules now?"

No one living in a safe house has set foot in an ancestral magical House. Safe houses are a refuge for those running *from* the Order. Going to Chateau Soleil isn't just giving them safe haven; it's defying history. Jordan hasn't moved, but he is silent, which I appreciate. I'm doing this for him, for me, for all of us.

"Once we arrive, you will summon a Healer to tend to his wound. That's all I ask for the safe haven."

"When would we have to leave?" Willam asks.

"Whenever you want. Even Dimara, if she'll come."

They are speechless. And I have my answer.

"I guess I'll go tell everyone." Willam's mouth is thin when he tips his hat, excusing himself.

Jordan sinks deeper in his seat, stroking his chin.

Knox pulls me aside. "I had to be in line. Willam's lead now. But I do believe in what you're doing. It's very courageous, Quell."

I'm not sure what to say. I'm not concerned with bravery or anything like that. I just want to live in a real way.

"And you're sure you're not interested in leadership?" She squeezes my shoulder affectionately. "You did good, Quell. I won't say exactly what I'm thinking, but I'm sure you can imagine."

My mother would be proud.

TWENTY

Nore

The winding road along the drive to Begonia Terrace was speckled with sun-kissed vineyards and lush hills, but Nore sat in the back of the driver's car with clenched fists. She watched the sky behind them. The ancestors weren't following them this time, it appeared. But she'd feel better when she crossed the property line up ahead.

Nore couldn't stop thinking about the cryptic message carved in broken glass on the pavement.

Soon.

Soon they would have her heart.

Soon she would have to fulfill the Pact.

The dead were getting more aggressive. Thankfully, the person driving the crashed car walked away, despite being pretty banged up. Ambrose Headship changed at age twenty-two. The serving Headmistress's heart was removed from the glass box and returned. And the new heir gave up theirs. Unless the Headmistress died first. *Ellery's plan.* Succession passed down to a child *or* it jumped family bloodlines. It did not change between siblings.

She had to die first, then her mother, to ensure Headship passed to him. And it felt like Ellery's hands were already wrapped around her throat.

Yagrin, who hadn't spoken to her much since they landed, turned to her now as they were nearing their destination. She longed for the boy who sat inches away to tell her it would be alright. To let her break, for a moment, in his arms.

"You never told me why the dead are after you, specifically. Does it have something to do with your brother?"

"Yes."

"He's sending them to capture you?"

"I think so. Or to scare me. I'm not really sure. But I know he wants to get his hands on me to kill me to force Headship to pass to him."

Nore's mind flooded with memories of the brother who'd stood in the way of their mother's cruelty, always telling her that she was good enough. Her eyes stung with tears. She tried to blink them away. But her chin dropped to her chest as she relived the horror she'd boxed away since she'd been on the hunt for the Scroll pieces with Yagrin.

"Are you alright?" Yagrin looked at her squarely. Her heart twinged.

She cleared her throat but couldn't lie this time. "I don't know."

"Would you like a book or something?" He patted his pockets. "I have this pamphlet I nabbed from the airport on aerodynamics that you might find distracting." He handed it to her, and she couldn't help but grin.

"Why on earth are you reading about nuclear fission?"

"Oh, I just needed a place to toss my gum."

She laughed, and it felt like weeds being pruned from her soul.

"Seriously, if you are not fine, that's—" He spread his fingers apart on the seat between them. "You're allowed to not be okay."

She studied his dark brown eyes as his gaze danced across her face, wondering what he was thinking.

She shook her head. There was no time for her not to be okay. Her being okay was the only way she was holding herself together, traveling with him, sitting so close while slowly dying inside of longing to be known by him completely. No secrets. No lies.

"You're allowed to be scared."

"This hurts me more than anything." When she heard the words come out of her mouth, she pressed back in her seat, hoping he wasn't *really* listening. She'd been too honest.

"I don't understand. You and your mother are close?"

All that Yagrin knew was that Ellery Ambrose had kidnapped their mother and Nore suspected he was going to try to kill her. She bit her lip. Then she opened her mouth and the truth fell out.

"I hate my mother. But I need her alive."

Yagrin's stare narrowed. "Go on."

"When she dies, our House tradition orders that I am Headmistress. I *refuse* to be Headmistress of a House that's never wanted me. My brother wants the gig, and he intends to kill me to pull it off." Her breath hitched. *What was she doing?* But by the Sovereign it felt *good* to finally speak the truth!

Yagrin leaned forward as if he was about to speak, only to turn and stare out the window again.

Her heart knocked into her ribs.

"You want the Scroll for yourself. To keep her alive."

She was too far upstream in the truth to lie now. "Yes, Yagrin, I do."

"You never intended for my brother to have it."

"Did you?"

His jaw clenched.

"I'm sure you can understand what it's like to walk in my shoes. You *hate* the Order and do anything you can to avoid it!" She bound her lips shut. She'd gone too far. She had to stop now, before his expression changed from confusion to heartbreak—that was a loss Nore couldn't take.

Everything else had gone wrong, *not* as planned. The one thing that *was* sort of going right was that she was near him. And despite the perpetual torture, there were moments of the sweetest delight. Like in the airport. And rummaging around Chateau Soleil. And puzzling out the roses. And listening to him try to compliment her intelligence. His jokes. His disdain for the Order was life-giving. She'd missed being so near it. In a way, Yagrin knew her in ways no one else did. He knew the persona she'd made up and the fugitive heir she was. He just didn't know they were the same person.

"Say something, Yagrin. Please."

The car stopped. A gate hidden in lush greenery towered ahead of them. Beyond it were rolling hills covered in vineyards. The window rolled down. Yagrin flashed his Dragun coin at a box protruding toward them, and the gate opened.

"You've never been here before either?" she asked. Resolving to focus on the task ahead, she slipped her fake diadem from her pocket and set it on her head.

"Never." He didn't look at her when he spoke, but she couldn't focus on that. They were there for the last piece before she'd have to face her brother. If Yagrin was done helping her because she'd lied to him, she'd just have to find a way to finish on her own. She wasn't a quitter.

"Begonia Terrace's security is a known joke," he added.

That didn't bode well for the Scroll piece being securely held. Nore's stomach was a knot. Beyond the gates, the sun hovered on a horizon of endless hills. The grounds were rich with color; flowers and overgrown vines covered every structure and lined every paved road. There were tucked-away courtyards rimmed in boxwoods and quaint stone cottages. In the distance were three separate houses, their facades almost entirely covered in foliage and flowers.

"Which house is the main House?" But as the car rolled to a stop in the half circle drive where the three similarly sized houses sat, Nore noticed that above each pair of grand doors the thick vines had been trimmed away to reveal an engraving. Where she expected to see Oralia's name, each house bore a word.

Corporeal.

Cerebvis.

Sensarus.

"Your guess is as good as mine." Yagrin stepped out and opened her door. Perhaps he wasn't furious with her. She was a mirror of his own hypocrisy. He wanted that Scroll for himself, too! He couldn't judge her for her having her own motives.

The car drove off, and she pondered every bit of Latin she knew. Studying the dead language had its etymological uses. *Corpus* was a root word often used for things relating to the body. *Cereb* often referred to the mind.

"Let's get on with it. This one's good enough." Yagrin started toward the middle house, *Corporeal*. She stuck to his heels. They walked up a few short steps and stood before the door. She gazed around for some sign of security or something, but there wasn't a soul in sight.

"Can you hear anything with your senses?" she tried to ask, but no sound came out of her mouth.

Yagrin tried to speak, but his mouth moved wordlessly.

Nore couldn't hear *any*thing, she realized. She watched the trees moving with no sound to the wind. She ground her boot in the gravel. Silent. *Audior magic.*

She felt around the door handle, grabbed it, and pushed. The heavy wooden door opened without a sound. They shared a glance before stepping inside. The hall was dark; warm lanterns swung from the paneled ceiling. They walked down the long hall until the foyer corridor opened up to a wide rotunda lined with doors. The room was larger than any ballroom at Dlaminaugh. It might have been larger than any room Nore had ever seen. There was a roped-off circle in the center of the room, but nothing was within it. A projection of the Sphere used to hang there, she realized.

Ding!

The sudden sound struck like a splash of red paint on a blank canvas.

Then she heard someone playing the piano. *Well.* She and Yagrin rushed toward the door where the music carried in. Inside was an auditorium with seats filled to the brim with people. And a stage where a lone person stood in a fine teal gown with a sparkly mask on their face, twinkling in the stage lights.

Their body swayed as they moved their arms in evocative motions. With every shift in their body, the piano music played; it was the only sound she heard. Suddenly she understood. The Audior magic was in place so nothing could interfere with the exquisite performance.

She wasn't really a music person, but the notes of the song took her heart on an adventure, filling it with sharp, short, low sounds, which made her feel nervous. Then the auditorium burst into a skitter of high notes. She thought of a bird shoved out of a nest, bobbing in the air, then spreading its wings for the first time. The tones were a melody that elicited a nostalgic ache. Audior magic—and all art in general—was not considered distinguished at Dlaminaugh. In their entire history, they'd only finished *one* Audior specialty. Art was looked down upon, but painting sang a song to her soul. So much so that she hid her brushes and colors in her stove.

Nore followed Yagrin along the back of the theater to get a better view. She couldn't look away. He appeared to be as captivated as she was, staring at the stage as he wove between the rear of the orchestra section. He stopped suddenly, and she ran right into him. For the second they touched, she felt her heart ram with life more than it had in a long time. They resituated themselves as the music stole their attention.

This is good, Yagrin mouthed. He *loved* music—the cello, especially. She of course couldn't know that, so she just nodded back. When the music finished, applause boomed, the theater coming to life with whistling and shouting cheers. Flowers flew onstage as a petite blond woman with the strut of a Headmistress joined the Audior center stage.

"How about *that* for the future of magic!" Litze was every bit as colorful as Nore'd heard. She wore a chartreuse silk pantsuit with a turquoise riband across her middle. Her lips were painted in a hot shade of pink, and an equally bright colorful diadem set in silver shined above her head.

The applause roared louder and demanded an encore.

"We don't want to wear them out, do we?" She hip-bumped the performer onstage and winked. Then she gestured for them to exit stage left before turning back to the crowd. "Pupils of top-tier marks, join us for refreshments in the reception area outside."

The crowd rose, and the aisles swelled with people. Two bodies swept between her and Yagrin, and when they passed, she lost sight of him. She hurried toward the exit, the direction she thought they were heading, the same door where they came in. But once she was in the rotunda, Yagrin was nowhere to be found.

Her palms sweat as a throng of débutants in boldly colored dresses and suits with masks and diadems to match swallowed her as they shuffled to the exits. The world around her pulsed with a vibrance that made it hard to breathe. By comparison, Dlaminaugh was a prison of drabness.

She spun, taking in the tapestry of people. No one hurried with books in hand, but there was every instrument she could think of, and funky paintbrushes with spiraled handles wound around wrists like bracelets. There were masks, *full-face ones*, like she'd never seen! They were plain, patterned; some appeared to be hand-painted while others were ornamented with jewels or flecks of gold. Emoters wore shimmery jewels on their bodies and faces. Hairstyles existed in every color, pinned, pressed, or curled high in creative shapes.

Nore stared at her gray dress and her plain red hair hanging over her shoulder. She tucked her head down and wedged her way through the crowd, peering for Yagrin. But there was no sight of him. She'd never felt so out of place. And that was saying something.

She stared so hard at a girl made up beautifully in silver and shades of blue that the girl grabbed Nore by the wrist tightly. She tried to wriggle away but stilled when the girl's palms shifted to purple.

"Are you lost?" the Emoter asked. "She's terrified, poor thing," she told a friend with her.

"I'm fine." Nore hurried away. She'd never seen an Emoter in person or been touched by one, as emotion-magic training was only offered in House of Oralia. Nore had read about it, fascinated, how there were Shifters so sensitive to emotion they could sense it in others. Still, she wasn't sure what all they could tell by touching her. And she needed her secrets to stay buried.

Corporeal House emptied into a courtyard with a paved stone path across a hand-painted pond. The crowd was ushered toward the reception. Nore walked along, peering harder at the mural on the ground, and noticed the fish were flicking their tails, swimming in patterns, their scales shimmering, putting on a show for her as she passed. *The art was alive.* Everything about Oralia was a performance—the displays of magic, the choice of wardrobe, hair, and make-up. Even a simple stroll from the auditorium to the reception. There was always something or someone to feast your eyes on. As colorfully enthralling as it was, being *on* all the time had to be exhausting.

She bit the inside of her cheek. She had so many questions for them about their lives between these walls, but that wasn't at all why they were there. She skimmed for Yagrin.

"Where are you?" she muttered. But there was still no sign of him. The stone path led to an outdoor area decorated with string lights and sweeping views of wine country. Refreshments sat atop tables, and music played.

She spotted Headmistress Litze Oralia. Maybe she could come right out with what she was looking for, like she had at the Chateau.

She worked her way through the people, searching. And ran smack-dab into a broad-shouldered, slender frame. Her arm stung. She felt it before she realized what had sliced her skin. The cut burned. The person who nicked her pulled a glass vial from their corset and dropped the bloodied tip of the small blade inside.

"Hey!" Nore smacked her hand away, but she was too late. The attacker blew her an air-kiss, spinning on her heel before freezing, face-to-face with someone Nore knew.

Drew, heir to House of Oralia, snatched the vial out of her attacker's hand, their simple black mask fading into their skin.

"I'll take that," Drew said. "Out of here, Shar."

"Your aunt said—"

"Don't care. You haven't even earned enough marks to be at a social following a performance. *Leave.*" Drew had changed their hair since the last time Nore saw them at Darragh's tea. Their dirty-blond braid cascaded over one shoulder. They wore a lacy blazer and fitted leather pants. Drew hardly wore make-up the last time Nore saw them. Today their face was made up modestly, not in the typical gaudy Oralian style. There were cat-eye swipes at the corner of their eyes and a new piercing above their lip. Nore almost didn't recognize them.

Shar glared at Drew. Then her annoyance dissolved into a sugary grin. She bowed as if signaling the end of a performance.

"Shar Wright, second of my blood, Anatomer candidate, theatrics type. I have a thieving role coming up and thought I'd try out the raw emotion of it on you. Didn't mean to alarm you."

Shar left with a flail of her arms in the most dramatic twirl.

Nore would bet anything that girl was lying. She held her arm, feeling sick all over again over her brother. Word had spread to Begonia Terrace that there was a pretty price on Nore's blood.

Drew offered Nore the vial. "I'm really sorry. Shar is a lot."

Nore snatched the vial and shoved it in her pocket before hugging around herself.

"What brings you to Begonia Terrace? My aunt didn't mention you were coming."

Nore wasn't sure what to say. Was Drew's concern authentic or another performance? "Idaho is so bland this time of year."

Drew cocked their head. "Come on, Ambrose. Why are you here really?"

Nore didn't know Drew well enough to divulge the truth. She could put on a performance of her own. "I've told you." She smiled, plastically. *Where is Yagrin?* They needed to get the Scroll and get out of there. Fast.

TWENTY-ONE

Yagrin

Yagrin looked for Nore in the crowd, but he couldn't find her so he set his sights on Headmistress Oralia. He hustled against the crowd toward the stage, where Litze had disappeared behind the curtain.

"Excuse me." He shouldered his way through. "Urgent business, please step aside." He wasn't familiar with Litze, but he'd worked alongside a few from the House, enough to know that acting confident went a long way with a House of performers. The arts weren't hobbies to them. It was a way of being. Everywhere was a stage. Every day was a chance to play a different role or be a different character. No one was less trustworthy.

He found Litze backstage, wiping off her lip color in a mirror.

"Well, this is a surprise. My second visit from the Perl family in a week. The last time I saw you, you were running around in diapers. Yagrin, is it? The eldest Wexton brother."

Yagrin's body went cold.

"Your cousin Adola was here." She scrunched her brows too tight to appear confused. Litze was making it clear she had relationships with key people. It was also a question—did he?

"You knew, I presume," she said.

"Of course."

She smiled, then opened her arms to greet him with a hug. "It's good to see you."

Yagrin leaned into the faux gesture of familiarity. He had no memory of meeting this woman formally. She may have attended a ceremony at his House at some point. But they'd never talked one-on-one.

"I wish I'd known you were coming. I would have welcomed you with all the fanfare our House has to offer." She hooked her hands. "We could have put on a performance of *The Lies We Tell*. You know the play?"

He did. It was a tragedy where two brothers fought each other vying for power until they ultimately killed each other. *Warning or threat?*

"Not my type of show," he said. "I rather like *Death Flower*." The play was about a paranoid queen who killed all her children for fear of a prophecy that said her fellow blood would one day replace her. Only to be killed by her mother, who was her closest trusted friend.

Litze was stoic. Then she smiled suddenly. Her House was full of performers, but Litze Oralia was the master of them all. "Your aunt is well."

"Are you telling me? Or asking?"

"I'm asking. I haven't spoken to her in some time since we stopped regularly meeting. I've been meaning to check on her. Your cousin said she is ill?"

Goose bumps raced up Yagrin's arms. Jordan swore Adola's heart was pure. But this didn't look good. His aunt wasn't sitting on her hands at Hartsboro while the world devolved into chaos after she *failed* at stealing the Sphere's magic. Even *if* her being sick isn't a cover story, she would be planning *something* to take advantage of all this chaos. That appeared to involve Adola running her errands, acting on her behalf. He felt sick.

"Walk with me. Tell me what brings you here. To feast your eyes and indulge your senses? Because if that is what you want, you're in the right place."

"No." He was tired of speaking in code. He wasn't his aunt, and he wouldn't be placated with Litze's niceties. "I'm working on putting things back right with the Sphere. To do that, I need your help."

"You know I love to help your family. Such honorable people."

He sneered.

"Nore Ambrose and I need to speak with you somewhere private."

Litze stroked the back of her neck. "Nore? I've heard she's very elusive."

"She—"

"You know . . ." Litze roped her arm into his. "Before we get into anything serious, please allow me to welcome you to Begonia Terrace *right*. We put on a whole dance for your cousin."

Yagrin's annoyance ticked. She was delaying. He chose his next words carefully.

"I am hoping to get back to work soon."

She shrugged, her cheeks rising as if he'd just complimented her hair. "The world is perpetually falling apart. Inside these walls, we don't take part in the chaos. Life is too short, and art is too beautiful."

"Are you saying your magic has been unaffected?"

She batted her eyes. "There have been challenges, but it will all sort itself out." She patted his shoulder. "Everyone is so quick to get themselves in a knot over things. History tends to repeat itself, Yagrin. And you know who survives? Those wise enough to get out of fate's way."

He stiffened. The truth wasn't working. Litze was as slippery as an eel. He knew how to deal with her type.

"You know, I *would* love a tour of the grounds. I'm sure Nore would love it, too."

Litze brightened. "Have you two been traveling together for a while?" She nudged him in the ribs and called over a server carrying a tray of fluted glasses.

"We have. It's been nice. How about tomorrow for the tour? It is getting late."

"We have a gala tomorrow afternoon. Some of the most renowned graduates are traveling here from *all* over the world. I'd love for you both to attend. We'll welcome you properly. And afterward, I'll give you the tour myself."

"You're so gracious, to receive with no notice," he bit out. "We look forward to it."

"I will have a garden house prepared for you and Nore."

"*Separate* garden houses, please."

"Oh? Alright." She shoved both glasses into his hand. Then she pinched his jacket, which was well wrinkled and a bit dirty. "I'll send Vestisers to your rooms in the morning to assist." She was playing a role that he wanted no part in. The blue in Litze's eyes darkened as she beamed at him.

He knew very little about this estate, its layout, its secrets. But they'd have to figure out how to find the Scroll themselves. *Quickly.*

Yagrin found Nore white-knuckling a glass beside Drew Oralia. Drew was the child of Litze's estranged sister, who resided in an isolated cottage at Begonia Terrace. Rumors were that Litze's sister had a devious secret on Litze, and that's why Drew was adopted to be heir. Others said Litze cannot have children. Yagrin had never met Drew, but he knew they reached out discreetly to the brotherhood more than a few times to get their mother some much-needed help. Drew was always dragged along into their mother's antics and likely tired of it. What Yagrin didn't understand was why Nore was so nervous next to them.

"Drew Oralia, pleased to meet you in person," he said.

"You look like you could use a bath." Drew sipped from their glass.

Yagrin forced himself to smile. "Nore, shall we?"

"She's having a drink with me. What is he, your security?" They sneered.

"He's my—" She looked at him.

"Date for the art gala tomorrow." That would raise far fewer questions. He held out his arm to Nore. She roped hers around his. Her eyes looked as if they were about to pop out of her head.

"*That's* why you're here," they said to Nore. "If you want to bury your head in the sand, you've come to the right place. My aunt's determined to behave as if nothing's happening. As if the world falling apart is some great show, and she's waiting for the final curtain to drop so she can applaud and go back to business as usual." Drew scoffed. "It's disgusting. And *not* smart. But what do I know? I'm just *her heir*, with nothing to do until she croaks." They tossed back their full glass. "Have fun, eh. I intend to."

Someone who was a spitting image of Litze but at least a few decades older waved at Drew to come over.

"I think they're trying to get your attention," Nore said.

Drew told them goodbye and went in the opposite direction. There was a nasty family feud there Yagrin didn't want any part of. He led Nore out of the reception on his arm as they waited for a concierge to take them to their rooms for the night.

When the coast was clear, she howled at him. "*Date? What* are you doing? And *where* were you?"

He explained how after they'd separated, he decided to find Litze. And how her evasiveness was unsettling. How she might be working with Beaulah. Nore took her arm from around his. The warmth of her closeness leaving him felt like being ripped from underneath a blanket.

"We have to be here through the gala tomorrow, at least. It gives us time to snoop."

"Figuring out our way around here is time-consuming." She chewed her lip. "We're going to have to rub elbows. Drew warmed up quickly. I'm hoping that means they're an oversharer. Maybe they can help." She tapped her cheek. "Every conversation is a canvas. Every new day is a bar of music waiting to be composed."

He watched her, perplexed.

"If that's the game, we have to play it. Otherwise, we'll stick out. We have to blend in, playing our own roles." She drummed her fingers on her leg. "Yes, this plan of yours to act like we are going to the gala as a couple is a good one, I think."

Excellent. They were in agreement on a plan. Attend the gala as a pretend couple. Schmooze to learn more about the layout of the estate, find out what they could about an Ambrose relic being entrusted to the House.

"You do this thing with your lips when you're thinking really hard, and"—he touched the skin between her brows—"you get a little divot here."

She stilled at his touch. "You're making fun of me."

"No! I think you're—" His heart stammered.

"Finish your thought."

His stomach twisted. The words were there, jumbled around in his heart but clear in his head. He thought a lot of nice things about Nore. "It was nothing."

"No, tell me. What do you think of me, Yagrin?" There was a glint of something in her eye; this was a real question she was asking. She genuinely wanted to know what he thought of her. His heart pumped faster.

His mouth was dry when he opened it. "I think you're witty and feisty. I think you're strong and that you carry more on your shoulders than you like to admit. I think you—" He swallowed. "You are the smartest person I've ever met in my entire life. I still don't understand how your neck supports a brain so big."

She chuckled, and it made him chuckle, too.

"There's so much more I could say."

She twisted her shirt. "Then say it."

He swayed. "I think you're exactly what the Order needs, but it's too broken to recognize that. I think you are relentless and determined and loyal to your own values. And I think you want to be understood but have given up trying."

She was closer to him somehow.

And now that the words were coming, he couldn't stop them.

"I think you love your brother, and what he is doing is hurting you even deeper than you admit. I sense that you hurt about a lot of things and bury them in intellect. I don't know, but I get the impression you've never truly had a close friend. Just by the way we work together." He stared at his feet because he wasn't sure he could look at her and say the next thing. "For so long I didn't want to even wake up day to day. I hated my family. I hated what the Order did to my life. But there was a person once, who—" He laced his fingers.

Nore shifted on her feet.

"She used to tell me that each day was a new day. A new chance to feel something good."

"Yagrin, I'm sorry." Nore was so close to him now the ends of her hair grazed his arm as the wind blew.

"When I was a child," he went on, "I used to curl up near the window when it stormed outside, to watch. The violent ones were enthralling. But the best part was when the buckets of rain stopped, the booming thunder quieted, and the winds died down. Everything became so *calm*." He held his chest. He could still feel it. "The cloudy sky would become this soft shade of gray. That's what I see when I look into your eyes."

Breath stuck in his chest. "I've said too much. I'm sorry."

Nore grabbed his hand. "No, you haven't."

He stared at her, and part of him ached. She was alive, present, in the flesh. The other part mourned because her face wasn't the one he wanted to see looking at him that way. But it was complicated. He meant what he said about Nore. He'd enjoyed being near her these weeks. It made him feel things he thought were dead. But if Red could live, his heart belonged to her and her only. He owed Nore nothing, but he wouldn't lie to her. She was special in so many ways.

He took his hand away and cleared his throat. It was awkward now. He was so good at making things awkward. "I'm assuming you didn't see your brother."

Of course she hadn't. She'd have mentioned that first. Could he be any more obvious about wanting to change the subject?

Nore let out a big breath and said, "I hoped to dig for information with Drew, but they seemed more interested in what I was doing here. Tomorrow I'll see what I can find out."

"Does Drew seem honest?" he asked.

"I'd say so, given how they greeted you." She smirked. The levity was nice.

"Are you saying I need a shower?"

She tucked her lips.

He threw back his head in laughter.

"When was the last time *you* took a shower?"

"It's rude to suggest a lady smells. Shame on you." Whatever else Nore said he didn't hear. He liked her. He liked her a lot. And now he was consumed with his own imagination. Nore. Bathing. Rubbing suds all over her.

"We should get to the garden house." He strode off. He *would* be taking a shower, a cold one.

TWENTY-TWO

Quell

The vines of black roses suffocating Chateau Soleil feel like they're wrapped around my chest as we approach its gates. I never thought I'd see this place again. Certainly not by choice. Jordan stops walking because I do. He's been my shadow, sticking close by while looking over his shoulder the entire trip. Willam, Yani, Knox, and the others travel at a distance, behind us. I sent Abby a note to let her know we'd be here, that she could meet us, but there's no sign of her.

"Your grandmother thought of everything, it appears." Jordan pricks his finger on a thorny flower, which sprouts two larger thorns.

I approach the gates and graze my fingers across the black roses. The blooms grow larger at my touch, curling toward me like they would the sun. Their vines and branches lengthen, reaching for me, winding around my wrist until I'm held to the gate by a tangle of prickly bush. The plant climbs up my arm, over my shoulders. When the stems tickle my neck, panic flickers in Jordan's expression.

"They won't hurt me." I'm not sure how I know it. But I do. Not a single thorn appears on the lengthening vine. Only more rosebuds, blooming as fast as they appear. Stems circle my neck and wrap around my chest. Willam, Knox, and the others watch warily until the plant stops. I hold still, breath heavy in my chest, hoping my instincts are right.

When suddenly, the nest of roses pulls apart the spindles of the Chateau's gate for us to enter.

Stepping inside the gates of Chateau Soleil is like walking on a bed of thorns. It hurts, like waking up from a nightmare that felt a bit too real.

The others trek across the sprawling lawn, which is a dense nest of weeds, their heads swiveling with curiosity despite this place being a far cry from what it looked like last Season. Yani especially. But I can't move. It all hits me differently, a congestion of emotion sticking in my chest. I wonder if my grandmother found out what happened to my mother before she died. I couldn't bear to tell her. I still won't say the words.

Jordan sets down his bag and takes mine off my shoulder. "Take all the time you need."

"I can do it," I tell him, trying to convince myself more than him. After all, this is where I met Abby and Jordan. This is where I bound with toushana at my Cotillion. This is where I realized I may not know fully who I want to be. But whoever I become, I will be free.

I reshoulder my bag. We take the meandering route around to the east side of the estate. The winding pavers take us past what used to be the rose garden. It's so overgrown, a dome of weeds has formed. Jordan keeps in step with me. The garden is enclosed by a chain hung with a lock. The dark roses peeking through the weeds twist in my direction as we walk past.

We reach the conservatory, and Jordan and I share a glance. It's where we spent time together, where he transformed the space into a beach with a tiny white house—my mother's and my forever dream—so that I could be inspired to pass Second Rite.

He walks so close to me my fingers reach for a touch. The backs of our hands brush. He doesn't move away, and that tells me more than anything he could say right now. Knox and the others continue toward the towering entrance of the estate. My feet are still lead. The fountain sculpture beyond the conservatory, of the mother with two little girls at her feet, is covered in so many weeds I can hardly see stone beyond the tangle of roses. I never looked at it closely before. Jordan follows me to it, fending off an attempted interruption by Dimara.

FOR MORIETTE

My grandmother's only sister. There are three stone figures. The littlest one must be Moriette. The taller girl, my grandmother, and the woman: their mother. My family. My legacy. All dead. *So much death.* I back away from the statue just as Dexler comes rushing outside with her hands full of her skirt. Jordan and I join the others at the entrance.

"Quell!" She plows into me, swallowing me in a hug, and as much as I expect to be put off, it feels nice. She is warm and soft and smells like the cinnamon treats Mrs. Cuthers used to keep on her desk. I rest on her shoulder, embracing her. She is the closest connection I have left to any of my family. I hold on tighter.

When we release the hug, she holds my face before hugging me again, and I can't help but smile. There are real tears welling in her eyes.

"Our Headmistress has come home. I have *so* many questions . . ." She rattles on, but my heart turns in my chest. All the warm feelings bleed cold, agitating my toushana. I clear my throat, hesitant to disappoint her so soon. But I haven't come here to be Headmistress.

Dexler looks at me with such hope, and I want to tell her, *Everyone I know dies.* Their deaths hover like a storm cloud I'm not sure I'll ever fully be rid of. How does that make me fit to lead a place like this? A place in much need of help. But I can't bear to crush her, so I keep my mouth shut.

"I'm Maezre Dexler, ninth of my blood, master Cultivator, curriculum regent of House of Marionne. I was Quell's instructor when she was here." Dexler's diadem appears from her tidied gray hair, its silver and opal gems duller than I remember. She offers a hand to Willam, but he ignores it. So she offers the hand to Dimara instead.

"Dimara, of no one's blood, fair cook and cleaner, expert at escaping Draguns, family of Knox and Willam's safe house." She picks her teeth. "Did I do it right?"

Kedd laughs. Rein frowns. "I'm Rein, pleased to meet you. I grew up in a safe house, so I'm not quite sure how's proper, but . . ." She curtsies and almost tips over. "We are grateful to be here."

"Speak for yourself," Dimara spits.

"Enough," Willam says. "I'm Willam."

Dexler gazes up at him with a look that suggests something is stuck in her throat.

"And I am Knox." She and Dexler, who's gone as white as a ghost, shake hands "These are my family. We have all lived in safe houses before here."

"I, uh, you . . . Right. Well. Quell?" Dexler hooks her hands behind her back.

"Could you show me where I'll be sleeping?" Knox says, cutting the awkward silence. "It's been a long couple days, and I'm tired."

Jordan moves away from me toward the doors of the estate, and I reach for him without thinking, grabbing his arm. He stills at my touch. My heart aches, but I snatch my hand away.

He clears his throat. "I'm going to see if my old room is intact," he says. *Alone, he means.* He hasn't said much about his pain from the wound, but when he doesn't know anyone's around, I hear him groan. Jordan skirts past Willam, who hasn't yet said a word about calling on his Healer, with a harsh glance on his way inside.

"There aren't many ready guest rooms, but I have a few session rooms I may be able to clear." Dexler leads the way inside, and Knox and Willam trail behind the others with me.

"Welcome to House of Marionne," I say to them. We proceed in silence. "Well?"

"This proves nothing," Willam says.

"That's harsh," Knox says.

"We had an agreement," I say.

"I didn't give you an answer, Quell. You assumed your goodwill would force one." He walks off to break up an argument between the twins.

"*You—!*"

"Give it time." Knox sets a hand on my arm. "Now, which room is mine?" She smiles in a way I don't think I've ever seen. "Being here in any other circumstance would be a death wish. This is a relief, I admit."

Maybe coming here won't end in complete disaster.

TWENTY-THREE

Quell

I refuse to put Knox in a session room. Knox and I exit the service elevator near the kitchens to the second floor and make our way to my old room. But the window is busted, and there is a wretched smell inside. My fingers graze my old dusty bedsheet. There are still two beds in here, where Abby and I dished on all the House gossip, stressed over exams, and where Jordan kissed me for the first time. I lock the door and try the next room in the Belles Wing. It's tolerable. Knox enters and gives the room a cursory glance.

"You've literally made history."

I laugh.

"I'm serious." Knox inspects the view from the window. She runs her hand along the dagger stand, desk, dresser, and ornate framed mirror. "It's just regular furniture." She chuckles, but tears rim her eyes. "All the people they hurt, the families they've destroyed, to keep their haves and have-nots separate. You'd think you'd at least have fancy furniture. A golden toilet, maybe?" She cackles again, so hard it's contagious. I barrel over.

"Your toilet was much better," I say when the mood settles.

"This was a bold move, Quell. Willam will come around. Since I found him half dead, discarded by Beaulah Perl's Draguns, he's only set foot outside of our houses for food. I always went to trade and deal."

Bumps skitter up my arms as I remember the cracked column scar at

Willam's throat. Perhaps he isn't the same Willam she knew before she was imprisoned. Because he *has* left the safe house. He's at least been to a tattoo shop recently to cover his scar. But I keep my mouth shut. She wants me to be hopeful. And I want that, too.

"He won't be easily won over. He can't. Or he'd be a terrible protector. You understand?"

"I do."

She pets my shoulder. "Your mother always believed you'd do great things."

My gaze hits the floor. I believe that. But I've realized since binding with toushana, she also made me spend my whole life hiding. "You talk about her as if you knew her well."

"You know what it's like in our house. That shouldn't surprise you. Willam knew her even better."

I sit on the bed, resting my chin on my hands, trying to make sense of this mother who saw something in me. She feared for my life because of how different I am. It was her way of loving me, but it also taught me to erase myself. Something I had to fight to overcome.

"They used to play chess until the wee hours of the night. Your mother was very good. She was like a sister to him for the short time we had her. Sometimes Willam would sing outside your door to help you get to sleep. Did you know that?"

I knead my hands together until the color leaves my fingers.

She moves to the window. "Tell me about that rose garden."

I join her, gazing out at the overgrown bushes.

"Your mother loved those roses. She talked about them at dinner once, and no one believed her. A rose that didn't smell."

I nod because I can't find words.

"She said she ran away a lot when she was a teen, returning after a few days. But each time, she told me, your grandmother would plant black roses in her garden, hoping that wherever she was, if trouble found her, the roses would help her escape death."

"If only it worked."

Knox grabs my hand. "Rhea told us she wasn't ever going back, joking about how many roses your grandmother would be planting. When you both left, the papers talked about Headmistress Marionne going on an indefinite sabbatical for mental health. Her fitness to lead was being questioned because she insisted on spending *months* uprooting her entire garden and replanting it. By hand. Alone. Your and your mother's absence were mentioned in the article, so I knew you hadn't returned home. Odd, don't you think?"

I watch the garden, recalling the strange way the roses seem to know who I am, ruminating over the grandmother I thought I knew. *Had I known her at all?* I stare, speechless, into the bleakness beyond the window, a once-beautiful garden choked by weeds. My grandmother kept so many secrets. So did my mom. I didn't know them at all. Toushana tremors in my bones, and the roses outside tilt in my direction.

A knock at the door makes my heart leap. It's Willam.

"Everyone's tucked away for the evening." Willam strides inside. "Quell, I was short with you earlier, and I shouldn't have been. I'm sorry."

Questions claw at my skull. The Healer. Jordan. I *need* Willam's help. But now is not the time.

"Let's talk once you've settled," I say. "In an hour or so."

Willam sighs, but agrees. He might need time to digest. He might actually care deeply about me and just be scared. But I can only give him so much time. Jordan's life and my magic are on the line.

And two women *died* so that I could be here to fight for what I want.

When I leave Willam and Knox, I find Dexler and ask her to ensure we have a private space to talk. Then I knock on the door of Jordan's old room in the Gents Wing, but no one answers. I wander the halls of House of Marionne, scorched and barely recognizable, until I find Jordan, who is warming his hands over a fire in a sitting room near what used to be the grand ballroom.

He invites me to sit in a nearby chair, but that distance feels like an ocean. Heat from the fire billows up my legs, and it gives me the confidence to slide onto the settee beside him, desperate for his comfort, even if we can't touch.

The toushana in my body is silent as I move closer to the fire.

"Are you feeling better?" he asks.

"Knox gave me a much-needed pep talk."

"Good."

That's when I notice a folded-up copy of the morning's *Debs Daily* in his hands. On the front is a picture of Audubon's mansion, burned to the ground. There is a smaller picture beside it: a bird's-eye view of the singed rubble arranged into the shape of a sun with a filled center. The mark of a Darkbearer.

I snatch it from him and find two huge photographs inside of the Dragunhead's face and Jordan's side by side. *Answers Demanded*, the title reads. *Neither could be reached for comment. "He was always a troubled boy but grew worse under his aunt's mentorship," says Richard Wexton, father to Dragunheart Jordan Wexton.* The interview goes on about how Jordan is a puppet for Beaulah Perl, blaming him for the world falling apart. It wraps up with vivid images of Unmarked bodies turning up across cities ransacked in the last few days.

I throw the paper into the fire. "You can't believe any of that. It is not your fault."

"If anyone should have been there to defend the innocent in the Sixth Ward, it should have been me. I took an oath."

"Yes, to protect and honor magic! Which is what you're doing."

"Still doesn't feel good to hear."

It's like they want him to crack.

We're no closer to healing him than we were when I intercepted him in the Sixth Ward. Now the Marked world is publicly pinning every vile crime on him.

"Jordan, I'm going to make Willam reach out to his Healer."

"Sure."

Encouraging him falls flat. I move even closer to the fire, recalling how warmth chases away toushana, and I reach to run my fingers through his hair. But he tips his head away.

"Warmth helps keep toushana calm and under control."

"We shouldn't take chances." He eyes the few inches of space between us on the seat and stands, moving to the mantel. "Have Dimara and the others ever used magic? Or has it all faded? They could be useful around here to get this place in better shape if you were thinking of—"

"*I'm not.*" I join him at the fire. "Jordan, I've lived with toushana in my body my entire life. I survived this place with it. I can help you understand it more."

"I don't want to understand it. I want it out of me."

"You need to understand it to control it."

"You haven't had *this* much toushana in you."

"Fire helps. Please."

He faces me. "Fine. I'm listening."

"Magic, as you once told me, hates indecision. Toushana is the same way. It wants to be used."

"Magic strengthens with use. If I use any magic by choice, it won't be that one."

"When dark magic is inside you, using it is how you control it. That's how you bend it to your will. As a dragun you summoned toushana from outside your body and expelled it, to keep it from attaching to you. Now, Jordan, you still have to use it to gain more control over how it behaves inside you."

He is silent. So I remind him about the forest behind Chateau Soleil, where I saw him push away toushana for the first time, and how I found solace there, satiating my toushana's need to be fed. "I can show you."

"No. It's already stronger somehow, without me even trying. I can feel it."

I let it go. Too much, too fast. First we need to heal him.

Jordan lifts his shirt to examine his side. Purpled, blackening skin hugs his ribs.

"I wonder if, since you're not feeding the Sphere's toushana enough, it's feeding *on you*."

Jordan gazes into the fire. "I don't like the way it makes me feel. Like I'm not in control. Do you know how long it's taken me to find *some measure* of control in my life?" Flames dance in his eyes, and it's the first time in a long time I've seen him look scared.

Nightmares from Hartsboro flash through my memory, and it draws me a step closer to him.

"This could kill me, Quell. The pain radiates through me so often now it's become how I expect to feel each day. I'm not sure how much longer I can—"

I settle a hand, fingertips first, on his back. His heart pounds, but he doesn't shrug my touch away, so I lay my full hand on him, right beneath his shoulders. They sink, and I press my body against the back of him, holding him. He sucks in a breath at the suddenness of my hug and becomes rigid.

"It's okay. This near to a fire, I think it's okay."

He swallows and allows me to rope my arms around him, carefully hooking them. His panic thuds through my body.

"It's okay to be afraid," I tell him, because I don't think anyone's ever told him something like that before.

"When it pours out of me, it brings out something in me that . . ." He shakes his head.

"Trust yourself more than you do."

He takes one of my hands, accepting this gesture of comfort, ignoring his worry for a second. And it feels like hearing *I love you* for the very first time. He presses my hand tightly to his chest. I nestle closer to him, remembering when he saw my rose gold diadem in the ballroom just paces away. And though he only had half a picture of who I was then, he admired my power and strength. A strength he clings to now with his fingers laced in my grip. *I have missed this.* Holding the person I love. Being this close to the only person alive who loves me back.

"We tempt fate, lingering like this." He unfolds himself from me, and before I can protest Dexler's voice rings behind us.

"Willam and Knox are waiting."

Dexler cleared her desk for the meeting. Willam and Knox sit across from us. The air in the room is more rigid than a whale-boned corset.

"Were you able to get a quick nap?" I ask to break the ice.

"Not easily. But we made the best of it."

"I apologize the House isn't in a more fit shape for guests." I dig a nail into my palm, realizing I'm apologizing for someone else's mess.

"The House was abandoned. Of course it's not in its best shape," Willam says, and my cheeks burn. Knox glares at him. I stomach the dig.

"How about we just skip to it?" I say. "While we're here, you'll be expected to help out."

"We assumed," Knox says.

"And part of helping out is seeing what we need and using *your* skills, *your* resources, to get them."

Willam mutters something, but before I can push, Jordan asks, "How certain are you that Dimara, the twins, Rein, and Kedd can't access magic?"

Willam's nostrils flare. "We don't use magic. It's not safe."

"How do you know they don't *want* to learn magic, Willam?"

"You overstep, Jordan." He braces his elbows on the desk.

"I don't think I have," Jordan says, matching Willam's posture. "I'm not sure I've stepped far enough."

I grab Jordan's arm and squeeze. He's cold. So very cold. His anger burns in my chest.

"It's a valid question," I say, trying to reassert some common ground. "But we won't force what we think on you."

"We don't even know what *you think* about us having our own House," Willam says. "I mentioned that to you, Quell, and you haven't even brought it up." He crosses his arms and leans back in his chair. "You bring us here for safe haven, but now you're questioning how useful we can be."

"And you think I'm overstepping," Jordan mutters.

"We don't want to be *absorbed* by your House." Willam stands. "We want a real say. Otherwise, we will leave. We have other safe houses ready to help."

"Sit down, Willam," Knox says impatiently. But he pounds his fists on the desk.

"Sit." Knox rubs her temples.

He does, fuming. "I meant what I said."

"You're nervous about trusting us," Jordan says.

"People who have persecuted us our *entire* lives," Willam spits. *"Yeah."*

"I am growing tired of him," Jordan tells me, shadows behind his eyes. "What have you done to show *us* you're trustworthy? The one thing we've asked of you, you haven't done." Jordan's hand moves to his side, and he flinches slightly. He huffs, exasperated, and storms out.

Now it's my fist pounding the desk. I understand Willam's hesitation. I didn't love Jordan's delivery. But Willam's resistance to healing Jordan and saving magic makes no sense. This has gone far enough. "Houses or no Houses, none of it matters if magic is *lost*. Jordan is *dying. Will you really do nothing?"*

Knox is on the edge of her seat. All eyes are on me.

I stand and shove my chair to the table. "A relationship starts with a step," I say. "I've made one. It's your turn. Summon your Healer. Until then, there's nothing to discuss."

I leave them there. I have to stick to my convictions. We need a Healer. And fast. If that makes me a bad person in Willam's eyes, so be it.

TWENTY-FOUR

Jordan

It's been an entire day since I stormed out of the meeting with Willam, and I'm still on edge. My side is bothering me, so I haven't left my room, haven't seen Quell. And Abby hasn't shown up either. I hope she's alright.

The sun sets outside my window as cold moves through me, scratching my bones. I adjust the way I'm sitting, but it doesn't help. So I get up and pace. Each step makes the space beneath my ribs ache more. When I pull up my shirt, a rancid smell hits my nose. The rotted flesh has spread. The skin around the wound is healthy and smooth. But it bleeds to black around my stomach, running down my side over my ribs.

Quell said to use it to control it. Is controlling it how I stop it from spreading? I swallow a dry breath.

There's a stretch of splintered paneling alongside the window in my room. Carefully, I inspect it. *Here goes nothing.* Unsure how to control toushana *inside* the body, I roll the tension out of my shoulders and focus on the hum of magic inside, like I would with proper magic. Warm granules flutter inside me like blustered leaves. Then a pressure shifts, and cold billows through my sternum.

Toushana wades through me, rippling through my limbs into my hands.

Visualize to mobilize. As much as I hate her, I can't get the ring of my aunt's words out of my head. *Magic responds to our intentions.* I hold an image in my mind of magic bleeding through my hands.

The chill inside me stirs violently.

I hold on to the sensation, tugging it to my palms. Fingers stretch between my ribs. My hands tingle. Then suddenly, in my palm awaits a whiff of darkness. *Magic is nothing without its wielder. Command it without hesitation.*

The shadows swell.

Numbness slinks up each notch of my spine, chasing away every warm feeling. I press the writhing magic against the wall beside my window, and it blackens, decaying on the spot. Magic pulses through me with an aching, icy bite. Rot spreads, racing up the wall like hungry flames. Toushana licks my insides.

Destroy it all.

My heart pumps faster as toushana coils inside me like a snake. I tremble, a deathly cold wrapping around me.

My vision blurs.

Fog forms at my lips, my body buzzing with a power like I've never felt.

No place has ever truly valued you.

A picture forms in my mind of a cloud of darkness engulfing the Chateau as several things happen at once.

A crash of glass.

A whip of wind.

The world is dark, fading into a memory.

Wails scratch my ears.

My frail arms hug my shaky legs. A familiar face breaks through the forest. My aunt, holding one of her wolves.

"I'm right here," I shout to her, waving. She unclips the wolf's leash, and it charges at me. Its paws hit me in the chest, and my back slams the ground. Snarling jaws snap at my face.

"React, nephew."

I breathe harder and reach for the wolf's face, clawing and kicking. Its teeth rip into my shoulder, and I moan in pain.

"It's him or you, nephew. End him. Use that fear, make it anger."

Heat burns through my body, numbing the pain. A strange blackness rushes through the air to my fingers, and the wolf howls in my grip. The rest is a fever dream. I blink, and there lies a pile of rotted bones. My aunt touches my temples, sparking a shoot of pain in my head. She signals for someone to join us. A Dragun I don't recognize comes out of the shadows and brings a magic I've never seen near me.

My head throbs harder.

I blink, and my room materializes back into focus.

The exterior wall in my room is gone. The window that was once there is broken in decayed pieces on the floor. A gust of outside air urges me to my feet. I gape at my hands, which have turned purple. I stagger backward, feeling my chest for a heartbeat. *Trust yourself more than you do*, Quell had said. She was wrong.

"That was quite the show." Yani, Willam, and a robed figure with stringy hair and icy gray eyes far too large for his long, bony face stand in the doorway. There is no sensation of magic, cold or warm, anywhere in my body anymore. I move away from the hole in the building. Yani watches me, mouth agape. Then she knits her brow as her gaze darts to the others.

"You didn't tell me I'd be working on the Dragunhead," the robed figure says under his breath.

A Healer. I can hardly breathe.

"Heart." My own twinges. "And not really anymore."

Willam scowls as the Healer spots the hole. "We're going to need a better place to do this."

"Is something wrong with Jordan?" Yani says.

"What is she doing here?" I ask. Quell and I told Knox that Yani should stay under Willam's watch until we can find a secure place to hold her. I'm not yet convinced she should be wandering around Quell's former home. But I didn't imagine him parading her around the estate, letting her in on my business.

"I was just checking—"

"I'm fine," I tell her. "Leave us." She scowls as she and Willam depart. The other man and I make space in the old Healer office.

He removes his hood, revealing a chiseled face with a sharp nose and beady eyes. Blond stubble covers the bottom half of his face. "I'm Zecky Meir, seventh of my blood." He wears a heavy dark cloak, black trousers, and boots. There isn't a memorable marker anywhere on him. Other than a speck of brown in one of his otherwise-pale gray eyes. He shrugs off his robe, hanging a thumb from his pocket as if he is here to hang out. His handshake is firm, and his posture is rigid despite his otherwise casual demeanor.

"I understand you have a toushana-related wound." He unpacks a satchel with curious metal instruments.

"Yes, sort of."

"How much toushana? And is it bound to you, or are you calling it to yourself? You're a Dragun, so I assume the latter, but I have to ask. I've heard things."

"It's inside me, binding to my blood."

Zecky stops polishing his instrument. "So the rumors about the Sphere's magic being stolen *are* true. You and the Dragunhead plotted—"

"My work relationships aren't your business."

"Only curiosity, my friend. Safe houses are ripe for the picking, thanks to you two."

"The last time I saw the Dragunhead, he stabbed me in the back. Literally. So no, we're not working together."

"Mmm." Zecky unrolls leather with tiny pockets. Inside are more silver tools in odd sizes and shapes. "Let me see the injury."

I lift the edge of my shirt.

"What do you mean—ripe for the picking?"

"Willam's the old-guard type, with a closed-door safe house policy. They don't take in anyone. Which is why no one in his house knows the first thing about healing or any magic, really. The newer safe houses are more progressive in our thinking. I am strategic and aggressive with who

I bring into the family. This news of the Sphere has filled out our ranks nicely."

"Glad I could help," I groan, eager to get these fake niceties over.

"Hmph," he says, inspecting my ribs. I try to exhale, but every hair on my body stands with unease. Zecky reaches for me with a round tool tight in his fist.

I grab his wrist. "What sort of experience do you have with wounds like this?"

"I am not in the business of proving myself to anyone."

"We just met."

Zecky purses his lips. "My ancestor's surname was Doyle. Kindred Doyle."

I sit up. "He was one of The Twelve. The Sphere's engineers." I think of the old Sphere engineer with the mottled skin and garden of strange herbs behind his home from the raid I did earlier this year. *Francis.* One of the brightest minds in magic, who worked on the Sphere. I can see his dead body on the backs of my eyelids. "How did you end up—"

"In a safe house?"

I offer a tight smile.

"I wasn't born into my safe house family. I fled to one when my curiosity sparked for how dark magic and Shifter magic could intertwine. It took over my studies, ostracized me from my friends. My success at the Rites came to a screeching halt. I was about to be kicked out."

"Someone should have turned you over to the brotherhood, in that case."

"Oh, there were a few cousins hoping to make a name for themselves by squealing on me. But my mother, thanks to Gramps Doyle, prepared me well for skirting the rules of the Order. I've seen many things," he goes on. "Nothing *quite* like this, but I'm confident I can heal you up." He rolls up his sleeves, and the insides of his wrists are covered in tally marks.

I shift uncomfortably. "So you work on Darkbearers?"

"My safe house family has to eat, too. I stopped practicing toushana to focus on research. But I know it well." He grabs his round tool again. "I should have you out of here by sunrise." He hands me a strap of leather to bite. "It could get loud."

I lie back with my heart in my throat. He pulls out a blunt tool with a wooden handle, turns it in his hand, studying it closely, then replaces it, only to pull another.

"This is curiously devastating," he says. "Both of the Sphere's magics are inside you. Your liver is fully attached to toushana. It looks like it's covered in black icicles. But your lungs and heart are covered in calloused earthy granules, stuck to their surface like barnacles. There is a battle inside your body." He slides the instrument deeper, and it nicks a bone.

I groan, recalling the stone with the Sphere's magic I buried in my chest. It's dissolved into my blood, unleashing the Sphere's magic all over my body.

"Your skin, bones, and muscle are holding it all in better than any human-made material ever could. Magic is alive, and it thrives in an organic environment. The most powerful man alive." Zecky smirks.

My stomach turns.

"How does it feel? Was this your plan the whole time?"

"I wasn't even sure I'd survive. I just needed to do *something*." The honesty slips out, and my heart knocks in my chest. But the Healer doesn't flinch. *The only person I could trust with the magic was myself.* I think of Quell as Zecky sets a flat stone on my ribs.

"There are all kinds of ways to do things your precious Order never taught you. In fact—" He slips a card out of his robes. "If you are ever curious, that is how you can find me."

"If you can heal this wound, that's plenty." I set the card aside. "I can handle the magics otherwise."

"I can tell you read a lot of books."

"I can tell you meant that as an insult."

"Magic strengthens with use, they say. But what they *don't say* is that dark magic senses your deepest desires. It is strengthened by the very *urge* to use it. No action required. Because of that, it can't be lied to. Think of toushana as your conscience. It knows you. Better than you know yourself. And you have a *lot* in you."

"You're saying it knows what I'm feeling?"

"It does, and it feeds on your deepest, most desperate feelings."

"That's preposterous!"

"Clearly I don't know what I'm talking about. Either way, don't be too down on yourself. Whatever happens." Zecky removes the bulbed tool and grabs one with pincers. I look away and grip the table.

"What's that supposed to mean?"

"The great gift of the magic city—Misa—wasn't its existence, where everyone used all kinds of magic out in the open. It was its fall. That's when people fleeing for their lives really *pushed* magic to its furthest extremes. Which ignited the foundation for our research. Tragedy is a gift. Because of the change that follows."

I fight the urge to sit up. "That's *ruthless nonsense*! You're saying I am a tragedy in the making? Aren't you healing me?"

He winks. "We can pretend this wound is your only problem, if you like."

My side cringes with pain. Zecky removes the tools, and the pressure releases. He slides his hands over my rotting ribs, and the air beneath his fingers shifts. Sweat beads on his head as my skin pulls together. The dry, dead parts flake off as the healthy skin grows in to replace it.

When Zecky finishes, the night sky outside is brightening. My skin's color has returned. The flesh is healthier and only a bit bruised.

"That should do it." He glances at the sky, which has only just begun to bleed from black to deep blue. "And ahead of schedule."

"Is there anything I need to do to it?" I ask.

"The bruise should fade in a day or so." Zecky smiles oddly, as if his lips don't quite know what they are doing. "But toushana is anchored in emotion, as I was saying. It feeds on the feelings we bury. And it ignores our inhibitions. And you have a lot of it inside you. To keep it calm, feed it if you can."

A deep unease settles over me. "What do you mean, exactly?"

"What your toushana urges you to do is what you really *want* to do, deep down." He tosses me my shirt. "Your most desperate feelings, the things we think of in a fleeting moment but dismiss, feed our toushana like a warm ocean feeds a hurricane."

"You talk about it as if it's something that can be controlled. If it could be controlled, the Order would have never decided that those born with it should be executed."

"You have too much faith in the Order."

"I have zero faith in the Order. That just seems logical. What does the Order gain by committing genocide?"

"This is a game. Everyone's playing. And genocide is checkmate."

I blink. He thinks the Order has only been after power all these centuries? "I can tell you don't read very much. Particularly history. Power is used, for better or worse, as a means to an end." *Beaulah taught me that.*

"Power gives the Order control. You think the Uppers didn't know toushana could be controlled? They knew. They were the ones who buried that secret. Then they ordered everyone with it to be executed."

I get up despite the pain stabbing my side. "But *why*?" The answer hits me like a punch in the chest. To create a system that *can't* ever be overthrown, you eliminate any weapons that can be used against it.

Getting rid of those born with toushana wasn't about *having* power.

It was about *keeping* it.

Now the power is mine. How can destructive magic exist safely when Darkbearers would use it so terribly? There has to be a way to create something better than the Order did. Or is Zecky right, and both sides of magic are destined to vie for power endlessly until they devour each other? The walls feel like they're closing in. Everyone has a different opinion about magic. Zecky, Willam, Beaulah, the brotherhood, Quell. Too many opinions.

"More questions, be sure to reach out. Now, please, try to twist your torso."

I start to turn at the waist, and it feels like a sledgehammer has been taken to my ribs. But the decayed flesh is gone. Progress.

"My magic has been spotty since the Sphere bled out. I wasn't sure how perfectly it would go. But it went swell."

"What kind of payment do I owe you?" I ask.

"Headmistress of the House took care of it." He flashes a stunning pair of earrings with bright rubies. He steadies me with a hand, helping me take the first few steps. Once I'm solid on my feet, he packs up his things. The card he gave me is on the floor.

"I meant what I said." He picks up the card and puts it back into my hand. "For the sake of my livelihood, I hope you have a solid plan for a *new world* of magic."

We have to get the Sphere's magic out of me and into something that can be safely preserved. Then there's the corruption that's infiltrated the Houses, the horrid way magic is being abused to hurt people, the oppression that has to end. My head throbs. Trust is a fickle thing.

Someone has to build a new Order.

How else will Quell live with toushana freely?

I'm still figuring out how I'll do it. But I crack my most confident smile. "I sure do."

"Well, then, I've just helped save the world."

TWENTY-FIVE

Nore

Nore walked beside Yagrin toward a cluster of guesthouses tucked away in the peaceful hilltop greenery of Begonia Terrace. But all she could think about was how close they were to finding the last piece of the Scroll. She'd pulled the entire stitching out of the hem of her dress on the trek over. She was filled with equal parts excitement and dread.

The House secretary escorting them, who donned an ornate mask of feathers, stopped at a petite gate overgrown with vines. Nore lifted its latch and followed a gravel path to two garden houses, facing one another. Each boasted a wide deck with a firepit between.

"Headmistress said you needed two accommodations?" The secretary dangled two keys.

"Yes," Yagrin said before she could respond. He was into her. She could see it in the way he looked at her, and that entire monologue he gave her earlier. She was winning him over. But the walk over to the guesthouses had shaken her nerves completely. The more she thought about the different ways this could go, the more she spiraled. The more she spiraled, the more she thought.

If he found out she was Red, could he really love her as Nore? Because she wasn't *just* Red. She was Nore, too. Heir to an ancestral magical House; daughter to a complicated, toxic family; bitter; and angrier than she cared to admit. She'd never been enough for anyone. Was it foolish to think somehow Nore could be enough for Yagrin now? She bit her lip so hard she tasted copper. *I have to hope.* Without it, she had nothing left.

"Breakfast is served in Cerebvis dining hall." The secretary turned to leave. Nore watched him go. When he was out of earshot, Yagrin handed her her key.

"Are you tired?" he asked.

"Sure."

"So there's nothing else really to talk about."

"Not really, I guess." She hated this distance between them.

"Sleep well." He climbed his steps, pulled the glass door open, and stepped inside. She watched as he walked the length of the house. There was a petite bedroom, a few counter spaces, and a single chair, all open to see, thanks to the wall of glass windows with pulled-back curtains. It was a fully functioning house, but bite-size. He kicked off his shoes and sat on the bed. When he gazed outside at her tiny garden house, Nore realized she hadn't moved. She waved, then hurried up the deck to her door.

It was cozy and filled with a floral scent. The bed was very soft, and the lamps and patterns on the covers were all artsy choices. Mosaic tile sparkled in the bathroom. When she exited the bathroom, she could see Yagrin across the way, reclined on his bed. It was silly for him to be all the way over there and her all the way over here, when they'd slept beside each other more times than she could count.

The memory of his body molded around hers clawed its way into her mind. When they lay together, they'd tangle their legs, and his fingers would graze her back so softly. He was so gentle. That's what she loved most about him. Dragun, heartless, cold. That was the mask. Inside, Yagrin was tender and sensitive.

He'd mentioned very little about his childhood when they dated. But she could tell that his parents were not very kind to him. There were rumors about the dark things that went on at House of Perl. She saw the fingerprints of cruelty all over his heart. She climbed in bed and rested her head back, trying to look somewhere else other than the boy she loved, yards away in a bed all by himself. She hopped up and took a shower.

When she was clean, she tied her hair up in a messy bun and slipped into a robe. She stepped out of the bathroom and screamed. Yagrin was standing outside her door. His face flushed. *Sorry*, he mouthed. She hugged her robe tighter around herself and opened the sliding glass door.

"Is everything alright?"

"I'm sorry. I didn't mean to . . . I didn't know you were . . ."

"Yagrin, it's fine. Is everything okay?"

"There's no soap."

"What?"

"My shower has no soap. I was going to see if—"

She snorted. "Sure, just a second." She grabbed the soap from her shower, which was still wet, and brought it to him. He took it from her, and their hands slipped over each other, trying to prevent dropping it.

He thanked her and walked away. Then he stopped. "I was thinking of lighting the fire. Would you like to—"

"I'd love to!" Clothes. She had no clean clothes. "Um."

"It's fine if you don't want—"

"*No*, I do. I just. I'll have to wear this."

"I'll be on my best behavior," he said, and she giggled.

After he showered, he threw on his same clothes, not bothering to fully button up. When he slipped back out onto his deck and headed toward the firepit, she joined him. He sat on the stone ring's edge, and she sat on the opposite end as he worked on the fire. He jostled around the logs and struck a match, but the flame kept dying out.

"Try giving it more air," she told him.

"Are you counseling me on how to build a fire?"

"Yes. Does that offend your masculinity?"

"No, I'm happy to sit my butt down." He handed it over to her. Nore shifted the logs and struck a match again. Then she blew on the glowing flame. Yagrin watched her with a grin.

"What?" She blew the fire again, harder this time. The flame flickered but resisted latching on to the log beside it.

"How'd an heir learn to build a fire?"

"My brother taught me."

"Sorry I asked."

"He also taught me to fish, to string a bow. I've chopped my own wood and skinned a rabbit."

"He likes to hunt."

Her brother did love hunting. The thrill of something running for its life. A shiver ran down her spine just as the flame swelled. "I think that's good."

"Does he know you don't have magic?"

"He found out when I was little. My mother wasn't happy about it. She would try to do terrible things to *make me* have magic. And my brother usually got in her way, on purpose."

"So what happened? Why are you at odds now?"

She shook her head. "I wish we had marshmallows."

"Did you not check your cabinets? Because *I* did."

"No way! You have some?"

"No crackers. But there was a half bag of marshmallows and chocolates in the small cooler."

She galloped past him and dashed over to his deck. "Find sticks!"

They met back at the pit, and the flames had settled nicely. Yagrin handed her two knobby sticks, and she shoved a stale marshmallow on them. He held both over the fire, while she opened squares of chocolate.

"What kinds of things did your mother do to you?"

She froze, remembering.

"If my questions make you uncomfortable, we don't have—"

"Your questions make me feel close to you."

Yagrin broke their eye contact. *There it is again.* Something that caused him to pull back from her. *It has to be Red.*

"She did many things. But the worst was probably being chained to a cement block as she rubbed heated Sun Dust all over my body."

"Deplorable."

"I left." She *had* to stop talking, but it felt so good to open up. Especially with someone whose heart she trusted.

"Where did you go?"

"Here and there. I just ran. Until I couldn't anymore."

"So your brother is trying to do you a favor?"

"*No*. He isn't. I don't want to be Headmistress. But I don't trust him to *bring me back from the dead*!" The chocolate squares were getting all over her hands. Yagrin brought the stick with a scorched marshmallow to her. She squeezed the marshmallow between the chocolate and pulled it off the stick. First on hers, then on his.

"I'll take that." He reached for his cracker-less s'more, but the chocolate was all gooey next to the hot marshmallow. "This is a disaster."

She giggled as he tried and failed to pull the quickly deteriorating treat from her fingers. It was no use.

"Open up." She shoved the sugary mess into his mouth.

"Mmmm." His lips lingered around her fingers. Meanwhile, in her other hand, her own confection had lost its shape.

"Your turn." He took her by the wrist.

"No, wait!" She wriggled. But the s'more ran smack-dab into her mouth, with more on the outside than in.

"You!" She scooped a finger of chocolate off her face and swiped it across his. He warmed another square of chocolate over the fire and returned the favor. So did she. This time she swiped it across his chest.

"We should probably get inside," he said, eyeing the place where her finger on his bare chest lingered. Then he took off his shirt. "You have a little something." He pointed, and she leaned into it. He smoothed his shirt carefully over her face, wiping the chocolate. He was slow around her lips, and when her face was clean, he used his thumb to brush a last bit of food from the corner of her mouth. She turned into his touch. But he cleared his throat and started cleaning his own hands and face with his shirt.

"Yagrin, stop running." She set her fingers back on his chest tentatively.

"What are you talking about? I—" But his next words left him. His brown eyes shimmered golden in the evening light. She let herself relax her hand on his body, finger by finger. He didn't move. She stepped closer until her whole arm rested against him. He was warm. His skin was so soft against the palm of her hand.

"Admit it," she said.

"Nore."

"It's the girl you mentioned, isn't it?"

"You don't even understand what you're saying." He grabbed her wrist tightly and started to pull her hand off him.

She resisted his grip. "Make me understand."

"I can't." He let go of her and looked away, but she closed the remaining distance between them, zipping their bodies together, and placed her other hand on his chest. His arms dangled at his sides as if terrified to touch her.

"Try."

"I can't tell you what you want to hear."

She let her hands explore his frame, following his strong shoulders, the curve of his arms, the sharp angle of his collarbone, the soft parts of his chest, where she used to lay her head. Her eyes stung with tears.

"Then lie to me. Just for a moment." She brought her mouth close to his.

"Nore."

"Please," she breathed onto his lips.

His chest rose and fell harder, his breath quickening, as his hands found her waist, finally giving in. His touch flooded her with a rush of feelings: longing, need, hope, comfort, as he traced her. She stopped breathing, wishing she could freeze time in this moment. Wanting to believe this could truly be real.

He slipped an arm around her and pulled her tighter to him. With the world on fire, this is what she'd wanted, the security of his closeness. The tightness of his hug rooted her to the ground, no amount of chaos could rip her from him—her anchor. *Don't let me go*, she wanted to say. Then their lips grazed each other. She couldn't bear the tease, so she dove for the sweetness of his kiss. And to her relief, he didn't push her away. He parted his mouth. Tentatively, at first. Then his mouth opened wider, deepening the kiss as his arms tightened around her.

The entire world disappeared, and she kissed him back the way she knew he liked to be kissed. She flung her arms over his shoulders as he lifted her off her feet. Her legs knotted behind him, and she ran her fingers furiously through his hair.

This was the Yagrin she knew. One who burned with passion. She became a fire finally getting air. He breathed into her mouth and she nibbled at his lips eagerly. The sounds he made as he kissed her covered her in goose bumps. She pushed her robe off her shoulder.

He froze, their mouths still connected.

"Nore, I love someone else." He pulled back. "And I don't think she'd like this very much."

She wouldn't care! She groaned as he set her back on her feet. "You love *me*!"

He looked at her wholly confused. "I *like* you, but—"

"Just *shut up*. Shut up, okay?"

She ran off to her small house, threw herself in bed under covers, and cried herself to sleep.

TWENTY-SIX

Quell

I've been waiting in the corridor outside the healing office since Jordan disappeared inside with Zecky. I need to know if he's okay and if we can move our focus to getting the magic out of him finally.

I haven't seen Jordan since he stormed out of the talk with Willam yesterday evening. I gave him his space, sleeping in the Belles Wing, unable to even enter the private family-only third floor of the estate for fear the memories would drown me in grief. Or worse, anger. But I held my ground with Willam. I meant what I said. Show you're on our side, then we can talk. And apparently it worked. Because just as I was fending off questions about what to do when one of the twins fell from a tree they were climbing, Dexler let me know we had a visitor.

It's well past midnight when Jordan exits the room.

I unfold myself from a blanket and chair, stretching my stiff limbs.

"Jordan." The edges of his face have sharpened. The shadows that hood his eyes are deeper or darker or something. It's only been a little over a day, but it feels like so much longer than that. Like a chamber of my heart hasn't been pumping. The procedure the Healer did took a toll on him.

"Quell." The air between us crackles with tension, and it pulls at me like a tether. I want to go to him, hold him, touch him. "I think I'm alright." He slips a card into his pocket and sways, catching himself on the banister.

"Are you sure you're alright? Did it go okay?"

"I would really like to sit down in fresh air."

"Of course." I lead us down the stairs and out to a garden bench beside the conservatory and rose garden. He settles back in his seat timidly and exhales.

"Can I see?"

He lifts his shirt. His smooth skin has only a slight bruise. "The wound is gone." He doesn't meet my eyes.

"We can focus on getting it out of you now," I say.

He doesn't respond. Instead, he stares at the rose garden.

"Now that you're mended," I go on, "we need to give Willam an answer about opening a new house. We could use their support."

"I don't recall saying we needed help beyond this."

"How could you still think that after tonight?"

"I'm not going to just hand over the Order to them, Quell."

"No one said that! Why does your mind jump to the worst possible scenario?"

He looks at me as if to say, *Have you seen where I grew up?* "I need sleep, I think. I'm sorry." He grunts, pulling his shirt down.

"What happened in there?"

He sighs.

"Nope, we're beyond keeping secrets. You said so yourself."

The green in Jordan's eyes darkens. I lace my hands together in my lap to keep from touching him.

"I did what you said. I tried using it."

"And—"

He jabs a thumb backward, and I turn in my seat to look at the Gents Wing behind us. A section of the estate is caved in.

"Is that your *room*? *Jordan*. What came over you?"

"I don't know. I visualized myself using it like I would proper magic, and then I blacked out."

My heart stutters. *My magic's never done that . . .*

"The Sphere's magic inside me isn't working for me like it worked for you. Something is off, I don't know. And then there's what the Healer said."

"The first time you use it—"

"I know you think you know, but, Quell, I'm telling you the sheer volume of magic pumping through my body is hitting me differently. I can't explain it." He tucks his elbow at his side. "It's not your fault. I don't mean to sound harsh."

"You don't sound harsh. You sound frustrated."

"I am." He walks, meandering, restlessly. I've never seen him this out of sorts. This out of control.

"What did the Healer say?"

"That toushana is driven by emotion. That what it urges me to do is what I want to do, deep down."

That makes so much sense. My toushana has always urged me to protect myself, even when I didn't have the courage to.

"Vandalizing this estate, my toushana lashing out to hurt you—" he says.

"No, Jordan. The damage to your room was on purpose. The magic lashing out was spontaneous. I bet the toushana is restless, that's all. I really believe that." He settles back on the bench beside me, and I slide closer to him.

But he slides away. "I'm not sure what you believe is enough anymore. I fear I won't be here to protect you from whatever's ahead."

"You *can't* say things like that. If nothing else makes it out of this mess, you and my magic *will*!"

Jordan's brow creases, and I realize I have been too honest. I allow silence to settle between us. I toss him a bag of candy that I found in the kitchens.

"What about you?" He tears the bag open. "Are you doing better being back here?"

"I try not to think about it."

"Quell, you are technically a Headmistress. You're going to have to face that eventually."

"I didn't ask to be."

"But you *are*. And that's not going to go away until you deal with it."

I stare out at the rose garden, ruminating over Knox's words about my grandmother's garden when she learned my mother wasn't returning, when she was worried we'd likely be killed.

"I feel like I *have* to have answers about the future of this House," I say. "That's the worst part."

"It's suffocating. Having the Sphere's magic inside me comes with this pressure like I've never felt before. No decisions I come up with feel quite right."

I exhale, hearing him put words to everything I've been feeling. My grandmother is dead. Knox thinks I'd make a good leader. I show up here, and Dexler makes it clear she's been *waiting* for me to come and take charge. All they're doing is derailing me from what I came here to do.

"It's like always being torn between impossible options," I say.

"*Yes.*"

"And feeling like a horrible burden on everyone. An heir whose magic cost her mother and grandmother their lives."

"Where someone is going to get hurt or be disappointed either way. It's so isolating." Jordan settles back against his seat. "You must have felt so alone here before."

I rub a rusted spot on the bench over and over. "*You* must feel so alone now."

"I'm never truly alone anymore, thanks to your stubbornness." He winks at me, and sun shines in my soul. "I'm sorry I never really saw you," he says, turning to face me fully. "I didn't know what it was like for you to live this way. But I'm starting to understand. Dealing with a fraction of this chaos inside me is so much to bear."

"Funny, after the time I spent with Beaulah, I feel like I should tell you the same thing."

"You don't owe me understanding. You don't owe me anything. I just regret I didn't have the heart to see when we were here last time."

"What use are regrets? What you see now is what matters."

"What I see now scares me, Quell. Even though it feels right." He glares at the damaged Gents Wing building.

"Maybe you see what you focus on."

Our gazes lock, and the questions about my grandmother, the lingering wounds over my mother's death, the endless worries about Jordan's life and magic melt away.

He stands, holding out a hand as if he's asking me to dance, and my heart skips a beat.

"Maybe you're right." Loving me comes with a steep cost. But that is not what I see when I look in Jordan's eyes.

"Let's see if I can manage to do this." He pulls at the Sphere's proper magic, and the air ripples like water around him. The sound of wind rustling trees shifts to the gentle croon of a violin. "No touching. But we can pretend."

I bite the smile at my lips as I hover my hand over his. He floats his free arm around my body without touching me. His back stiffens, and the light in his eyes returns as he steps to his left. It reminds me of our first time dancing. I follow, sliding to my right. Picturing the sparkly ballroom around us in all its glamour. Then I slide back, then forward. We turn in the dance. It's a bit stumbly at first, but we find our rhythm as we did the first time we danced. He extends his arm to turn me, I spin and bend backward, imagining he is holding me. I spring back up and dance again toward him, stopping so fast he catches me at the waist for a breath before pulling his touch away. I savor the feeling.

We dance to our self-made music. And I pretend he holds me close to his chest.

We laugh though nothing is particularly funny. And I imagine being curled up with him.

We smile until our cheeks hurt. And I tell myself I could do this forever.

When the sun rises, we collapse back onto the bench, still a breath apart, but I feel closer to him than I have in a long time. It's not the dance

I would have chosen. But it is the dance I needed. There is a song my heart sings, and only he seems to know the words. And I want to hear him sing it over and over. If that's what love is, then maybe when you love someone, sacrificing for them doesn't feel like a burden.

Jordan eyes a card in his pocket. And as we sit in silence soaking in the sunrise over the rose garden, my mother and grandmother come to mind. I cross the grass to the latched garden gate. The tangled black roses rotate in my direction, their petals folding under themselves, blooming more radiantly. Jordan is beside me.

"Why do the roses follow me? And why did she dig them all up and replant them?"

When I take the gate lock in hand, it shifts into gold dust. The chains fall to the ground, and the garden's gate swings open.

"Jordan, I need your help."

"With?"

"We're going to dig up this garden."

TWENTY-SEVEN

Quell

It takes my toushana nearly an hour to decay a way through the thicket of vines hiding the garden gate. Jordan and I waited to start working until the lights were out for the night so that we won't get any questions. I have too much on my mind already. Like how to keep magic *and* Jordan safe. What to do about Willam pressuring for support of a new House. Or how to get Dimara to stop making snide, unhelpful comments to Knox and Willam behind my back. Where in the world is Abby? And what in the world is taking Nore and Yagrin so long to send an update on the state of the Scroll?

Inside the garden gate, a worn path runs between the rows of roses. This is going to take a *long* while even *with* magic.

The toushana ripping out of my hands dissolves the garden's sprawling branches into dust. The power *feels* like an answer to a question I've run from asking my entire life—*Who is she, that girl in the mirror?*

She is free.

She is no one's pawn.

But loving her is destructive, choking the life out of everything, like the garden's weeds. A burden. I rip out another root, savoring the way wafts of darkness rake the gnarly roots into nothingness.

Jordan wrestles vines beside me with his bare hands, hesitant to use the toushana inside him. Every few branches that he chops, one sprouts into a thicker one. As black bleeds from me, I shove down thoughts of my mother, the agony she faced in her final moments in that wolf lair at Hartsboro the last time I saw her things. I swallow the lump in my throat and tug harder at the thread of ice worming its way through me. And I remember my grandmother's body lying near the breaking Sphere. I make short work of a bush. Then another, until my fingers ache and they start to purple. I shift my focus away from my hands full of bruises that pale in comparison to what she suffered. Destruction. That's my goal.

"What are we looking for, exactly?" Jordan asks. For once he is in casual pants and a dark shirt that hugs his chiseled body, outlining his side where the wound is healed. The bruise has improved even just in the last few hours.

"My grandmother is intentional, even dead. There's a reason these roses know me. And I'm going to find out."

I claw and rip, and wrangle, and destroy branch after branch as my grandmother's groan of pain when she died plays on repeat in my head. My fingers bleed, but I don't care.

"*Quell.*" Jordan offers me water. "Are you alright? What are you really looking for out here?"

Confirmation that I meant more to my grandmother than it seemed.

I start on the next bush, and Jordan grabs a spade. My grandmother spent time with me as if I mattered to her. As if she saw something in me. She plotted to save me when she learned about my dark magic, but she ignored me as I grew up. She was a complicated woman. But she was also careful.

She loved me.

For as much as it cost her, and as bad as she was at it—she loved me in her own twisted way. She would not leave me without her help now. I know it like I know the magic humming in my bones.

We work in silence until I clear the whole row. And the next two.

The world sways as I realize there are dozens more rows to go.

"Both of us using toushana would be faster," I tell him.

He lifts another pile of broken branches, walks it to the corner of the garden, and adds it to the mountainous stack. "My hands are just fine." They're covered in cuts and scrapes. We continue until my arms ache. My entire body throbs by the time we finish the next row. Dirt is caked under my bloodied nails. He tosses back water, hands it to me, but I'm too busy roving through the empty rows, moving around the soil to feel for anything buried beneath it. But there is nothing. *There has to be something here.*

"Quell?"

On my hands and knees I shove the dirt around, moving larger piles of it, searching, hoping, wishing. But there's nothing but rocks and sticks underneath. I beat the ground with my fists.

"Quell, *breathe.*"

A knot rises in my throat, frustration and grief trying to choke me. I rock back on my heels and try to inhale. Jordan moves right next to me, and the nearness of him helps some. But when I exhale, the disappointment welling up in my chest bursts out in a shaking sob. Grief's an unwieldy guest that arrives without notice and overstays its welcome. I'm not sure I can lasso it into submission anymore. I cry, then I scream, punching the dirt again and again until I can't see my mother's face in my mind anymore. Until the memory of her voice fades and the longing ache for her touch dissipates.

"You need a break. We can finish tomorrow." He holds his side where he has healed. But the fatigue shadowing his gaze makes me look at the time. He's been awake for over a day. He was told to get lots of rest. How quickly I can become so selfish. How easily I harm the one person alive who still dares to love me.

"You're right. Sleep is important."

He offers me a hand up, and it surprises me. Though he rips it away so quickly the touch is gone before I can savor it. He sets aside his shovel.

"I'm staying until everything here is destroyed. You should go." I pull on my magic and grab the first plant on the next row, one of dozens still left.

"I'm not leaving you to do this alone." He says something else, but as I approach the next row, its blooms turn toward me.

All at once.

I take another step toward the flowers. Their stems lengthen before my eyes, reaching toward me, and my heart skips a beat.

What if destruction isn't the answer?

I extend a hand, and a petal grazes my fingertip. I get close enough for the roses to explore me, slinking along my arms. One vine encircles me timidly, trailing along my chest, wrapping itself around my body. Another vine follows, more confident than the blooms before it. Then a whole section of blossoms stretches in my direction, reaching for and winding around me.

Suddenly everything stills.

The ground rumbles, and the earth beneath my feet shifts.

I gasp.

Jordan clings to my side as the ground opens up.

A gold chest inlaid with fleur-de-lis is buried deep below.

"Lift on three. One, two—" We dust it off. A thorny vine hugs the chest like a chain. Jordan touches it, and its thorns lengthen to razor-sharp tips. But the lock dissolves in my grasp, and the chest pops open.

Inside is a ring of gleaming brass keys.

JORDAN TRIES HIS best to convince me to go to bed as we reenter the estate. The morning sky ripples a soft blue with ribbons of orange. I race up the stairs. These keys fit into a certain-shaped lock I've only ever seen on the private family floor of the estate. The third floor, where my grandmother's quarters are.

"Quell." He takes the stairs two at a time to keep up with me. "You haven't slept or eaten in hours. Your grandmother died to save you, but she was also full of trickery. What kind of legacy is she roping you into if you use those keys?"

I stop.

"You want to be free. What are the chances that key is a way to that?"

He isn't wrong. More harrowing truths about my grandmother, about the Order, could be on the other side of those doors. Some way to tie me further into a life I never wanted. But I need to know. If I don't, I'll always wonder what my grandmother really wanted from me.

I feel his love. The ache in him to truly hold me rams in my chest. He would protect me from anything if he could. Even myself.

"Thank you. But I have to do this, and I need to face whatever it is alone."

My hand is on the banister. He strokes it once more, gently. "I don't trust her or any of her secrets."

"She left this for me to find."

"She's done *terrible* things."

"Yeah, well, so have we." She was complicated. But she was a part of me. If she's made a way to help us after her death, it's my responsibility to find it. "The entire world wants what's living inside your body, Jordan. It's just us, and a few others, against *everyone*. We need as much help as we can get. Even from a monster." I leave him there.

And because I know him, I know he won't move from that step until he sees me come back down.

THE DOORS ON the third floor are locked. I start with the first door and slip in a key. The room is bare, with patterned floral wallpaper and a stale smell. The light switch doesn't work anymore, but the window provides enough for me to see. There is a small wardrobe in the closet. I try the next bedroom, but it is completely empty.

I inspect three more rooms before I come to one piled with dusty furniture. There are labeled boxes stacked to the ceiling on one side of the room. And a bed, dresser, and small side table arranged to be used on the other side. The closet is full of old toys and storybooks with brittle pages.

But the strangest thing about the boxes in the bedroom is that none of them are taped closed. Several are propped open, as if they were recently rummaged through. On top of one box there is a neatly folded soft pink baby blanket embroidered with fleur-de-lis in golden thread. When I flip it over, I gasp.

R

Rhea, short for Rheanne. My mother. *This was my mother's room.*

My knees are weak, so I sit on the bed, my mother's bed when she was a girl. Yellow paint is peeling from one of its four posts. There are little ponies painted on the headboard. One of the posts unscrews when I touch it, two sleeps from broken. I smile, working the post back and forth.

The pillows are a soft satin, and I wonder if I ever slept here with her. For a moment I consider running down the hall and trying each key in every door. Maybe I have a room I never knew about, too. But I tuck my knees into my chest where my mother once sat.

Eventually, I pull open each drawer on a small bedside table and find a stack of old photographs. In one picture, my mother is no more than seven or eight years old, in a frilly dress with a lace bodice and satin-capped sleeves, jeweled gloves on her tiny hands. She wears an older-style bonnet hat, ornately decorated with bows, ribbons, and some flowers. In one photograph she appears to be a young teenager. She wears the house riband across her, a beautiful bonnet, and elbow-length gloves. The joy in her smile is what strikes me most. There are creases around her eyes as she hugs Grandmom tightly. It makes mine sting with tears.

I grab the box with the pink blanket and settle on the floor with it to see what else is inside. But when I grab its top to open it, my feet go numb beneath me. I should stop. If I stay here too long, how will I ever leave? How can I heal if I keep ripping open the scab of the same wound?

How can I heal if I don't?

I open the box.

Inside are paper dolls with crookedly drawn smiles, a pearl necklace, and several folded sweaters. The next box of my mother's things is easier to open. This one is full of colored drawings and what appears to be my mother's old schoolwork. Something shines from the bottom of the box. A hair clip with a butterfly made of pearls, similar to the one my grandmother always wore.

I make more space on the floor for another box. This one is full of diaries and folded letters teenage Rhea wrote to herself.

Apparently she used to go by the nickname "Rae," and she had a best friend who failed out at Second Rite. She never saw her again. My mother *did* induct when she was seventeen, a year later than Grandmom wanted her to because she was late to emerge. There is a sketch of a diadem on the page with a date, and my heart skips a beat. The drawing is painted gold like Grandmom's, with clear-colored stones.

I drag a blanket to cover my legs and finish one diary before picking up a tattered covered book with a sticker on the front. I don't know what time it is. And I don't care. Her loopy handwriting is scrawled across the pages in every color ink, decorated with hearts and doodles. She talks a lot about débutante training as something in her past on these pages, so this diary must be from when she was close to my age. It's unclear whether she passed or failed Third Rite, but she gave me her dagger, which means she can't have passed. She took up House duties, working as Grandmom's assistant, I read in her diary. She even mentions Dexler a few times, who apparently competed with Maezre Cuthers to be Grandmom's right arm.

Cuthers walks around like she has a stick up her butt. But little does she know, my mother would much prefer it to be her foot.

I snort at a mother I never knew and never can know. I scrounge through more boxes until I find another diary covered in sticker hearts. A bunch of folded letters spill out. These are from someone special. A boy. He always signed his letters: *Yours, Teddy*. She snuck out to meet Teddy many times. Grandmom caught her once and locked her in her room for a week. But Teddy visited her even then, posing as a House of Marionne student. She ran away with him at some point after her Second Rite exam, but they were found and brought back by Draguns within days.

Teddy . . .

She'd never mentioned anyone by that name. Not even a friend. Any questions I ever asked about my father went unanswered, so I stopped asking.

He drew boxy little hearts by his name on each of the letters. I stuff them back into the book and return it to the box. That's when I notice a hatbox wrapped in a mauve velvet ribbon tucked behind the door where I came in. Its top has slipped off. This box shines with a newness that's eerily out of place. Inside is not one of my mother's bonnets. But instead a bouquet of dried black roses, tied with more ribbon. Attached to the flowers is a card.

For Rhea.
Upon my death.
Yours,
Mommy

But it's the writing of the card that sends a shiver up my arms.

My life's greatest work.
12 Sparrows Circle

TWENTY-EIGHT

Jordan

Quell is too hard on herself. I wait on the stairs for her until the world sways. She doesn't come down. By noon, I drag myself to my bed and sleep. Finally.

When I wake, a day has passed. My bruise is almost completely faded. Smooth skin covering my ribs. There's no pain. Quell hasn't come by. There is no note. I'm not sure what other problems having the Sphere's magic inside me could cause. And I'm *not* willing to "feed the toushana," whatever that means, as Zecky suggested. I need this magic *out* of me.

I turn his card in my pocket, pondering how trustworthy Zecky could be. He's really smart. He knew stuff about toushana even I haven't heard. *Willam would know.* I look for him but find Yani.

"There you are," she says. "You're a ghost around here."

"I'm looking for Willam." I try to walk past her. She gets in my way. "What do you need?" I ask.

"I just wanted to know what's wrong. I heard you have some kind of wound. Is it from the Sphere's magic?"

"That's not your concern."

"I want to help."

"Busy yourself with cleaning up around here, help Dexler, or learn to knit for all I care." I keep walking.

"I know he healed you of something. Is the Sphere's magic hurting you? I heard you screaming."

I stop.

"I know you think you can't trust me. But you can."

My blood writhes. "Eavesdropping on me doesn't help your case. Spend your time getting in good with Willam. Maybe he'll take you under his wing once this is all said and done. I'm a lost cause, Yaniselle."

"Then I'll prove it to you. I'll *show* you."

I don't bother with a response. Before I round the corner, she says, "Willam's in the library."

When I reach the library, he is sifting through books on the shelves with Knox.

"What are you looking for?"

Willam drops his book. Knox is much more cool and collected. "We're looking for historical texts on House organization, land acquisition. Those sorts of things."

"I came to talk *and* thank you." Maybe niceness helps. "Zecky did a solid job."

"So then, you've come with your answer about our House."

"I've come to say I'll consider it. But I'm still recovering. Quell is dealing with a lot being back here. Give us more time. That's all I ask."

"That's reasonable," Knox says before Willam can respond. The shirt he wears today dips below his throat, and I notice some kind of sprawling tattoo across it. But he tucks his chin down, adjusting his collar before I can make out what it is.

"Was there anything else?" he asks.

"Tell me more about Zecky. What's he like?"

"Brilliant. A bit arrogant, but the really smart ones usually are. He plays it too fast and loose opening up his safe house to new people. But I wouldn't trust anyone else with the lives of my family."

Knox studies me. "Jordan, you're not alright."

"I will be." I leave them and read Zecky's card again. If he can help me,

I can start rebuilding. He proved himself once. Feeling out trusting him with this is at least worth a shot. What other options do I have?

Cold magic hums in my chest as I slip out of House of Marionne under a dimming blue sky. Toushana tugs sharply in me as I glare back at the estate. Quell won't be happy about me doing this behind her back. But I hurry out of the property's gate into open acreage, where I can cloak. I reread the card.

The chorus of bells chime.
There, never brighter, has the Sovereign shined.
The well listens, the well sees, the well knows how to find me.

I pull at the shadows, hoping my cloak works as it should. A prickle of cold claws at the underside of my skin. *Tippets Square.*

To my relief, the world disappears.

It's not dawn, and the Minneapolis streets are full of people. I steady myself, waiting for the cloaking magic to wear off. That's when I notice a patch of fabric from my coat is missing, severed nearly at its seams. Not all of me made it with the cloak.

Magic is weakening.

I slip into the crowd with my collar pulled, careful to stick to shadows. With a quick stride I cross an intersection to enter Tippets Square. The entire block is home to dozens of churches, attracting tourists from all over. At dawn, the church bells chime a special melody all at once. At the center of the square is a courtyard with stone statues—each an artistic interpretation of what Sola Sfenti would have looked like when he roamed the earth centuries ago. The plaques at their feet label them as mythical gods from some kind of Unmarked lore. I pass a couple trying to stop their child from decorating a statue with chewing gum.

Beside the stone statues is a sparkling fountain shooting water in the air. I check the card again and sit on the fountain's edge. A few minutes pass, and when the bells ring, I set the card in the water. It dissolves, sinking below the surface. Then a ghost of Zecky's face appears where the card vanished.

"Bay Hill Church, front steps."

I hustle out of the square, toward an ornate stone building surrounded by hedges. I climb the steps about halfway and busy myself reading its plaques. Someone clears their throat behind me.

"Are you feeling alright?" Zecky asks, pretending to admire the carved detailing in the stonework. "I didn't expect to see you so soon."

"I came for assistance with another matter," I say, keeping my back to him.

"Yes, your situation is precarious," he says.

"You can do all kinds of things that are out of the ordinary?"

"Extraordinary, you mean."

"I want it out."

He traces his jaw. A beat of silence passes between us. "And what are you going to put the Sphere's magic into?"

My heart ticks faster. Trust is a risk. *Sovereign*, don't let this be a mistake. "Your great-great-however-many-greats-grandfather made the Sphere once. I don't see why his successor can't make another one."

Wind shuffles the trees. Somewhere birds chirp. But Zecky doesn't respond.

"We can assemble a team, like they did before," I add.

Zecky still doesn't respond. I face him.

"And in exchange?" he asks.

"Working on the new Sphere isn't glory enough for you?"

"Glory doesn't ease hunger pangs."

"Name your price."

Zecky walks up the church stairs and strolls along the promenade beside a lush green courtyard. "I want a House."

"You're making your own houses, I've heard."

Zecky scoffs. "Willam and his friends are idealists. I'm a realist. I want an *ancestral* House. Something with roots. Something proven. I hear one could be available. That someone close to you might be willing to abandon their post."

House of Marionne. His words slice like a knife between my ribs.

He could never. Unless Quell wanted to. But Zecky didn't have to know that. "Get this magic out of me without any issues, and all things are on the table."

"You should follow me." He quickens his pace, and I hustle to keep up.

But as I disappear down the steps, I spot a familiar face patrolling the fountain, the same I thought I saw at the airport, that guy who used to hang around Abby. *Mynick.* I hurry behind Zecky.

Deep underground below Bay Hill Church is a maze of stone hallways. The church is actually a hollowed-out locked building concealing a safe house beneath. Zecky guides me through a main room with two ornate doors on either side. We enter the northernmost one, which opens up to winding, dimly lit halls. The air has a biting chill, so cold it causes the toushana inside me to stir. Wailing groans behind each door we pass send bumps up my arms.

"This side is a healing clinic. We're used by every safe house in a thousand-mile radius. Churches get traffic all the time. It's a good cover. The southern entrance is where we've made our home."

"You don't sound very mobile. That's a risk."

"We're nimbler than you think. Evading the brotherhood has become much easier thanks to you." He smiles, and I feel sick. "I've collected some of the ripest, most lethal minds in magic you'll ever meet. Who should we fear, Mr. Wexton? *You,* our newest patient?"

When we stop at a small room with an examination table, toushana lurches in my chest. My feet are frozen. In a new Order, labs like this wouldn't have to be underground.

"Inside, please."

"Shouldn't we assemble an engineering team first for the new vessel?"

"Constructing the Sphere took my ancestor nearly a year. First, I need to have you thoroughly examined by an expert Retentor and Cultivator to ensure we *can* get the magic out of you without damaging it."

My heart thuds, the cold inside my bones pricking me like needles urging me to run.

"I assure you there's nothing to fear. I am not a man of brute magical strength. *You* could level this entire building in seconds. If anything, bringing you here is more of a risk to me than to you. I'm just a Healer who takes advantage of opportunities as he comes across them."

I note the nearest exits, Zecky's relaxed posture, his steady breath.

He gestures again for me to go inside.

With clenched fists, I do.

"I'll need to pull Erla and Ube for this. They're my best brains. And then there's the matter of the vessel. We'll have to find the right thing. If you'll excuse me, I'll be right back." He closes the door, bolting it shut with a clang, and the sound ricochets in my chest.

I imagine Quell's face when I bring her this temporary vessel, the strength I'll feel having this chaos *out* of me. Maybe Zecky could come for another visit and explain how it works to her. Maybe he has ideas about how to free families like his and Willam's while stopping the carnage of Darkbearers.

Zecky returns with a spindly fellow in a blue tunic and leather slacks. His petite shoulders and small frame make him look younger than he is. White stubble covers his jaw on his otherwise bald head. A slick black mask slopes across the top half of his face, fading into his tanned skin as he enters. He slips on glasses. Behind him is a woman who looks a lot like him. Her blond hair is cut in a low fade. She wears deep green pants and a jacket to match. A gold diadem sits on her head, and jeweled earrings in the same hue dangle from her ears.

She holds a gold diadem with colorful stones in her hands.

A diadem *not* connected to anyone's head.

An icy feeling—that is not magic—seizes in my bones.

"Erla and Ube are siblings," he says. "And this—"

A wide-hipped, dark-haired woman in red robes boasting a magnificent silver, jeweled diadem enters the room. "Is Runetta Bell," Zecky goes on. "She was dropping off a few things, heard you were here, and says you know each other?"

She gives me a hard look. I've never seen this woman before.

"Yes, we have been friends a long time." She hugs me as Zecky is pulled into a whispered argument between Ube and Erla. "Auspicious meeting you here," she says under her breath. "I'd heard you were looking for a lady a few weeks ago."

"I don't think that was me."

"Oh, it was you, Dragunheart. In the Sixth Ward."

"Lady Ruby?" *The Trader I was looking for.*

"In the flesh."

The world teeters on its edge. How vastly my circle has changed in months. A fugitive, partnering with the most sought-after names in the Order. I'm not sure if I should be honored or disgusted.

"The girl in the alley."

"There wasn't enough of her left to bury." Lady Ruby's mouth thins. "I overheard your exchange. When Darkbearers attacked, I had to flee. The cargo I carry is precious." She gestures to the diadem.

"You brought them that?"

"Some safe houses pay *well* for magical artifacts." Her fingers circle her chin. "You know, I tried tracking you once I realized the rumors about you are true, to offer my help. You're incredibly hard to find. And I find things for a living."

"I think we've sorted out their confusion," Zecky says, forcing his way between us. "We can get started."

Lady Ruby smiles. But worry deadens her eyes.

"If you'll excuse us, Runetta," Zecky says. "I assume you've said your hellos." She is practically forced out the door by Ube. Erla wipes a cloth over the multicolored stones in the diadem at a back counter with shaky hands. I'm sure working on magic under these circumstances is an intimidating task, but her nerves set mine on edge.

"Lie down here, please," Ube says. Erla backs away from the counter and stands against the wall, rigid.

"Erla, make yourself useful or leave," Zecky orders, and she barrels out the door. I stand beside the table he's asked me to lie down on.

"We need to see how the magic in your body is moving," Ube says.

"Zecky's seen all that."

"We need a fresh picture since the recent healing. It should only take a minute."

"Ube, check on your sister," Zecky commands, inspecting the diadem before setting it back on the counter. "I'll help him relax."

When the door closes, I climb onto the exam table and lie flat on my back. Cold thrashes inside me. *This is a mistake.*

I try to sit up.

But I can't move.

TWENTY-NINE

Yagrin

Yagrin lay in bed all night, tossing and turning. When he finally drifted off, he dreamed he fell asleep beside Nore but woke up the next morning to her bones. When he climbed out of bed, he stepped onto his deck and stretched. Nore was already grazing a tray of fresh fruit and in discussions with a Vestiser. She didn't even look his way. He felt sick for hurting her.

"You're awake finally." His Vestiser appeared out of nowhere and ushered him back inside.

When he had his style for the evening picked out, his wardrobe maker shifted him a casual pair of slacks and a crew neck to wear that day. He dressed and hurried out to the latched gate to wait for Nore. But he waited and waited until he realized she'd gone to breakfast without him. *I deserve that.* If he was more like his brother, he'd have been more restrained developing feelings for someone.

But her mind was *beautiful.* Listening to her talk and watching her think inspired him. It felt so easy with her, as if he'd known her a lifetime. He'd never felt this way about anyone other than Red. Nore was like her but different. It was hard to explain. He lost his appetite, climbed the deck of his small house, and buried himself back under the covers.

When evening came Yagrin awoke tangled in his covers. The sky outside was dim. He'd slept through most of the day. When he sat up in bed, his gaze snapped to the small house across the way. His heart pattered in his chest when he saw Nore curled up on her bed, reading. He craned for a better view of what she'd been doing. He'd spent every day with her the last several weeks. It was strange to just *not* talk with her at all. Feelings aside, weren't they a team?

He rose from his bed and stood in the window. She didn't look up. He had a sneaking suspicion she could feel him watching, but he turned his attention to the evening ahead, showering and pulling on his dark suit. He polished his mask in the mirror, trying very hard not to look across the way at her. He checked his watch, and at a quarter to seven, he stepped out on the deck and returned to the latched gate. She wouldn't leave him tonight. She wouldn't risk their plan. They'd agreed they had roles to play to get in the good graces of Oralia and find their piece of the Scroll.

He heard her before he saw her, heels clacking on the garden pavers. When he turned, the sight of her took his breath away. She wore a dark green gown with a simple silver headband on her head, reminiscent of an Ambrose diadem. Her long red hair was swept up into an ornate style. Her face was made up in soft natural colors that looked like she wasn't wearing anything on her face at all. He gaped, the closer she came. The beading on her gown was intricately woven with gems that sparkled brilliantly in the moonlight. The neckline plunged down her torso, revealing a gold pattern that was hand-painted onto her skin.

He tried to find words, but none of them seemed adequate to describe how beautiful she was. He unlatched the gate, and she walked through. The back of her gown was a mirror to the front, continuing the ornate detail and body paint. A gold comb was tucked into her hair, and from it hung shimmery emeralds. He opened the car door for her, but before he could find words, she slid inside and pulled the door closed.

The scent of her filled the car, and it felt like fire on his skin. She looked at him. Despite her make-up, her eyes were slightly puffy from a night of crying. His heart fractured against his ribs. Nore deserved better.

He opened his mouth to speak but thought of Red. It had been so long since he'd seen her, held her, spoke with her. And there was Nore, in the flesh, only inches away, with a strong heartbeat in her chest. Maybe it was better this way. He liked her. And she really liked him. His heart twisted. He *loved* Red desperately. Their moments together were stars on the darkest of nights.

As long as Red was a possibility, Nore couldn't be.

He closed his mouth and stared out the window. They rode to the main house in silence. Tonight they had a role to play, and if they succeeded, he'd have the Scroll and he wouldn't have to fight these feelings anymore. He had to go through with taking the Scroll for himself. He owed that to Red, whose life was stolen too early because of him.

Maybe he could figure out another way to help Nore avoid becoming Headmistress. Maybe he could still kidnap Isla or take on Ellery himself. He didn't want to leave her without any options, but he wasn't ready to give up on his plans either.

When they stepped out of the car, the melody of a piano beckoned them to a rotunda. This one was as beautiful as Corporeal House. The event was decked out in towering floral displays, sleek chandeliers, linens, sashes, painted sculptures, and more, all in an explosion of rich, deep colors. Aerial silk dancers hung from the ceilings, and ballerinas performed to music on raised platforms all over the rotunda. Everywhere was art. He caught Nore smiling. He smiled, too.

A few guests lingered on the fringe of the room, chattering and sipping. But a dozen couples danced in the center. Eyes followed them as they entered the gala. And he couldn't blame them. Nore was the most beautiful girl he'd ever seen. His heart thrummed. This was their moment.

He held out his hand. "Shall we?"

She met his eyes for the first time that night, slipping her fingers into his. "I hope you're a good dancer," she said.

"You're about to find out." In truth, he hated dancing. Of course he was good at it. The way he was raised left him no choice. He was skilled in all social graces. He just didn't care for them very much. But tonight he would dance better than he ever had. They would sell this act. And the pain he was causing Nore would be done. He still had Ellery to deal with, but he had ideas about how to pull that off if worse came to worst. He lifted his chin and led with his left foot.

The music took him. It had been so long since he'd danced. He moved with the melody, holding the steps a bit longer than the box step called for. And she followed his every movement without missing a beat. He pulled her closer to him, his arm tight around her waist. She fit against him, in his arms, just right. Like she belonged there. She swayed with his movement. Backward. Forward. Then they turned as if they were one.

As the music switched to a peppier cadence, Yagrin released her waist and turned her out, letting go of her hand. She moved like the music was inside her, bouncing around in her bones. She held her skirts to show off her footwork, tapping her heel and toe in a rhythm to the measure. He laced his fingers behind himself, the music nudging him with the next step. They touched elbows, rotated and touched elbows again. The teases of closeness with her only made him eager for the next count where he could pull her close again.

She curtsied, and he extended his arms, inviting her back to him. She grabbed his hands and held on with a tightness, a request to never let her go. And it ruined him. He wanted to hold on to her, too. He wanted to live in the present. Nore was here. Now. He squeezed her hand with both of his, clinging to their grip.

Her whole countenance brightened. Her smile deepened, tiny lines reaching her eyes. It felt good to make her feel good. The more eagerly she danced, the more the music began to feel like it beat inside Yagrin, lightening the weight on his shoulders. He danced harder, letting himself breathe in this moment and enjoy it for what it was. He worked his body, each dance step, sharply, precisely, until he lost any awareness of the world around them.

"You're good," he said.

And this is . . . fun.

Her cheeks were pink. He could feel her racing heart through her fingertips. He zipped up the space between their bodies, holding her close to him. Their faces touched, cheek to cheek as they swayed for the next four count. The heat of her made his own heart leap. The music jumped. They spun bodies pressed together. The notes rose higher and faster, and they went around and around and around, quicker each time. She giggled, scents of honeysuckle and lavender swallowing him. He slowed them down, and when they'd nearly stopped, he spun her out and let her go one last time, preparing for the finish.

"Can you do it?" he asked.

"Can *you*?" She smirked in that sly way she did, and it made him grin.

He steadied himself, bracing to catch her. She padded toward him quickly. His hands grazed her ribs as he gripped her tightly. She trembled. Her stare bored into him as he lifted her in the air.

"I have you."

She let go of his shoulders, swept her arms overhead, and bent back for the finish.

The audience around them exploded in applause. He brought her body down, sliding against his, carefully. He set her on her feet. Her arms roped around his shoulders, placing her lips a breath away from his. They froze as the final measure of the song played. The audience roared louder when it finished. Litze Oralia watched from the refreshments table, slamming her hands together.

He couldn't breathe. Everything he wanted to say tangled in his head.

"I am so sorry that I hurt you," he said as more applause roared around them.

"Yagrin—"

"Listen, please. I really like you. I like being with you. But you deserve someone who isn't holding back from you."

"You don't have to hold back from me," she said as he loosened their embrace.

"I do." If Red couldn't be brought back to life, then he wouldn't want to be with anyone else. But those words would hurt her more than they would help. He was many things. But loyal to those he loved most of all.

"Because—"

"Encore," the audience shouted. "Encore!"

Nore squeezed his hand, and the joy in her eyes sent a thrill racing across his skin. He pulled her into him in an embrace, and the applause turned to cheers. Nore nuzzled his neck. Her mouth found his ear.

"We are their feature presentation," she said, pressing against him, and it felt like a puzzle piece of him just slid into place.

"Alright, alright," he announced, and signaled for the Audior to play something slower this time. "Ready?" he asked her.

"I've been ready, Yagrin. I am just waiting on you."

His heart did funny things in his chest. The music began, and they swayed slowly for the first few beats. Several joined them on the dance floor. Nore's arms were around him, and he let himself gaze squarely into her eyes.

"I couldn't have done this with anyone but you." That was true. There were things about Nore he adored that were different from Red. Nore was the right person for this moment, for this situation he found himself in in life. He wouldn't regret that. How could he regret feeling things for someone like her? She was a walking anomaly that defied everything about the Order. He loved that about her most. Her audacity. To just exist as she is. That was something Red would never be able to understand. A whole part of him she would miss.

"What are you thinking?"

"That I wish this song would never end." His chin hit his chest. It felt wrong to say. But this moment was so sweet, so unaffected, so pure, he wanted to keep it. His life had been a continuous reel of disappointment. Even with Red, he had to leave. He couldn't just *be* with her all the time like he wanted. But with Nore . . . His chest ached.

"You're torturing yourself," she said. "I can see it in your eyes."

"It's just very complicated."

"It's not." She stopped dancing.

"Nore?"

She exhaled. "There's something I have to tell you."

THIRTY

Quell

Twelve sparrows. Twelve. Perfection, completion. There are twelve main stars. Twelve sparrows is twelve birds. Birds fly. Without a cage they are free. If they dare to be. Small birds with brown plumage. Songbird sparrow. They sing! Singing is joy. Unless it's a lament. Sparrows are sorrow. Or are they hope? Sparrows mean protection. 12 Sparrows Circle . . .

My mind won't stop. I tossed and turned for two nights. Jordan came looking for me, but I sent him away. When I went looking for him, he was not in his room or anywhere.

Just before morning, while it's still dark out, I take my traveling coat and leave Chateau Soleil. I am here now with one foot wedged in my grandmother's shoe and the other still on the ground. I need answers. *I need closure.*

There are five 12 Sparrows Circle addresses, or some variation of that street name, that I could find. Two are homes in Virginia and one in Pennsylvania. Another is the address of a diner in Washington. But it's the fifth that pricks my senses. It's in New Orleans and doesn't show on a map properly. The address brings up an abandoned lot of land. But that same piece of land is where St. Louis Cathedral sits.

When I arrive at Jackson Square, the streets are silent and empty. The gentle rushing of the Mississippi can be heard in the distance. The cathedral towers over me. Why would this church be my grandmom's greatest work?

There are no hidden symbols of suns, filled in or otherwise, anywhere in the stone architecture. There is a tall clock tower with sunrays for clock arms. A small sign sticking out from the landscaping mentions a side entrance. I follow the sidewalk to a garden at the back of the church. My toushana flickers, and I hold it close, worried coming here makes me too exposed. I let shadows unfurl in my hands as I listen for footsteps to be absolutely sure I'm out here alone. The back of the church is as beautiful as the front, with its steep angles, colorful stained glass windows, and statuesque detail.

That's when I see it.

The gable over the rear doors bears a beautifully carved fleur-de-lis, not unusual for this city. But it's the Latin inscription beneath it that raises the hair on my arms.

SUPRA ALIOS

A cut above the rest. The House of Marionne motto. My grandmother didn't build this building. But she built *something* here. The garden landscaping doesn't give me any clues. There are statues of dead old men, but other than that, it's an ordinary yard shrouded in greenery. *But the fleurs.* My toushana urges me forward. Once I'm up on the steps of the back side of the cathedral, I notice more ornate carvings on the church doors. The picture is familiar: a man is hunched over, holding a giant sun on his back. At his feet a younger person hugs his legs. Around them are crowds of people. *Sola Sfenti and his apprentice, Yaque Paru, when the two discovered the magical sun stones buried in the earth.*

I touch the doors, toushana still whirring in my hand.

The doors flutter like a veil before fading into a dark shadow.

Now, my magic tells me. And I trust it, stepping through.

The world beyond the magical veil is not the inside of a church. The world reappears in vibrant shades of blue. There is a narrow sandy road that leads to the ocean beneath a crisp, cloudless sky. *A cloak veil, like in the airport. I've been transported.*

Square houses with flat roofs and small windows run along the dirt road. In the front of each house is a fenced yard. The front lawns are full of black roses interspersed among the plants. The beachy village is busy with people working in their gardens, sharing a meal, tossing a ball over a net, playing with small children, and sitting in the sunshine. Several are my age.

Closer, I notice most don black diadems or masks.

The hair on my neck stands.

What is this place?

That's when I see the magic. Some use toushana to rip out weeds in their gardens. A few others work together repairing a fence with Shifting magic. There is an older woman who transfigures the face of a tiny little girl, giving her whiskers and furry ears. The child bounces off to play with someone else. All this magic. All kinds. All together.

But it is the next house, nearest the ocean, that stops me dead in my tracks. A woman in a long blue dress gathers flowers into a woven basket. Her gray-streaked black hair is pulled back in a low bun. I recognize the way her frame hunches over as she stoops to the ground. I move toward her, unable to stop myself, my pulse racing. Her profile is familiar. Specifically, her nose.

Which is the exact shape of mine.

My heart hammers. My hands are slick. The world sways.

"Mom?"

THIRTY-ONE

Nore

Telling Yagrin the truth couldn't be any worse than the torture he's going through. Nore didn't have him the way she wanted him now. And if she told him, she still risked not having him. She had to fess up and hope for the best.

"Yagrin, I don't think I've told you what I love about you."

His brow creased. The music shifted, and they danced the next section several feet apart. The dance floor was a tapestry of ornate masks. It felt like every single one of them was looking right at her and could feel the thud of her heart pounding against her ribs.

"I've never met someone who despises the Order's hypocrisy the way I do."

They moved into the next part of the dance. He stepped backward; she stepped forward, following his steps.

"And—" Her voice cracked. "I love that you don't look down on me because I don't have magic. It feels like I am more beautiful to you without it. It feels like we could run away from all this together and pretend the Order, magic, none of it ever existed."

"How do you—"

"Let me finish. I love that you are not easily fooled. You don't wear intellect as a shield like so many in my House do. I grew up in a world of plastic people enslaved by their need to be better than the next person. I could care less." She squeezed his hands. "And *you* get that! No one else

I've ever met gets that." Her heart sank. "When I am with you, there is no Order. Or awful mother. Or terrible brother. Or looming dead."

He tucked his lip.

"I don't desire magic. I decided a long time ago, I don't need it. But if there was a magic that could make you understand how sorry I am for what I've done to you—" Her eyes stung.

"Nore?"

"I love you, Yagrin. I have only ever loved you. And I will always love you." She swallowed. "Even if you can't forgive me. Only with you have I ever felt *free*."

His hands stiffened in hers. He stopped dancing. "Forgive you for what, exactly?"

When she opened her mouth to speak, shadows shifted in the distance. The skies darkened as the dead descended upon them.

Her heart banged violently in her chest.

Yagrin turned, following her gaze. "They're here. Impossible."

"My brother. Somehow he's done this. They want my heart, Yagrin."

"Your *heart*?"

She grabbed him by the sleeve. "Have you ever considered *why* Ambrose can stretch magic in ways others can't? Our Anatomers can change *others'* faces when the rest of you can only change your own. Our Retentors don't just *remove* magic; they can *repair* it. Our expansive intellect has a *source*." The crowd continued dancing, a few glancing up with the expectation of rain. "We have a Pact with our dead. They get the Headmistress's heart, allowing them to cling to a shell of a life. And our members get to channel *their* power to push magic beyond its limits."

His gaze widened. He let go of her hand. She hadn't even told him the worst yet.

"But you don't have magic—" His mouth fell open. "Your ancestors would be furious if your heart is given—"

"They'd devour me alive." She fought tears. "My mother needs to live. They have her heart. It needs to beat forever."

Yagrin put distance between them.

"Who knows this?"

"My brother wants to be heir. And we don't have any female cousins anywhere near the immediate bloodline. A dozen times removed, all males. Because of that, succession would pass to him if I'm out of the way when our mother dies."

Yagrin didn't move. Frozen with shock.

"But he promises to bring me back to life with the Scroll after he's secured Headship."

"Bullshit."

"He might actually mean it, but I'm not taking any chances. I told you before, people get one time to show me who they are. If he would kill me, his own sister, I can't be sure he'd bring me back. Or what my condition would even be after."

"He's not going to kill you. He's not even going to touch you."

"If they are here, he has to be." An audience of masks watched them. How many of them knew her brother was out for her blood, like Shar had? Did Litze summon Ellery? Getting the ancestors to cross the threshold is probably what delayed him here. Yagrin pulled her closer. Her stomach knotted. The next admission she made would rip him away from her forever. But she'd been this truthful, she owed him the rest.

"Ellery could be anyone on this dance floor," she said, studying the ornate make-up, which even without Anatomer magic was a perfect disguise. The music played sweetly. She grimaced.

"He *is* here somewhere, daughter," said a voice that felt like a dagger in her back.

Nore turned to face her mother. Isla Ambrose—or someone who looked like her—stood in front of her with a decorative party mask on her face and a plain gray gown dangling at her feet. Nore blinked.

"May I cut in?" she asked Yagrin.

His grip on her tightened. "Sorry, I really like this song."

"Nore, I came here to help you," her mother pleaded.

But Nore grabbed Yagrin's hand and exposed his palm. "Show me the truth."

He got her meaning and unleashed darkness, dripping destructive magic from his fingers. Her mother gasped as his toushana grazed Isla's skin with a hiss. But no disguise was torn away. It was actually her. Isla cupped her cheek where the dark magic burned her skin ever so slightly.

"*I swear* it's me."

Litze Oralia joined them on the dance floor with a stern expression.

"I've done what you asked," she said to Isla, who held out her hand in response. Litze pulled out a brittle piece of old stained paper and handed it to her mother. Nore's heart leapt. *The Scroll!*

"Where's my son?" Isla asked.

Litze flapped a hand in the air. "You're a poor ad-lib in a flawless script. This is a party. Please take your family matters elsewhere. I've done what my ancestors were sworn to. I kept the piece safe and delivered it to you, specifically, by request." She wiped her hands together. "I am finished with this mess."

"If you're here to help me," I told my mother, "let me see that Scroll piece."

But Isla tucked it into her dress pocket before Nore could snatch it. "Neither you nor Ellery can be trusted with this very dangerous magic. You are both behaving like petulant children. You will honor the rules of our House and do your duty. Or so help me, Sovereign, Sage, and Wielder, I will disinherit you both."

"Do me the favor," Nore said. *"Please."*

"You wouldn't do that to me, Mother." Ellery's voice curdled Nore's blood. Her brother lifted a decorative mask with sequins and gems off his face, and Nore realized he'd been dancing around them for some time. Watching, plotting, waiting. She needed that Scroll piece from her mother and the one he had on him. Then she needed to get out of there!

When the dead sauntered onto the dance floor, the music came to a screeching halt. Some guests fled, but a small crowd watched as if they were enthralled by some kind of show.

"I am your true favorite." Ellery gestured at the audience for them to laugh. And they did.

Yagrin stiffened beside her.

"We should show gratitude to Headmistress Oralia and her hospitality by leaving this dance floor," Isla said.

"And rob them of the performance of their lifetimes?" Ellery clapped. His dark exuberance twisted Nore's spine. "We're going to give these loons a show," he told her under his breath.

Nerves cinched in her gut.

"The tension is masterful," someone uttered from the crowd. Nore looked for Litze or Drew, but she didn't see either of them. She scanned for an exit, standing closer to her mother, eyeing the pocket she'd stuck the Scroll in, wondering where Ellery had hidden his.

"Ellery." Her mother glared. "You *said* you wanted to come here together to ensure things ran smoothly. We are *leaving*." Her mother started to storm off, but Ellery didn't budge. He only had eyes for Nore. A flash of silver inside his sleeve caught her eye.

She stepped backward at the sight of the blade.

"You have half of what we want. I don't see any reason we can't work together," Yagrin said, a protective arm around her waist.

"*Wexton*. Your reputation precedes you." Her brother sneered at her. "*This* is who you've spent your time with?"

He knew Red loved someone, but until this moment he hadn't known who. Ellery's lips curled, and when he reached for her face with his hand, she almost wished it was the blade. He dragged his magic down the slope of her nose, and she tried to pull away. But he gripped her by the back of the hair.

"You've lived a half life, pretending. That's not freedom, sister."

He held her roughly and forced her still while he changed her face. Red's pouted lips. Red's deeper-red ringlets. Her cheeks. Her shoulders. All of Nore became the dead girl again.

Yagrin uttered a sound that made Nore's heart stammer.

He stumbled backward and gaped at her. Pale.

"You—"

"I was *about* to tell you."

"Plans have changed," Ellery said.

Pain ripped down her back. She gritted her teeth, refusing to give him the enjoyment of hearing her scream.

"We have all the pieces; we can work together," she said. "You're my *brother*. My safe person. My escape from *her*." She jabbed a finger in her mother's direction, and the tears rolling down Red's cheeks felt like flames.

Ellery dug out the Scroll piece from Perl and the half piece from their House. Yagrin cocked his head, feeling his own pockets for the parts they had. Nore eyed the piece in her mother's fist. She considered all four of them. She could picture them side by side. Together they formed a piece of parchment.

But with a hole in the middle.

For a fifth piece.

The world dented at its edges. She couldn't think. What did that mean?

"We are not done," her brother said. "The pieces are in each of the Houses. *All* the Houses."

Her body rocked in his grip. No! She hadn't considered it.

"Duncan?" How did you find a relic in a House that's been disbanded for generations? Her pulse raced. He glared at her. Without the Scroll he couldn't bring her back to life, but he could still kill her, right now, and become Headmaster.

"I thought you loved me," she forced out.

"I do. And I love this House. More than you love the House, clearly." The dead handed him something reminiscent of a glove but made of shadows. He slipped it over his hand. She couldn't breathe.

"You're blinded by your pain, little sister. I'm freeing you."

Ellery moved his gloved hand in a circular motion. The air glowed in a way she'd never seen. Then he shoved his shadowed hand into her chest. Her body shook as he gripped her heart and pulled it out.

The audience gasped. Nore had forgotten they were there. Someone screamed in horror, and people fled in every direction.

"No!" Isla screamed, an earsplitting shriek. She blinked, then blinked again, eyes widening as if she was seeing for the first time.

Nore's vision blurred.

The world dimmed.

The dead took her heart from her brother's hands and placed it in a glass box. Her mother's heart vanished the moment Nore's entered. Ellery smirked. Isla gasped for air. The last thing she remembered was her mother falling on top of her with a face full of tears.

THIRTY-TWO

Quell

I stand unmoving, worried I'm gaping at some kind of dream. Or magic trickery. I blink harder, but the scene doesn't change. My mother—or an illusion of her—stands ten strides away from me in a dark blue dress tied at her back, with her hair pulled into a low bun. I saw her bones amid her shredded things, with my own eyes. The wind picks up but sweat still beads on the back of my neck.

Is this real?

My mother sets down her woven basket. She tents her gaze with a hand, staring in my direction. Then she hikes up her skirt and gallops toward me.

"Quell!"

When my mother slams into me, I shake, a deep sadness unraveling in my bones. This can't be real. But I don't move, not willing to shift an inch and risk shattering this dream. Words claw their way up my throat and gush down my face as tears. I wipe my eyes, noticing the way she rubs circles on my back just like she used to. The way she embraces my head, holding it tightly against hers. The familiar gray of her hair, the worn lines of her face, her chewed-off nails, the mole beside her right ear. She even smells like she used to. Like flowers after a fresh rain. Like hope and resilience, and everything in me that's good.

This is my mother. I'm hugging my mother.

"It's me, baby. It's me." She holds me. Her voice is soft, her love tender. But I am a rock in her hug, arms stiff at my sides. Hope scrapes at my ribs, stabbing at the organ thumping in my chest. I tighten my fists. *I've seen this trick before. I've fallen for this lie.*

"Raquell, look at me." She presses her forehead to mine. "I am your mother. I carried you thirty-nine weeks and two days. You came into this world feet first and screaming. I had you at Chateau Soleil with the best attending Healers in the Order. We left there just before your sixth birthday. We visited places but eventually settled on our own."

I pull away from her, but she doesn't let go of my hand. "My mother's dead."

"When we lived in California, there was a lemon tree in our front yard. On your way to school you would look for the sourest one to gift to Ms. Newman, your—"

"Science teacher." Tears cascade down my face.

"Yes, because she was not very nice, and so you thought it would be funny. You've always shaken things up."

"Mom?" My body tremors.

"Yes, baby."

"I saw—" But the images that come to mind steal the words I managed to find. I can't speak the horrors out loud.

"Your grandmother saved me. And brought me here. I can explain everything."

A tidal wave of emotions knocks my knees from under me as I collapse into her arms. I melt into her. If this is a dream, I never want to wake up. She strokes my hair, and I realize she is touching my diadem, which must have slipped out without me noticing.

"You are so beautiful," she says, admiring its gems. The knot I've been since we parted ways feels like it might finally come undone. *"Mom."* I hug her tighter. We stand there until she coaxes me inside the small house behind her. My mother's living quarters are cozy but comfortable. The window in her sitting room overlooks the ocean in the distance.

"What is this place?"

"This is my legacy. This is Nova Misa."

"There are hundreds here that your grandmother has hidden over the decades. Most are gifted with toushana, which of course is a death sentence out there."

Her words jumble in my head. "My grandmother poisoned them with toushana. And then killed them."

Her nose crinkles. "Is that what she told you? She is not a perfect woman. But she covered her mistakes with honor, not murder."

A cover story. That was her cover all those years. "She took the blame."

"My mother was not concerned with how others saw her. She didn't mind playing the monster because she knew who she was inside and what she was doing. That was her hope for you, and where she went wrong with me. She wanted you to know yourself fully. And love that person." My mother squeezes my hand. "I am so sorry, Quell, for not coming to find you. But when Darragh rescued me from that wolf lair at Hartsboro, she risked everything. I hated her before that moment. I didn't trust her."

"Why? You never told me."

"I don't trust the Order. Growing up, all I knew was that my mother wanted me to follow in her shoes. Sometimes, Quell, people wear masks for so long, they forget where the truth ends and the lie begins. She had toushana. And she watched her little sister, Moriette, be turned over to Draguns for it. A six-year-old little girl, sent off to die by her own mother."

I recall the statue in the garden at Chateau Soleil, an ode to her grief. Grief is an odd thing; people deal with it their own way.

"Her saving me after I ran from her my entire motherhood told me how much I meant to her. She knew she was dying and was making preparations. She told me that she built a legacy she wanted me to carry on and that it wasn't until I left Chateau Soleil with you that she realized *I* was the one who could run this place for her. Since my name wasn't in our House's Book of Names, the induction log for our House—because back then I took classes but *refused* to formally induct—Headship couldn't pass to me. And my name wasn't on the Sphere either, since I didn't finish Third Rite. It's like I wasn't an Order member at all. I am practically untraceable. But the ways she had to bend toushana to keep doing that took an even greater toll on her magic and her health. It destroyed her from the inside out. She wanted to use whatever life she had left to fix things with me. And make sure both of us could walk in our legacy. She told me the best thing for you was to teach you to trust yourself instead of deny yourself. I'd done a horrible job at that, living on the run. Not letting you experiment with your magic and get to know who you are.

"When I was little, your grandmother never appreciated me either. My magic wasn't dark, but it wasn't as impressive as hers. And she thought impressive magic was the key to my safety. So she pressured me to be great. And I despised her for it. And every chance I got, I ran." Something shades her expression. "But I always came back. I love my mother. Every daughter does, even when we don't want to. But when you were born and I realized you were different, I wasn't willing to allow her to put that pressure on you. I didn't know if she'd follow the rules and report you to the Draguns. I didn't know where the perfect Headmistress mask ended, and I wasn't willing to find out. So we left, Quell. And I raised you to forget every part of you that is special. I am so sorry for that. Deeply."

I fidget with my clothes.

"She told me that you bound with your toushana. At first I panicked. I was scared that you weren't strong or capable enough to figure out how to survive. Then I realized: choosing to bind with your dark magic tells me everything I need to know about my daughter."

Fresh tears prick my eyes.

"You didn't need me to protect you. Your grandmother was right. You needed me to *set you free*." She looks at my diadem again and allows silence to join us.

"Should I get us tea?" she finally asks.

"Sure."

As hard as it is to face her words, they suture me back together. I wouldn't have found my own footing with her. The trouble I went through pushed me to discover who I was. Who I am.

When my mother returns with hot cups, I sort through the memories of the harsh grandmother I knew. The mother who left me to fend for myself, burying herself in a lie. And I hold the cup so tightly, my skin burns against the porcelain.

"You let me believe a lie while you live here, hiding."

"A sacrifice. Your grandmother wanted to work on getting the Immortality Scroll for you, if worse came to worst, so she needed me here. The girls here were not born with the privilege of our name. This is the only safe place for them, until the world out there changes." She takes my cup from me and holds both of my hands. "Again, I'm so sorry."

My mother pours another cup of tea. It wouldn't be what I would have chosen, but I understand it. We drink and chat about the silliest things for the longest while. I tell her about how much I love dancing. How much I love Jordan. And somehow I admit we've kissed. That part is embarrassing.

Then the conversation shifts to where I've been and *how* I've been. And what I am doing here now. I update her on everything about my time at Hartsboro, the battle at the Sphere, teaming up with Nore and Yagrin to find the Scroll, Darkbearers after Jordan, and retreating to the Chateau with Willam's safe house family, talking until my mouth is dry. She doesn't interrupt. At one point she clutches her chest.

She takes a sip before setting her tea down. "You mentioned Darkbearers are after Jordan. It sounds to me like the *Dragunhead* is looking for *you*."

"What makes you say that?"

"He sent a letter to your grandmother before she died, for *me*, looking for *you*, while you were at Hartsboro, I suppose. Dexler recovered it. Do you have any idea what he would want with you?"

"*None.*"

"You are *strong*, daughter. Bound to toushana with a heart for people. He wants the power that lives in you, I bet."

"Well, he won't have it."

"The Dragunhead is dangerous, Quell. When we fled Chateau Soleil that first night, I thought we'd sleep in a Tavern, that somewhere magical would be safer. But when I snuck into a warehouse back room, the Dragunhead was there. As if he'd been *waiting* for me. At first, I thought your grandmother had sent him to arrest me for kidnapping you or something ridiculous." She hugs around herself. "I tried to leave, but he forced me to sleep there while he watched. When I woke he was gone. Your grandmother also told me that he made not one but *two* visits to House of Marionne over the years while we were gone. You *must* stay far away from him."

A breath of silence passes between us. *Another who wants to use me.*

"You are welcome to stay here. Jordan could come, too. *But* my legacy is here; *yours* is out there. You have the choice what it will be. It's your life."

Toushana curls in my chest, comforting me.

"I could never repay—"

My mother's finger touches my lips. "Hush that foolishness." Her love radiates through me, and I'm warm all over. She has sacrificed so much for me, living her life on the run and now serving here. My grandmother, too. But there is no regret in her, only relief.

Perhaps sacrificing for the person you love *isn't* a burden.

Perhaps it's a choice.

And everyone should be free to make their own choices.

The way my grandmother and mother chose me. They sacrificed to give me the power to make my own choices. To choose myself and fight for who I want to be.

What do I want?

With so many clamoring to use me, it's time to make decisions. And own them.

"What do you choose, darling?"

The weight of the world is on my shoulders, so many people's expectations. *Save the magical world. Repair the ancestral House. Bring justice. Broker peace.* My legacy will be mine because that is freedom.

"I choose love."

I choose Jordan.

THIRTY-THREE

Yagrin

Red's body lay collapsed on the ground, and Yagrin couldn't move. Isla's hands roved her own chest, her mouth gaped open. He stepped closer as deep red ringlets shortened and lightened to a rusty shade of auburn. Red's full lips faded into Nore's as she lay there, eyes closed. Yagrin couldn't feel his heart beating. He watched her lashes change, her body morph, Ellery's Anatomer magic wearing off.

The last several weeks tore through his mind. The way Nore warmed up to him quicker than he did to her. The way she seemed to know things she shouldn't know as well as she did, like how he spent his time, his deep hatred of the Order. The way she looked at him as if she knew the secret parts of his soul. The way she kissed him. And the fury she ran off with last night when she told him that he loved *her*.

The world swayed. He looked for something to steady himself. *It was her all along.*

Red wasn't real?

His throat was dry. *Or was she?* He stared back at the body on the ground, and his pulse skittered.

Isla peeled herself off Nore and charged at her son in a fit of sobbing rage.

"You! How could you?"

"I saved your life, and you would accuse *me*?" Ellery flinched, throwing the glove off his bruising hand. "*You* ruined her life."

"I did all I could to break the Pact!" She gestured at the dark whirring above them, which were the ancestors, he now knew, circling overhead like a brewing storm. A glass box floated in the air, held in their shadows. Yagrin crept away from the argument, keeping an eye on the dead. He checked Nore for a pulse. A thump beat in her wrist.

"I *tried* to protect her by helping her access her magic," Isla went on.

"She *doesn't* have magic, Mother. That's the point you seemed to miss! Your desperation put that *poison* in her."

Toushana. Yagrin went cold all over. *Nore had toushana implanted in her?* He'd never seen her use the dark magic. And judging by the way she watched him use it, she knew very little about it.

"By mistake." She grabbed Ellery by the shoulders and shook. "I have given my entire life to protect her. Can't you see? The private cottage. The lies about sabbaticals. I knew this was coming. I knew they'd feast on her if her heart ever went in that box. And *you knew that too*!" She jabbed his chest. Then she held her face, shaking with sobs.

Yagrin hovered a hand over Nore's mouth. She was breathing deeply, as if she was sound asleep.

"She hardly had a life," Ellery said, hooking his arms behind his back.

"I was trying to find a way to get it out of her." She wailed. "I was truly trying, Ell. You've killed your sister! You've *killed* her." She fell to her knees. But Ellery grabbed his mother by the arm, snatching her back to her feet.

"Pull yourself together, woman. You're hardly recognizable. This is why *I* should be heir. I'm doing her a favor. When I find the Duncan piece of that Scroll, I'll bring her back."

Isla paled.

Yagrin's heart leapt. Ellery was going to kill his mother. Right there in front of everyone. *I have to get Nore out of here.* The ancestors were moving closer to Ellery. Nore's heart pulsed inside their gold-rimmed glass box. Maybe there was still something he could do. He hated being lied to. It shredded his soul to know that he'd been deceived.

But his love for the girl he was holding, whatever skin she was in, burned hotter than his hate.

He eyed the glove Ellery used to reach into Nore's chest on the ground. But when he reached for it, it vanished. He scooped Nore into his arms. When he turned, the scene around the argument had changed dramatically.

Ellery's hands were still behind him, but silver hid between them.

"You have no idea what it's like with your heart in that box," Isla yelled as Yagrin tried to shake Nore awake. "This is the first time in a long time that I've seen the world clearly. When your father—"

"*Don't speak about my father*," Ellery shot back. "You *shut* him out of both our lives after Nore was born." As Ellery spoke, the ancestors moved his way. Nore still didn't move, unresponsive. But Yagrin focused on her gently beating pulse.

"I never wanted to," Isla said as the cloud of dead shifted away from Ellery now and toward her.

Indecision. The ancestors weren't sure who the Head of the House was. Nore's heart was in the box, but she was unconscious. Isla was alive, so succession hadn't happened. And Ellery brought them here. Yagrin's grip on Nore tightened. He heaved her over his shoulder.

"You are not the logical choice anymore," Ellery said.

Yagrin distanced himself from the commotion, and the shade of ancestors shifted, rushing his way. But when they reached him, they stopped.

Ellery grabbed Isla by the collar. She clawed at his wrists. "Your reign as Headmistress has ended, Mother." He raised the dagger above Isla, and something shot past them in a blur, slamming into Ellery's side. The redhead tumbled sideways, bleeding, a dagger stuck in his arm. He pulled it out and flung it aside.

"Drew!" Headmistress Oralia reappeared, dashing over. "We promised the Perls that he would be *safe* here."

But they dusted themself off, meeting the malice in Ellery's eyes. "No one's committing murder on these grounds." They pointed. "*You can leave.* Anyone else with you isn't welcome here. House of Perl be damned."

Litze looked like she'd seen a ghost.

Drew dusted themself off. "I'm nothing like you, and I'm done hiding that. Try standing for something for a change. Oralians not interested in cosigning murder, with me."

Yagrin moved closer to Isla, who watched breathlessly as the crowd thinned. Nore said she needed her mother alive. He tugged at Isla's sleeve, pulling her toward him, when Nore gasped, like a drowned person coming back to life.

Her eyes batted open. "Yagrin?"

As Nore came to, the ancestors closed in around their trio. It felt like standing in the eye of a hurricane. He searched for the right words to describe what he felt for the disguised girl who he'd had an entire relationship with. Tears welled in his eyes. He'd betrayed someone who trusted him by using an alternate persona, too, once. Red gave Nore the chance to live without magic, without the guillotine of people-pleasing hanging over her head, away from the pressures of Order life. He understood what that felt like. He knew it, and loathed it just as much. She gazed at him, and the knot of frustration in his chest melted away the longer he stared into her gray eyes. Knowing what he knew now, how could he be anything but relieved? A tear rolled down his cheek. He loved her. And for the first time in his life, he was holding the person he loved with no lies between them.

He set her on her feet, keeping an arm around her. Isla watched without a word. The ancestors tightened the circle, protecting them from Ellery's fury beyond their shadows as they held fiercely to the glass box with Nore's heart.

He traced her features with his fingers. Red wasn't real. *This* was who he loved. It felt like the sky parted just then and the sun was shining right into him, brightening the shadowed crevices of his soul.

"Nore, I know about you being Red. And it's okay."

"I'm so sorry."

"You're alive. That's what matters."

Her mother stifled a sob.

"How? How am I alive?" She felt her chest. Suddenly, the shadowed bodies around them thinned, and the air began to clear, the ancestors shifting their position. The party around them quickly became less of a haze. Nore pulled herself away from Yagrin completely. Isla was sobbing harder. The dead formed up behind them, and it felt like a wall of ice at their back.

Ellery was pulling himself up off the ground, staggering, when he spotted Nore on her feet, not dead. He glared. She backed up into Yagrin. He stood firm beside her.

Nore held out her arms, staring at them as if she was seeing herself for the first time.

"Yagrin, it's *happening*," she breathed. "I feel strange." She was becoming Headmistress of House Ambrose.

"You *witch*," her brother roared. "You don't even have—"

Then the tiniest drip of black bled from Nore's hands. She shuddered against him. *Her toushana.* The truth struck him like an axe.

"The seed of toushana in you was enough to fulfill the Pact," Yagrin said.

"The ancestors accepted it," Isla muttered with relief.

"An immature, undeveloped, infinitesimal amount of poison that wasn't even mine," Nore said.

"It was enough," Yagrin said, reassuring her. "*You* are enough." But she ignored him. Ellery struggled to stand, bleeding more, as Nore played with the darkness between her fingers. Her expression scrunched in curiosity, then in disgust.

Ellery raised his dagger, but fear flickered in his eyes.

"Imagine the cold growing," Yagrin told her, wary of an impending attack. "Cling to it. Channel its power through you." He called on his as well.

But Nore stiffened as the dark magic bleeding out of her thickened.

THIRTY-FOUR

Nore

Cold pressed through Nore's fingers, and it felt like holding something sharper than a blade. She brandished her hands, holding the chilled feeling slithering around her ribs. She'd never felt the dark magic in her like this. It had been hardly an inkling inside. It was certainly never something she could control. But something about the ancestors, and the Pact, had amplified its presence.

Her brother growled, jabbing with the dagger in his fist. Isla backed away, hiding behind the dead. Nore let the cold dark shadows curl in her grip. She hated the way using magic felt. She closed her fist and snuffed the darkness out. She didn't need magic. She never had. And she wouldn't start relying on it now. Yagrin unleashed his own toushana. It thrashed in his palm.

But as Ellery reached her, the dead formed around them once again. An impenetrable fortress of Ambrose between her and her brother.

"This is not the end of this," he said. "I have allies with means at their disposal that would give the *dead* nightmares."

Words stuck in her throat. She'd never imagined herself standing in the shoes of her mother. She hadn't expected to survive it. She hated the Order. She hated the way she'd never felt a part of her House, truly. But standing there with an army of dead at her back, she'd never felt prouder of her surname.

Nore watched as her brother departed, trying to swallow the lump in her throat, but it wouldn't go down. The crowd was returning to assess the chaos. She scanned for Headmistress Oralia and spotted her in the distance, talking with her hands to someone Nore couldn't make out. The someone boasted a tall diadem of warm amber stones. But the woman was resting on a walking cane. Nore craned for a better view.

"Beaulah," Yagrin whispered in her ear. "We really should leave. *Now.*"

He was right. But where would she go? Back to Dlaminaugh? Where would Ellery go? Then it hit her. *She* was in charge, whether she liked it or not.

"Ancestors, go home. Keep Ellery Ambrose off the grounds." She held her skirts tight in her fist, waiting to see if they would listen.

The dead rose from Begonia Terrace and swept away, holding the glass box: the seal of Nore's Headship. As Beaulah Perl marched toward the dance floor where they were, Yagrin tugged harder at Nore to leave. They dashed off into the growing crowd, rushing toward the winding road the car had brought them down. Isla trailed behind them, hardly able to form words. Nore didn't have the stomach for her mother's sudden emotions.

Beside her, Yagrin exhaled. "I can't believe you're okay."

The sound of his voice skidded down her spine like a serrated knife. The eagerness in his expression made her stomach curl. She glanced at the heart, in the box, held by her shadow escorts.

Suddenly she remembered her mother's face before she'd fallen unconscious. There were tears, actual tears, from a woman who'd never even given her a hug . . .

Nore and Yagrin had been tangled around one another last night. Now the thought made her feel ill. Physically sick to her stomach. It was confusing. She wanted to be with him. In her mind, she understood that. But the only thing she felt looking at him now was pure discomfort. The truth jabbed her in the chest.

I can't love Yagrin.

That part of her was sealed in a box until *her heir* took her place.

When they cleared the entrance gates, Yagrin stopped them.

"I'm going to try to cloak. Hold on to me."

"Thank you, Yagrin. For everything." She placed a hand on his shoulder and only grew more irritated. He held on to her. Too close. Too tightly. She should love it. Yesterday this was all she wanted. But she fought the urge to rip his hands off her skin.

As darkness swept to his fingers, he whispered, "To Dlaminaugh."

Moments later, her home materialized around them, their feet crunching on snow. Several dead awaited her. Her mother ran to the concrete and glass palace ahead of them. Nore put distance between her and Yagrin. She wouldn't tolerate any more lies between them, not after they'd just cleared the air. She had to be honest. She was a long way from having an heir.

He reached for her.

She moved out of the way.

"Nore?"

"Yagrin." She held her chest. "I can't love you back." She pressed her hip bone, remembering the hemlock tattoo in the shape of a heart. A reminder that love wasn't something she would ever have. This was just another form of defeat. And no matter how much it made sense to her brain, she felt nothing for him. It was wrong. But this was her curse. And she was frankly tired of fighting for hope. Love was an impossibility. He stepped toward her. She stepped back.

"Your heart, I understand," he said. "But you'll try, won't you? After everything, you have to be willing to try."

She scowled. He had proven trustworthy and helpful. Keeping him around could be practical. Before she could stop herself, futile words tumbled from her mouth.

"Sure, Yagrin. I'll try."

They hurried up the mountainside to the posterior gate. She had her coronation ceremony to plan and a brother who wanted to kill her still on the loose.

THIRTY-FIVE

Jordan

While Zecky rests against a wall, turning the diadem in his hands, panic seizes in my chest. Ube works a Retentor brush over my body in circular motions. A warm sensation gusts through me as the stone slides along my body. I try to hinge at my waist again, but it's no use.

"Hold still."

"I can't move. Why can't I move?" I am stuck, flat on my back on a table, with only my neck and head able to rotate. Erla hasn't returned. And Ube doesn't make a sound as he works.

"He is nearly done," Zecky says, watching from a distance.

"What's the diadem for?" I ask, turning my head to look in his direction.

"Shh." Zecky grabs me by the jaw tightly and urges my gaze straight up. He lays his free hand near the scar where the Sphere's magic entered my body, and toushana lurches in my chest.

"It's agitated," Zecky says, and my body tremors with pain. A buckling sensation snaps between my ribs like a cement block shattered in half. Heat rushes through the crater in my chest.

"*There* we are." Zecky brings the diadem closer.

The icy wave of my toushana slams into the bluster of heat prickling my body, drowning the proper magic's heat. I try to speak, but Zecky smothers my mouth, clamping his grip tighter. Whatever this is, it isn't an examination. Cold and hot wrestle in my bones. I try to pull myself up, but the table won't let me move.

"*There*, right there," Zecky hollers. "Put it in place now."

The world sears of sound and color as a tear rips through me like being carved open with jagged teeth. Ube shoves the diadem, jeweled tips first, beneath my ribs. The cold refuses to budge.

"Out of my way." Zecky shoves Ube aside. "Leave the dark one. *The other* is the one that legitimizes us."

They're stealing the magic.

Weight shifts against my ribs as Zecky shoves the diadem deeper into me, away from my decaying ribs. It knocks the wind out of me and feels like I've swallowed a knife all at the same time.

Cold.

My body.

All over.

Everything is *so* cold. A bluster of grainy heat rushes through me as Zecky pulls the diadem out. The metal glows. Pressure releases in every crevice of my body as piping hot magic gushes out of me and into the brightening stones of the diadem.

Zecky fumbles the diadem, now smoking in his hands. Ube scrambles for something to help him hold it, when a jewel pops out of the metal frame, exploding all over Zecky's hands.

He shrieks.

Another jewel buckles at the intensity of the magic. Zecky crushes the diadem in his hands, holding it tightly against him, and I can hear the *hiss* of the metal on his skin. He tries to shove it inside a metal box. But more stones spill between his fingers. I watch the horror of their plan backfiring, when I suddenly realize my pain is gone.

It feels like ice has replaced the marrow in my bones. But it doesn't hurt.

I try to sit up, but a final gush of cold magic renders me flat on my back again.

Everything grows hazy.

And colder.

So much colder.

Zecky and Ube manage to get a handle on the diadem, locking it inside the box.

"*Out!* Before he wakes." Something hard hits the floor.

"I don't understand," Ube says. "You want to—"

"*Go now.*" Zecky urges him out the door, knuckles white on the metal box.

My arms are lead. I glare at the box, trying to move, but the world sways. So I focus on slowing the pace of my breath as I search for an inkling of warmth, a tickle of granules inside. I feel nothing. They are gone.

The Sphere's proper magic inside me is gone. What's left of it is in that metal box.

Fog forms on my lips.

Cold unfurls in my chest, lugging itself from the space inside where it wedged itself as Zecky gapes in shock, holding his seared fingers. I feel more balanced as the toushana spreads through me in a way it never has before. No longer wrestling for a place inside my body. But spreading over each organ, coating every bone, slinking underneath each muscle and into every limb. *Up. I need to get up.*

But my body feels like dead weight. Like no matter how much power I hold in my hands, it will never be enough to protect what matters. Like I *am* the useless nothing my father insisted I was. I see Beaulah's face and then the Dragunhead.

Darkness dents the edges of my vision.

A deathly cold races through my veins. It feels like all I have left. So I whisper to the dark magic.

"Help me, please."

Shadows seep from my pores, and the table at my back crumbles. When my feet touch the ground, shadows swallow my steps. And I feel steady for the first time in a long time. Memories of Beaulah and the Dragunhead fade as the world sharpens in focus. Sounds are crisper. All kinds of smells unfurl in my nose. But the one that licks my insides with delight is the fear beading on Zecky's forehead. He drains of color as he stumbles backward, away from me.

"Please, hear me out." He white-knuckles the box, offering it to me. "I'm more on your side than you think. I could have made a deal with the Dragunhead when he came looking for you. But I refused him. That should matter. *Please.*"

"You baited me into trusting you." I snatch the metal box. But Zecky wasn't the only one baiting me. I inhale deeply, piecing together the chaos of the last several weeks.

The Sixth Ward. The other cities. Darkbearers hurting innocent Unmarked. Audubon's mansion being burned.

These attacks were also bait.

Darkbearers have been trying to use my sense of duty, my desire for justice, to draw me out in the open for *weeks.* They want the Sphere's magic. Badly.

Zecky collapses to his knees with praying hands. I should really thank him for helping me see. I've been so worried about Beaulah, when Darkbearers are burning down the world to lure me.

"Our team is brilliant," Zecky says. "They have discovered all kinds of things about the Sphere. I gave them access to all my ancestors' research."

My ears perk up.

"I recruited the best brains *away* from the Order. I can help you."

He could. But I could never trust him again.

"Together we are an unstoppable team. I would give my life for that opportunity."

"You just did." I reach for him. Shadows slither off me toward him. Darkness hoists him up by his throat. His face purples, choking on useless apologies.

"I, Jordan Wexton, former Dragunheart, sentence you to die for theft of sacred magic with ill intent." I close my free hand into a fist and rotate my wrist. The bones in Zecky's body twist in the direction of my grip until they snap.

End him, magic whispers.

His bones pop and crack as the light leaves his eyes. Leaning into an urge never felt so good.

Zecky is a mastermind. He plotted from the moment he met me. And the toushana in me knew it. That's why it was so unsettled when I arrived. Instead of listening to my instinct, I buried it. *Never again.* The skin falls from his bones where my darkness touches him, and he collapses on the floor. I open the metal box to inspect the diadem, which has half as many gems as it did before. My heart knocks in my ribs.

This is all that's left of the Sphere's proper magic.

The jewels are still warm from the heat of the magic it absorbed. Could we multiply it somehow? Is there a way to restore what was lost and grow what we have?

My side aches with a dull pain.

My heart skips a beat.

I lift my shirt and study the smooth skin where my wound used to be. A subtle pain is still there, but there is no bruise.

I stretch my torso again, searching for some dregs of *my* proper magic, but the faint hum of the grainy dust I used to feel flutter around in me is gone. A weight of cold shifts in my chest, and it's oddly comforting. Toushana rolls through my body, settling into its every crevice, and the chill answers in an instant, dark mist rising from my fingers. My own binding ceremony tugs at my memory. But I inhale and play with the darkness in my hands before snuffing it out and tucking my shirt.

Before anything else, the Sphere's toushana must come out of me, too. With so many hunting me, my body is the least safe place for it to be.

I glare at the corpse. Thankfully, I just witnessed an extraction procedure that can do it.

The corridors of the safe house are busy. There's no sign of Ube or Erla, his sister. Ube seemed in on it. But he also seemed confused. Lady Ruby is nowhere to be found. My toushana is quiet, at home in my bones, as I stroll past the other exam rooms. I wouldn't have gotten out of there alive if I hadn't asked toushana for help. *And* let it flow through me, freely.

I push away the last traces of grief over the boy I was—who studied and strengthened his proper magic to be better than everyone else. *This is what I have now.* I'm not letting it go. When the Sphere's toushana is extracted from my body, I will make sure a piece of it stays. Dark magic is propelled by my deepest, most desperate instincts.

I won't second-guess them ever again.

And right now they're urging me to find Quell.

THIRTY-SIX

Quell

Tippets Square is empty as the sun rises over the buildings. When I returned to Chateau Soleil, Yaniselle told me she followed Jordan here, where he disappeared inside a church. And didn't come out. Panicked, she returned to find me, and we traveled back here together. I linger near a fountain's edge, looking for some indication where Jordan could have gone. But it's an earsplitting scream that sends a jolt through my ribs.

Leaving my mother in Nova Misa was hard, but I made my choice, and it isn't goodbye forever. The Dragunhead is after my magic, and I won't stand for it. No one else is dying to fight my battles for me.

I will stop him myself.

I will glide on my own wings.

The air shreds a second time with a bloodcurdling scream.

I look for where the noise is coming from and in the dim morning light spot a girl with cropped dark hair standing over a charred body on the sidewalk that rims the square. She's covered in bruises, and the closer I get, I realize I know those thick black-liner-streaked eyes, combat boots, and mixed-metal jacket.

"Abby!"

She turns, and morning light illuminates her whole face. It's really her. I run harder, slamming into her.

"Quell?" She sobs against me, hugging me tight.

"You're okay."

She shakes, falling to her knees. I smell the body's stench before I see it up close.

"It's Mynick."

I gasp. *"What happened?"*

She points at the church. "He tried to get in there, and when he crossed those steps, he caught on fire."

The last time I saw Mynick, he pretended to help me look for my mom at a ball, when he was really plotting a raid to capture me. "You hate him."

"I do, but he showed up at the Tavern one night for one of the shows. I was hoping to slash his tires or something to make myself feel better. I couldn't help myself." She folds her arms, and I hug her again. It hurts to see her so upset over someone who isn't even worth her time. "But when I went looking for him, he was meeting with some people who mentioned Jordan. I've been following him ever since, to see what he was up to. I worried he was setting Jordan up to be raided like he did to you, but no one ever came. Now he's dead." Her grip on my hand is iron. "Quell, have you been reading the papers?"

Darkbearers. "I have."

"I was in one of those neighborhoods that got destroyed. I watched Mynick and those guys—" Her voice cracks. "She was just a little old lady, Quell." She breaks. "Why? Why would he do this?"

I hold her tighter. "Some people only feel good about themselves when they make others feel bad."

"He wasn't like this before. It's that poison. That *toushana*. He should have never touched it." She looks at my hands. "I don't mean— I'm sorry, Quell."

Every person in the Order has been taught that toushana should be despised. It's going to take time for her to see how wrong that is. "I'm just glad you're okay. Check his phone."

"Good idea." Abby digs through what's left of Mynick's pockets and pulls out his phone. "Who is that?" She points to Yani.

"Jordan's ex. Long story."

"Do we like her?"

"We definitely don't like her."

Abby gives her a condescending sneer, and my heart swells. I've missed having a friend.

"Jordan went into the church—" Abby says, and Yani takes that as her cue to invite herself into our conversation. She looks at Mynick.

"Knew he wouldn't last. The overly eager ones never do," she mutters.

I approach the stone edge of the fountain. "Walk me through it again, Yani."

She explains how Jordan hung back at the fountain and then went to the church steps.

"He used a card to get in or something."

"How did the card work?" I ask.

"If I knew that, we'd know who he was meeting already." She folds her arms, dark hair draped over her shoulder. She is annoyingly beautiful.

"Why are you here?" I ask.

"Where else was I supposed to go?"

"Literally anywhere. You lose your home, and you follow Jordan like a kicked puppy? You either have no self-respect or are up to something."

She scowls.

The cold magic inside me awakens. "What are you after?"

"I've told Jordan everything. Sounds like he didn't share."

"*Rude*—" Abby starts, but I stop her.

"I know Jordan," she goes on, "better than you ever could. I *made him* into who he is. You're all wrong for him."

"This from someone who worshiped at the altar of Beaulah Perl."

"From what I heard, we weren't all that different a few months ago." She quirks a brow. "Besides, I've turned over a new leaf."

"Your opinion doesn't matter."

"It doesn't need to matter to *you*. Only him."

"It doesn't matter to him."

"Then why didn't Jordan rat me out to Willam and the others as a heartless traitor who could never be trusted?" She's so close to me I smell her flowery scent. It turns my stomach. Nothing she says matters. If he is foolish enough to fall for her, he was never truly mine. I busy myself skimming the area again, but I can feel her glare still on me. Abby encourages me with an eye roll.

"You can't understand him," Yani goes on. "Especially now, with so much power—"

I tighten my fists, keeping my back to her.

"You don't know what it was like growing up—" she rattles on.

"*Don't I?*" I say to her face. "A childhood living in shadows, being seen by others but not ever really being seen at all, impossible expectations, feeling like you're losing some part of yourself, being haunted by nightmares of things you've seen, isolating, self-deprecating, dabbling with darkness and *liking it*."

She swallows.

"I'd rather be burned alive than sing the Order's pledge anymore." I smell a lock of her hair. "You still smell like Hartsboro."

Hatred burns in Yani's eyes. When suddenly behind her a figure shaped like Jordan appears across the Square. He strolls with steps sharper than a blade, holding a box.

"Something's wrong," I say, trying to reconcile the sublime expression on his face.

"Or something's right," Yani says.

"What is he holding?" Abby asks.

I book it toward him. His mouth bows in a clever smirk. He shimmies the box, and when we are close enough, he whispers, "The Sphere's proper magic in an ancient diadem." He clears his throat. "All of it that was inside me is gone."

I look back. Abby watches, gaping. Yani gasps.

"What? How? Wait. That means—the Sphere's toushana is still in you?" I hover a tentative hand near him and feel cold radiating off his skin. "Are you okay?" I ask. He has the Sphere's toushana inside him. *Only* toushana.

"Quell, the extraction procedure they used to get this out of me is the same one we'll use for the toushana. There were a few mishaps, unfortunately. Some of the magic was lost." He turns the diadem, and I can see gaps for missing stones. "We'll have to refine the procedure a bit before executing it again. But we know *how* to do what we want now. This is the best news."

He smiles. I hesitate. "We should get back behind the gates of the Chateau." The protections my grandmother put in place should hopefully help keep him from the Darkbearers hunting him and the Dragunhead after me.

"W-We have to leave!" Abby drops Mynick's phone, and it hits the pavement with a thud. She's as pale as a ghost. I pick it up, and despite the damaged outer case and cracked screen, I make out his last messages.

Mynick: Target found. Confirming, the magic in his body seems to be doing fine. Appears physically intact from what I can tell. Apprehend?

But it's the response that chills my blood.

Them: Send me your location. He is my Heart. I will do this myself.

Mynick: Tippets Square.

My heart drums faster. My mother's warning about the Dragunhead haunts me, connecting with something Jordan said some time ago. *Darkbearer attacks are too coordinated to be random.* My stomach plummets. The last several days crash together in my memory, the conversations about Jordan I kept overhearing, the swift way word spread, the absence of Draguns, Mynick's death. Darkbearers are moving like a unit, an army, well organized.

Darkbearers don't want Jordan.

Their boss does.

"He is behind the Darkbearer attacks."

"*Who*, Quell?"

"The Dragunhead."

PART THREE

THIRTY-SEVEN

Ellery

The slow drip of rainwater outside worked Ellery's nerves. His plan to force his sister's death by handing her heart to the ancestors had failed. They accepted the seed of poison in her as payment for the Pact.

He burned with irritation that he hadn't considered that possibility. The toushana was so immature, it hadn't even grown. He didn't expect it to be enough to satiate the ancestors' desires. But toushana was a powerful magic with massively destructive potential.

Even the dead coveted it.

The cut he'd somehow gotten on his arm during the scuffle with his sister stung. He rubbed more salve onto it, watching the Dragunhead—Sal was his name, but he preferred to be called by his role—tear off morsels of a loaf of stale bread and feed it to a crow in a wiry cage. He hummed a melody, and it made Ellery want to glue the man's lips shut. *How dare he be so chipper?*

Outside lit up with howls, scratches, and all manner of sounds once the sun set, and Ellery's mind was restless. The Dragunhead's cabin was a forgotten pile of wood in the middle of nowhere. There wasn't a city for hours. He wanted to pace, but the tight quarters were too small. There was one tidy bed, made up perfectly in the corner beside a few pieces of countertop. When Ellery slept here, they took turns, resting one at a time. Two armchairs were wrapped in blankets between dusty shelves.

Books were wedged on the shelves in any angle they'd fit, squeezed on top, beside, and flattened open. The place was cramped. Its musty smell was what he hated most. He loathed coming here.

But his sister was insulated by the ancestors now.

He had nowhere else to go.

They weren't honorable creatures, but they demanded loyalty to their agreements.

He'd angered them by telling them that Isla was ill and Nore planned to outrun the Pact. So they followed her. He deepened their trust of him by offering them an ancient magic that only required a vial of Nore's blood to help them cross thresholds where she was. They were eager to keep a close eye on her. It took Ellery weeks to learn the ancient magic. And more weeks spreading word of a reward for a vial of her blood. He was stunned when after several unsuccessful attacks it was someone posing as a hotel maid who brought sheets Nore'd slept on stained with blood.

When he got the call from Litze Oralia that Nore showed up at Begonia Terrace, he had them come along to put the final piece of his plan into motion. They were so close. But his oversight had pulled the rug from under him.

Sal side-eyed him now. He knew all kinds of things about magic Ellery had never learned before. That was part of why he was willing to work with him. He'd shown him a magic to replace Nore's heart in the box while keeping his mother's intact. That was when he thought his mother could be swayed to help him. He scoffed. *Should have just let the old hag croak.* The Dragunhead whistled now, twisting the lock on the bird's cage before settling into one of his armchairs. He pulled a wooden dragon out of a basket, along with a stubby carving knife. He worked the edge of the blade along the dragon's head, wood shavings curling up and off it.

In truth, Ellery hadn't expected things to get this out of hand. He loved his sister, and he wanted to free her. But she had to trust him. Now that she was Headmistress, he had to kill her outright and hope Headship would still move to him. Usually when a parent was killed, Headship moved to one of the children—a daughter if available. If not, the son. It didn't move between siblings, he thought. But the Dragunhead insisted he not worry about that detail. That all magic is manipulable with the right skills.

"You're quiet tonight," Sal said.

Ellery bit back the first retort that came to him and grunted instead.

"A disappointing night for you, I know." The Dragunhead blew dust off the wooden figurine before continuing to work on one of its claws, tilting the blade back and forth quickly over the same spot to bring the wood to a sharp point. "It is unfortunate to hear the Mynick boy died. He could have proven very useful."

Ellery had no one else in his corner. Bitterness wasn't prudent. "Do you have meetings tonight?" he asked, to hopefully change the subject.

"I thought after an eventful day like we've had, a quiet evening to think would be nice. It is going to rain. You like the rain, don't you, Ell?"

"Sure."

"It's good for thinking."

"And what are you thinking about, pray tell?" *Quell. Jordan. That's all he talks about these days.* "They fled to Chateau Soleil. We can't get into that estate easily, my sources say."

The Dragunhead's brows rose quizzically.

"I still have a few connections," Ellery said. "I'm well liked, believe it or not."

"Of course I believe it."

Ellery's chin rose.

"Do you know anything about Quell's acquaintances?"

"Maybe. She has a friend who dated Mynick, I think."

"Write them down, would you? Any and all, please." The Dragunhead tossed Ellery a pen and paper.

"Sure." Ellery tensed, writing down a few names he'd heard who knew the Marionne girl.

The Dragunhead took the paper and tore each name into its own slip. Then he placed each one into a separate jar and set it on his highest shelf. Some of the things he did were very strange, but Ellery had learned a long time ago not to question him. With his seasoned experience, his depth of understanding of magic was extraordinary.

"And what about House of Perl, what sources do you have there?"

Ellery's heart ticked faster. "Why?"

The Dragunhead smiled.

"I don't know who I know that's still there. But I can look into it. Anything else?" Ellery stewed. He sure was doing a lot. What was he getting out of this partnership? Besides magic advice here and there.

"I can tell your mind is going. Careful to avoid acting on assumption. This was not the big failure you think it is. Timing is everything. I had to be sure the magic could live in a Marked body and that proper magic could be removed. The girl is very important, too."

Ellery grumbled. "I want to hear more about your plan to get rid of Nore. How are we going to get to her with the ancestors determined to keep her obedient to the Pact? Where do we even start looking for the Duncan piece of the Scroll?"

Ellery intended to lead his House through this chaos of the Sphere breaking. Ambrose could chart that course like no one else. But how could they focus on stretching their intellect when their Head had no magic at all? His sister was really clever, but that wasn't the same as knowing how to do things *magically*. He ground his jaw every time he thought of it. *He* was the natural choice. But as a child he'd always been overlooked by his mother and ignored by his father, who was focused on trying again for an heir. He'd proven himself eventually. But he was done doing that.

He would take what he wanted.

"Don't worry about the Duncan piece of the Scroll. That was never the best use of anyone's time. I told you that before. Now you believe me?"

"I guess so."

"I have a better plan. Trust that I have my hand in *many* places." The Dragunhead set a hand on Ellery's shoulder. "Saving the world is not for the impatient. Are you still up to the task?"

"I am," Ellery said between gritted teeth. He didn't care about the world unless it threatened to rip magic away from him. That was the only reason he was willing to put any energy into the Dragunhead's plans for Jordan and Quell.

"On second thought, the rain is slacking, and the soil will be nice and soft." The Dragunhead set down the wooden animal and tossed Ellery a shovel.

Ellery balled his fists, but he followed him out the door.

THIRTY-EIGHT

Nore

Marching toward Dlaminaugh across the bitter winter snow felt like being escorted to prison. She'd never been safe between the walls of her House, but especially now.

Her brother's plan to shove her heart in the ancestors' glass box had failed to kill her.

But Ellery still wanted her dead.

Somehow he'd manipulated magic to allow the ancestors to cross other thresholds. She needed the Duncan piece of that Scroll more than ever now. At least she and Yagrin would be on the same page about that.

The ancestors glided along before her as if charting her course. As if they knew if she had a moment to decide her future for herself, she would turn around and run. She was several steps faster than her mother and Yagrin, despite her hesitation to come back to this glass-and-concrete estate of horrors. The box with her heart was covered in a dark fabric and wedged in the grip of one of the shadowy figures, hardly perceptible, blending together like a half-told truth.

Drew's bravery haunted Nore. The way they stood up to her brother. The way they dared to stand for something even if it defied everyone's expectation. She was marching back into her home as a fraud. If they knew, they'd probably *turn her over* to her brother.

Draguns stood sentry on either side of Dlaminaugh's concrete gate. With the rumors she'd heard about the brotherhood, she was surprised they hadn't abandoned their posts. Their stares slid to her mother first, then to her before hitting the ground. She had to believe there was some way out of this mess—*stuck* in the exact role she'd been avoiding her entire life. If she had a heart, it would have cracked.

She spotted the gravel path that wound around the estate to her cottage. She veered toward it, and the world darkened. Her body hit solid air as the ancestors blocked her detour. The only path that was clear was the path forward—to the shiny, opening glass doors of House of Ambrose.

She marched inside, where a long line of House members, students, maezres, and staff waited rigidly to receive her. She stopped. And Yagrin nearly stumbled into the back of her. *How did they know?*

Maezre Tutom, her governess when she was small who was determined to help her acclimate to magical studies the last time she was here, waved at her. But Nore couldn't move. Another woman who was older than Nore but not quite as old as her mother approached. Her dark hair, pinned under a servant's cap and dull silver diadem, fell beside her face as she curtsied. She quickly shoved it back in place. Nore recognized her as one of the maids always at her mother's beck and call. She couldn't recall her name. Caisely or Paisely or something. But she realized this maid would now be *her* shadow.

"Headmistress," she said. "I'm Ainsley, and I'm here for whatever you need. Head Maid Maura Shoom retired, so I'm lead now. I trained closely under her, serving your mother for the last ten years. And before me, my mother served your mother and the late Porsha, your grandmother."

"How—" Nore's voice cracked. She cleared her throat. "How did you know I am to become Headmistress?"

Ainsley blinked. "Mr. Ambrose."

"My brother?"

"He told us that he and Headmistress Isla were leaving to change House leadership. He instructed us to wait for their return. Then *you* arrived. Is your brother alright, ma'am?"

Her heart fluttered. Her brother could rot in the deepest pits of hell.

She didn't want this. She didn't want any of this. Her entire life, she'd never been good enough for this role—magicless *her*. Now the whole House watched her arrival, staring with expectation gleaming in their eyes. She still didn't have magic they would find admirable. *When* would she be done living a lie? She bit the inside of her cheek just to feel something.

"They'll only know you're terrified if you hesitate," Yagrin whispered into her ear.

She shrugged him away, with her eyes forward. The ancestors slipped inside the building, billowing along the ceilings like smoke. She took a step. They inched along. She took another step, then kept going, her fists full of the skirt of her dress. She avoided every face she passed as the long corridor took her wherever the ancestors intended her to go.

Ainsley stayed close. The shadows shifted when they rounded on the Hall of Discovery, and it hit her. *My heart has to go into the vault, sealing my fate.* She'd almost been foolish enough to be comforted by the ancestors' presence guiding her home. But they weren't protecting her; they were keeping her accountable to her word.

Yagrin and Isla whispered behind her, and she bristled with irritation. She glared at them and hardly recognized her mother. Isla's hands were linked, worry lines carved her face like a pumpkin, and there were tears in her eyes.

I am so sorry, Isla mouthed.

When they reached the vault, Nore held up her hand to the wall behind the glass, where she'd opened it so many months before. The wall rippled, and her hand dipped inside. The dark bundle the ancestors held emerged from the shadow it was in and was thrust into her hands. Nore stepped through the rippling wall and set the glass box with her beating heart down without looking around, keeping her gaze turned toward the exit. Then she dashed back out. The ancestors swarmed around her before vanishing in a haze.

On the wall behind her was a message carved by the dead into the plaster with something sharp.

ALWAYS WATCHING

She tried to slow her breath.

She recognized some of the faces in the audience of Ambrosers, who'd followed them to the Hall of Discovery. There was pride in some of their expressions. One girl's chin raised, books tucked tight to her chest.

Nore smoothed her clothes.

"They're waiting for you to acknowledge them, ma'am." The tiny voice was Ainsley's. Her maid. "Was there anything you wanted to say?"

"No, there's nothing I want to say."

"Then you must say that. It's tradition for a new Headmistress to address the House when they take over."

Nore's heart must have returned because *something* was lodged in her throat.

"Perhaps at coronation?" Ainsley suggested. "Once you're more rested."

Nore nodded, still unable to find words. Her clammy hands slipped against each other as she clasped them. Yagrin moved beside her.

An odd feeling came over her. An unsettling twist in her gut and a deep sense of mourning for the child she was. This was the future she was reared for. She'd marveled at it when she was very little, before she realized she was different. And now it was meaningless, completely void of anything that actually mattered.

"Breathe in for four, out for six," he said, sensing the hold her anxiety had gotten on her. She did it, and the tightness in her chest began to unwind. She hadn't felt like this since—dark memories tried to haunt her. She shoved them away.

Her mother was still among the crowd. Anger reddened Nore's cheeks. She was *not* the nervous, fidgety daughter her mother mistreated. Wasn't she the *Headmistress* of House of Ambrose? Becoming Red, being who she wanted with Yagrin, had ignited a fire in her to bury those anxious parts of herself, once and for all. She stood straighter.

"It's been a long journey and an even longer few weeks," she said. "I will address you at coronation. Get back to your studies."

"Tomorrow," her mother announced from across the hall. "Coronation *tomorrow*."

"Tomorrow, right." Nore paled and rushed off.

"Nore?" her mother called, hustling to catch up with her as the crowd dispersed. Yagrin stayed close but silent. And as much as she wanted to shoo him away, she didn't.

"I can stay and help you prepare."

"Why is it tomorrow?"

"House laws. In the case of a Headmistress taking over in times of conflict, coronation is fast-tracked. Or in your case, when you've already taken part in *other* ceremony sacraments, the process must be completed immediately—the first sunrise after."

My heart is in the box, she means.

"Right now, you're like partly Headmistress until the ceremony. As much as we wear gray, we like to keep things very black-and-white."

She would be thrust into this whether she wanted to or not. She looked at Yagrin, and in his golden-brown eyes, she could see into his soul. It longed for her. She felt sick.

Her mother touched her arm. "There are certain *preparations* that a mother could be helpful with."

"I can manage myself." Nore left her mother there, but her maid and Yagrin stuck to her heels.

The trio halted at the door to the Headmistress's private quarters.

"Ma'am, all your mother's things have been moved to her new quarters. I can show you around, if you'd like? Privately." Ainsley looked from her to Yagrin.

"Please don't call me *ma'am*. I am Nore. Just Nore."

"Yes, Headmistress." Ainsley curtsied.

It was a partial victory.

After many suspicious looks, Ainsley closed Yagrin and Nore inside her new room. Nore exhaled. She could not feel love, but her memory seemed to be working just fine. And she knew how she *should* feel, being alone with him *finally*. It was a relief she didn't have to hide. Yagrin watched her with his back against the door. She busied herself surveying the furnishings. She'd seen her mother's room a handful of times as a girl, and it was just as cold as it always was.

The brutalist-style bedroom was basic, with a simple stone headboard. The whole room wept gray. Parted gray shutters flanked the windows. Beside the cold stone fireplace there was a fraying gray blanket and two circular pillows on the floor. Beside a slab of concrete desk with a metal chair beneath, shelves stuck out of the wall like blunt teeth piled with books.

She crossed the room, and her foot nudged a book beneath her bed. There were stacks of more books in every corner of the room. Yagrin gave her space to take it all in. On a tall pile of tomes was a small frame. In it was a picture of her mother holding Ellery on her hip and Nore wrapped in blankets. The glass of the frame had cracked, and parts of it were chipped. She set it back down as a draft whipped in from the windows. She moved to the hearth and poked a dark log. She rubbed the lighting stick along it, but nothing happened. When Yagrin joined her, she almost yelped. She'd forgotten he was there.

The nearness of him toyed with her senses, sending tiny bumps up her arms. His smell was one she used to miss when he wasn't near. There were a few of his shirts she still had in her things somewhere.

"I know how to start a fire."

He ran his steady hand along her shaky ones, gliding the igniting stick slower and smoother along the log. "I know you do."

She bit back her retort and resisted everything in her that wanted to throw him out of her room. He had been helpful, and just because she couldn't feel love didn't mean she had to be cruel. *I hope.* She clenched her jaw as she thought of her mother.

"This log is too big," he said, his body so close to hers, she could hear the rise and fall of his chest.

"I was thinking the same thing." She struck the log hard with the poker, but the bark hardly chipped. She heaved the poker over her shoulder to swing harder, narrowly missing Yagrin. He grinned as he caught the stick in his hand. Their fingers brushed, and it sent a thrill up her arms. It was no more than two days ago that she'd wept, hungering for a moment like this with the unveiled truth between them.

"Try your magic," he said.

"I am clever. I don't need magic."

"Fair." Darkness trickled from his fingers, and the log snapped in half. He leaned in closer to her, guiding her grip of the igniting stick along the now-broken log. He eased it backward and forward in a smooth rhythm, and she moved with him, his chest firmly at her back. "But if you have it, you may as well. I can show you how."

The back of her neck heated. She ripped herself away from him as fire finally ignited in the hearth.

"I won't lead you on, Yagrin."

He stepped toward her. She stepped back.

"You're not leading me anywhere. I am here by choice."

"I'm not sure you should be."

He winced.

She folded her arms, but her cheeks burned with shame. He loved her. And he deserved someone who could love him back.

"You're not yourself," he said, with a kindness that deepened the sickness she felt. How was it possible to know something so strongly with the mind, but the heart just won't follow? She raked her hands through her hair.

"Do you remember that time you let me take you into the city and we climbed to the top of that tower? We dangled our legs over the edge of its rails. The view was breathtaking."

She remembered. They'd snuck into a fancy neighborhood, over its security gate, breaking its cameras just so they could access the water tower. They climbed until the soles of her feet ached. She'd never seen anything like it before. Afterward, they picnicked on the ground, and one thing led to another. He searched for her eyes. Her gaze fell to her hands, which were carving moons into her arms.

"That was a lifetime ago." That night at the water tower, she was speechless. Now all she could seem to recall vividly was the grime the rusted ladder left on her hands, the cut she got on her leg when they reached the top, and the disgusting stench coming from the water. There was no sparkle in remembering. The Pact had robbed her of that. It was as if the color had been drained from her life. As if the gray rags she wore now veiled her eyes.

Yagrin ran his soft touch up her folded arms, but stubbornness kept her still. She was ice, and his touch was fire. "We can take it slow." His other hand grazed her skin, drawing gentle circles. Then he cupped her arms, both of them at the same time, in his strong hands.

"I'm not sure I can survive this," she said. "I've failed at so many things in life, I've lost count."

He held her tighter. "Not the things that matter." His stare bored into her with an earnestness that made her blink, expecting to cry. No tears came. No feelings rushed in.

"I won't fail at us, too." She peeled his fingers off her skin, recalling the memories that flooded her as they touched.

"You agreed to try," he said.

"I need time alone."

"I'll see you at dinner, then."

"I'm taking it alone here."

He pleaded with her wordlessly. Nore was sure she didn't have a heart because in that moment it would have shattered.

"After dinner?"

"No, Yagrin!" She should send him away from here, kick him off the property. But she could not do it. He was the only person who knew her. Feelings aside, he was trustworthy. And right now she needed people she could trust. "I'm sorry. I will see you soon." She marched to the door and opened it. Yagrin didn't move. He started to speak several times but

stopped himself. When he joined her at the door, he reached for her hair and ran his fingers through it.

"I was going to throw everything away until a free-spirited redhead made me realize there are things in life worth fighting for more than revenge. That bitterness is worse than death. I will wait my entire life for you, Nore. Because you gave me mine back."

He stepped through the door, and she watched him go down the corridor. There was a part of her that wanted to call him back. She knew how he made her feel. She could not deny that he was on her side like no one else had ever been. She knew he would never betray her. She knew how he could make her feel like the only girl in the world with a kiss. He could tend her wounds with the way he held her. He could make her feel things physically that made the world itself cease to exist. She couldn't string him along. It was selfish. Rationally, the kindest thing she could do was to push him away.

But as he disappeared around the corner, she shouted, "Wait!"

Yagrin's chin slid over his shoulder.

"Tomorrow, could you be there? Beside me, I mean."

"Of course. Sleep well."

Ainsley was nowhere in sight when Nore shut the door. She walked the length of her room, replaying the last day. She passed the picture of her mother, her, and Ellery, and picked it up. There were no creases of joy in her mother's face. Just a stoic, icy expression as Ellery grinned and she herself stared bright-eyed at the camera. Nore sat on the edge of her bed and pulled the picture out of the frame and saw a faded message written on the back.

The sun shines, and it reminds me of you.

Storm clouds, thundering rain, behind them all, the sun remains.

She held a handkerchief to her face. But nothing came. So she hugged her knees and glared at the angry, unwieldy, powerful fire across the room until her eyes were heavy. Then she lay down and curled up on her mattress, handkerchief in one hand and the picture in the other.

THIRTY-NINE

Jordan

The church clock bells chime again in the distance. Tippets Square thins of tourists as emergency personnel arrive to deal with Mynick's body. Quell's eyes burn with worry. She is wary of trusting this extraction plan with Zecky's safe house team. But I will make sure there is nothing to fear. I *will* make a world that is safe for her, even if I have to burn this one down with my bare hands.

"I need your help," I tell her, fighting the urge to comfort her with a kiss and promise this will be over soon.

Abby watches us, and Yani eyes the box where the diadem is.

"Just Quell," I say. "We're going to round up everyone inside. They know the procedure. They are the sharpest magical minds I've seen. If they can do the procedure once, they can refine it to make it safer and do it again."

"You want to take them prisoner?" Quell asks.

"Do you have a problem with that?" Yani asks.

I pull Quell aside to the church steps to speak alone. "We can ask them to come along. But if they refuse . . ." Toushana stretches in my chest. "They will come anyway."

"Jordan."

"There's no time to debate this. Do you trust me?"

"With my life."

Her words stoke the flames to my fire. I must be careful with her trust. Honor it, protect it, while not betraying my own instincts. She is teaching me how to love all of her. I hope I am not so wretched now that she can't do the same for me.

"Are you with me?"

Quell looks at Yani before answering. "I am."

The labyrinth underground rings with chaos. Its main artery, where we agree to gather, is full of people scurrying down its several hallways with panic. Quell takes the halls on the right, and I take the ones on the left. Yani agreed to stay outside and watch for the Dragunhead. Quell insisted Abby stay with her.

It takes longer than it should to empty two dozen rooms of people and essential things. At each new room I open, I am met with wide eyes of fear. As the hall swells with people, I urge them along faster, directing them toward the entryway.

Quell is waiting there with a throng she retrieved from the rooms she emptied. Mothers, children, young, old. A mother holding her small child attempts to dash out, to escape, shouting something in Latin too fast for me to understand. Toushana rears up in me when I grab her by the arm, but I make sure my hold on her is gentle.

"Please, I am not here to hurt you. I am here to help free you."

She snatches her arm away. "I *am* free."

"There is a very dangerous man who could be outside at any moment. He will not spare anyone here to get to me and that girl." I indicate Quell. "We are taking you somewhere safe. Please cooperate, for your daughter's sake."

The little girl in her arms watches a shiny button on my shirt. I pull off the silver circle and hand it to her. She grins. The mother settles. Everyone packs into the foyer of the underground lair like sardines. Still no word from Yani or Abby.

"They don't like this, Jordan." Quell joins me.

"Because they don't understand what's happening. They'll see."

Worry has carved a space between her brows. "They may not. You're disrupting their lives, ripping them from their home."

"Don't you mean *we*?"

"Yes. I'm just saying, tread carefully." There is tenderness in Quell's gaze. That's why she deserves the world. She is everything this Order needs. I long to touch her, to lace my fingers between hers and press our heads together, to inhale and breathe her in. But I am not sure how much harder my magic will pull on hers since toushana is all I have left.

When every room is emptied, there are half a hundred, maybe more, gathered. How many of them have healing Shifter magic or some other magic? How many have toushana? Are there Darkbearers in this room? I skim their eyes for malice, but all I see is fear. A little fear is good. Their actions will show their true colors soon enough.

For now, safety.

"I am relocating this operation somewhere safer," I announce. "We're moving you all to House of Marionne. Chateau Soleil is an estate in the southern quadrant. But there are walls around the property that should provide better protection than you have here. There you will have more space to roam, meals around the clock. You can be done living like this."

"We're pulling down the walls between our worlds," Quell adds.

Heads swivel in every direction. Some exhale. Others glare. But when I spot Ube and Erla side by side in the crowd, my heart hiccups. Several of those staring at us have heavy-lidded red eyes.

"Is it true? Is Zecky dead?" the mother with the small child asks.

"He was sentenced to die for trying to steal the Sphere's magic." No use in lying to them. "I carried out the sentence myself."

"*He's not a thief*," the crowd roars angrily. "*You're the criminal!*"

Quell's nails dig into my arm. My heart thuds, but before I can speak, Ube elbows his way through the crowd.

"I was there!" he shouts. "Zecky did try to steal the magic out of this man, which is all the magic that's left in the world. Zecky tried to make me help him, saying we were doing a routine procedure." He shakes his head. His sister's eyes dart in his direction before her sad gaze hits the floor. "I didn't want any trouble. I am sorry, sir."

The room erupts in whispers. Ube is *much* less stoic now than he was when he was cutting into me. And humble. Was that the real him? Or is this? Still, his vote of confidence may be the boon I need.

"How'd *you* get the magic if you didn't steal it?" someone yells.

"I can answer questions when we get where we are going. But *we have to* leave *now*."

"I'm not going anywhere," someone protests, and cold licks my insides.

You're going whether you want to or not. But when I open my mouth, someone else speaks.

"I don't see the point in staying here if Zecky's gone. That means the work is gone, which means the money and food will dry up, too."

"You're promising a lot," a younger girl chimes in. "What will you require of us in exchange?"

Chatter erupts, echoing the question.

"You're going to help me save magic." A collective gasp sweeps across the safe house. "You have the research, the skills, I've seen them."

"Will we be paid?"

"Your pay is the honor of participating in making history. I'm also overlooking any of your past crimes." I can hardly swallow, saying that aloud. "The law says you should all be killed for using dark magic here in secret. For operating in secret at all." No one speaks. Quell shakes her head subtly, and I worry I've gone too far. But they should understand this is a mercy. "If the Dragunhead found you here, it would end very differently. Ube, is that your name, sir?"

"Yes."

"Are you a leader here?"

"No."

"Maybe you should be. I saw what you can do."

His sister looks at him. Ube doesn't respond, but he pulls back his shoulders ever so slightly, standing taller, and it's the final victory I need.

He joins me at the front to stand beside me. Many follow him, including his sister, whose gaze is still pinned to the floor. I look for Quell and expect to find her as pleasantly surprised as I am. But she's not engaged with the crowd at all anymore.

She stares into the distance at nothing in particular, somewhere else completely.

When we emerge from beneath the church, the body has been taken away and the square is refilling with tourists. The hair on my arms stands. Abby and Yani join the rest of us as I scan the perimeter.

Across the square, leaning against a lamppost, is a familiar spindly man with long gray hair pulled over his shoulder in a braid. He wears a fine coat covered in House sigils.

He tips his head in my direction.

My heart stops.

The Dragunhead.

I stagger backward and bump into Quell, who is giving out instructions.

"Quell."

She stares quizzically, but when I turn back to the lamppost, there is no one there. I blink.

"Jordan? What is it?"

"I thought I saw the Dragunhead," I tell her under my breath.

A divot creases Quell's brow as she scans the area.

"It's nothing. I must have imagined it."

She eyes me strangely before taking another look around.

"Let's get out of here."

NAVIGATING THE CITY using the airports like Knox taught us makes getting the large crowd South much easier than I expect. I watch closely for being followed, but the commute is smooth. Seeing the Dragunhead still haunts me. If it was him, why wouldn't he approach or *do* something?

Perhaps I *did* imagine it. The mood of travel is as riddled with excitement as it is with fear and mourning.

This is all new. Zecky was special to them. And I killed him.

I want to reassure Quell, but she seems to have moved on, laser-focused on getting to Chateau Soleil as fast as possible. When we reach the estate, its overgrown hedges and walls of black roses have not changed. Quell gets us inside easily enough. But she hasn't spoken to me or Abby the entire trek back.

"Is something wrong?" I ask her as she holds back the gate's spindles, allowing the crowd through.

"Later." She hasn't told me about anything that has happened. I don't know how she and Yani linked up to find me or where Abby came from. I'm just relieved she's alright.

As the last person comes through the gate, the black roses close behind us like a curtain. I'm about to say something to Quell, when she spots Willam outside and rushes in his direction with a look of fury on her face I've never seen.

FORTY

Quell

As I storm across the lawn of Chateau Soleil, my mother's words ring in my ear like a song I hate that won't leave. *The Dragunhead is after me.* And while the walls of Chateau Soleil have my grandmother's prickly roses, I'm not sure that's enough to stop the leader of an army of Darkbearers if he decides to show up here.

Jordan said he saw the Dragunhead . . .

If that's true, why isn't he pursuing us . . .

What if the enemy is already inside?

Willam has made his desires plain—he wants his own House. He's already started making moves. But he was hesitant to say with whom. He's been at odds with Jordan since day one, but he was willing to come here with us. And then there's his shirt, which is always buttoned to the collar, over his new tattoo. From what I recall it has sprawling lines stretched in every direction.

Like a sun.

Is it a shaded-in one?

Willam stands on the colonnade with a hand shading his brow, watching a throng of Marked from safe houses descend upon the estate.

"Quell, what's the meaning of this?" Knox says as she exits the Chateau.

Jordan catches up to me. "Quell?"

"Unbutton your shirt, Willam."

He gazes in both directions before arriving at the obvious conclusion I'm talking to him. He has always been nice to me, and he received me warmly. Maybe I'm wrong. *Please let me be wrong.* His skin reddens. Knox glances between us, perplexed.

"What are you talking about?" Willam looks down when he talks. I can't see the rays or the edge of his scar.

"I want to see the tattoo you have over your scar."

"We don't need to do this here, Quell," he says.

"Willam?" Knox's curiosity deepens.

"What better place than in front of everyone else that will be staying here with us for a while?" I gesture at the group. Dexler joins us outside and clutches her chest.

"*Goodness*," she says. "Do we need rooms for *all* of them?" she asks no one in particular. But my eyes don't leave Willam.

I allow the cold to bleed through my fingers. "Shirt. Off."

He exhales sharply through his nostrils, rips his buttons open. On his neck is a sun with curved rays.

And a shaded-in center.

A freshly inked Darkbearer mark.

The same marks on the bodies in the Sixth Ward.

Has he been feeding the Dragunhead information on us all this time?

Toushana bites my bones. I ball my fists, resisting the urge to unleash on him. Knox helps Dexler order the others inside the House. A few give her strange stares before streaming inside. When the doors to the Chateau close, Knox grabs a fistful of her clothes, staring at Willam. I can't tell what she knows.

"This is not how I wanted them to find out," Willam says to Knox. She is stone. "It's not what you think. Let me explain." He takes a step toward me.

Toushana unfurls from Jordan in an explosion of shadows, forming a wall of darkness between us and Willam. "Your *breath* is a gift."

Willam's complexion drains of color.

"There are massacres with that symbol left as a signature," I say. "People who are trying to rob Jordan of the world's magic and do who knows what to me. And you have the audacity to *stand here!*" People who have *such* a horrible reputation for carnage that I couldn't live my life freely. I was born judged by *their* actions. And he has struck up an alliance with them? He is *on their side?* Jordan is beside me, and the nearness of him calms the rage hammering my heart. All this time. The lies. The pretending to understand my plight. The offering me a place while supporting the very people who give toushana a bad name.

"It would delight me to rot his bones," Jordan says.

"I want his answer. I want to know how he looked my mother in the face; how he smiled when he told me he was glad that I was back. I want to hear how *that person* decides to betray me!"

"Willam," Knox says. "I *told* you we couldn't hold this secret. Out with it, *all* of it."

Jordan pulls his toushana back inside himself and puts more space between us and them.

After a heavy breath, Willam says, "Knox can see if a person's heart is pure. That's a branch of toushana magic that died generations ago. It felt like an erasure of her legacy to let it go, so in our safe house, we made the exception that her magic, which is very useful, could be used." He lowers his voice. "The others don't know."

They're lying to Dimara, Kedd, and the others about using magic . . .

"And there are more like Knox who are Darkbearers, technically speaking, bound to toushana, but who want *nothing* to do with the carnage you're seeing in the papers! They are just like the rest of us, trying to find a place in the new world that won't villainize them." He stands straighter. "So I agreed to ally and help them. Officially. This is our mark." He raises his chin to let me see the tattoo fully. It's a sprawling sun with curved rays wrapped around the side of Willam's neck.

My heart rends. "These people are signing this mark on bodies."

"The Darkbearers doing that are not with us. I swear. The Dragunhead must be having them do that to frame us."

"How could I believe anything you say? You said you'd allied with other safe houses. You meant you've allied with Darkbearers."

Willam's chin hits his chest. "I shouldn't have lied."

"And what do you do for them?" My gut swims.

"For the *good* Darkbearers, I host meetings, connect them with others in our network. Help when needed."

Jordan folds his arms. "And how can you be absolutely sure that the Darkbearers you're helping *aren't* the ones ransacking Unmarked neighborhoods?"

"I know these people. I'm careful."

Jordan *tsk*s.

"You knew about this?" I ask Knox.

"She knew I'd considered it. But she didn't know I signed on until she came back."

"I'm sorry, Quell." There are actual tears in Knox's eyes now. So glistening and large I feel a pang of grief.

Beside me, Jordan fumes.

"Technically speaking, you're a Darkbearer, too," Willam says.

I never labeled myself or joined anyone's cause. All I did was bind with my toushana because it is part of me. But I remember studying Darkbearers at Hartsboro. How Beaulah tried to make me embrace being one, which had nothing to do with appreciating who I am and everything to do with manipulating me for control.

"Just because the world calls me a name," I say, "that doesn't make me a monster."

"Exactly, Quell. Isn't it the same for others?" Knox dabs her tears from her cheek.

"Of course it is." I slip my hand in hers and squeeze.

Jordan stiffens beside me.

"But you should have told me up front. We have to be careful. Where are these *good* Darkbearers?"

"Around," Willam says. "Hiding." Willam touches the spot above his tattoo, and I notice a tiny stenciled star drawn there. "A beacon in the dark."

"No more communication with them. For now."

Willam nods.

"*Speak up*," Jordan says.

Willam scowls. "No communication. Understood."

"And it's not my business, but it seems like you should tell Dimara and the others the truth that Knox uses magic," I say. If some of them can still reach magic, they deserve to know that's an option.

"I don't like this," Jordan mutters. As I'm about to respond, Dexler bursts through the doors of the Chateau with cracked glasses on her face and her dress's skirt singed.

"You're needed inside, Quell. There's some serious disagreement among everyone over rooms. It's getting heated."

"We need to be very careful with these two," Jordan whispers to me, and I hardly hear what Dexler is saying. "They lied to you. *Convincingly.*"

"You can see remorse all over Knox's face."

"I see regret for getting caught," Jordan says. There's something that's hardened even more in him in the last day. And I can't put my finger on it.

"That is heartless, and you know it."

Knox at least is sorry. That I know for sure. But sorry doesn't erase the damaged trust. With the world in pieces, trust is the only thing we have. And ours has been cracked. That has to be rebuilt. "We're not arguing about this here in front of everyone."

"Quell?" Dexler blinks, waiting for a response, but my heart races as I try to fend off panic.

What if Willam has trusted someone who is as good at lying as he is?

If Willam has worked with Darkbearers, did Zecky?

We can't get toushana out of Jordan or save magic *without* help. We have to trust *someone*.

"I'm sorry, Maezre, Jordan and I have a lot to discuss. Things just got far more complicated. I'm sure you can sort out the issue. Maybe Knox can help." I rush past all of them, to a side entrance of the estate, with Jordan on my heels and Willam's confession still burning my ears.

When Jordan and I are alone in the dorm I've been using, I burst into tears.

"What are we doing?" I say. "All these people are here. We don't know who we can trust. The two people we thought we could trust have been keeping this major secret. And—my mother is *alive*, Jordan."

He stills. And I tell him everything my mother and I discussed: how the Dragunhead wants both of us and how my grandmother actually *hid* the débutants she accidentally gave dark magic to. My heart rams in my chest harder, and Jordan touches his chest.

"Is she okay? Are they all okay? Does she want to come here?"

"She vowed to my grandmother, before she died, that she'd protect Nova Misa for the rest of her life. They both agreed the House was my—" The walls suddenly feel like they're closing in. I sit in the nearest chair.

"Quell, breathe." His hand hovers near me, and I would give anything to nestle against it. Words fail me. I need his comfort. I need him to hold me. I need something buzzing through my body besides anxiety.

He is hardly breathing when he dries a tear from my cheek. "Is this okay? Do you feel anything?"

The tenderness of his touch makes my heart thud stronger. He holds his hand there against my skin, and I savor it, not daring to ask for more. Not willing to tempt fate to rip away this moment, too. I inhale, letting the scent of him drown the erratic panic in my veins. Closer—I want him closer. This distance feels like my heart beating outside of my body. Like a hug with one arm, instead of two.

I lean against his hand, unable to resist, melting into his embrace. He's rigid with fear, but he lets himself hold me. His free hand strokes my hair. I don't speak, afraid to shatter this stolen moment between us.

When he lets me go, I can still feel his heart pounding in his chest. He puts more space between us. "You're okay. I—it was okay."

"You used toushana so strongly out there. It probably helped satisfy it."

"I didn't mean to." He pales. "It just bled out of me instinctually. I told myself to trust it. But I was afraid it might . . . I don't know."

"I'm okay. It protected me. That must have been what you wanted, deep down."

His color returns, and his thudding heart settles, then he asks, "Are you feeling better?"

The weight on my chest is lighter. "I am. But what are we doing here? Seeing my mother only makes me more determined to have a life that's mine. I want to be free, Jordan. Not in a new kind of safe house for toushana. Not running for my life or hiding. I want to *live*. Don't I deserve that? Don't *we* deserve that?"

"I want that, too."

"Then the world has to change. And the Dragunhead *has to* be dealt with."

"Dead. He has to be dead."

Silence hangs between us.

"I could face him."

"Not with all of dark magic inside you. It's too much of a risk. We have to extract the Sphere's toushana and put it in something safe. Then rewrite the rules for this backward world. Nova Misa shouldn't *have* to exist. Jordan, the people Knox and Willam are trying to help deserve freedom, too."

"And Zecky?" His jaw works.

I sigh. "You have to see what I mean. You're trusting toushana now, too?"

"Because I know what I am and am not capable of. Same goes for you. I don't know them. Willam never struck me as honest. And now I see I was right. People like that can't be trusted with toushana. It'll corrupt them."

"The magic will corrupt them?"

"*Yes*. Like it's corrupting those people razing cities. I've told you before, it takes a lot of self-control to be this close to this much power and not be incensed by it. But none of this matters if the Sphere's magic is not safe.

We *have to* be careful. Keep our eyes on one another. Trust *no one*. Willam can prove himself. Time will tell."

"We've brought Zecky's people here."

"To do a task. Then they are free to go."

"Into a world that would destroy them? Or force them to hide in a place like Nova Misa? I'm not for that. I won't stand for that. It's not right."

"So you suggest we hand out trust like candy?" he asks.

"What is your plan, then, huh?" I ask.

"I trust you. You trust me. We have all of magic between us. We can decide who gets to use it and who doesn't. I was thinking of a set of rings, tied by tracer magic, perhaps. Each family with a ring can pass it down in their bloodline. If the family misbehaves, the ring is taken away."

"The Order by another name."

Anger flickers across his expression. He takes a beat, scoping out a spot to store the metal box with the diadem and locking it in a cabinet. "We'll need to find a better place for it. But this is good for now."

I blow out a breath. And step closer to him. He doesn't step back, but I can feel his nervousness.

"Are you sure you're alright being away from your mother like this, after—?"

"I am. It's time I fly on my own." When this is all said and done, I will see her again and we will bury our toes in the sand. "We extract the dark magic and kill the Dragunhead. That frees us and them. Whatever else needs to happen with a new Order can be figured out after that."

The green in Jordan's eyes shimmers. "Alright." He raises a thumb to my lips, and I dare to lean into it. He rubs it roughly across my mouth, and I burn for him in another way. Then he blinks. "I'm sorry, I didn't mean—"

I smirk. "You must have wanted to do that, too, deep down."

He takes a full step backward. "I'm sorry, I feel things so strongly now." He stuffs his hands in his pockets. "I thought about . . . and then, next thing you know, I was . . . never mind."

"I'm going to move up to the Headmistress suite to make as much room as possible for everyone. I don't want to sleep up there all alone."

"We're already playing with fire, Quell. We *must* be careful. You have to get through this unharmed."

"If you're worried about your toushana getting out of control, use it *more*. It worked tonight."

He shifts on his feet uncomfortably.

"Meet me tonight. I'll show you." I tell him about the broom closet and how to get to the forest behind the Chateau, where *my* secret lived when I was here last Season.

He agrees reluctantly before rushing out the door suddenly without another word.

FORTY-ONE

Jordan

When I shut the door to Quell's room, I run. Down the dorm wing, through the foyer where the projection of the Sphere used to hang, toward tall exit doors with the conservatory beyond it. The fresh air hits me in the face, and it's the slap I need.

I cup my face where her head just was. I can still smell her hair on my fingers. I pant, trying to return my racing heart to normal. But toushana wrestles my insides like an ice storm.

I hadn't meant to touch her lips.

An urgent memory of how it felt kissing her had wrapped around my chest, and I couldn't feel anything else. My toushana lurched. I blinked, and my thumb was at her lips. I *desperately* wanted to kiss her. I've always wanted every part of her, but I've never wanted her *this* strongly. When we're not near, it's impossible to feel whole. I see the certainty of who I am in her eyes. She is the sun, and I am the moon. Without her reflection, I have no light.

My magic thrums, filling me with an urge to run back in there, take Quell in my arms, and kiss her like I really want to. To hold her like I've longed to. To be near her like we used to be.

I'm close to the conservatory and decide to enter it. Inside feels like stepping back in time. This is the first place she let me get really close to her. I shove around the overgrown grass with my shoe, recalling transfiguring it to sand, making this entire place a beach so that she could focus on her exam. I linger.

Until the sharp pain in my side returns.

Sharper and longer than it did when I was dealing with Zecky.

I lift my shirt, inspecting my side. The skin is smooth; there is no sign of a bruise. I blow out a slow breath, staving off worry of the worst.

Then it pinches again.

I need to talk to a Healer.

I leave the conservatory and walk as casually as I can to find Abby. Commotion fills the halls of the Chateau once I'm back inside. Somewhere, over a barrage of voices, Dexler shouts instructions for an assembly line to make dinner go smoothly. I skirt past and stave off a few stares as I look for Abby.

The sun is a glow on the horizon when I find her. She's in the old Healer office. The door is hanging from the hinges, but over the wreckage, I spot her mending a trunkful of dresses.

"Do you have a minute?" I ask, dissolving the broken door hardware with toushana to detach it fully before setting it carefully against the wall.

"Jordan." Abby's dark bangs stick to her forehead. "Sure. Dexler is trying to find some clothes for everyone. She found these. I told her I could help clean them up a bit." She sets aside a plum gown with blue beading. "What is it?"

I duck my head out into the hallway, and it's empty, for now. But I don't want to risk being overheard. "Can we speak privately?"

She takes me to the back of the office, inside a room untouched by the damage. There are piles of half-unpacked boxes with herbs and vials of liquids beneath an exam table. Along the walls are more racks of dresses, slacks, and shirts. I close the door and twist the lock. "Are you settling in alright?"

She laughs. "What can I help you with?" Her gaze dips to my side. I lift my shirt and show her the tender spot where I felt pain beneath my ribs. "There used to be a wound there."

"It looks fully healed." She presses the area. I wince. "Lie down for me."

I get on Abby's table, and she begins to work her Shifting magic over my skin. I can feel my ribs tugging at the nudge of her magic. A cold sensation rushes to the area. She *tsk*s.

"Something wrong?"

She doesn't answer, trying her magic again. "Try to stay very still."

The pull at my bones wedges an ache deeper into my organs. I hold my breath, trying to swallow a groan welling in my throat. She grunts, exasperated.

"Hmph. You can get up."

"Well?"

"There's no easy way to say this, but the Sphere's magic is still wreaking havoc inside you."

"He fixed it. I just think there's some residual tissue or something."

"Jordan, Zecky lied to you."

My neck breaks out in a cold sweat. "What do you mean?"

"Your skin is shifted to *appear healed*. You're still rotting on the inside."

I steady myself on the wall. Black dents the edges of my vision.

"I tried moving the tissue around to repair it. But the minute I shift it back, it dissolves again. The magic that caused the wound is stronger than my Shifting magic." Abby won't meet my eyes. There's something she's not telling me.

"Say it."

"Jordan, it's killing you."

I don't move. I can't. "Will the bruise re-form?" How long before Quell is able to see what it's doing to me?

"Eventually, yes. It depends on how aggressively the toushana is binding to you. It's just too much in your body, I suspect." She taps her lip. "I don't know if Zecky *could* heal you and just didn't. Or if he *couldn't* heal you at all and just pretended to. Give me some time to look into the magic. The best thing is to get it out of you as soon as possible. The longer it's in you, the more damage it's doing." She hands me a vial. "Use this salve for the pain in the meantime."

I turn the cream in my hand. "I should go."

"You're going to tell Quell, right?"

Cold scrapes at my insides, writhing with irritation. "Of course. *You* will say nothing. *No* mention of this, Abby. I mean it."

"You have my word," she says. "I'll see what else I can find out."

I tuck the vial into my pocket and head straight for the broom closet where Quell is waiting. If there's a way to make the toushana inside me more manageable, I have to consider it. Especially since it's still killing me. I can't have it exploding in bursts like it did outside with Willam.

It's only beneficial if I can keep it in check. Otherwise, there's no difference between me and the shaded-sun-worshipper scum out there.

Quell is waiting in a new dress, one I haven't seen. It's a soft mint color that brings out the gold in her deep brown eyes.

I hope this isn't a mistake.

She's holding the metal box with the diadem. "Didn't want to leave it, just in case. My dorm room doesn't lock."

"Good thinking. I was worried you would think of a reason not to come."

"Oh, I have thought of many. But I'm here."

Outside, the night is thick with fog. The forest is a litter of destroyed trees. We walk for a long while until we reach a stretch of forest that appears untouched. Thick trunks rise in the air, towering over us, sprawling into sprays of branches. The moon can hardly be seen through the cover of leaves.

"What now?" I ask.

"Destroy some of these trees."

I wipe my clammy hands on my clothes. She steps back, and I call on the cold in my blood. It lassos in my chest and oozes through my limbs. The feel of it traveling to the tips of my fingers sends a shiver up my spine. It pools in my hands, thrashing, and my heart skips a beat. *All the Sphere's dark magic. So much power, in my hands.*

Unleash, it whispers.

Relaxing every muscle in my body, without holding anything back, I do.

Darkness expels from me like vomit. Toushana bleeds from every part of me, filling the forest. The fog thickens, and I lose sight of Quell. I try to speak, but I am frozen, a vein spewing blood. Everything the Order's cost me claws at the walls of my mind.

Hartsboro.

Beaulah Perl.

The Dragunhead stabbing me in the back.

The lies of Darragh Marionne.

Yaniselle's betrayal.

Almost losing Quell.

I groan as darkness thickens, rushing out of my skin so fast every pore on my body burns.

Destroy it all, the magic whispers. *Make them hurt.*

The world dents black at the edges. A growl tears from my throat. I'm so cold all over I am a floating body without feeling at all.

Somewhere Quell yelps.

The world is a haze of confusion and anger, and I can't see a thing. But I can feel the delight in my bones. The way the dark magic licks my spine. The corners of my lips tug up in a smile. Through the haze I faintly hear shouting.

Quell's voice.

"*Let up!*" she screams. But before I can pinpoint where my limbs are and how to stop this flow, fire erupts in the middle of the forest. The woods glow as flames consume one tree, then lick the next.

"Jordan, you're starting a fire. *Stop!*"

I hear her, but I don't see her, my senses dull like an overused blade. I focus on the ripping feeling as toushana tears through my skin. *Stop*, I plead. *Stop now!*

The cold slows.

The cold obeys.

I rediscover feeling in my legs and stagger into a stump. The warmth of the nearby fire quenches the rest of my toushana. The dark magic slinks back inside my body, and I blink, seeing the forest—or what's left of it—for the first time. Fire still burns in the distance.

Quell jogs toward me. "We have to get out of here."

"What happened?"

"I don't know! Your toushana was destroying the forest so fast, and then it sparked, and there were flames."

"We can't let the fire reach the house."

My mind spirals, sifting through every single thing I understand about dark magic. It's destructive in nature. It should be able to destroy fire, right? But the heat stifles the toushana's ability to breathe. The cold and hot don't mix. *Think!*

"Jordan, turn the trees that are not on fire to ash. We can spread those ashes all over to create a barrier between the estate and the flames. If there's nothing left to burn, the flames will go out."

"You're saying—"

"Destroy the forest before the fire does."

I call on the chill again, and it answers with precision. Quell does the same. Together we make short work of decomposing every tree, plant, or piece of brush in the line of the fire. When we're finished, a pile of ash runs in a long line through the forest, forming a barrier. When the most distant glow of fire is finally gone, I collapse on the ground beside Quell in a wasteland of destruction with a clear line of sight to Chateau Soleil.

Windows at the back of the estate glare down at us. "We should get back inside."

By the time we make it in, Quell takes me to the third floor, where the only sound is our feet on the shiny tile. Darragh Marionne's suite has a gaping hole through the bathroom wall. We slip inside and make our way into the Headmistress's private suite.

Everything hurts, including the spot under my ribs. Quell inspects a small room off the bedroom.

"It'll be safe in there," she says, emerging from the room where the diadem is. "I've been kept prisoner in there, there's no other way in."

"Very good." Fighting a grimace, I apply the salve Abby gave me and sit down on the bed. To my relief, after some time, the throbbing pain subsides.

She disappears into the bathroom, and I hear shower water running. *I should leave.* I hesitate. If all that toushana use doesn't buy me a moment with her, a chance to sit next to her and just breathe her in, I'm done for. I lie back on the bed, tempting fate, and glare at my hands. *What did we just do?* My fingers are bruising, purple at their tips. A jittery feeling like drinking too much coffee buzzes beneath my skin, and I can't be still. I see glowing flames on the backs of my eyelids and the memories that prompted them: despicable things from my past I want to forget. Haunted, I promptly open my eyes.

Quell emerges from the bathroom in a towel, and I sit up. "How did it feel?"

"Like my blood was made of rage."

She sits beside me, her hand on the bed inches from my leg. "When I used to do it, it felt like gorging myself on a delicious meal."

"It was freeing in a way," I say. "I had all these memories come to me. Things from the past."

"Hartsboro."

"For the first time it felt like I could *do* something with that pain." It felt like chipping away at the bottom of an iceberg. "Thank you, by the way."

Her fingers walk across the blanket to mine. I pull back from her touch, waiting for my magic to react. But it doesn't. Part of me hesitates to be relieved. The other part burns with a need to drown in Quell for the next few hours.

"When you keep it fed, it's easier to quell." She grins.

Here goes nothing. I take her hand in mine fully, running my fingers across her palm. Waiting. But no cold thrashes in my body, as if the magic living in me is fast asleep. I can't even feel it. I scoot closer to her, too scared to breathe. Too scared to believe this is real.

She knots my shirt around her fingers, pulling me closer.

"Quell, we have to be careful."

"I know." She leans so close her breath warms my lips. "But it's safer now than it's ever been."

The smell of her awakens an ache I am barely holding at bay. Something stronger than magic lurches in me.

Love her as if time doesn't exist.

As if she is the only thing in the world.

I trail her neck with gentle breaths, still worried this is too good to be true. She smells like sunshine, a salty breeze, and wet sand. The cold in my bones still slumbers. I bury my face in her curls, letting her crisp sea spray fragrance raise the hairs on my skin.

I stare at her perfect lips, desperate to share my love with her and feel hers in return. "If I could give in to what I'm feeling right now . . ."

She tugs hard on my jaw. "Then what?"

"You'd be peeling me off you tonight."

She leans into me, and I cradle her head in my hand, bringing her mouth a breath away from mine. Close enough to curl her long brown hair around my fingers and feel her lips against my fingertips. "You don't know what you're asking."

She parts her mouth. I trace her jaw with a gentle touch, then down her neck. She moves closer and brushes her lips against mine. Our mouths melt into each other in a kiss. She slopes her arms over my shoulders, and I lay her gently onto the bed. Everything about her is perfect. My hands rove her calves, savoring the physique of her muscles, then her thighs, which are softer than silk.

My heart feels like it could burst out of my chest.

What if it wasn't enough? What if I give in now and my toushana becomes agitated and I can't pull away from her fast enough?

I lay my head on her stomach. "I can't, Quell."

She runs her fingers through my hair. "It feels so nice to be close to you this way."

If she only knew how I've longed to hold her like this. I plant a kiss beside her navel, caressing the skin there. She hugs me tighter, pretzeling her legs around me. I plant more kisses on her fingertips.

Until she's fast asleep.

At sunrise, I slip out of the room with Abby's words on my mind. There is no time to waste. Our guests have hopefully had a good first night's rest.

It's time to get the extraction practice started.

FORTY-TWO

Nore

Nore awoke while it was still dark outside to the sound of a rough tap at the door. She stretched an arm across her bed, but no one was there. She blinked, the haze of sleep blurring her vision. The knock at the door grew more insistent. She got up and accidentally kicked the untouched dinner tray at the foot of her bed. Ainsley rushed in with fresh juice and a bowl of veggies and fruit.

"Are you ready, ma—Headmistress? Today's the day!" Ainsley held a robe, and Nore blinked the dregs of fog from her eyes as she slid her arms into the sleeves. She stared at the bed, confused.

"Was anyone in here when you brought me dinner?"

"No, no one. You were fast asleep. I didn't want to wake you."

It had been a dream. She'd slept in Yagrin's arms, curled up next to him while he stroked her hair like he used to do.

"Let's get you in the bath."

"I am bathing myself."

"Well, I'll at least prepare the water." Ainsley did not stop talking.

Once Nore was clean and her skin bright red from scrubbing it with jasmine-soaked petals to ensure there were no impurities in her skin that would impede her magic, her head was spinning with details she wasn't well versed in. She held the maid's wrist, urging her to take a breath. She noticed Ainsley's eyes were red and her hair wasn't freshly done.

"Did you not sleep well?"

"I did not sleep at all, Headmistress." Ainsley pulled a gray frock out of the closet that was the drabbest yet most delicate thing Nore'd ever seen. "I stayed up refreshing on coronation procedures and protocol. There was so much to read, I hardly got through it all. A maid only gets to prepare a Headmistress for something like this once in their lifetime, if they're lucky."

Nore couldn't believe her ears. "Ainsley, you will sleep tonight if I have to watch you sleep myself. In fact, I refuse to see you after dinner. You're in bed by eight. Alright?"

She curtsied. Nore held out her arms as the itchy fabric slid across her freshly oiled body. She'd never attended her mother's coronation, obviously. But she knew the fashion in her House like the back of her hand. *That* she had memorized since she was knee-high.

"And your hair? In the simplest style?" Ainsley asked. "Your grandmother wore hers in a single ponytail. Your mother wore it the same but added bangs. A way to give it her own flair. For you—"

"I want curls."

"I'm sorry?"

"You heard me. Curls down to my waist and blue flowers in my hair."

"Headmistress, that would upset things. Early into your reign, you don't want people talking. Dissenters are like a flock of seagulls once they get started. I prayed in the Caelum this morning with Priest Winkel that you would have a peaceful reign, even if the world outside is falling apart. I prayed that you would chart a course for us to see it through."

A hope sparkled in Ainsley's eyes that stuck Nore like a knife between her ribs. If Nore was going to make the best of this position, shouldn't she wish for the path of least resistance?

"A simple ponytail is fine."

"What about bangs?"

"Bangs were my mother's. Straight back, but maybe a braid."

Ainsley smiled. When she finished getting her ready, Nore stood in front of a mirror, her stormy eyes tracing the plain gray gown. It was made in the most abrasive linen variety available. A Vestiser had crafted it for her mother for a special occasion. But the occasion never came, apparently, because Isla never wore the dress. Nore ran her hands along the corset, taking shallow breaths against the iron that was used in the place of whale bone. Her sleeve hems were kept frayed, threads spilling over her bony wrists. The gown was trimmed a smidge higher in the front, Nore noticed, as Ainsley slid a pair of well-worn heels on her feet.

"I think you're ready." There were tears in Ainsley's eyes.

"You are wonderful. Don't leave my side today."

"That is not allowed."

"Aren't I the person who makes the rules now?"

Ainsley blushed, and it gave Nore an idea. Her hair might be straight as a board, but she bit her lip and pulled the servant's cap off Ainsley's hair. Dark natural curls cascaded down her back. Her maid gasped. Nore grabbed some color from the beets on her leftover dinner plate and smoothed it on both of their cheeks, then a little bit on their lips. It wasn't exactly make-up like she'd worn as Red. There wasn't any of that at Dlaminaugh. The more plain the outside, the richer within, was the *lie* her House boasted. The light color on their cheeks could be mistaken for a deep blush.

"*Now* I'm ready."

"This is scandalous," Ainsley whispered.

Nore grinned. "Isn't it?" She roped Ainsley's arm around hers and opened the door to her room, where the dead waited for her. She and Ainsley walked between them, their stares like daggers dragged across her skin. When she turned the corner, she exhaled. Yagrin, her mother, and a pair of House Draguns were waiting for her.

Isla gasped at the sight of her and offered her a wrapped box. "You're breathtaking."

"Thank you, Mother. If you'll excuse me." She walked past her and stopped at Yagrin.

"Is that blush on your cheeks?" he asked.

"I don't know what you're talking about."

"You have to be very careful hanging out with this one," he told Ainsley. "She'll get you in a world of trouble."

Ainsley pressed her lips together, forbidding herself to smile.

"How did you sleep?" Yagrin asked as they walked. The dead followed like the train of a ceremonial gown.

"Fine." Memories of her head against his chest flitted through her mind. "And you?"

"I dreamed of you."

Nore looked away.

"Would you like to hear about it?"

"You must enjoy frustrating yourself," she said.

Ainsley's gaze darted between them.

"Would you say it's a hobby?" Nore asked.

"Yes. One I'm really good at." He smirked.

"Well, I have enough hobbies, so I'll leave that one with you."

Ainsley's brows kissed the longer she listened to their conversation. When they reached the ballroom, Yagrin kept talking, but Nore could no longer hear him. She forced a smile, taking in the space. Hundreds of metal chairs were in long rows, nearly all filled with guests from the House, their families. There were simple reception tables draped in gray. No flowers. No frills, as if the entire ceremony was drained of color. And yet this was the finest she'd ever seen the ballroom decorated.

Her palms grew slick. A knot cinched between her shoulders.

"Nore?" The old voice spun her around. Priest Winkel made his way toward her on his cane. Priest Kimper was right behind him. Of each of the three priests, Winkel was the one who always snuck her candies before dinner and brought her surprises from his travels. He was Priest to the Sage—a master craftsman and skilled warrior god with a deep value of truth and law—spending half the moon's cycle in prayers and the other half traveling to study cutting-edge magical research. Priest Kimper communed with the Wielder—a female god associated with war and fate, foretelling doom, death, and victory. Kimper was an odd woman of few words. But she had a booming voice when she spoke. She passed Nore roughly with no more than a head nod before taking her seat in the front row.

Nore craned for Priest Pizor, who she hardly saw growing up, and found him already seated near the front. He prayed to the Sovereign Sola Sfenti night and day. The Priests all resided in the Caelum, where the bodies of their predecessors were buried among the texts. They only left the library for work or very special occasions.

Like your sixth birthday, Winkel had said once.

"You've returned to us. I always knew you would." He kissed her cheeks, and there was a little girl inside her that wanted to throw her arms around his neck and squeeze. But she only smiled politely. He slipped something into her fist discreetly before heading to his seat. A gem sparkled in her hand, changing from greens to blues depending on how the light hit it. She held it to her chest.

"Headmistress, I am going to check on things to be sure all is in order for you," Ainsley said, and the maid hurried off before she could stop her. Completely forgetting she'd asked her to stick by her side.

"I haven't seen you smile like that in a long time," Yagrin said. "Is that who gave you the elephant with the trick snout that you kept on your fridge?"

There was no hiding with him anymore. It made her feel naked, exposed.

"Yes. And the leather-bound journal was from his trip to the Netherlands when I was twelve." Nore lost sight of Winkel as the crowd swelled. She couldn't move.

"This will be over before you know it," Yagrin said. "Remember to breathe deeply."

There was so much concern in his expression. It made her feel ill. "I'm not staying for the brunch reception."

"Then I won't either. Where are you going after?"

She wanted to tell him she was going to lock herself in her room and try to slip back to her dream from last night. But instead, to spare him, she just said, "To sleep." It was so nice of him to come and be there beside her. That's what she needed. She wished she could give him more. "Thank you for being here, really," she managed.

But an usher came along and dragged him to find his seat.

She was all alone at the back of the ballroom, waiting for the procession to begin. She gripped a nearby empty chair. She focused on Yagrin's words, inhaling and exhaling slowly. When sunrise streamed through the ballroom's windows, a chord of music silenced the audience.

It was time.

Yagrin was right. The ceremony was over quicker than she expected. She recited the House creed and took her oath. Her mother cloaked her in the House robes, and she rose as Headmistress. And other than almost passing out when she stood to be applauded by the crowd, she'd survived. When the ceremony finished, couples rushed to the dance floor, and she stuck Ainsley back to her side, asking her to please stay. She scoped for a chance for escape. But every eye in the place was on her. One dance. She could stomach *one dance*.

Dancing partners lined up, her House's finest and brightest ladies and gentlemen. But no one approached her. She didn't approach them either. Instead she chewed her nail down to the nub. The thought of enduring their conversation, their questions, their touching, made the world swim.

"They're waiting for you to choose," her maid said. The music hung suspended in the air.

"Bring me *him*." She pointed at Yagrin, who'd become a wallflower. Ainsley's mouth pursed in thought.

"Forgive me for asking, Headmistress. But is he your *person*? Every Headmistress has a person. Even your mother—"

"Please don't finish that sentence."

A single brow rose on Ainsley's face.

Nore shifted on her feet. "That is not needed. I just, um, *if* I had a person, which I *do not*, it would make logical sense to be him. Do you understand?"

"Oh, yes." Ainsley's lips puckered. "I think I understand."

"Just get him for the dance."

Her maid hurried off, and in moments Yagrin's hand slipped into Nore's for a promenade around the dance floor. But when she pressed her body against his, holding him tightly, it stole her next breath. They swayed as the melody of the song began, easy and soft. Their chests were pressed so close, Nore could feel his heart beating for both of them.

"You're nervous," she said.

Hunger unfurled in his eyes as the tempo grew peppier. Nore danced like there was no one around them, following his feet, the direction in his hips. She got lost in the glee of the movement. It was easy. Everything was always so easy with him.

Yagrin spun her out, then back under his arm until her back hit his chest. His breath warmed her shoulder as he hugged around her for a four count. They swayed left to right, right to left.

When the refrain of the song called for their bodies to separate, it felt like another piece of her had been ripped away. The song dashed to the finish with a skittering harmony. His palm rested on the small of her back as they glided with the music from one step to the next. As if she hadn't just lived through the horrors of her brother trying to kill her and being locked in a prison as Headmistress for the rest of her life. That was one of the things she enjoyed most about being with Yagrin. The weight of her life at Dlaminaugh disappeared.

The moment the music stopped, Nore pulled away from him. But he held on to her fingers as they turned and bowed to the applauding crowd. Once the dance floor swarmed with other couples, she took her chance to leave, tearing her fingers out of his grip.

"Where are you going?"

"I told you."

"I don't understand. The dance. Did it mean nothing?"

"It was—" She exhaled. "A much-needed reprieve. Thank you, Yagrin."

But the hurt in his eyes hadn't faded. She turned to go.

"You told me you'd *try* to remember," he shouted at her back.

"I am."

He caught up with her. "You are not. You are running."

"I am protecting you, Yagrin."

"I don't need you to protect me."

He did. Life had dealt him a crappy hand. He deserved love. And that was something she couldn't give him. Letting him love her would only torture him in the end.

"There is no logical reason I should invite you back to my room."

His teeth pulled at his lips. "So the thought crossed your mind, too?" He brushed the back of his hand gently across her reddening skin. It lit a fire inside her.

"Have a good day, Yagrin." She didn't look back. She couldn't. She wanted him, even if she didn't feel an ounce of love for him. Because she knew he loved her. And no one could ever love her more. But it was selfish to take his love and not be able to reciprocate it. When she fell into her bed, she begged for sleep and sweet dreams.

But they did not come.

The moon was high in the sky when the handle on Nore's door shook. She sprang to her feet. She'd been lying there glaring at her ceiling. Yagrin's audacity was almost admirable. She opened the door, but Yagrin was not on the other side. Instead there were the two House Draguns escorting a fellow her age with auburn hair and eyes the color of emerald pools.

"Headmistress Ambrose." The Dragun spoke. "Your final sacrament of coronation."

Nore froze. The fellow stepped inside and shut the door. He bowed, then strode across her room, taking in the size of it. It wasn't ornate, but for an Ambrose it was a masterpiece of hard, sterile architecture.

"I'm Vincent."

"Vincent, I am trying to understand why you're in my room."

He huffed a laugh before pulling his shirt overhead, unveiling a carved body forged with much diligence. Then he grabbed the buckle of his belt and slid it off. Nore squeezed her eyes shut. And reopened them. But he was still there.

When he grabbed the zipper of his pants, she finally found words.

"*What* are you doing?"

He furrowed his brow, but Nore didn't move, and his mirth faded. He shifted on his feet. "Uh, I received a letter that I've been selected to further the House bloodline with the Headmistress. To make an heir. It is a great honor, they explained. A tradition created by a Headmistress a century ago, where the leaders of the House select the most astute genetic pairing for you to ensure the *best* possible heir. I speak nine languages. I have mastered four strands of magic, but have never coveted interest in the brotherhood. I plan to continue my studies in—"

"Please *shut up*!" She pressed her temples. *This can't be.* She paced in a circle. Nothing in her wanted to be Headmistress *that* badly. What would Yagrin think? He slipped down to his underpants and sat on her bed. She marched back to the door, but the knob didn't turn. "I did not agree to this."

"I don't know what to say." He stared, shocked. "I have a duty to make a child with you. I've signed an oath."

She beat on the door. "Open this door! Ainsley? Get me my maid!"

But she remembered she'd sent her to bed early.

FORTY-THREE

Quell

I skip breakfast the next morning and find Dexler, who is repairing a section of crumbled wall with a Shifter ring on her finger. Yani is there as well, helping remove debris. She's supposed to be with Willam . . .

"There you are," Dexler says. "I hope you slept well?"

"I slept fine. She's helping?" I point at Yani.

"Yes, she's been a huge help. I needed a hand, and the tall, gangly fellow told me she said she could. Thank you."

I watch Yani restore a threshold over a session room door. She's covered in sweat and dust. She descends a ladder and moves down the wall to repair another hole.

Dexler watches me, watching her. "It's alright that she lends a hand, isn't it? She's so skilled with Shifting magic."

"Yes, of course. Also, there is a wall down in the Headmistress's suite, by the way."

"Oh yes, I was going to ask if you knew if anyone else here has any Shifter magic. Or Cultivating. I have extra rings." Dexler speaks with confidence, but the way she holds her shawl around herself says how uncomfortable she finds this arrangement. First I return with a handful of safe house members. Then I return with a whole lot of them.

"Some of them might have magic. Zecky did, so I am sure."

Dexler's eyes darted. "Would you perhaps talk to them? Maybe ask. I don't get that they like me very much."

"I'm sure that's not it. This is all just new." I pat her shoulder, but she doesn't appear moved. "I was headed outside to inspect the roses to enhance our defenses. But sure, I can take a moment."

Dexler leads me to a lounge not far from the dorm wings, where she gathers everyone. I spot several familiar faces and some I don't think I've ever seen. Neither Willam nor Knox is here, and that doesn't give me a good feeling. The chatter quiets when I stand to speak, and it feels odd having so many attentive eyes on me at once.

"By a show of hands, who can access some kind of magic?"

About half the crowd's hands rise. "That's two dozen, at least," I tell Dexler.

"And you're sure about this?"

"I know it's a bit different, Maezre. But they're here to help."

"Drawing on toushana count?" someone asks, and Dexler tenses.

"It all counts."

More hands rise. "Sort them into groups by the type of magic they can access. Shifters will be the most useful, I assume. There's lots of repair work to be done." I look for relief in her expression and find some. "I really should get to the gates."

Dexler waves her hands, directing the crowd to separate their lines so it's clearer who can do what. Then she hands each a sheet of paper to document their names. Dimara, the twins, and Kedd haven't moved.

"So what, we're useless, then?" Dimara says, still sitting across the lounge, nowhere near the lines.

"The landscaping is a nightmare outside," Jordan's voice says behind me. "I'll get you a rake."

The twins are thrilled, bouncing up from their seats. But Kedd isn't amused. Dimara sneers, considering her next retort.

"You're good at cooking, aren't you? That doesn't require magic. You can help there."

"You think I want to be your chef?" She scoffs.

"That's not what she means, and you know it," Kedd says, excusing himself with the twins. "I'm going to talk to Willam."

Dimara drags herself to the line for those without any known magic. Or those who have signs of magic but haven't yet emerged.

"Have you seen Ube?" Jordan asks. The fellow who stepped up to Jordan's side at Zecky's safe house. I did see his face in the crowd. I spot him and his sister, who looks so much like him, in the Shifter line. "He's a Healer, right?"

"Think so. He and his sister were the only two Zecky brought into my exam room." He flags him over.

While we're alone, I turn to him and say, "You left me last night."

"No, I stayed until morning."

"Beside me?"

"On the chaise. That counts."

"Hardly. I'm working on defenses around the estate today," I tell him.

"I'm getting the extraction team set up."

"Dinner?"

He adjusts his coat. "Uh, can't. Not tonight."

But before I can ask why, Ube joins us.

"You asked for me, sir?"

"I have questions about the extraction procedure. Should we bring your sister?" Jordan asks, as they depart. I'm on their heels when a shoving scuffle breaks out in the non-magical lines. I loosen my clenched fists and step in to break it up.

"What exactly *is* the problem?" I ask.

"She was trying to get ahead of me in line," a young fellow from Zecky's house says.

"He's lying," Dimara says. "She said order by first name, and because *I know the alphabet*, I stepped in front of him."

"She never said that!"

Dexler tugs at her pearls. "If it's not this, it's something else. All night, spats about one thing or another. Willam's house doesn't care for Zecky's. They seem to have very different ideas about coming here." Fatigue lines Dexler's eyes.

I scope the room and spot at least three other irritated exchanges about to implode. There are children climbing the grand piano in the hall outside the lounge and another sticking a bauble from the fireplace mantel in their pocket. "They have too much time on their hands. They need things to do. Come up with things for them to do. Please."

"What kinds of things?"

"I don't know, Maezre. I'm *sure* you can think of something. You worked so closely with my grandmother for all those years."

"But I never worked from that perspective, ma'am. I did what I was asked. I'm no Headmistress."

Her stare burns my skin. "I'm confident you will think of something." I set a hand on her shoulder, hoping she knows how much I appreciate her help and how it allows me to focus on keeping magic safe. "Willam and Knox should be able to help figure out how to keep them occupied. I'll ask them to find you."

Dexler curtsies, and I am *finally* out of there.

The rose garden is an empty field of dirt. It feels like part of the estate is missing. Something should be planted there. I'll mention that to Dexler, too. When I make it to the perimeter of the estate, to the outer gate, the roses greet me, blooming wider as they turn in my direction.

I run my fingers across them, pulling at a thread of cold. Toushana grazes the petals' tips, and they swell in size. I blink. It's the first time I've seen my destructive magic do something *con*structive. I try releasing more magic. The flower expands, growing unnaturally large, twice the size of my hand, before its petals wither and die, crumbling to ash. Toushana somehow gives these roses life *and* kills them. Odd. The gate dents my periphery, and the sharp spindles run along the edge of the property like spears. The rose is thorny and sharp, but could other things take on toushana constructively without being destroyed? The iron spindles of the gate are grimy to the touch. I stream dark magic to it, fog wrapping around the iron.

And it snaps in half, creating a hole in the gate. One spindle dissolving into ash touches the one beside it, and it crumbles, too. I run toward it with my bare hands, trying to find some way to stop it. But by the time the magic fizzles out, it's destroyed several feet of the gate.

I claw my skin. I came down here to *strengthen* our defenses, *not* destroy them.

The roses.

An idea strikes me, and I scramble to grab the vines of roses now dangling on the ground across where the gate used to be. If I can multiply them, maybe I can disguise the gap in the gate until I can find a Retentor or Shifter to repair it. The roses are delicate in my hands. I cup a bloom in my palm and smooth dark wisps of magic across it. The bloom grows, and the cinch in my chest untwists. I fill it with enough magic until it's nearly twice its size. Then I stop. I don't want to push my luck this time. I repeat the process with the thorns, touching them carefully; they grow in size and sharpness, lengthening to deadly tips. It takes a long while, but once I finish, a tangle of black roses, as thick as the gate, hangs between the broken edges of the gate's frame.

It's not perfect, but it's something.

I need to know more about how the roses work and if there are other ways to use dark magic to help. When I turn to hurry back into the estate, a curtain in an upstairs window flutters.

Someone has been watching me.

FORTY-FOUR

Jordan

I keep Ube two steps ahead of me as I direct him to the session room where the extraction procedure will take place. He smells like a fresh shower, but he is in the same clothes he wore the last time I saw him.

Inside, I run my hands along the walls, feeling for some kind of fortifications like steel or iron that help keep the magic contained to the room, like at Hartsboro. But the wall is just stone.

"Concerned about the procedure going wrong?" Ube says.

"I want to be prepared." No magic will leave this room. I sit on a stool at one of the tables. Ube doesn't move, fidgeting with the belt loop on his pants.

"I—I've wanted to tell you, one-on-one, I didn't know he was *stealing* it," Ube says. "I'm really sorry how that all went." He is either terrified or deeply contrite.

"A gift in hindsight. I learned something very valuable. And so did you." I watch his every movement.

"No kidding." He straightens his glasses. "Never use low-density stones for highly concentrated magic."

"And never cross me."

He nods, hooking his hands.

"Tell me more about what went wrong with the procedure."

He gestures at a chalked wall. "May I?"

"Sure."

Ube writes out an equation. He underlines and circles a set of numbers, then draws an arrow to another equation. The longer he writes, the faster he goes. He works furiously, circling more, underlining certain things multiple times. At one point he erases a section, then starts again. When he's finished, the wall is covered, every inch, in some kind of math that's completely foreign to me, with symbols and diagrams interspersed.

"The density of the stones, as I mentioned, was an issue. But the rate the magic was entering the stones was the bigger problem. The Retentor brush was removing the magic faster than the stones on the diadem could absorb it."

"How do you remedy that? The toushana will be stronger."

"I'll have to run some tests to look into it. I'll need help from someone skilled with toushana. Zecky only took in people who could touch it, ex-Draguns, people like that."

I watch the bead in the center of his eyes for the slightest averted gaze. Any hint of a lie. Ube appeared to be *well* trusted by Zecky.

"I'll find someone for you. What other resources do you need?"

"We need something that can hold the toushana."

"What about the diadem specifically made it work so well?"

"Its age. Ideally, I'd have another ancient item or something with *old* magic. Magic was more concentrated in the old days. So the metals forged to support it were full of all kinds of strengtheners. They don't make things like that anymore."

Very astute. I hadn't put that together before. We hone blades for Second Rite, by folding in enhancer stones, to *put back* some of the stuff that's been stripped from magic over the years. "So it's about finding the right item."

"And the right people, carefully monitoring the process. I have a few people in mind to lend a hand with this one."

I recall Erla leaving nervously when the procedure was underway. Just *after* they were arguing with Zecky about using the diadem in the first place. Ube studies his equation on the wall.

"Maybe there is something here? This *is* an ancestral magical House, after all. Surely there is some piece of history they've kept."

"Is there nothing else you can use? Something less sentimental to the Headmistress?"

"I don't think so. But I'll confirm. And I didn't realize Quell's really Headmistress. Doesn't seem like it."

Cold ticks in my chest. "Your opinion of Quell never needs to come out of your mouth while you're on these grounds."

He shuts his mouth, and I crack my neck, trying to remember that he wants to help me.

"I will work on what we've discussed. The next time I see you, I want a clear answer on whether you can use something else for the Sphere's toushana. And I expect you to run a sample extraction procedure at least a dozen times without any accidents before we do this. Am I understood?"

"Yes."

I wait for him to say more. But Ube only stares, and I spot something very honest in him for the first time: *anger4*

Erla appears in the doorway, dressed in neat pants and a simple top. She wears a different pair of chunky earrings. Matching jewelry dangles from her wrist. "I heard you two were looking for me?"

I leave them there on my way back toward the dorms, and I grab an envelope from Cuthers's old office, now Dexler's. I write to my brother. We need to meet up. He needs to know what we've learned about the Dragunhead and Darkbearers. I also need an update on how the Scroll search is going. Lady Ruby crosses my mind, and I consider grabbing another envelope. *Could she have something we could use? Runetta? Roberta? Bell? What was her name?*

"Oh, I was looking for you," Dexler says as I exit the office. "This came."

She hands me a letter with my name on it in a handwriting I don't recognize. Inside is a simple request to meet, but the signature makes the hair on my arms rise.

Monument Park Saturday at seven.
Come alone.
—Ellery

FORTY-FIVE

Yagrin

Nore's expression when she'd left the coronation reception that morning haunted Yagrin. He splashed water on his face. He took a long bath. Then he did a long run around the estate in the frigid cold and came back for a hot bath again. Nothing helped.

So instead of eating lunch, he came back to his room to read up on House of Duncan. But he was accosted with memories from Begonia Terrace, Nore's body collapsing, the horrors that ran through his mind as he rushed to her to search for a pulse, the deadly fury in her brother's eyes as he shoved her heart in the box hoping it would kill her.

He closed the only book he'd found in the library on Duncan. Had Yagrin gone mad? He was definitely madly in love with her. And she was madly in love with him, too. But the ire in her expression when she left him on the dance floor felt like a dagger in his chest. *She doesn't mean any of the things she's saying.* She can't. When they danced, he could feel the way she clung to him, the way she curled toward his touch, the way she trusted him. *Something deep down inside her remembers how it feels.*

He held his chest, imagining he could still feel her, smell her. He wished he would have learned her secret sooner. He would have whisked her away from this horrid Order. They could have run, hid, disguised themselves. It wouldn't matter as long as he had her by his side. But now here he was living in an ancestral House just to be near her.

Maybe their love was strong enough to break the curse of the Pact.

He had to make her remember the feeling. To free them both.

He hungered for sight of her. When the clock above the hearth struck seven, he slipped into the halls toward the dining hall, ignoring the inquisitive eyes and studious stares. Yagrin walked with his head down out of his guest quarters building and into the main building, where the dead waited. He couldn't see them very well, but he had grown used to the oddly placed darkness, which hovered along the hallways, and the sudden chill in the air. He knew they were there.

As he rounded on the family's private dining room, he spotted Nore's maid.

"Evening," she said, her arms full of fresh linens.

"Is she in there?" His thumb jabbed backward toward the room ringing with the ting of dishes behind them.

"Not yet. She may be exhausted, honestly. Coronation day and night are quite busy."

Night? "I'm sorry, what?" He leaned in to hear her better.

"It is nothing personal, Mr. Wexton. I know the Headmistress is fond of you, despite what she says."

That sent a rush of heat through him. But her words tangled his thoughts in a knot. What did she have going on coronation night, and why would he take it personally?

"I am Ainsley, by the way." She stuck out a hand, and they shook. "I know the guest quarters are not quite what you're used to. If you need anything, don't hesitate to ask for me."

Her hospitality caught him off guard. "Nore likes a thin pillow, by the way. If they're too thick, she gets pain." He touched his upper back. "Right here."

"Comfort isn't one of our pillars of value, Mr. Wexton. Also, Headmistress hasn't mentioned that. I'm sure she's managing just fine."

He was about to ask if they had masseuses on staff, but he swallowed the question. He'd almost forgotten who he was talking to. He'd check on her when he saw her at dinner.

"Would you at least notify me if she's ever restless at night?"

"Tonight I cannot. But I can ask about it for future." Ainsley curtsied and left before he could thank her. He sauntered into the dining room and filled his plate, waiting for Nore to arrive. Isla was sitting at the far end of the table.

"You haven't returned to Hartsboro." She slipped a bite of meat into her mouth.

He wouldn't be leaving Dlaminaugh unless Nore made him. "No, not yet." But he wasn't sure what Isla's relationship with his aunt was like, so for now his business would be his own.

"How is your family doing with everything happening in the world?"

"I am not sure."

"I've heard about the Sphere."

"And you're mentioning it to me because?"

"Well, your brother is at the center of those rumors."

He straightened in his seat. "I despise games. If you have a question, ask it."

She set down her teacup. "I apologize if I've offended you."

Yagrin's fork froze on the way to his mouth.

She let out a long exhale. "I'm still relearning social graces. It's been so long. Love is the first emotion to go." Her gaze moved beyond him. "Then it's guilt and shame. Sadness is a funny one. It would come intermittently, but it would never fully go away." She dabbed her mouth with a napkin and stood. "I only meant to say that I hope your brother is doing okay. If he's anything like you, I will hold him up in prayer."

Yagrin wasn't breathing.

"You have been very good to my daughter when many were not. Myself included. I may never earn her trust again. But from what I've seen in the last few days, if she has you by her side, she'll be alright."

Words stuck in his throat. After staring blankly, he managed to say, "How do you know how I feel—"

"When you go without love for so long and then suddenly you can feel it again, you *never* mistake what it does and does not look like. It's in the way you look out for her." She tapped her ear and pointed to the hall where he and Ainsley were just speaking. "If you'll excuse me."

Yagrin watched her go, speechless. He finished the rest of his food in silence, ruminating over her mother's words. When he finished, Nore still hadn't showed. Now he was worried. But he stewed his anxiety by reading in the Caelum for one hour. Then another.

By midnight, his thoughts of Nore led him inside the main building. The halls were far from silent, students wandering to and fro with arms full of books. He wasn't sure what he was looking for, but something in him was unsettled. When he spotted a girl with luscious red hair curled up in a lounge chair over a pile of leather books, he had to look twice to be sure it wasn't her. He wandered near Nore's quarters and spotted Draguns outside her door. They staggered their stance as he passed. And that stopped him in his tracks.

"Mr. Wexton? What are you doing out of bed so late?" Ainsley appeared behind him, holding a flat pillow.

"Why are there Draguns outside her room?"

"Just Headmistress business."

Shouting voices behind the doors rattled his pulse. He marched up to them, despite Ainsley's lightning-fast grip on his arm.

"Open the doors."

"You know we can't do that," one of the Draguns said. Yagrin thought he might recognize him.

"Mr. Wexton, please. If Headmistress catches me disobeying a direct order, I'll be in such trouble."

"I will ask once more," Yagrin said.

"I don't open the door unless—" the Dragun started.

Something crashed inside Nore's bedroom, shattering, and it sent ice skidding up his spine.

Yagrin summoned toushana, and streams of cold answered in a sputter. His hands filled with weak shadows. He focused on the icy feeling to grow the dark magic, but it didn't swell. The Draguns reached for their magic as well, but their hands came up empty. Yagrin took the second of distraction and shoved his fist up the nose of one and whipped his elbow against the head of the other. Then he shoved his way inside. Blood drained from his body at what he found. Nore stood over her bed with a lamp base heaved over her shoulder.

"If we could just try—" some fellow in her bed, wearing only heart-dotted underwear, was saying, pulling at her wrist.

As she swung the lamp base at him, he ducked, scrambling out of the covers, eyes wide.

"Get out!" she screamed.

"*No!*" the intruder yelled back.

Yagrin noticed some kind of rope in his hands. Questions flooded Yagrin, but his body was well ahead of his mind. He dashed over and shoved the fellow to the ground before climbing on top of him. Yagrin slammed his fist into his face. He groaned.

"Did he hurt you?" he asked, hopping up.

Nore brought the lamp base down again. This time it struck the fellow's head, and the metal shaft snapped in half. He howled in pain. She snatched the rope from him.

"Headmistress, can we help?" Draguns rushed inside, one holding a pillow. Ainsley was gone.

"Stand back," Nore shouted as she tied the fellow's wrists together with the precision of a sailor before tugging it tight. Then she lugged him to the door.

"You will drag him through the halls like this all day. If anyone wants to control when and how I make an heir for this House, this is a *kindness* compared to what I will do to them."

"Yes, Headmistress," the Dragun gushed. "We are so sorry. The oath—"

"I don't care about your oaths. I don't care about your traditions. This is now *my* House!" She slammed the door in all their faces. Yagrin was breathless. She was furious, but fully clothed, thank goodness.

"Did he touch you?"

"You think he'd be alive if he touched me?" She lifted the sleeve of her nightgown. "I nicked my arm on the broken lamp." She held it out to him.

Yagrin ran his hands along her soft, smooth, and unmarred skin.

"I tried to be nice, offering him tea to sit down and talk through whatever this tradition is. He genuinely seemed confused. But instead of taking the cup, he grabbed me by the wrist." She huffed. "So I whacked him, good."

"Uh, yeah. I doubt he'll ever be signing up for anything like that again."

Her frustration melted into a guffaw. It took about an hour for their conversation to move on and Nore to settle from the stressors of the day. When she did, Yagrin was sitting in a chair by her fire, holding a picture of Nore as a baby and her brother sitting on her mother's hip. After a shower, she sat beside him on the floor.

"Thank you for checking on me, I'm not sure I said that."

He waved the words away.

"I mean it." She stretched her neck, holding her shoulder. Yagrin had long noticed the lack of any pillows on her bed. She was in pain. Red always had neck pain if she didn't sleep just so. Now he knew why.

"May I?"

Her gray eyes said yes. She didn't answer, but she moved in front of him, sitting beside his toes, her back pressed against his shins. He gathered the long locks of her hair and moved them aside, exposing her bare shoulder. He bit his bottom lip to try to stop thinking about kissing her there.

As he moved his hands over the muscle between her shoulder blades, she arced backward, lengthening her neck. He studied the new lines of the face of the girl he loved. He'd known Red's every dip, blemish, and curve. And he adored each one of them. But Nore's lips were shaped a bit differently. Full and pink. And soft. So very soft. *Goodness, she is beautiful.* He closed his eyes as he kneaded her muscles, and the moment he'd let himself kiss her at House of Oralia flooded his senses. Desire burned in him, but he focused on getting the hard knot out of her back. He dug his knuckle deeper, and she moaned in relief.

"There." She straightened against him, pressing against his firm touch. He worked the heel of his hand harder, up and down in a smooth motion, deeper with each movement.

When he finished, her fingers found his. She cupped his hand and turned to face him.

"I don't know if I can do this." Her stare burned with fear. "Being Headmistress."

"You can do anything. But do you want it?"

"I don't have a choice."

Yagrin laced his fingers between hers, and she let him. "We will make you a choice."

"You cannot fix this. I'm bound by a Pact. They have my heart." She shook her head. "There's no way out. There's no way for us. For this." She laid her head on his lap, and he raked his fingers through her hair, drawing circles on the crown of her head the way she liked.

"It's okay to be terrified. It's okay to not have the answers. I was made a Dragun and never wanted any of it. My future was decided for me before I was even born. It's okay to not like that. And resist it."

Her lashes batted as she looked up at him, listening. She was really listening. Not thinking of ways to get rid of him or mean things to say to push him away. He could see the girl he loved in those eyes.

"You are a fire that will not be extinguished," he said.

"Fire needs air. I can't breathe here."

"Then let's break you out of this cage. Maybe there's a way out of the curse."

"Somewhere under my mother's thick skin is love for me. I see it when she looks at me now. And I loathe it. It's too late. But it made me realize that if she couldn't find love for her daughter because of the Pact and she damaged me the way she did, how is there hope for us? I don't have hope, Yagrin."

"You don't need hope. I have enough hope for the both of us. You just need trust."

She sighed and tried to look away. But he gently pulled her by the jaw back around to face him. "I know you like no one knows you."

She blushed.

He smiled as he let his fingers trail her neck. His throat went dry. "I *meant* I know you have what it takes to beat this. I will fight for you to remember every day."

She kissed each one of his fingertips. Somewhere behind those steel eyes, the girl he loved was still in there.

"Let me help you remember."

"Please." She slipped her shoulder out of her gown. "I want to remember it all."

FORTY-SIX

Nore

Yagrin stared so intently at Nore, it felt like the sun shined on her bare skin.

This was probably foolish. But she couldn't pretend she didn't wish she felt something for him. Maybe he was right. Maybe her body remembered. More than anything, she wanted to believe being together again with him, like this, would make her feel *something*.

They stood, and he pulled the tie out of her hair. His scent wrapped around her as his arm brushed past her cheek. She inhaled deep. Rosewood and something soft, like vanilla, with a spicy bite underneath. Cinnamon. Tiny bumps rose on her skin. Her natural curls, which had returned since her shower, billowed over her shoulders.

As they stood there inches apart, flooded with memories of the life they used to share and questions about the life they had now, she searched herself for some effervescent flutter, some bubbliness in her stomach. But there was no first-time feeling as they stood there more honest with each other than they'd ever been. What she felt was much deeper: a secure, confident knowing unlike the uncertain flutters of frilly love. This was rock solid. Whatever it was between them would not be easily moved. Not because it was new. She'd never been excited by that. It was because it was confident and certain. Their bond was unshakable. Not even her losing her heart could take this man away from her.

His arm snaked around her back, the touch of his fingers trailed the base of her spine. There was a promise in the way Yagrin touched her, every moment anchored, not by adventurous infatuation, but by a steady love that was impossible to break. Even if she couldn't feel it. She knew. And tonight, she hoped knowing would be enough.

He savored her with his fingertips, trailing them across her collarbone, down her shoulder, stopping every few moments to stare into her eyes. She cupped his face, the warmth of his breath on her hand.

"You are real," he said. "You are here."

"I am."

Her body burned with want to feel him. But for the moment he only hugged her, burying his face in her hair. He nuzzled against her neck, dragging his mouth across its hollow, back and forth. Her breath shortened as he teased her. When he finally pressed his lips in the softest kiss on her shoulder, it hit her like fuel on fire.

A demanding warmth pooled in her. She searched for that same want in her chest. But it wasn't there. She gripped his arms tightly, suffocating any space between them. *I love him*, she told herself as he lifted her off her feet. She wrapped her legs around him and tossed her arms over his broad shoulders, trying to recall how this felt before she'd been locked in this prison. She felt her covers at her back. But when he opened his mouth and kissed her properly, the world disappeared.

Their tongues danced. And her body tingled all over. They kissed until her lips were swollen. She came up for air and searched herself for some sentiment. Some feeling.

But there was nothing.

Only passion.

Fiery passion.

And for someone else, maybe it would be enough. But passion wasn't what she craved. Intimate emotional love was. She went in for a kiss again, holding him close as he gently bit her bottom lip.

"I love you," he breathed between kisses. The words to reciprocate tried to form in her mouth. But they did not come together.

"Is something wrong?"

"No." She pressed his mouth against her neck again, wishing it were true, wishing she couldn't feel her hope fading that this could work. But her heart, that hum of love in her chest, the sweetness that could bring tears to her eyes when he held her, wasn't there.

She pulled away.

"Nore?" He set her gently on her feet.

Her mind raced, searching her body once more, her empty chest, for some inkling of the emotion she'd lost. She swallowed to wet her dry throat. Her body still tingled with the dregs of pleasure. But that was all . . .

Sheets were tight in her fist. *Feel something!* But there was nothing there. She felt nothing when she looked at him.

"You're not okay," he said.

She was anything but okay. It wasn't working. She stood and gathered Yagrin's clothes. She couldn't do this.

"Yagrin." She handed him his things.

"I don't understand. Was it something I—"

"It's me. It's always been me. You are perfect." She tried to turn away to march to the door, but he grabbed her by the arm.

"You don't feel anything between us right now?" he asked, finally getting her meaning.

"I feel regret. Deep regret over letting myself hope." She felt all the wrong things, none of which filled her emptiness.

Yagrin's eyes widened as he swiped something from her cheek. Her tear glistened on his finger. And he did the strangest thing. He smiled.

"Regret can't exist without love." He dressed and left. Nore closed the door behind him, curled up in a ball right there on the floor, and cried herself to sleep.

FORTY-SEVEN

Quell

It's been two days since I destroyed the gate outside of Chateau Soleil, and I haven't had the stomach to tell anyone. Not even Jordan. But I've hardly seen him. He's been spending the entire day with Ube and Erla, and he hasn't returned to my room and has had an excuse for dinner both nights.

Thankfully, the vines keep the gap in the wall reasonably covered. I've drowned my shame in the library but can't find a single book that mentions the roses. *The irony.* Everyone looks at me as if I could actually serve as a good Headmistress, when the first thing I've done is destroy the protections the previous Headmistress put in place.

I need answers. We need as much between us and the Dragunhead as possible. I scoop up another pointless book and shove it in my bag and hunt for Dexler. She and Cuthers worked closest with my grandmother over the years. Maybe she knows something.

I find her overseeing a group repairing damaged chandeliers in the formal dining room.

"Headmistress," one of them says before dipping into a bend that I realize is supposed to be a curtsy, the rim of her pink velvet dress skimming the floor. She grins. "Did I do it right?"

"Where did you get that dress? And who taught you how to—"

She frowns.

"Yes," I say, realizing I've taken all the wind out of this girl's sails. She can't be much older than me, with streaked chestnut hair and intensely green eyes. "You did it just fine."

"Maezre Dexler gave me the dress."

"Quell." Dexler glides the back of her hand across her forehead. "I was beginning to worry they'd trapped you in that room upstairs instead of just repairing the wall."

My cheeks burn with embarrassment for the second time today. "Thank you for doing that."

"Abby fixed up a bunch of old garments I found around the House." She dusts her dress. The one she wears today is finer than the one we found her in when we showed up. This one is made of lush purple taffeta with silver threading. "It's starting to feel a bit more like home around here." She brushes my arm. "I hope you feel that way."

I smile tightly, unsure how to tell her that when I think of what's on the other side of this chaos we are in, I see Jordan, sand, and blue ocean. I want the others here to be alright, to have access to magic, but I won't be roped into a life I didn't choose.

"You're doing a great job." Making this place feel more like a home will help the others settle in. All around, it is a win. I did notice, on my walk to and from the library each day, that there was less debris in the halls, more of the sconces were working, and the scorched walls in the foyer had been stained a beautiful glossy wood. The House is transforming, and it's like watching a person inches from death come back to life.

"*Wait* until you hear what else I've planned." Her lips pucker with excitement, and I'm relieved. "I was able to get some of the maezres to agree to put on a few classes during the day so there's something to study. Since there's a mixture of abilities and some with none, we're doing an elixir session for anyone, one on Shifting, and I was going to see if I can find enough good silver to do an old-fashioned seven-course-meal session. Like old times. For the little ones, I'm trying to find a good place on the grounds for a magical sensory station, where they can play with magical objects and see if it wakes up any dormant magic inside them. Who knows, we may yet have someone *emerge* in all this chaos."

She is brilliant. "See? I'm not even needed around here."

Dexler rambles on. "It's already been more chipper."

"Less fighting, for sure." I only overheard a single yelling match in the last twenty-four hours, down from three the day before that. "Just be sure they're choosing to participate. Don't force them." Some of them may want nothing to do with the Order's traditions, rightfully so. "Same with the clothes. It's their choice, right? They can wear whatever they want."

"Um, sure. Yes, of course." She squeezes my arm, and I don't think I've ever seen her so excited. "You haven't even heard my wildest idea yet. Though I'm not quite sure we can pull it off. *A ball!*"

I blink. A thousand reasons why a formal dance seems like the most frivolous waste of time run through my mind. But her glee and the calmer atmosphere over the last day shut my mouth. If she believes putting on a dance is what the guests need, then so be it.

"Great."

"You don't think it's bizarre, do you? At a time like this? When the world is such a mess?"

I shrug. "Maybe that's when we need a ball most of all."

She squeezes her hands to her chest. It is refreshing to see her *not* overwhelmed. I was beginning to feel bad for the woman. But she signed up for this life, overseeing a House. I didn't.

"I did want to talk to you about my grandmother's roses, if you don't mind."

She gives instructions to the others and leads me into the hall. "Alright, what exactly is it you'd like to know?"

"They protect the estate."

"They never did until your grandmother died. But yes."

"I also noticed that they take on toushana, absorbing it. And it causes them to *grow, not* be destroyed. I've never seen anything like it."

She pulls at the ribbon on her dress. "You start talking about that dark magic stuff and it gives me an uneasy feeling, Quell, I must tell you. In my day, we didn't discuss such things."

"My grandmother had toushana. You do know that, right?"

"I figured it out by going through her things after she died, trying to get her affairs in order." Dexler looks away. "It felt wrong invading her privacy."

"You were trying to help, it's fine. Did you learn anything about the roses?"

"I learned how to trick them to let people inside. I also learned that they reproduce prolifically. Other than that, no. I did find a gardening journal your grandmother kept. She was big on documenting things. I have it in my office. I'll drop it off in your room."

I thank her again and round the corner, where I spot Ube leaned against the wall. I freeze and clear my throat. "How long have you been waiting here, Ube, is it?"

"Yes. And not too long."

But long enough.

His propped-up foot finds the floor. "I'm sorry, but I couldn't help but overhear your conversation about the roses."

"Yes, and?"

He rubs his palms against his pockets. "I, uh, also saw you the other day at the garden wall. I happened to be leaving the Sunrise Corridor and looked out and noticed you were having trouble with the gate. There's a hole in it, I think."

I search him for dishonesty.

"I think I can help."

I can't afford to turn down any knowledge that could help keep us better insulated. "I'm listening."

"The roses feed on toushana, like normal roses feed on water. If they're overwatered, they'll die. Much like if the black roses get too much toushana at once, they'll decay. Is that what happened?"

I nod. His countenance brightens as he pulls a paper from his pocket. "Here, I drew a diagram for you. Only give each flower toushana in proportion to its size. Instead of feeding it lots of toushana at once, feed it toushana in small doses over several hours, even several days. It'll let the petals absorb the magic more slowly." He flips the paper over. "*And* roses are not the only thing that can absorb magic that way. But they have to be the purest metals. A gate won't work. Jewelry usually works better."

How closely was he watching me? The picture he's drawn also has a list of other ideas. I take the paper with narrowed eyes.

"I'll look into all you've said. I won't keep you." I leave him there, equally moved at this help and creeped out. Was that him in the window? It had to be.

When I clear the dorm wings, I spot Jordan passing the stairs and dash after him.

"Jordan!"

"Quell, *there* you are." He hurries toward me but stops suddenly to keep some distance between us.

"You say that as if we don't live in the same house. Why haven't I seen you in two days?"

"I've been busy. So have you. But there's something we need to talk about." He reaches into his jacket and pulls an envelope addressed to him. "Ellery wants to see me."

I go cold all over. Ellery Ambrose, Nore's brother, who has their mother prisoner or something wild like that.

"He sent this two days ago. I needed to wrap my head around it and think before I brought it to you. I'm going to meet with him."

"You're *absolutely* not going to leave here and meet with him. I am breaking my brain trying to make this place safer for everyone, but mainly *you* and all magic. And you want to go waltzing out there? You already have a target on your back."

"I understand it's a risk. But he could have much-needed news about the Immortality Scroll. I have all this power inside me, Quell, if I have to, I will use it. He wants to meet tomorrow at Monument Park. I can take someone with me if that gives you peace of mind."

"Jordan, *no*. I order it. As your Headmistress."

"Oh, now you're my Headmistress?" he asks, teasing me.

"I've always been your *head* mistress."

He bites his lip, and it makes me want to kiss him.

"Ellery is working against your brother and Nore, which sort of makes him our enemy, too. You think the Dragunhead hasn't figured that out?"

He strokes his chin. I grab the note from him, and our fingers brush, stealing the moment. His eyes are an odd shade of green today, more bluish than usual. There's fatigue in his smile, tired lines hugging his eyes.

"That letter tells us everything we need to know. Ellery is desperate. He needs help. He has no allies. There's no way the Dragunhead is telling him to set this up to trap you. He has been trying to draw you out of hiding all this time. If he thought a meeting with Ellery would do it, wouldn't he have done that a long time ago? This is a cry for help from Ellery, which you're not going to give him. You only risk getting into some kind of fight with him that risks magic."

His silence lets me know I've convinced him.

"Fine, I won't meet him. I don't deserve you. Have I told you that lately?"

"Not nearly enough."

He blows me an air-kiss, and I resist the urge to run my fingers along his jaw, to cup the back of his neck and pull his mouth down to mine. I stare at his lips, and it takes me a moment to realize he's talking again.

"I did also write to Yagrin," he says. "We have to update him and get an update. I won't put that in a letter."

My heart pumps harder. He is right.

"Did he say he'd meet?"

"I haven't heard back yet."

"We'll have to plan it just right. Maybe late at night so that no one knows you're gone. And you can be back before sunrise. *No one* can know you're leaving."

"You speak as if you don't trust some of these wonderfully kind and genuine safe house people we've brought here."

"You're mocking me." My thoughts move to Ube. Then Yani. "I'm just being cautious."

"I like that." He closes most of the distance between us. His scent lathers me in a need to touch him. Tonight he smells pungent, like dirt, sweat, and something underneath. His finger finds my chin, and it takes my breath away.

He's touching me.

There's no fear in his eyes, only confidence. He slides his finger from my chin down my neck, painfully slow, stopping at my collarbone. Every place he touches turns to fire.

"You haven't come back to my room. Even to sleep on the chaise. Why?"

I know the answer—he is not convinced it's safe to be so near me for longer stretches of time.

"We will have dinner soon. Just us."

"I will hold you to it."

A wicked smirk bows his lips. "Please do."

I walk him to his dorm, where he insists on sleeping, and tell him about my horrible time with the gate, Ube's advice, the eerie feeling I had about him lurking. Then I immediately felt bad. Ube has only offered help. Unlike others. I also mention Dexler's improvements, which he's noticed as well.

"I'm going to try his recommendation first thing tomorrow."

"He and his sister are *sharp*. It'll probably work."

"Does that make you trust them more? Can you see them being part of a House permanently?"

"I trust no one. *Our* House is you and me, as far as I'm concerned."

I fold my arms when we reach his room, perturbed he still hasn't budged on his ideas about what happens *after* we save magic. We have to do *something* with the magic. Shouldn't we leave things better in the Order than we found it? More equitable.

I glare at the ornate walls and polished decor we pass. It screams

Darragh Marionne. She was the House. And the House was her. Magic is in our hands. We can mold it into something better. But we don't have to hold it in our hands forever. Whatever we do, it starts with trust. Without that, we can't build anything.

"You're working with Ube on the most important procedure of our lives. We have to know if he's trustworthy. And if he is, you need to treat him that way. Then there's Yani." *She lingers in the shadows.* "I don't like her, Jordan."

"I've told you, I can handle Yani. She is desperate to please. That could be useful."

"No. Not ever. Period."

"But you're ready to hand over a whole House to Willam and Knox? Who've teamed up with *good* Darkbearers, so they say, and lied to us about it? Who are *lying* to their own people about it as we speak?"

Footsteps tap in the distance.

"We're not supposed to be fighting about this, remember?" he says.

My jaw works and an idea strikes me. "You can learn a lot about a person when you show them a little favor." I will show him how Ube and Erla have done nothing but comply with us uprooting them and forcing them to help us with the Sphere's magic. If anyone deserves a chance to prove themselves, it's them.

"What are you suggesting?"

"Dexler's gotten the dining room almost fully repaired. Let's christen it with a nice dinner. We'll invite each of them: Ube; his sister, Erla; and Yaniselle." Talking with Ube and Erla in an unpressured situation will help him see what I see in them—*and* what I see in Yaniselle.

"Fine." Jordan opens his mouth but shuts it. And it feels like a win.

FORTY-EIGHT

Nore

Nore's covers still smelled like Yagrin. It had been a couple of days since they'd rolled around in her bed before she forced him to leave, after coronation. The next morning, she couldn't bear to leave her room, still in pieces. Her absence was ruffling feathers, though.

Three families had dropped out of pursuing Rites. One of their largest donors sent a strongly worded letter to Nore. It still lay open on her desk. Priest Kimper requested a meeting with her, which she refused. Her mother had come to her door, but left when Nore didn't answer. Nore also noticed the dead hovering outside her window more than once. She couldn't hide out in her room anymore. She had to lead the House. Or at least pretend to.

Ainsley busied herself around Nore's room, tidying and preparing her clothes for dinner. The maid hadn't said much or even looked at her since the incident.

"Is this gray off-the-shoulder dress more to your liking?" Ainsley asked, dangling a ratty dress whose only saving grace was the interesting neckline.

"Sure."

"I'll find something better, Headmistress."

Nore rose from her bed and joined Ainsley at her closet. She closed her hand around Ainsley's as she struggled to pull the dress strap onto the silk hanger. "Are you alright?"

"Yes." Her maid didn't elaborate, tucking her chin down and shoving the dress in the closet to pull another.

"Look at me," Nore said.

Ainsley obeyed with tearstained cheeks.

"Ainsley?"

"I am *so* sorry. I can't believe you didn't know! The former Headmistress usually goes over these things. You should have been given a rundown of his qualifications beforehand. I don't see you and your mother talking much." She sighed. "I should have asked to be sure."

"You have nothing to be sorry about."

"You cannot be all you are required to be if I am not supporting you *perfectly*." This House's obsession with superiority bled into one with perfection. And it made Nore want to claw her eyes out. Ainsley *tsk*ed, noticing a slight snag in the seam on the next gown she pulled. The maid worked magic between her fingers, smoothing her thumb over the thread. It wriggled free from the dress, and the hole in the garment widened. Ainsley groaned, trying again.

Nore snatched the dress from her hands and tore it as best she could. The rip in the air sent a thrill through her bones.

Ainsley gasped. "Headmistress, that is one-hundred-year-old linen."

"I don't care." She asked Ainsley to sit in the chair by the fire and pulled up a seat to sit beside her. "It is not your fault that I didn't know. My mother tried to warn me, I suspect. Anyway, if it is anyone's fault that I didn't know, it was mine."

Nore could see the shrug of disbelief in Ainsley's shoulders, her gaze stuck to the torn dress on the ground. It mattered too much to her. It all mattered too much to them. House of Ambrose was a prison. And she was its warden!

She grabbed a dress from her closet and held it to herself. "I think this is quite nice. Did you pull this one?"

"I did. From a few Seasons ago in your mother's old things."

"You have such a good eye for fashion, Ainsley. This is perfect." In truth, the dress was just as drab as the next. But Nore didn't care. Before she was Headmistress, the fashions in her House never bothered her. But now that she was trapped, every dot of monotonous gray was another form of restraint, a reminder her life had been drained of color and she had no say. But the sparkle in Ainsley's eyes now as she readied the dress for dinner that evening made up for the dress's lack of shiny beading.

Ainsley smiled to herself as she crossed the room to change the sheets.

"Leave them another night, please."

When Nore finally emerged from her room, she found Priest Winkel combing his bushy eyebrows as he waited outside for her.

"Winkel, I could have met you in the dining room. You must be tired, standing all that time."

"Oh, I am much more fit than I look, Miss Ambrose." He stuck out his arm, and she hooked her hand onto it.

"I also . . ." he said under his breath as they walked.

Here it is. A chastising about how I'm not doing a good job. It was actually shocking she hadn't gotten one from her mother yet.

"Before we are in the company of so many, I wanted to just check in with you. There are concerns swarming."

"Because I had my chosen suitor put on display in his underwear?"

"The research and interviews revealed that Vincent is a cooperative and natural leader in all his athletics at his traditional school. His maezres here spoke *most* highly of his character when we did our research. He presented like a bright, compassionate young fellow. What did you not find suitable?"

"I had no idea of this tradition. My mother never told me. I asked him to leave. But he *refused* to leave my room, climbing into my bed practically naked, *insisting* I make an heir with him!"

Winkel froze, gaping. "Your predecessors have been unwavering in their commitment to employ logic to make the best heir. These things are usually celebratory and *certainly* consensual. The boy may have been confused, but disregarding your unpreparedness and ignoring a direct order from his Headmistress to leave is *inexcusable*. A few *more days* of punishment seem in order. I truly apologize. The priesthood take heir matters *very* seriously. We try to make the best selection possible."

"Did you decide for my mother?" Nore wasn't sure where the question came from. She'd never known her father. She'd never even heard a whisper of his name.

"We did."

A follow-up question stuck in her throat, but she pivoted. "Had I done what you all recommended, what would have happened to Vincent after?"

"Sometimes they're offered a position at the House. Marriage is an option, but historically only two Headmistresses have chosen that path." He patted her hand affectionately. "Most often, they leave and live a life well provided for away from here."

"What will happen to him since I've refused?"

"He technically broke an oath. So he will be dismissed from the House once the investigation is done. Because of the unique circumstances, we are looking into an ancient magic that takes the edge of memories away. Beaulah Perl has offered to help us with things of that nature in the past. Your mother always refused her help. But—"

"And I do, too. We do not deal with Beaulah Perl. Period." She'd learned enough from Yagrin to know that woman could not be trusted. A monster. And with Adola's standoffish encounter weeks ago, she didn't trust them at all.

"The other priests and I thought . . ." Winkel studied her expression. "As you say, it will be, Headmistress."

"I should be consulted on these things."

"Yes, of course. We just wanted to give you time to settle in."

"I am settled."

As the dining room came into view up ahead, he leaned into her ear. "There *must* be the promise of an heir, Nore. And soon."

"My mother didn't have me until well into her forties. Why am I being rushed? Coronation in our House does not happen until age twenty-two, except in extreme cases. Like mine." She thought of her brother, and a chill ran down her spine.

"She didn't wait that long by choice. Fertility issues have plagued your bloodline for generations. You must start early."

"*I refuse.*"

He stopped and looked over his shoulders before standing squarely in front of her. The intensity of his stare made the hair on Nore's arms rise. Under his breath, he said, "Nore, the dead only grow more restless with the news of the Sphere. They are already inside the walls, which is *unprecedented*. You are playing with fire. You need to cement their commitment to you with a magical heir."

"You *knew*." He knew about her lack of magic. And the seed of toushana in her, from her mother.

"Sweet child." He tapped her nose. "Of course I knew. I kept Pizor and Kimper in the dark. Kimper can be abrasive with matters that require a gentle touch. I am only sorry I couldn't do more to help you. I aided Ellery as much as I could. But he grew cold even to me."

Nore didn't have words. "He's lost now."

"The Sage is a craftsman, a maker of things, who upholds truth *and law*." He held her arm tight but gently. "Do you understand what I mean?"

Nore shook her head. She'd stopped doing the empty worship rituals as soon as her mother gave up on forcing her to go. She'd forgotten most of the recitations she'd memorized when little. All she knew was that it was good to pray to the Wielder in times of danger, the Sage when in need of help, and the Sovereign always. But she never did any of it anymore. She'd tried praying to the Wielder once, terrified of her mother, and it didn't help. Why would she do it again?

"The dead require his blessing to accept anything that does not fit the natural law. At Begonia Terrace when the dead accepted your heart, they did not have the Sage's blessing. When they returned with a heart like yours, it angered the Sage. I've been begging mercy for you and the dead in my prayers."

"Thank you" were the only words she could think of. What did it mean to have a god angry at you? She hugged her free arm around herself.

"Is there anything I can do?" she asked.

"Pay your penance, attend services, and say your prayers, every day, like I taught you when you were a girl. Ask for mercy. The Sage values truth as much as law. Show him your true self, Nore. Hold nothing back, and I believe he will honor you as heir. You are a warrior at heart. He will respect that."

Winkel's nails dug half-moons into her arms.

"So sorry." He released his tight grip. He'd gone pale as he smoothed the sickle indentations from her skin. "I worry about you, dear girl. That's all."

"The ancestors have accepted me. But if the gods don't honor me as heir, then what?"

"Then we are at war."

A war between the dead and the gods.

Nore's feet were cement.

"One more thing. There are whispers that families are detaching from our House and allying with your brother, supporting his claim to Headship. They are pointing out your choice of punishment for Vincent as evidence that you are not fit to lead."

"A stranger is sent into *my* bed who feels entitled to my body, and *I'm* drawing criticism?"

"It is not right. But that is the narrative. It seems his boldness is inspiring more dissenters."

She was the boldest Ambrose. But she'd had to make up an entire persona to confidently be that person. Her maid suggested that being bold would fracture the House. Winkel was suggesting boldness projects strength. Which was it? It wasn't possible to please everyone. She could hear Drew's urging to their aunt rattling around in her head. *Stand for something.*

She eyed the drab gray walls as they passed. *I will show them, in small ways, just who I am.*

"Do you know where my brother is?" She knew she needed to ask the question, though she dreaded the answer.

"I do not." As someone passed, he pulled Nore along to keep walking. When they were fully out of earshot, he said, "Consider talking to your mother. She's been through much of this."

She wasn't going to tell him no to his face. Talking to Isla wasn't just having a conversation with the woman who gave birth to her, it was reliving the heartless pain she caused. Nore nodded and showed Winkel to his seat at the simply set table just as the first course was being served.

Panic ricocheted around in her mind like a bullet. She *did* need to talk to someone about all this. Someone she could trust who was both discreet and wise.

She knew who.

Priest Winkel's words about boldness stuck to Nore's ribs like hunger, no matter how much she ate. After dinner she joined the staff for drinks. It brought a few nervous glances, but by the fourth cup of kiziloxer, the awkwardness faded and a magic-off ensued. At one point there was music. And when she left, she'd managed to get Ainsley to agree to stay longer and take the night off. Nore dragged herself back to her room. Her first day at really being Headmistress was a lot. And she'd actually had fun with the maezres, House secretary, and maids. But was it enough?

When she arrived at her room to get ready for bed, the lights were all out. There was no fire lit. Ice skidded up her spine as she felt her way through the darkness to flip on a lamp. When she reached in the direction of it, it fell. She blinked, and only the moon's light dusting the windows gave her any form in the shapeless darkness.

She crossed the room, stumbling into a chair and something else that moved through her bones like the gust of a winter storm. The toushana in her tremored. She couldn't remember the last time she'd felt the dark magic awaken in her. It was such a small nudge, she wondered if she'd felt twinges of it many times and just ignored it. When the log she was trying to light erupted into flames, the room glowed. She stood and exhaled, then turned.

And came face-to-face with the dead.

Air punched out of her lungs. Dark shadows moved everywhere, slinking along the room. One sat on her bed toying with the cord of the lamp shattered on the ground. Darkness closed around her like a cloud, and it felt like suffocating. Her toushana wriggled in her chest. But she wasn't sure what to do about it. She started at the depthless, faceless shadow hovering before her and cleared her throat, remembering her talk with Winkel. He made it sound like they could understand her, even if they couldn't communicate back.

"Can I help you?"

She felt a nudge at her back pushing her to walk. She followed as the ancestors led her to the window.

Letters wrote themselves on the snow-covered glass.

GROW THE MAGIC

"You want me to grow the toushana inside me?"

The lights in her room flickered.

"Okay." What else could she say? She didn't want to imagine what they would do to her if she didn't. They had *her heart*. "Okay, I will."

The doors to her room flung open, and the darkness departed like a night breeze. She hurried to close them, when Ainsley appeared to tuck her in.

"Headmistress, are you okay? You're pale!"

Nore threw her arms around the maid in a tight hug. She'd never felt more in a cage.

"You're shaking, miss."

"I want it out of me. I want it out of me now!" Her chest heaved. She had to concentrate to slow her breath. She could be the ancestors' pawn, or she could get this magic out of her and find a way to live. She needed the final piece of the Immortality Scroll. The House of Duncan piece, wherever it was. She needed an insurance plan.

She'd fought too hard to have a life that wasn't hers.

She would say what she must to get by. She would play the game of winning Ambrose loyalty, appeasing the ancestors, praying to the gods. But she would plot her escape.

"I need him, Ainsley."

Her maid nodded before rushing off.

When Yagrin appeared at her door, she wanted to run into his arms. But she had to be careful with his heart.

"You've been crying." He rushed toward her.

But she stopped him. "Three things."

"Alright," he said.

"The dead want me to grow the toushana. I need to understand the risks. I need to know everything, the stuff nobody writes down."

He nodded.

"And when you leave this room, I need you to find the last piece of the Immortality Scroll."

"And three?" Yagrin asked.

"No conversation, and you will be gone when my maid arrives in the morning."

The brown in Yagrin's eyes deepened.

"You will spend the night here, with me." It wasn't what she needed. But it was all she could have.

So she would take it.

FORTY-NINE

Yagrin

Yagrin propped up a book at the desk in Nore's room and turned another page. He skimmed for mention of the fall of House Duncan in the lamplight, but there were only scant details, like the dozen other books he'd been reading for hours. He slammed the book closed and gazed over at Nore, who was still sleeping.

Outside the night sky began to brighten. He returned the book to the stack Nore retrieved from the family's private library, buttoned up his coat, and pressed a kiss to Nore's hand, which dangled over the side of the bed, before slipping out the door.

He'd spent the last four nights with her, up late searching after a passionate yet emotionless time together. And he'd had it. She still didn't feel anything for him, from what he could tell, despite her eagerness to keep him in her bed. But hope flickered in his heart, because before drifting to sleep, she'd lie on his chest and ask him to stroke her hair like he used to do. It felt like they were frozen in time, on a never-ending loop. Yagrin had to break them out.

He wasn't sure how much longer he could look into the girl's eyes who he loved and see no love there. Nore was planning to escape, but her plan had no teeth. Telling her that hadn't gone over well. So he did as she asked, night after night, at the desk in her quarters. It was useless. Chasing down the last piece of the Scroll from a House that had been decimated decades ago felt impossible. Finding it wasn't the best way to save her life if it came to that—breaking the Pact was.

That's where I should shift my focus.

He always trusted his gut. He needed to now. But that risked disappointing her, when she'd decided to keep him close and trust him.

He strode fast through the House, which whirred with the sounds of early morning, when an idea struck him. No matter what time it was, the halls of House Ambrose always had students lingering. He took a detour past the dining hall, the grand ballroom, a few smaller specialized libraries, and ascended the stairs toward the Caelum.

When he reached the highest floor, he noticed low-hanging clouds outside hugging the tall windows. His legs ached. But he hustled toward the library's doors. It was the grandest place of books he'd ever seen, with sweeping views, a lounge full of desks, and endless walls of books. Stairs built into the walls zigzagged between shelves. There were gaps every several feet with large plaques engraved with a Priest's name, birth- and death dates. *Burying the dead inside.* He grimaced as he climbed a set of stairs wedged between the history and medicinal sections. The second-floor shelves were more tightly knitted together. Finding a staircase required moving a few chairs. He climbed to the third floor and found that most areas were roped off. A clerk sat typing at a writing desk.

"Clearance?" She held out a hand, still typing with the other, not even looking up at him.

"I, um, am a guest of the Headmistress and am searching for texts on her behalf."

He wasn't sure it would work, but the House staff had been so accommodating thanks to Ainsley vouching for him. The Draguns had even stopped asking him questions. The clerk's head swiveled in his direction. He could go wherever Nore went, it seemed. But the Caelum is where they drew the line.

"Headmistress will need to escort you. This area is restricted."

Creaky stairs groaned in the walls. Yagrin couldn't see where the noise was coming from. This floor was cozy compared to the others, and each of the areas of books was sectioned into rooms. But he'd heard the priests' offices were hidden up here.

"You may go." She went back to typing. Yagrin's irritation thrummed. But when he turned, he spotted a bushy-browed man in long robes, poking his head out of a door. Priest Winkel gestured for him to quietly hurry over, his gaze darting to the clerk, a mischievous smirk on his face. Winkel led him inside, and they tiptoed through adjoining rooms of texts until it dead-ended at a concrete door.

"Nore sent you, I heard you say? For what, may I ask?"

He knew Nore adored Winkel, but he wasn't sure how much to trust him. "She wants to know more about the Immortality Scroll." *And I want to know more about breaking the Pact.*

Winkel twirled his white beard around his finger. "You won't find anything written down. What you need is a true library." He tapped his temple and offered Yagrin a seat. That was the first time he really looked around, taking in the priest's office. He wasn't sure what he imagined it would look like. House of Perl was hardly religious, and they didn't believe in the Sage and the Wielder, nor that they needed a priest to communicate with any god.

But Winkel's office was not just an office; it was a home. This is where the man lived. And where he would die. Yagrin walked the circle of his living room. There were leather seats arced around the fireplace, a velvet armchair beneath a window. And there were a few plants. A hall led to several doors. Yagrin sat down by the fire. He shifted in his seat, the thickness of the cushion supporting his back. It was oddly comfortable and colorful.

Winkel poured them a lavender tea and offered him a pipe, which Yagrin refused. Peckle could temporarily dull the mental faculties. He wanted his head clear.

"You don't ever tire of being stuck up here?" Yagrin asked, leaning on the cushy pillow at his back.

"Privacy is underrated. Constant distraction is an obstacle to the mind and the faith."

Yagrin braided his fingers.

"What really brings you here?"

"The Immortality Scroll."

His eyes glinted, staring at Yagrin's chest. "Your motives are torn."

Yagrin's hands began to sweat. He wiped them on his pants.

"There is no need to be nervous. I am here to help."

"How can you *see* my motives?"

Winkel stood and trailed a finger along a row of spines. When he plucked a book off the shelf, he parted it and handed it to Yagrin.

"The short version is fine. I've had my fill of mind-numbing reading today."

A crater appeared in Winkel's cheek. "I know you're Nore's right arm. That's apparent to everyone except Ginger." He gestured toward his door, where his clerk sat paces away. "So I will speak freely. Do you know *why* magic being in the blood is one of the best and worst things to ever happen to this Order?"

He shook his head.

"Before magic was in the blood, you had to *have* magical Sun Dust to do magic. Ancient scholars wrote harrowing accounts of children being taken hostage to ransom for Dust. Everyone wanted the source of magic. The brightest minds of the time found a way to infuse magic in the blood so that it *reproduces* with DNA in order to be passed down genetically. There was nothing to steal anymore, but—" He sighed. "That is when the real horrors began. It took a few generations, but eventually deadly lines were drawn. All of a sudden there were certain types of magic that were acceptable and others that were not. Families who had a long lineage of having magic were shunned because the magic that showed up in *their genes* was no longer in the acceptable category."

Yagrin knew there were the haves and have-nots.

Winkel tapped his eyelid. "Long ago, there was a seeing magic, achieved by applying Sun Dust to the iris in a precise measurement over a specific amount of time. The magic formed a kind of toushana in the bones. But in the *eyes*, it created *sight*. Because toushana is destructive, it allows the person's sight to *destroy* any deceptions or lies and see through to the truth. Sometimes it turns the eye an icy blue. It is no longer studied, and because it involves toushana, it is banned. You can hardly find books on it." He winked. "Unless you're up here. It's how I know Nore is the best thing that could happen to this House. I'm determined to see her through."

"She doesn't want Headship."

"She doesn't want it as it is now. But deep inside there is a love for the House that shunned her. She has always been forced to prove herself."

"Proving Ambrose is shortsighted, not intellectually superior."

Winkel conceded with a wave of the hand.

"I won't try to convince her to do anything she doesn't want to do, if that's what you're asking."

"I am not asking anything. I am merely trying to help you see more clearly so this conflict in your spirit is settled." He crossed his leg, pausing for a moment before continuing. "I think your challenge, dear boy, is to help her find the freedom to explore what she really wants. Right now she is scared. Being led by fear is a true prison."

Yagrin rocked back on his heels, thinking. As much as he loathed the Order, someone like Nore could transform things for the better. He didn't want to care about the Order. But if he cared about Nore, he had to be willing to support whatever was best for her. Yagrin planted his elbows on his knees, studying the old man.

"Tell me more about the Pact between the Headmistress and the dead." Being so honest made him sick to his stomach, but he held the bobbing feeling in his throat as Winkel pondered.

"One of the House family's best-kept secrets. Not even the brightest minds downstairs know about the Pact." He left the living area, beckoning Yagrin to follow, and walked through a simple kitchen into a praying room. There were kneelers by the windows and candles burning next to an open tome.

"This is one of my favorite Unmarked books." Winkel flipped a few pages and then stopped where there was a picture of a man wrestling a beast that was three times his size at least. Yagrin followed the story from illustration to illustration, turning the page. The final picture showed the man standing over the slain beast. "How'd he beat him?"

"Impossible. He couldn't without a weapon or some kind of magic."

"Who knows how big the beast actually was? Who knows how small the man was? Only the author and artist. Look deeper. What do you see?"

The man was covered in blood, bits of his flesh hanging from his skin. A feral look burned in his eyes. "A desperate will to survive."

"The ancestors are like anyone else." Winkel gave him the book. Yagrin pondered. They just wanted to live as long as they could. In a half-human form, if they must. He hadn't considered how human their interests were. He was about to leave, but remembered his promise to Nore.

"Do you have any idea where the Duncan piece of the Scroll could be? Nore wants it." Now that the well of trust had been opened, Yagrin couldn't stop himself.

"Mmm. I imagine she would. Your own relationship with members of the Duncan family might be more illuminating. After all, you are a Dragun."

He shrugged in confusion. Then it hit him.

Shelby Duncan.

A débutante at House of Marionne when Quell was there. She died gruesomely, turned to dust. The scandalous murder was pinned on Darragh Marionne because it took place on her property. It wasn't true. Jordan told him a ruthless House of Perl Dragun named Felix had killed Shelby.

"It's time for my prayers," Winkel said, ushering him to the door. "But let's do this again sometime. If only to get under Ginger's skin."

Yagrin's mouth bowed unnaturally. This man was helpful. And kind.

"Thank you for your service." Winkel shook his hand.

Yagrin blinked. "Uh, sure. You're welcome." As a Dragun, Yagrin had never felt like he was serving anything other than his aunt's greedy motives. This felt different. This felt good.

"How did you—" Ginger started as he passed, leaving the upper floors.

But he hurried down the stairs.

If he could come up with a way to appeal to the dead's humanity and break the Pact, nothing else mattered. Everything in him wanted to throw away this needle-in-a-haystack search for the Scroll and focus on the Pact. But Nore would be devastated that he ignored a direct favor she asked.

If Winkel was right, maybe he could give finding the Scroll one last shot. He could find Shelby Duncan's family and bring them a priceless gift in exchange for a meeting with whoever was in charge of the House family. When he arrived at his room, there was a sealed letter on his desk in his brother's handwriting.

We need to speak. Urgently.
Tell me where.
—J

Yagrin picked up a pen to reply, then froze. Things had changed so much since he and his brother struck a deal to part ways with the same goal in mind: find the Scroll to save Quell. His brother would be furious. They should talk in person.

Jordan knew Felix better. Maybe he had ideas about a way to loosen Duncan's family's tongue. It took him a few hours, but he found and dug through past issues of *Debs Daily* to the one announcing Shelby's murder. Darragh Marionne was alluded to as the prime suspect because Shelby was killed in the forest behind her estate. He skimmed the paragraph until he found a mention of Shelby's father's name before dropping two messages in an Ambrose outbox.

FIFTY

Jordan

My side hurts. More than it has in a long time.

I sit myself up on the blackened floorboards in this abandoned house, wondering how long I've been unconscious. Cuts and scrapes cover my arms. I dig the salve out of my pocket, squeeze the last little bit there is on my skin, and rub it in. I stand, surveying what's left of the two-story home I found in the woods a few miles from Chateau Soleil.

The home I just destroyed.

From the outside, the blue Colonial looked like something on a postcard. Now it looks like someone took a torch to the siding. South of House of Marionne's property, through the forest I already leveled, is an overgrown trail to a small neighborhood of eleven houses on a cul-de-sac. At first, I panicked. The thin forest around Chateau Soleil meant this hideaway could overhear things happening at House of Marionne. But I snuck around the cul-de-sac, peering into the homes one evening.

And they are all empty.

Deserted.

The first time I entered one of the houses, I was looking for a place to spew the darkness, something to burn. I long to hold Quell, to be near her, to give her the comfort she looks to me for. If satiating my magic for an evening could allow me to lie with her for an hour, I will feed it all night long, *for days on end*, until my bones ache and I can't feel the hum of cold in me at all anymore. I'm not sure it will work, so I hesitate to tell her what I've been doing and risk disappointment. But we'll know soon enough.

It's been four days of this. My hands aren't even the same color anymore.

First thing each day, before coming here, I check on Ube and Erla's progress with extraction practice. This morning Yani was helping them since she's skilled at calling on toushana. I allowed it, but plan to check back in on things.

The worst part of satiating this dark magic in me is it forces me to relive my worst memories over and over in my head. At a point, the world goes black with rage, and I can't hold back. Then I wake surrounded by carnage. The next day I do it all over again.

It's like getting control of toushana means giving up control of everything else.

The door of the house I destroyed today is jammed, half the structure collapsing in on itself. It took all night to meticulously decompose the living room and kitchen inch by inch. I made sure to be thorough, to feed the darkness *as much* as I could. The rest of the house will be short work tomorrow.

But the more I feed it, the hungrier it gets.

I ram the front door with my fist to shove it open. Early-morning air hits me in the face. Across the street is my work from the last three days—a heap of rotted houses. Sometimes I picture Beaulah inside one of the houses, being swept into the rot as it spreads from my fingers. It makes me smile. I am wretched to be delighted by such a thing.

I jog the trail back toward the Chateau. Still no reply from Yagrin. The day to meet with Ellery already came and went. I didn't bother replying. Quell is right. He is desperate.

When I reach the southernmost wall of the estate, I pull myself up and over it, using the rose vines as leverage, smoothing a bit of toushana across them to thicken their stems. The Chateau is a dot in the distance. I race toward it, follow the broom closet back inside, and slip down the halls to the Healer office. But Abby's door is back on its hinges and locked. The lights are off. My hands ache. My side, too. I detour to Sunrise Corridor to check on Ube and Erla in the lab. Abby can't have gone far for long.

The siblings are in the session room, bickering. Between them is a large boulder on a table. Erla is wearing an oversized T-shirt. No frills on her wrists or ears, as if she woke and came immediately here. Ube jabs fingers at her, yelling to make his point.

"I *don't* like it," Erla taps her foot. "It's *not* smart." She sucks in a breath when she sees me.

"What is it?"

Her brother clears his throat. "We have some disagreement about amending the procedure. She thinks the rock size is going to be a problem."

Her foot taps faster.

"But the larger the item absorbing the magic, the quicker the rate at which we can siphon magic into it."

"I need a break." Erla storms toward the exit.

I step into her path. "Show me. Run a trial right now."

"Am I late?" Yani strolls past me, brushing my shoulder as she enters the room.

Ube fidgets, rolling the large rock to the center of the table. "Yaniselle, stream some toushana to the boulder when I say." He grabs a tool with jagged teeth. He sets it on the rock. "Now."

Erla crosses the room, far from us, watching with her arms folded across her chest.

The claw clamps down on the rock, snapping it in half. Black streams from Yani's fingers to the metal contraption, sliding along its razored teeth and inside gashes in the rock. Black spreads like an ink stain over its surface.

"More," I tell Yani.

The rock cracks once. Then it explodes.

Yani's toushana gushes as stone flies in every direction. Erla squeals. Ube groans. Cold slithers over my spine.

Useless.

Waste of space.

I shake my head, trying to mute the whispers. But toushana fills my fists.

"This is all you have to show for *three* days of running this process?" I say. "There's no time for mistakes like this!"

Ube stares at the floor. Erla's chest rises and falls like a hummingbird's wings. Yani glances between them, holding a scratch on her arm.

"Did you know this would happen?" I ask Erla.

Ube glares at her.

"I strongly suspected it."

"Start listening to her. *Run it again.*"

"A vessel more compositionally similar to the object we are putting the toushana in would be better. Have you come up with something that we can use?"

Excuses.

Choke him.

It hasn't felt right to ask Quell for a keepsake from here that could be hunted or eventually destroyed when she is still grappling with how she feels about this place. "You were supposed to tell me if there is anything else more easily procured that we could use. A gem perhaps. Gems absorb magic." Like the cave in Aronya we nearly depleted of resources.

"There is nothing I can think of," he says.

"The next time we run this procedure, I will use *you,* Ube, instead of a rock! Stay here all night if you must."

He doesn't move. "Uh, we were going to finish up early for dinner with the Headmistress tonight."

Quell's dinner. I'd almost forgotten. "Plan to eat quickly."

A rap on the doorframe fractures the tension. The magic bleeding from my hands siphons back inside.

"Jordan?" It's Abby. She eyes the mess warily. "Do you have a moment?" When we leave the room, it takes a few paces before the anger burning through me at them subsides. When we reach the stairs, she pulls me aside.

"I was wrong." She struggles to meet my eyes. "You're planning to extract the toushana inside you because if it stays inside you, it'll kill you eventually. But . . ."

She tucks her lip, hesitant to go on.

"Tell me."

"It won't work. It's too much. The Sphere's toushana is so strong and already partly bonded to you that it *can't* be removed without killing you. This procedure you're planning will be the death of you. Jordan, either way, you—"

"Die."

WE'RE FIRST TO arrive. I enter the dining room with Quell on my arm, and it makes my pulse race. I am dead, no matter what.

"Are you alright?" Her palm rests on her chest.

"I'm fine. Do you know if any letters have come for me?"

"I haven't seen any."

Quell hugs tighter on my arm, which only makes my heart rattle faster. I remind myself where I spent last night. It should be safe to be near each other for a couple of hours of dinner.

"Did you hear about the brawl in the Elixir session yesterday?" she asks.

"An actual *fight*?"

The doors open again, and our guests enter, greeting us as they pass.

"Two are unconscious in the Healer office. One of Zecky's mixed an elixir and tossed it in Dimara's eyes, who of course went feral, attacking them back," she says through a plastic smile. "If you weren't so busy with Ube and Erla, you'd know."

There is no pleasing these people. They are here, have access to magic, work a few hours a day, but otherwise can do whatever they want as long as they don't leave. The ingratitude is grating. "Can't Willam and Knox help Dexler make sure their people are under control?"

"*Our* people."

Now isn't the time to tell her that my feelings on roping in *all* safe house people into a new Order haven't budged. It's not prudent. Once all the guests have arrived, I lead us to the dining table set with a four-course meal. Ube, Erla, and Yani are already seated. Yani wears a black dress ribbed with red detail. Erla has thrown a suit jacket over her T-shirt with a pair of slacks. Ube wears a tailored tux as fine as the one I'm wearing, with a watch on his arm that's blindingly glitzy. Their discussion promptly stops when I pull out Quell's seat and take mine. Erla watches Yani with a perplexing expression somewhere between curiosity and annoyance. Yani sits back in her chair staring daggers across the room at Erla, who I realize is wearing little to no jewelry. Ube straightens his silverware, ignoring both of them.

As appetizers are passed around, no one speaks.

"How has your research been, Ube?" Quell asks as the olives and spiced nuts from the aperitif are cleaned up. His eyes dart to me. I lean closer to Quell, our arms brushing.

"We have to secure something for the magic to go into," I say. "Ube, why don't you tell her your bright idea?"

"I thought you may have some kind of ancient relic here in this grand House we could use."

He just wants to snoop. Why? Quell's face scrunches, and she shifts in her seat. Maybe now she understands my skepticism about Ube. I won't *give* power to people with questionable motives.

"I'm not sure about that." Quell rubs the heel of her hand back and forth on her legs.

Yani doesn't look up when she speaks. "You don't have to explain yourself to him."

I set my fork down beside my plate, and after chewing my gristly meat, I break the rigid silence again. "How did the afternoon extraction trials go?" I shove around the food on my plate, with eyes only for Ube.

He slides a shaky knife along his meat and takes a bite before answering, which grates my nerves, stirring my toushana.

"We need to run it a few more times."

I almost force Ube to tell Quell how terrible this morning went but decide it's better she isn't worried about the extraction procedure.

"How do you think it's going, Erla?" Quell asks.

"We will be working through the night." She sets a bite of cantaloupe and smoked meat into her mouth. "I am optimistic." She turns to her brother. "Did you try calibrating the last stone *before* infusing it?"

"What, do you think I'm inept?" He stabs his food and shoves another bite in his mouth.

Erla is the conundrum. Her quietness feels more calculating than timid. By the time the third course has been laid out, my second hasn't been touched. The tension at the table is more pungent than the rind cheese on my plate.

"May I take this, sir?" a servant asks before whisking the plate away, and the third course is set down before me: a salad with greens, beets, and more cheese.

"Yani, you are quiet. Ube says you've been a good help to their team."

She bats her long, dark lashes at me. "I'm glad. They seem to need all the help they can get."

"We have things under control," Ube says.

Erla slips a bite of food into her mouth.

"They're going to cut each other's throats out," Quell whispers. "You are working through the night, then, too?" she asks Ube.

"Even if there is a stone we can use, there is no guarantee they are findable in the quantity and precise density we need."

Yani plays with her napkin instead of eating. "That's funny," she says. "Isn't it, Erla?"

Erla stills, her grip frozen on her fork. "I have been busy with density analysis. As I told you earlier, whatever your issues are with my brother, leave me out of it."

"Tell them what you told me earlier, Yani," Ube snaps.

She flinches. A look of guilt I know well.

"I think a more interesting topic of conversation would be why you told your sister Triveyna has the stones we need. You've even mapped the route and location."

"Triveyna?" Quell squeezes my arm beneath the table. This was a battle of who would out who first, and Yani's decided to take the first strike.

"It's one of the Order's mining caves, like Aronya," I tell Quell.

Ube dabs his mouth with a napkin before pulling out a sketched map from a satchel beneath his chair. "This is a map to assess the area, not to pinpoint travel. I wanted to be sure a trip to Triveyna was needed before mentioning it. I assume we have time constraints."

"Liar." Yani slams her fork down on her plate. "Erla, tell the truth."

"Erla," I press. "If you know something . . ."

"My brother did mention the stones could be in Triveyna. But I didn't know anything about him planning to go there."

"Because I wasn't *planning* anything." His words bite. His sister sighs and pushes her plate aside.

"Jordan, look at me," Yani demands. "You know I'm not lying. Ube is the liar at the table."

"She makes a fair point," I say. "It doesn't look good, Ube."

Quell stands. "This dinner is over. See yourselves back to your room. I will talk to Jordan privately and then discuss with each of you what's next. Am I understood?"

They all nod. Except Yani.

Toushana flutters under my skin, skimming my fingertips before disappearing back inside. Quell tosses the napkin on the table and storms out. Behind her is Ube. Erla starts to speak, but when she spots Yani, who hasn't moved from her seat, she leaves.

Yani exhales. "I'm so glad that's over."

"You were told to leave by the Headmistress of the House."

She gets up, pushing in her chair. "You need those stones from Triveyna, it sounds like. I don't know what he's up to. Send me to Triveyna to get them."

If I send anyone anywhere, it would be to find Lady Ruby. She is the real hope. I study Ube's map, which he left on the table. It doesn't have travel coordinates or notes about cloaking restrictions. It looks like more of a visual scope of the area, as he said.

"You can't leave to get the stones," she says. "This place will buckle at the seams. They don't like you. They dislike her less, but they despise you most of all. She's too soft."

"Quell?"

"Don't deny it. You're fire, and she's . . . lukewarm water."

Insubordinate.

She's never truly respected you.

Or the girl you love.

I won't listen to insults about Quell. I excuse myself, pausing at the door.

"*If* I need the stones, I'll consider sending you, as long as Quell likes the idea." It's still too early to tell. But if someone *has* to retrieve an item, Yani makes the most sense. She's so eager to prove she can be trusted. That's more than I can say about Ube.

She blocks the door. "Thank you for listening to me at dinner." She plays with the collar of my shirt. Then she fingers the top button and leans into my mouth, inches from my lips.

"I can be as quiet as a mouse," she whispers.

Protect Quell. At any cost.

Cold hardens in my chest.

I grab her in the Dragun choke, gently but firm enough to get her attention. Shadows seep from my body, swallowing the floor. "You are loyal to Quell above all else. Any hint of betrayal from you, and—" I squeeze, then release her and leave.

When I reach my room, there is a letter from my brother waiting for me, full of questions about how to get House of Duncan talking and an address of where to meet him. I check the time. I need to tell Quell I'll be away another night.

FIFTY-ONE

Nore

Nore strode the halls of Dlaminaugh, checking on the state of things, hoping her audacity was working in her favor. She needed everyone convinced she was *into* this Headmistress gig. A dozen dead trailed behind her. They were with her every time she left her room now, and they became belligerent if she didn't have some kind of toushana study material on hand.

Before Yagrin left to meet Titus Duncan, he gave her a pile of books. She didn't need magic. She never had. She never would. It irked her to pretend that she did.

She held two tomes tight to her side as she headed toward the Hall of Discovery. The corridors were full of débutants between sessions. Truly, she had only cracked one of the books open. She spent her late nights in her room reading up on Pact law, waiting for Yagrin to return from his trip.

She turned the next corner, and the shadows closed in around her so tightly, her bones turned cold. "I can't think with you breathing down my neck, some space *please*."

The fog of the dead around her thickened.

She'd spent the entire time of Yagrin's absence being as present as possible on the grounds, meeting the students, socializing with the staff. The numbers of Electus and Primus were thinning every day, and if they were switching to her brother's side of things, that didn't bode well. Secundus were nearly done with induction, preparing for Third Rite Cotillion. So the weighty decision of unenrolling wasn't a popular one. If she did need her House's help to fend off her brother, at least she would be surrounded by the best. She wasn't sure where Ellery was. Or what his next attack would look like. His growing numbers wasn't a good sign.

She strode faster, popping into the specialty wings, trying to be warm and supportive to the students. Each room was filled to the brim with débutants folded over books, as if the only answer to righting the upside-down world was the intellect of an Ambroser. Débutants watched her, some with curious stares, others stoic. She noticed someone in a simple silver mask had a riband in a smoky orange hue across her chest, instead of the previously mandatory gray. The girl blushed, and Nore winked.

When she reached the Hall of Discovery, with its new bright blue wall—her other subtle attempt at boldness—she stopped. Someone had set up lounge furniture, study tables, and fresh flowers. The area was teeming with chatter over some new discovery in enhancer stone labs.

They *liked* the color.

When she reached her office, the dead did not enter, hovering near the door, and she let out the tiniest exhale. Her desk was piled with a fresh stack of letters from complaining families about the new dress policies, allowing for fabrics in House colors, and rumors that painted walls would be added to the dormitory wings soon. She pushed the envelopes aside and searched her desk for any word from Yagrin. It was supposed to be a quick overnight trip. But it had been two days, and the lack of updates on his progress made her want to scratch her eyes out. Had he run into Ellery? She sat back in her chair before realizing the time. She exited her office, but the dead formed a wall in her doorway.

Her nails dug into the spines of the stack as she grabbed them from her desk. "I have them, alright!" She hated being a puppet, living a life that wasn't hers. "How am I supposed to study if you never give me space to focus?"

The shadows swarmed around her before disappearing. She blew out a breath and marched faster to her room, thankful they listened to her that once. The doors to her bedroom were slightly ajar. She set the books down, a smile biting her lips. *Is Yagrin back?*

"Hello?" She scanned for his things but didn't see them. She heard commotion and running bathwater in the bathroom. "Yags?" But all feeling drained from her when she noticed his shoes weren't in their usual spot, and his coat wasn't hanging in the wardrobe. "Who's there? *Identify yourself!*"

The running water in the bathroom stopped.

She waited for an answer. None came. Nore's pulse thudded as she ripped a lamp from the wall and white-knuckled its post, anchoring it over her shoulder. She padded to the door. Tiny bumps raced up her arms as she eased the bathroom door open with her shoulder and found Ainsley shifting together a broken handle of a brush.

"Oh, there you are!" she said. "I was beginning to worry."

Nore sagged against the door in relief.

"I didn't mean to scare you!"

Nore slowed her breath. She didn't need *anyone* sneaking up on her. "Please be sure to close the door. Has Vincent been dismissed yet?"

"Tomorrow, Headmistress."

"Good." She folded her arms, wondering if he thought she was a monster. If it would lead him to sympathizing with her brother. Everyone had the impression her mother was *awful*. And they were right. But Isla couldn't care less what people thought of her. There was something to that. She leaned on the doorframe, waiting for Ainsley to finish.

"Did my mother receive her suitor selection better than I did?"

"You'd have to ask my mother. But you made history with your response." Ainsley nudged her with a playful elbow. "In a good way, many whisper."

That made her feel a bit better. Nore tried to picture her stern mother's face when her surprise guest arrived at her door. *At least she'd known.* A question ran through her mind. A question that had run through her mind a few times as a child. One she never asked. It made her gut quiver. She shifted on her feet to fend off the feeling. But as Ainsley rambled, the question chipped at Nore's mind like an ice pick until it tumbled out of her mouth.

"Was he my father?" Nore asked. It took her mother so long to conceive. She could have had a dozen lovers by then. Unless she had a reason to keep the original around for all those years? But that would mean her mother was fond of him. That would mean she'd made peace with what they could have. *Maybe it got easier?*

"I am not sure, ma'am."

"What *do you* know about my father? Anything?"

"Just that he was a student here. An Ambroser."

As Ainsley finished her cleaning, Nore forgot about House duties, the tall stacks of mail she should probably go through. Instead, she took a long bath, had a cookie for dinner, and opened the windows to let some of the icy night air in. The entire time her mother was on her mind. She was the only person who knew, to some degree, what Nore was dealing with. Could she trust her? Should she?

But pondering her mother's time as Headmistress only drove her curiosity about her father. And what that could mean for her and Yagrin. Once Ainsley was gone for the night, Nore thumbed through the books on her bookshelf. The ones that were private property of the House stayed in the Headmistress's quarters. She pulled a thick leather one: the Book of Names for her House, a registry of each person who had entered induction at House of Ambrose since its inception. She flipped through to find the year her mother was coronated. There were seventy-three débutants at the estate that year. She ran her finger down the columns of names. But they were all meaningless to her.

She had an idea. She pulled her mother's coronation ceremony invitation from a keepsake file of stationery, and in fine print at the bottom was a name, like there had been on hers. She didn't know what to make of the name at the bottom of her invitation at the time. She assumed it was some participant in the ceremony or something. *Commended: Vincent Malarky*, hers read. She held her mother's invitation to the lamplight. Her hand trembled.

Commended: Kendall Dorset

She pulled the Book of Names, the induction registry, back onto her lap and flipped, unsure why her hands were slick and what exactly made her want to know so badly. But there was no record of anyone named Kendall or Ken at all. Even with a different last name. She chewed her nail. *Cotillion.* She added a dozen more books to the growing pile on the floor. Maybe there was an oversight with his registry and somehow he wasn't in the Book of Names. But there would be a record of Kendall's Cotillion, unless he dropped out. In which case she could check the Hall of Shame in the courtyard, with the names of every person who tried to make it in their House but couldn't.

But Nore flipped through Cotillion announcements until the sun began to rise, and there was no mention of anyone with the name Kendall. There was no indication he ever inducted or finished at the House. She tossed the book aside. She hugged her knees.

Kendall Dorset, possibly her father, was a ghost.

She'd never wanted to talk to her mother more.

NORE'S MOTHER JUMPED at the breakfast invitation. As Isla made her way to their meeting, Nore still held the note Priest Winkel had dropped in the seam of her door that morning.

Such a regal shade of blue.
Proudly,
—W

Nore refolded the note, trying to settle her nerves. With Yagrin gone they were more on edge than usual. A third day passed, and still no word from him.

Talking to her mother was the most nauseating idea she'd ever had, but she couldn't stop thinking about the fact that her mother's suitor selection was untraceable. With her House hemorrhaging people and Ellery determined to get rid of her, she needed all the wisdom she could get. Even if it came from a person she only knew how to hate.

Her mother was already seated in the breakfast room. The head seat of the long family table was empty. Nore gulped, realizing the last time she was in this room, she sat where her mother was sitting, and the chair the servant just pulled out for her is where Isla had sat.

"Good morning," Nore said, smoothing her linen dress.

"I was *so* glad to get your note this morning."

She'd almost chickened out of the idea before bed. But after a solid night's rest she still woke up with the burning feeling that needed her mother's insight. And she sort of *wanted it*, too. The elusive identity of her mother's selected suitor was just the bait for her conscience. In truth, she'd wanted to ask this woman questions for years. This was her chance.

Nore sat. Her mother passed her a tray of thinly sliced meats. She took a few to be polite. But her stomach was swimming. She shouldn't accost her mother with questions. She couldn't be rude. That wouldn't go anywhere. But she also would not pretend everything between them was fine.

"So how have you been settling in?" Isla asked.

"I hate it." She bit her lip. She hadn't meant to be that truthful.

"I hated this place for *months* after coronation, too."

Nore slid a piece of fruit into her mouth. "Did you?"

"Very much. I hated what it did to me."

Nore's gaze hit her lap. "I wasn't prepared for this role."

"Blame me for that."

"I do," she spat, able to meet her mother's gaze again. The servers in the room stared at one another. Isla nodded with a somber glisten in her eyes. Nore stuffed her hands between her knees, kneading them together as if that would settle her nerves. That's when she noticed something odd about her mother's dress sleeves. Where the frayed edges would normally spray across her delicate wrists, they'd been hemmed neatly and lined with blue velvet ribbon.

"What are you wearing?"

Her mother stood and turned in a circle, showing off the adjustments to her gown. The gray of her corset was threaded with the same blue as her sleeves, forming intricate patterns along the ribs of the gown. Nore was speechless as her mother sat back down.

"Just following the rules," her mother said, bringing a teacup to her mouth. "I've always loved blue."

"Your favorite color is gray, I thought."

"I'm sure you did."

Nore studied the woman she'd sat across from for so many years. Did she know her at all? She sliced a pear before sliding it in her mouth.

"I would love to help you learn your new role," her mother said, pushing her muffin aside. "It is a lot at times."

They shared a laugh. Nore released her iron grip on the edge of her seat. "Thank you for meeting with me."

"I'm grateful you even considered it. Though I am curious what brought this on."

"I think it's obvious."

"The boy has been sent away is my understanding."

Nore pushed around the food on her plate, itching to dive into what she wanted to know. "Did you send yours away too?"

Her mother's face flushed, and Nore had her answer.

"So you went along with it?"

"It made sense. I wanted an astute heir." Her mother smiled. "I was also expecting his arrival, so it wasn't as alarming. But most of all, I hoped it would please my mother. I spent a lot of my life doing things I thought would please others."

"I can't relate."

Her mother crossed her legs. "What questions do you have? I'm an open book."

"Clear the room," Nore ordered, and the servants exited, shutting the doors tightly. "Everything. Ellery's plans. He's winning Ambrosers' loyalty somehow. And the dead want me to *grow* this poison in me."

Her mother clutched her chest.

"Families are furious. Pizor and Kimper are not very helpful. And then there's the Scroll."

"The Immortality Scroll?"

"Yes, we've found most of—"

"Leave that alone. You're chasing a dead end."

"That's what everyone says. It's impossible. But I'm stubborn, remember?"

Her mother sighed. "You don't even begin to understand what you're up against with the Scroll. And Kimper takes a certain finesse. I can help you win her over. Pizor cannot be won over. He thinks what he thinks, but he usually won't dissent on a vote with Kimper. Your brother—I don't know where to start with him. There is so much I should tell you. I'm not sure this is the venue. Nor is it the place to discuss that thing you've been asked to grow. Word of that spreading would risk more than just unseating you. People would demand a public death. House rules for betrayal."

Nore's head throbbed. Would Ellery tell them? Without proof, it was no more than a rumor. And Ambrosers usually demanded their intellectual curiosity be fully satisfied.

"Despite what you think, your brother loves you. He thinks he is doing what's best for you. He is wrong."

"I don't know if I agree with that." Nore's eyes burned with tears, and the suddenness of it unsteadied her. She grabbed another slice of toast and buttered it quickly. She'd loved her brother and wanted to believe he loved her. He was her only friend in the entire world for so long. The truth was a sharp pain in the place where her heart used to live. His betrayal cut her too deep to ever heal.

"How are things going with your inner council and the rumors of the Sphere?" Isla asked.

"We haven't discussed it."

"Nore, it's your duty to usher the House's future. That requires planning. The world is on fire. The Sphere was drained of magic *on these grounds* just months ago."

"I'm more aware of what happened with the Sphere than you realize." Nore tensed at the strain returning to her voice.

"What does that mean? Does this have to do with that Wexton boy you're keeping around?"

Nore wasn't ready to tell her mother about Yagrin, Jordan, and Quell and all their plans. "It didn't mean anything."

"Oh, come on." Her mother's silverware hit her plate. "How can I help if you keep me in the dark?"

"I am not going to fight with you."

"Then let me help you."

"I will. My way." Nore released her grip on the fork tight in her fist. They ate for several minutes in silence. She wasn't prepared to be Headmistress, but she certainly wasn't prepared for all her mother was looking for—a relationship. But she needed to understand things only her mother could show her. It was smart to allow her mother to assist. She pushed back her chair and grabbed her napkin. "Meet me in my office each morning at the top of the day."

"And how about a check-in later in the day to see if there's anything that's come up that shouldn't wait until morning?"

Nore felt the push like a squeeze on her ribs, a hug she didn't want.

"I could join you for dinner, perhaps? Here. So it's more casual."

"Sure." Nore dabbed her mouth. "Mornings and dinners. Starting tomorrow."

"Excellent." Her mother slid her chair back as well, wiping her hands.

"One more thing. Kendall Dorset. The man sent to you on coronation night."

Her mother didn't move. "What about him?"

So that *was* his name. Not an alias. "Why is his name not in the Book of Names? Nor is there any record of him finishing Third Rite."

Her mother left her chair and joined her at the head of the table. She moved a rogue tendril out of her face. "Some doors are better left shut," she said. "See you tomorrow." She turned to go.

"I am your House Headmistress. You will answer me truthfully."

Her mother stopped.

"Is Kendall Dorset my father?"

She swallowed. "Yes. May I go?"

"Did you erase his name from the Book of Names?"

Confusion drew her brows together. "*No.* How could I?"

"Maybe you called in a favor with Darragh Marionne."

"Nore, I did no such thing. He did not finish. There is no Cotillion record. May I please go?"

It wasn't enough. But they'd made progress, and that felt more important than anything.

"Sure." When Nore left the dining hall, her mother's words still irked her. So she walked to the courtyard where the Hall of Shame plaque was on the facade of the building. There were hundreds of names of people who'd started at their House but dropped out, all alphabetized.

Kendall's name wasn't there either.

FIFTY-TWO

Quell

I'm halfway to the stairs, with that sham of a dinner with Ube, Erla, and Yani still ringing in my head, when I spot Erla storming away from a conversation with her brother. I wait until he stomps off toward the dorm halls and follow her.

She is crying.

"Erla?"

She tries to curtsy.

"Please don't. There's no need for that."

She dabs the tears from her tired eyes. "My apologies. I'm fine."

"You don't need to apologize for being upset." The shirt beneath her jacket is stained. I realize she isn't wearing any jewelry on her ears or wrists. She's never looked more haggard. "What is going on between you and Ube? Are you okay?"

She opens her mouth but closes it several times. There is a lounge down the hall, but there are people in there.

"Come on." I lead us to a storage closet a few doors down from Dexler's office. Once we're inside, I try again.

"What is it?"

Erla pulls at her clothes. "I am not comfortable with dishonesty. And so as much as I would like to answer your question, it would make me feel pressured to lie to my brother about this conversation. Silence, I find, is the best option."

"I can't help you if you won't talk to me."

"I never asked for help. Please, may I go?"

I don't know what to say. Something is very wrong, and I suspect I've misjudged Ube. She leaves, and when I exit the supply closet, Dexler is there.

"Is there something that needs cleaning, Headmistress?" She is holding a letter. The handwriting on the envelope is familiar.

"Uh, no, I've handled it." I reach for the envelope, studying the handwriting, which looks like the same writing on the envelope Jordan got days ago. "Didn't we get something from him the other day?"

"That's what I thought." She looks down her nose through her glasses. "This one is for you, not Mr. Wexton."

"Thank you." I leave her there and rip it open with my heart thundering. Why is Ellery Ambrose writing to *me*?

Your lover stood me up. Perhaps you're the wiser in the duo.
Wednesday at dusk. Monument Park.
Unless you're content breaking up fights between safe house junkies,
hoping one of them is smart enough to save you.

I grow cold all over. The devil's in the walls. Ellery has some kind of spy here? I race to my room, and to my relief Jordan is there.

"Quell." He greets me with open arms, and I bury myself in them without thinking. He rests his chin on my head, and the world quiets for a much-needed moment. If the Dragunhead has someone *inside* our walls, what use are my defenses? I can't breathe. I press my face harder against his chest, feeling his heart thud against me. Savoring the life that pumps through him and my magic.

I will save this man. I will save him and myself. Whatever it takes, I will have the future I want. One that is *mine*. I won't choose between love and freedom. I will have both.

"We should start small." He peels me out of the hug after a few precious minutes.

"I don't understand."

He plants the tenderest kiss on my forehead before establishing space again between us. "Soon you will." When he pulls his warmth away from me, part of me feels chipped away. He gestures at the letter. "What is this?"

I hand it over and fall into a seat at the foot of my bed.

His silence sends bumps racing up my arms.

"I assumed the Dragunhead hadn't shown up yet because he was worried about getting past the walls. But he's been working from the inside out."

Jordan's expression is stone, but the way anger burns in him makes my heart tremble. He stares into the fire in my room as if there is a truth in the flames.

"Jordan, say something. Please."

He crumples the paper, and I expect him to toss it in the fire. But he destroys it himself, turning it to ash in his fingers. The darkness follows him as he paces, like a train of death, blackening the ground beneath his steps. His burning rage beats in my chest.

It's Yani, I want to say. But jealousy is insidious. Could that be clouding my judgment? Does Ube make more sense?

"Lock everyone in their rooms." His glare doesn't leave the fire. The shadows have swarmed so thick he is a floating body levitating on darkness. "Meals will be brought to them. Dexler will escort anyone helping with the extraction to the lab for ten-hour shifts. She stays with them the entire time. No breaks. No clothes with pockets."

"Jordan."

"I am not asking."

"They are *actual* prisoners if you do this."

"So be it. Someone is feeding information to the person who wants to kill us."

"But punishing all of them for the betrayal of one . . ."

Jordan's gaze finally leaves the fire. His shadows retreat as he suffocates the distance between us. His hand runs tenderly along the bridge of my nose. Then he traces the rise of my cheeks and the slope of my jaw. He caresses my neck, then his fingers dance across my collarbone, before he slides his hands down my arms and laces his fingers between mine. He brings our bodies together. My heart skitters when his mouth moves to my ear.

"If anyone attempts to hurt you, I will do far worse than lock them up."

Breath sticks in my chest. I don't know what to say, and yet I have so many questions. How is he comfortable with us so close?

"I have to leave tonight to meet my brother. Do as I've said."

"Jordan." This feels wrong.

"Quell, do as I've said."

I nod. Then my heart knocks into my ribs. "The ball," I mutter. "Dexler planned it for tomorrow night. I have an idea."

"That's too much of a risk until we know who the rat is."

"No, the ball is our chance to draw the rat out of the shadows." I squeeze his arm. "Trust me on this."

"Only if I'm back in time. Otherwise, not a foot in the hallways unless it is yours or Dexler's. Not even Knox and Willam." He peels his arm away from me and hurries out the door.

FIFTY-THREE

Yagrin

Yagrin double-checked the address on the note in his pocket as he neared the downtown San Diego Tavern. The Duncan family had been invisible since their House was destroyed decades ago. He promised information about Shelby's death and just hoped it was enough to get Titus Duncan to show. He didn't know another soul in the Duncan family. This guy was his only chance to get the Scroll.

Yagrin took off his thick wool socks and heavy coat and shoved them into a dumpster before stepping through a trick wall between condominium high-rises. He unbuttoned the top button of his shirt and rolled his sleeves as he followed the long corridor up several flights of stairs. He reshouldered the strap of his bag, which was digging into him. When he reached the top floor, a cloud of chatter greeted him.

This Tavern was like any other but with palms and lots of open air. Empty gambling tables overlooked soaring views of the harbor. Drink and peckle trays on tables were untouched. *It is still early.* He didn't see his brother. He'd told him to meet him here. Facing Titus together would be more convincing.

Head down, he walked straight to the bar and set his bag on the ground between his feet. Copper and something worse stung his nose. He tugged at the zippers on the duffel before turning in his seat to scan the place. Titus Duncan was a behemoth of a man in both attitude and stature, he'd heard. Notorious for his boisterous, booming voice and heavy hands. Yagrin counted twelve people. None of them Titus Duncan. All of them Traders.

"What are you drinking?" the barkeep asked.

Something was off. This was where Titus's note said to meet. Yagrin pulled his coin from his pocket and turned it in his hand, clearly enough to ensure the bartender got a glimpse of its face but discreetly enough to make sure no one else saw. The bartender rang out a towel, throwing a glance over his shoulder toward a door behind the bar. Yagrin hesitated, checking the Tavern entrance once again before reluctantly following the bartender to a back room, where a dark-haired fellow sat with his meaty arms folded across his chest.

"It's about time you showed." Titus rose from his seat, towering over Yagrin, and clapped him on the back with an iron slap. Yagrin swallowed, hoping his plan would work. Because he couldn't overpower this guy with his shoddy magic. Not by himself, if it came to blows.

Yagrin set his bag on the table, and it landed with a thud.

"Look at you. Brother to the keeper of the world."

Yagrin leaned across the table. "What?"

"Your brother stole the Sphere's magic. And he's putting together a whole new Order."

Yagrin shifted in his seat. Was *that* why Titus agreed to meet with him? To get favors from Jordan?

"I'm not here to talk about my brother." Jordan either wasn't there yet or wasn't coming. He thought of how much Nore was counting on him. "I'll get straight to it. I want a meeting with the Duncan Elder."

Titus's thick fingers circled his chin. "Demisse is dead. It's Rajna now."

"Where is she?"

"Around. You said you wanted to talk about Shelby. Are you here on behalf of your brother?"

"No."

"Because that bastard has some explaining to do if the rumors are true that he's mixed up with the Marionne girl."

There it was. Family rivalries were like weeds, impossible to kill. The rule was House blood for House blood. But Darragh Marionne didn't kill Shelby.

Felix did. At Beaulah's order.

Yagrin sat back in his seat. This was playing right into his hand. The desperate were the easiest people to exploit.

"Have you heard from House of Perl lately?" Yagrin asked.

Titus flinched. "No. What's that got to do with anything?"

"I'm sorry for what happened to your daughter. I must be frank. My aunt used you. Just as she uses everyone."

"She gave us a shot at Darragh Marionne. That toushana-spawn killed my baby girl."

Yagrin shoved the bag across the table at Titus. "A gift. Open it."

He peeled the zipper back to reveal a rotting head with bloody slicked hair.

"Shelby's actual murderer. You're welcome."

Titus pushed back from the table, holding his nose in disgust. "I don't understand."

"My aunt ordered Felix to keep Shelby on a leash while she worked her way up in the House of Marionne ranks. If she got in the way, she was to be killed. At the time Shelby died, Darragh Marionne was facilitating Cotillion. Quell Marionne was there as well. You might have heard about it? The whole world has. Follow the timeline. It's not hard to see between my aunt's lies when you really think about it. She hasn't been in touch since the Sphere shattered. You lost more people than she did. I saw with my own eyes. And when it came down to taking the Sphere's magic, she had her Draguns around her, not any of your people. She doesn't care about you or your House. She doesn't care about me either. She cares about power."

Titus gaped.

"I'm very sorry about Shelby," he added again, for good measure.

Titus's fist batted the head against the wall. He pounded the table and stood, kicking over his chair. When he settled, his back was to Yagrin, who couldn't breathe. He'd played all his cards. He hoped it would be enough.

"Wait here." Titus slammed the door.

Yagrin ducked his head out. There was no sign of Jordan. So he sat back in the chair, hoping he would actually make it back to Dlaminaugh after upsetting Titus so much.

Yagrin almost left multiple times, but after a long while, the door flew open, and Titus returned, holding a phone. His expression had changed. There were actual tears in his eyes.

"Rajna is on the line." The big fellow swallowed hard, and it moved Yagrin's heart. He wasn't sure it was compassion or relief, but either way it was one step closer to getting the answers Nore needed. "She's hesitant to meet in person with anyone right now. Until things in the world shake out a bit more."

Hedging their bets, like Oralia.

Titus held the phone in one hand and pinched his leaking eyes with the other between sniffles.

"Yagrin Wexton, son of Richard Wexton, nephew to none other than Beaulah Perl. Thank you for connecting dots that have haunted our family for some time." Rajna's voice was raspy with age. "What is it you'd like to discuss?"

Yagrin slid forward on his chair closer to the speaker. "I am helping Nore Ambrose retrieve a piece of parchment that was entrusted to each House a long time ago. My understanding is that the Duncan piece was given to someone in your family after it was disbanded."

"Did you say Ambrose?"

"Yes."

"This isn't about Perl business?"

"I'm no longer affiliated with House of Perl."

Rajna was silent for a beat too long.

Yagrin's grip tightened on the edge of his seat. "You know the piece I'm speaking of?"

"I do, but it's strange having a Perl come around asking."

"I'm with Nore Ambrose. *With* her, if you get my gist."

"It's true," Titus said. "Heard all about the Wexton brother who fled House of Oralia. Ghosts and attempted murder in front of a live audience."

"I see," Rajna said. "What about it?"

"Where is it?" He went for it. "Nore is Headmistress now and would like it returned."

"Oh dear. I wish I had better news, especially after you've been so generous with us. The Living Scroll is what I've heard it called. And that was lifetimes ago. It is gone. It's been gone."

Yagrin lost feeling in his hands. "I don't understand. We've found the other pieces. All we need is yours."

"Yes, we've heard this before. Listen, I'm sorry, kid."

Maybe she was wrong. "What do you know? Start from the beginning."

Rajna's voice was muffled a moment as she said something to someone trying to interrupt the call. "I need to wrap this up. Look, it's a farce, alright?" She sighed. "When Sola Sfenti stumbled upon the glowing stones in the dirt in the ancient days, he sent his apprentice back to their village to retrieve help to excavate them. Sfenti was dead by the time the boy returned with help. From then on, the boy made it his life's work to discover the secrets the glowing stones held. Generations later, that boy's descendant assembled a group of five. Surnames Marionne, Cantion, later changed to Ambrose, Perl, Oralia, and my ancestor, a Duncan."

Yagrin's heart stuttered.

"He told them his ancestor discovered magic and did all kinds of tricks to win their trust. Then he asked them each to keep a piece of a Living Scroll safe, and in exchange, he promised legacy and glory as future leaders in the magic world someday."

"The House leaders were chosen by popular vote by the Upper Cabinet in the nineteenth century."

"You think democracy runs the world? Naive for a Perl. Fate is puppet-mastered by those who hold all the power. The *victors* write history."

Yagrin shook his head but didn't dare interrupt again.

"They all agreed and made the deal. Only, the boy called them back together years later, when he was deathly ill, to demand the return of their pieces. He said he needed more time to make good on his promises to create a magical world. This was lifetimes ago. The Houses hadn't even yet been formed. Most didn't even believe magic was real. The group refused him. He unleashed a dark magic on them, forcing them to agree."

"What happened to him?"

"Who knows? But I can assure you the Scroll you're hunting down on the word of the inaugural Ambrose Headmistress is a fake. The original Scroll was written on goatskin. Not parchment."

The world blackened at its edges.

"I'd bet you're collecting replicas."

"Everyone in the House believes—" But Yagrin's experience in his aunt's House shut his mouth. If enough people believed a lie, it didn't matter if it wasn't real. Yagrin's mind burned with questions. But his curiosity was snuffed out by the slosh in his gut. Every House had its own smoke and mirrors to unveil, it seemed.

If this was true, the Scroll was a dead end.

And the only way to save Nore was breaking the Pact with the dead.

FIFTY-FOUR

Nore

Nore ripped her covers off in the middle of the night. She pulled her robe on and walked to the window. The gate was closed. There were no fresh footprints in the snow. Yagrin still hadn't returned.

She ventured into the hall and paused, waiting for her shadow of death. But the ancestors didn't come. She descended the stairs to the lower floor and exited her estate. The snow chilled her toes, despite her shoes. By the time she got to Yagrin's quarters, she couldn't feel her face or her hands. She knocked at the door and twisted the knob. It was unlocked. The room was in disarray, with clothes all over the floor. But he was not there.

She wanted him back. She needed him back. She left his room and made her way back across the snow. Had something happened to him? Yagrin could take care of himself, but Ellery had become someone she didn't recognize.

When she approached the doors of Dlaminaugh's main building, she froze, realizing there still weren't any dead swarming around her. The ancestors weren't outside her door. They weren't hovering outside the building either. She gazed around her in every direction, but didn't see a single one.

The toushana inside Nore twinged, like a shard of glass stuck between her ribs.

She pushed the door open and found the estate dimly lit. A huddle of Electus occupied a circle of lounge chairs.

"Excuse me," she said to them.

"Headmistress! Sorry, didn't see you there," one said, a simple white mask bleeding through their skin.

"Have any of you seen ancestors looming around here?"

"The dead haven't been in this corridor since noon, Headmistress," a round-faced girl with dark bangs said. "I've been here working on Anatomics since then."

"There was one outside during the lesson earlier in the graveyard. Remember? You mentioned it when we were using the diffuser stone."

"Right."

"*One?*"

"Yes, one."

Nore's mind whirred. She thanked them and excused herself, when the girl with bangs cleared her throat. She stood up from her study chair now, showing off her gray dress, which was cropped at the shin. There was blue stitching along the bodice in leafy patterns.

"I hope it's alright," she said. "I did the changes myself. My mother's Oralian, an expertly trained Vestiser."

Nore watched the girl turn, showing off the nice movement of the fabric. She ran her fingers across the detailing. But what caught Nore's eye was the erectness of her posture, the slight pucker to her smile. She was *proud*.

"It's the prettiest dress I've ever seen between these walls," Nore said.

"I was thinking of dyeing the tips of my hair to match the detailing."

"Only if you save some of that dye for me, too."

She curtsied. "Yes, Headmistress."

"Nore. Please call me Nore. I'm a handful of years older than you."

"Respectfully, age doesn't make a Headmistress, intellect does."

"What is your name?"

"Lauren, ma'am."

"And who is your lead maezre?"

"Maezre Ogle. I'm sorry if I've offended you. I only meant that you were chosen before it is custom, which means you must be wickedly sharp. And from what I've seen, you have a refreshing way of thinking about things."

Nore felt a lump rise in her throat. She'd never stood in these walls and heard such kind words about herself. And certainly not like this now. When she was hardly worthy of the role she had. It was a facade. It was all a facade. Except she had recognized the brilliance in Winkel's push to be bold. She knew what it was like to feel like you were dancing to a humdrum melody stuck repeating the same step. Something as simple as *color* brought fire to her soul.

"It takes cleverness to recognize it. I am going to tell Maezre Ogle you're very impressive and he would be wise to keep an eye on you."

She beamed. "Also, my understanding is the ancestors thrive under the moon's light. So they are most present at night. But the last three nights I've studied here, the halls have been more vacant each time. Maybe they moved back outside?" She hugged around herself. "Having them around all the time indoors is taking some getting used to."

"They won't hurt you." *It's me they're after if I disobey their request.* "Don't worry." Nore thanked Lauren again and left them all there. The estate was large, and she hadn't roamed its every nook and cranny since she was very young. The dead had to be around there somewhere. She was going to find them.

Perusing the halls of Dlaminaugh usually felt like walking a brutally fragile tightrope. But this time she admired the way the towering ceilings had new inscriptions in Latin along each doorway. The glass walls that wrapped around the estate provided sweeping views in nearly every direction. Tonight, everything glowed beneath the moonlight. This place was magnificent. She wandered, awestruck, allowing herself to imagine ways she could change things if she wanted. She stopped abruptly on the first floor near the kitchens when she spotted shadows. Not nearly as many as the usual few dozen who stuck to her side and roamed the halls. There were ten or so ancestors slinking back and forth past a window that led to the ice gardens and graveyard.

She called to them. But they didn't acknowledge her.

They were fixated on something outside.

She pressed her nose to the glass. The night was silent. The ice garden's sculptures of the gods were hardly discernible from the fresh blanket of snow.

"What is it?" she said, watching the foggy glass for a response. But the dead ignored her. At least she'd found some of them. Maybe more would be visible come morning. She almost turned to go when something shifted in the forest. She wiped the window with her sleeve and peered again.

The trees were swaying.

And they glowed with the faintest light.

"The trees," she asked the dead. "Do you know what's going on with the trees?" She watched for a written response.

Their silence made the hair on her arms rise.

"Well, I guess I'll just have to find out for myself, won't I?"

When she opened the door, icy air hit her face. The dead followed her. In some twisted way it was a relief. She crossed the courtyard, which ran through the garden, watching the rustling branches in the distance. When she reached the edge of the garden, she had no clearer vision of what was happening; her mind raced as she stared at the trees beyond the graveyard.

She shouldn't be out here alone.

There was only one person she could talk to about this.

NORE'S FIST HIT her mother's door, and Isla answered by the third knock. She was fully dressed, with a scarf on her head.

"Can you hear them?" she asked. "The dead."

"No. But I can't find more than a dozen of them."

"You can't hear that?" Isla held her ears. "They're somewhere, humming somberly. I was a Cultivator, but Audior magic was my sharpest gift. It never left me fully. I thought that's why you'd come. That maybe the gift was strong in our line."

Nore held her tongue. Her mother couldn't help but wish some kind of magic on her. The débutante Lauren's words were like a blanket, the hug from a friend she hadn't realized she needed.

"Come with me. You have to see this." She took her mother by the arm before she could disagree. But when they reached the window where she just was, the dead were gone. Nore pointed at the trees, still shuffling.

"Could it be wind?" her mother asked. But Nore pulled her mother outside into the cold.

"Something is in that forest."

Her mother straightened her glasses and walked the length of the courtyard, stepping down onto the stone path that led to the ice gardens. Nore followed.

"That area used to be a graveyard as well. But it was uprooted and the trees were replanted forever ago." They followed the path through the ice gardens, and Nore pulled her robe tighter over herself as she passed the gods' glassy stares. The grave headstones on the ground were arranged in perplexing patterns around the gardens. She began reading the names. None of the last names were Ambrose.

"Who do these graves belong to?"

"Those close to the family." Her mother fidgeted, moving closer to the building.

"Such as?"

"The priests' extended families. Star pupils. Heir sires. Please, enough of this nonsense." She glanced at the forest. "Back inside."

Nore had always assumed the graves' names that didn't share her surname were from outstanding débutants or something.

"It's stopped." Her mother pointed at the still trees. Closer now, it was easier to see that the patch of unsettled trees were younger than the thick forest behind them, several feet shorter, baby trees against the taller conifers. The glow flickered before disappearing.

"We should really get inside," Isla said, rubbing her arms.

Nore watched the forest. Then she studied the names on the graves. Her mind was firing, trying to make connections and sense of things that didn't feel connected. But a nagging at her conscience persisted. Heir sires meant her father's name was here. Kendall Dorset. The Kendall with no record at the school, no name in the Hall of Shame. She uncovered the faces of the headstones in the ice garden to read each one.

There was a connection between the dead and her mother's secrecy about her father.

"Nore, it's cold. What are you doing?"

But Nore moved from one grave to the next, trying to follow the erratic pattern. *Abbot. Zempry. Myn. Bradshaw. Grig. Loigre. Carson.* Every third grave was the next chronological alphabet. But the rhythm of the names in between made her head hurt. *Dorset. Where is Dorset?* Isla had only ever told Nore how unworthy she was her entire life. Had her father thought the same? Was he anything like Isla, or did he have Nore's quirks? Did she get her cleverness from him? Did he have magic? Is that why his name wasn't anywhere, because he, too, struggled to produce? But what needled her most is why her mother was so uncomfortable here around these graves.

"You were ready tonight when I came to your room. Why?"

"I don't know what you mean. I— There was just— The noises . . ."

"You know something about the missing dead."

Her mother paled.

Nore's tongue poked her cheek as she kept looking.

"Nore, please. Let this go."

Frost bit at Nore's nose. Her throat was drying. She couldn't feel her limbs. But she kept going until she'd read all eighty-seven headstones in the ice garden.

"His grave is not here," she said. "He didn't finish his studies here. He isn't in the Hall of Shame. *And* if he is dead, he is not buried here." She planted her hands on her hips. "*Who* was he? And why are you determined to hide it from me?"

All the warmth she'd seen in her mother was gone. The tenderness she'd worn since getting her heart back faded to fear. Isla didn't speak. She only shook her head and tried to retreat inside. But Nore grabbed her.

"*Answer* your Headmistress!"

"I refuse to speak on such things until I am sure." Her mother snatched her arm away and fled back inside. Nore saw red. It was infuriating that she could keep secrets under such circumstances. She fought the urge to chase her mother down and force her to share. That's what Isla would do. Instead, she bundled up before heading to the stables. She was going to find out where the dead went with or without her mother. The dead were holding her captive as Headmistress, forcing her to be someone she wasn't. If they were vanishing, she was going to the vault to steal her heart back and get the hell out of there.

She found her horse, Daring, and he met her with a flick of his tail. Her hands were sweaty in her leather gloves as she climbed on top of him. Daring took off, out the front gate, past the Draguns, who stood sentry there. She rode through graveyard after graveyard to the outermost reach of their property, where tangles of naked trees appeared to claw the sky with their branches. Dlaminaugh grew small in the distance. She rode around the perimeter of the property, traversing between the headstones of her most distant relatives. Names she didn't recognize. When she reached their property line, she turned Daring to the east, to make her way toward the part of the forest overlooked by the ice garden.

A sour smell wafted past. The dead were close.

"Easy." She pulled back on the reins. Darkness shifted ahead of her. She squinted, willing her eyes to adjust to the moonlight, as she eased her steed closer to the shadows. There were two dead lingering in the forest, barely discernible between the trees.

Leaves rustled.

Something grunted.

And then a familiar voice cut through the night, curdling Nore's blood.

She swung off her saddle and tied Daring to a tree before hiking up her skirt to keep it from rustling the leaves. Her lungs burned with trapped breath as she slinked closer to the voice. She had to see him to be sure.

Her brother's auburn hair was pulled back in a long braid. He wore gray leather. Across his chest was a plate of bronze marked with three yew leaves intertwined. Nore flattened firm against the nearest bark, careful to stick to the shadows. She fought the urge to heave. Had he found the last piece of the Scroll? Had he found Yagrin? Was he there to kill her?

The world spun, but she dug her nails into her skin. *You are Nore Ambrose, Headmistress of this House and author of your own fate.* She forced herself silent as she moved closer for a better look. The dead pair loomed around her as if they were watching, too.

Her brother wasn't alone. He was speaking privately with a girl. Around them were at least a dozen others. The girl's back was to her. But she could tell that she boasted a glittering gold diadem with the largest dark jewels Nore had ever seen. Dark hair knotted at the base of her skull. She wore leather pants and a fitted blouse with exaggerated sleeves and collar. She turned to a profile view, and Ellery pulled her in for a kiss. Nore made out a sigil across her chest—House of Perl's cracked column but wrapped in a vine of thorny roses. She shifted, revealing sleek velvet skin and dark, striking eyes.

Adola Perl.

A twig snapped under Nore's foot. Adola's head swiveled, but Ellery marched off, talking to someone. There were others? Nore crept closer. There were several more, nearly thirty that she could count in the dim moonlight, each holding large spades.

Ellery spoke with his hands, giving instructions. Nore was too far to hear, but the masses understood, and each marched in various directions. Adola scanned the forest. Nore ducked beside a thick fir, hugging her knees. She *knew* Yagrin was a fool for trusting anyone with the last name Perl.

Nore peeked as Ellery drove one of the spades into the ground. She watched as he dug deeper and deeper. Questions flooded her. But when he finished, covered in dirt, Adola lowered herself into the hole in the ground. Ellery helped her back out. She reappeared with something flaccid in her arms.

Suddenly, one of the two lingering shadows contorted, twisting in the air.

The dead ancestor writhed as if fighting off an invisible foe.

It slammed into a nearby tree with a force that was not human.

Then it swayed *hard*.

"Hurry." Adola emptied her arms onto the ground. "We don't have long before morning."

The tortured shadow ricocheted from one tree into another, scraping at bark, fighting harder. Leaves poured like rain as the forest shook. Flames erupted on the pile Adola dropped. The dead fell to the ground, morphing into a groveling dark mist before slowly blowing away. The stench of rot grew, but Nore couldn't look away. When the bones were a pile of ash, Adola put out the fire.

Only one shadow remained.

The other dead was gone.

They killed its spirit . . .

Nore backed away and tripped. Ellery gazed in her direction, but she stuck to the darkest shade in the forest until she reached Daring. The ancestors were not her friends, but they were the only defense between her and her brother. The closest thing she had to an ally.

And her brother was *killing* them.

FIFTY-FIVE

Jordan

My brother is sitting at a bar in a tavern sipping from a stemmed glass when I find him. Yagrin's ability to disassociate is envious.

"How'd he like the gift?" I ask, sliding into the seat beside him. "I got here as soon as I could."

Yagrin looks as if he's seen a ghost.

"What happened?"

"So much." He rakes a hand through his hair. But doesn't meet my eyes.

"Yagrin?"

"I would have written, but with Ellery out there, I couldn't risk getting intercepted." My brother speaks to the floor, and my heart tremors in my chest. This is the brother who couldn't keep my birthday gifts secret from me each year. He takes another sip from his drink.

"I have some of my own updates," I say to break the ice.

He pushes his seat out from the lip of the bar a few inches. His heart hammers harder. And because of the trace, I feel it in my chest.

"Go on, then," he says, and I tell him about the Sphere's proper magic being removed, relocating the safe house to Chateau Soleil, and planning the toushana extraction. How we are held up at House of Marionne, which is in a state of disrepair.

"Headquarters is in shambles," I add. "The brotherhood is a joke."

"Always was one," he mutters, and a strangled laugh escapes me. My brother smirks, and it chips away at the ice between us.

"I found Maei's body, deflated like a sack of skin." A shiver finger-walks my spine. "The Dragunhead is actually after Quell *and* me. The Darkbearer attacks are to draw me out. Be *careful*, Yagrin."

"He always rubbed me the wrong way." Yagrin buttons and rebuttons his sleeve. "When he realized that daddy business didn't work with me, he left me alone."

My jaw hardens. That was a dig. A fair one. The Dragunhead played me like a viola, and I sang his praises like a song.

"What a mess," he says. "What else?"

My side throbs, and I'm not sure if it's my decaying rib cage or guilt. I try to find the words to tell him about my conversation with Abby. How I need the Scroll now more than ever. But the words stick in my throat as I stare at the brother who counted on *me* to hold him up his entire life. I flag a bartender and order two drinks.

"Tell me how the search for the Scroll piece is going," I say.

He meets my eyes, but his deaden on impact. "Nore Ambrose is Red."

I blink. "Red?" I lean toward him to make sure I heard him correctly. "*Your* girl, Red, the Unmarked?"

"Nore may as well be Unmarked. She has no natural magic either. No one knows that, of course."

His words are a train wreck in my head. Red, my brother's love, who the brotherhood killed, is alive. And she is actually *the heir* to House of Ambrose? She has *no magic* and has somehow hid that her entire life. I sit back in my seat, unable to shut my mouth. He explains how her brother gave her the persona. How she used it to have a life away from the Order.

Red is alive.

My brother's love. His *only* love is alive.

"I'm happy for you," I manage, his words still sinking in. My brother deserves true happiness and a life that's his own. The sag in his shoulders and shift in his posture confuse me. His heart still thuds. My stomach twists. Something isn't right.

Red being alive means . . . "You're still looking for the Scroll pieces, aren't you? You haven't run off to Dlaminaugh like a couple of newlyweds?" I chuckle. Yagrin doesn't respond, and I sip my drink. Cold stretches in my chest, riling itself up.

"Ambrose has an agreement with their dead. That's why their magic is so advanced."

"What kind of agreement?" My grip on my glass tightens, and it feels like I'm standing on the edge of a cliff I'm about to be pushed from.

"Ambrose Headmistresses turn over their hearts to their dead ancestors. In exchange, the House gets to channel the magic of all their dead. Breach means death."

"But Nore doesn't have magic. So—" The world rips in two. Nore becoming Headmistress should be a death sentence. I shove myself up from the bar. "You have the Scroll! You used it to save her!"

People stare in our direction. But the ice seizing in my veins whispers, *Choke him.*

"No!" He shoots up as well. "Though, would that have been such a bad idea? To do something for myself for once!"

The glass cracks in my fist. Shadows bleed from me in every direction. Table bussers come by to clean up the mess, and I pull my brother into the corridor to the bathrooms. "*Everything* is riding on this. And you're worried about yourself?"

"Isn't that what you're worried about? The girl you love. I don't deserve the same?" His finger stabs me in the chest, and I stare at a brother I've never seen.

"You've planned it this way the whole time, haven't you? You've never been honest. You've been plotting with Nore behind my back!" *How could I ever have trusted someone so selfish?*

"You're wrong. The Scroll is a bust. It was found centuries ago. We've been chasing a fraud. Duncan told me tonight. But if I *could have found* that last piece of the Scroll," he spits, "I would have used it without thinking twice!" He tries to push me off him, but I tighten my hold on his shirt.

Cold claws at my bones. "The Scroll is a fake?"

He pulls pieces of parchment from his pocket. "These are pieces of Caera Ambrose's historic scheme to look like the cleverest Marked to ever live."

I shove him back into the wall. "If you're lying to protect your little redhead, I'll gut the life from her myself." Shame burns in my chest. I did not mean that.

All the tenderness in my brother's stare dies. The hard, bitter Yagrin I've known the last few years glares at me. Only he doesn't change into one of his personas. He doesn't hide his feelings.

A thousand apologies and regrets run through my mind, but only "Am I clear?" makes it to my lips.

FIFTY-SIX

Yagrin

Jordan's eyes burned with a madness that stuck like a knife between Yagrin's ribs. He'd seen his brother furious at their aunt, at their father, even heartbroken over Quell. But he'd never seen such rage in his brother. The numerous times Yagrin found himself lost, cast aside, broken, his brother had saved him. Shouldn't he save Jordan in return?

As Jordan let him go, Yagrin wrestled with love for his brother and the dignity he deserved but had never demanded.

"Thanks for all the years, brother. I can never repay them. But I'm done being your errand boy."

His brother fumed. Murder glinted in his eyes. Yagrin couldn't breathe. If Jordan came at him, he'd give it all he had. Nore deserved that. *He* deserved it.

But something prompted his brother to turn and march out.

He wanted to believe it was love. That some part of the boy who used to play hide-and-seek with him and tell him stories at bedtime was still in there. But he couldn't live for that hope anymore. He had to start living for himself. Yagrin peeled himself off the wall and straightened his clothes. He splashed water on his face and wiped the sweat from his brow.

He was going to find a way to break the Pact with the dead.

He and Nore would come through this *alive*.

That was all that mattered.

Yagrin cut across the snowy fields of Dlaminaugh with sharp steps. The dead had their claws into Nore now, demanding she grow the toushana inside her. He had to figure out what they wanted *more* than they wanted Nore. They were basically human, which meant they could be swayed if he could appeal to them in the right way.

He stopped.

I know what they want.

Nore's seed of toushana.

They demanded that she grow it.

They wanted a heart with *powerful* dark magic. He hurried faster across the snow despite feeling like he might hurl. He would convince the dead to return Nore's heart in exchange for a heart with the *strongest* dark magic there was.

His brother's.

FIFTY-SEVEN

Quell

I toss every copy but one of *Debs Daily* on the estate grounds in the fire. I had them *all* brought to me when I opened mine this morning and saw the headline.

WEXTON FAMILY MANSION BURNED TO THE GROUND WITH ONE CONFIRMED DEAD INSIDE

Jordan's family home, the article explains, was destroyed in a sudden overnight blaze. *There is no apparent cause for the arson*, it says. *Inside are the confirmed remains of a faithful father, servant of the brotherhood, and brother to House of Perl Headmistress Beaulah Perl, Richard Charles Wexton II.* Jordan's father. There is no mention of his mother. Only that they are still searching for remains.

When my fireplace eats the last corner of the paper, I fold the only copy and tuck it in the bottom of a drawer and exhale. *He will hear this terrible news from me.* I twist the pearls around my neck. I know he didn't care for his father. But this isn't news anyone wants to hear. The rest of the *Daily* is equally harrowing—more Darkbearer attacks on neighborhoods across the States. Morgantown in West Virginia. Lexington, Kentucky. There was one in Nashville last night. And two suburbs in central Alabama this morning.

Each is farther South.

Closer to Chateau Soleil.

He is coming.

We are not ready. There is still a hole in the gate. A rat in the walls. We don't have anything to put the Sphere's toushana *into*. There is nothing I can do, besides what I can do. And it doesn't feel like enough.

I sit in my full black gown, as best as I can, and flip through my grandmother's journal about her roses to *do something* useful. But another book from the stack I found in the library yesterday grabs my attention: a biography on the Dragunhead. I slide it onto my lap and read about the childhood and adolescent musings of a man who is determined to capture me.

I pull my shawl tighter around myself, when the door opens. Jordan enters, decked out in a fine dark tux with a white bow tie at his neck. His shoulders still hang with the deep heaviness he returned with from meeting his brother early this morning. When I woke up, I found him in the chaise across my bedroom, staring out the window. When I returned from breakfast, he was gone.

The drawer with the article inside it taunts me. Now does not seem like the right time. But who am I to choose that for him?

"You look lovely," he says, but the divot between his brows betrays his attempt at appearing okay.

I cross the room to be nearer to him. "You never told me how it went with Yagrin."

He won't look at me. "Later. Let's set the trap."

I knit my fingers and fill my lungs with air. I cannot spend this entire evening with him and not mention this. I have to tell him. "Can I hold your hand?"

He stares at his before offering it to me. "Sure."

"You don't fear this anymore." I lace my fingers with his.

"No."

I wait for him to say more. For him to explain why he will tolerate brief touches confidently. Why he promises I will understand soon. But I tuck my need to know away.

"We shouldn't delay." He pulls the diadem with the Sphere's magic out of his pocket. "A replica." He twists it, its gems gleaming. "Can I see the real one again?"

We enter my grandmother's bedroom—where we have stowed away the real diadem with the Sphere's magic. I unlock the door to the smaller room off her bedroom, where she once kept me. He goes inside, and I follow, connected to him, trying to find the right words. He grabs the real diadem and holds it beside the fake.

"They're imperceptibly different."

"The real one has a nick." He shows me a spot on the edge of the headband before locking the real one back away. Back in the living room, he sets the fake on the coffee table inside a half-opened metal box. We release hands so I can arrange the room in a bit of disarray to make it look like I left in a rush.

"You think it will work?" he asks.

The plan is to leave my quarters unlocked with the diadem's metal box in plain sight. The Dragunhead wants the Sphere's magic, and we're serving up half of it on a silver platter. We made the ball mandatory, after all, to pull this off. We will watch the dance for who slips away. We'll follow them to catch them red-handed. "It will work."

I pull the desk drawer open where I've hid the article, wrestling with withholding such urgent news. So much is riding on this diadem trap succeeding. *After. I'll tell him after the ball.* Getting rid of the rat will feel like a win.

"What is that?" He peers over my shoulder.

I shove the drawer closed. But he pulls it back open and finds the folded newspaper, so small the headline is hardly readable. I snatch it away. Jordan stares at me quizzically.

"Quell?"

"I wanted to tell you later."

"What's happened?"

"Jordan, sit."

He does. I sit beside him and take his hand again. He lets me, but his grip is rigid, and his palm is sweaty. I can't think of a way to say it that sounds good. So I just spill.

"The Dragunhead has burned down the home where you grew up." I cup his hand with both of mine. "And your father was inside at the time. He is dead."

Jordan rips his hands from mine. The green in his eyes dulls as he glares at the folded paper in my hands.

"Did it say anything about my mother?"

"They are still looking. Jordan, I'm so sorry." I give him another moment to say something, to ask questions, but he doesn't move. And it only rattles my pulse more. The weight in his chest grows so heavy I feel it, and *I* can hardly breathe. "Would you like to read the article?" I offer it to him.

With a vacant stare, he takes it from my hands and tosses it in the fire. Then he offers me his arm. "We're going to be late."

THE BALLROOM IS beautifully decorated in lush dark fabrics. Black silks billow from the ceilings, and roses from the garden fill elegant vases on the tables. Dexler asked for my creative vision, and I told her to design it around my diadem. I hoped it would feel more welcoming, like a powerful House with a refreshing makeover.

"Dexler really remixed things," I say to Jordan, who is stiff on my arm, a hollowed shell. Every time I say something to him, I get a short reply.

"She did."

Now is no different. The tables are decked out with tall centerpieces ornamented with crystal, which shimmers against the rich black fabric everywhere. Everyone is dressed in dapper suits in all styles and radiant gowns in gorgeous patterns and colors. Sweet music floats in the air, coming from an Audior who has to be one of Zecky's. A few dance.

But despite the atmosphere of festivity, most linger on the perimeter of the ballroom, shuffling their feet, side-eyeing the food reception line and scarcely filled chairs.

The reality is, until an hour ago, they'd been locked in their rooms for twenty-four straight hours other than the handful of people escorted to do work in the extraction lab.

"Is everyone here?" Jordan asks. There are two sets of grand doors to the ballroom: the main entrance, which feeds into the reception line, and a pair of smaller carved doors on the north side of the ballroom, where two servers enter and exit. Both doors are closed as the servers set out the last trays of hot food. I count each head in the room.

"Yes, every single body on the grounds is in this room."

Willam sits at a table, picking over a biscuit on a tiny glass plate. Knox is beside him. They don't speak. I've been so busy I haven't had time to check in with them. Dimara is beside Knox, ripping a piece of chicken off a bone and shoving it into her mouth. The twins and Kedd also sit at their table, staring into space, resigned.

"They are miserable, Jordan."

"Not my problem."

No, but sort of your fault.

I smooth my dress. Before the news tonight, he hadn't been himself. He's been less willing to listen, harder to compromise with, and now he won't talk to me at all. The world is in pieces. We should be closer than ever. But I'm not sure I've ever felt more distant from him.

"If we want the culprit to feel safe enough sneaking off, we need to liven up this atmosphere. Dance with me." I pull him toward the dance floor, and he refuses, rigid in place. I am asking a lot of him after the news he just learned and clearly hasn't processed. "Well, keep an eye on the doors. I'm going to try to perk things up."

He glares at the main entrance to the ballroom.

"No one is going to try to sneak out with you standing guard like that. Grab food or sit down. At least pretend to be distracted." I reach for his hand, and it's ice cold, the toushana in him highly agitated. I pull out a chair at the nearest table. Jordan meets my eyes with a steel glare, but he sits. I flag one of the servers to set a plate and drink in front of him. And I hurry off to try to inspire some revelry. The first table I visit is Willam's.

"I hope your night was alright."

"Nice ball. Right back to the old ways, huh?" Willam eyes me warily. This is the first ball they've ever been to. I hadn't considered whether they'd want to go to a ball at all. Another pair makes their way to the dance floor.

Knox dabs her mouth with a napkin. "How long will we be restricted in our rooms?"

Dimara watches with a sneer.

"I'm not sure." I whisper to Knox, "We need to be very cautious right now."

"Oh?" She says in a tone that is colder than her stare.

"Yes. We've come into some information. We need to be careful with people we *don't* really know."

"You're perfectly fine locking us in our rooms after basically kidnapping us?" Dimara scoffs.

Am I? I didn't want this. But Jordan . . . And now he's . . . The longer I think on it, the sicker I feel. "Things will be back to the way they were soon."

"Something tells me this is the new way of things," Willam says, tossing his napkin on the table.

"You understand what I mean, right?" I pull at Knox's arm, but she only gazes at me, eyes first, then my heart.

I suppose we could ask those who I do know are on our side to spy. Would Dimara help? I want to pull my hair out. Jordan would never go for it. He is the one with the world's magic inside him. We're halfway up this stream. We have to swim it now.

"This isn't my choice!"

"No, it's just your House." Knox returns to her plate. "You should get to your guests." She slides a bite into her mouth without looking at me.

I march over to Jordan and spot Yaniselle attempting to talk to him. She tenses when I approach. He stares past her at a thin crowd moving toward the dance floor.

"Shouldn't you be enjoying the dance?" I ask her. *Or stealing the diadem?* "Everyone in the entire House is here."

She looks at the doors and elbows Jordan to make sure he doesn't miss it.

"I'm sure one of them interests you as a dancing partner," I say.

"Sure. Have you seen Ube?"

"He refilled his glass with punch three minutes ago," Jordan says, still not looking at either of us.

"I guess I'll go find that dancing partner." Yani disappears into the crowd.

"Do you think she bit?" I ask.

He doesn't respond. He must feel awful.

"Jordan, I'm really sorry."

"Don't be. I hated him."

"But you—"

"I'm fine."

The fury roiling through him sears my chest. He is the farthest from fine. But how do you tell that to someone who has never been allowed to make space for their feelings? I can't find words he'll understand, so I grab him by the arm and jerk him with all my strength out of the chair. I nearly stumble into the table like a giraffe on roller skates. But he stands to help steady me on my feet. *If my words won't convince him, maybe my love will.* I throw my arms over his shoulders, hoping we haven't pushed the amount of physical closeness past whatever limits he's set on it.

I grab him by the jaw and squeeze, wishing I could kiss him right here, right now. Wishing I could smother him with my affection to remind him even if the people who were supposed to love him didn't, I do. Maybe that's enough. But a smooch is definitely beyond his boundaries.

"You *will* dance with me."

He tries to pull his beautifully sculpted face from my fingers, but I don't let him.

"Because despite what you say, I know you want to."

He stops resisting and finally settles in my arms. There is pain, sorrow, anger, so many things warring inside him.

"Only for one song." When he escorts me to the dance floor, he stops suddenly. I follow his line of sight, and my heart hiccups. The door to the ballroom is slightly ajar. Both servers are still in here. One is assisting in the food line. The other is in a conversation with someone.

Ube is missing.

And so is Yani.

"We can't both run that way."

Jordan releases me. "Go through the other doors. You first. I'll follow shortly after. Act casual. Watch but don't apprehend. We need him *in the act* so there is no denial."

I squeeze his hand. "This is it." He squeezes back with his deadly cold hands. All that is in his eyes now—is anger.

I take the steps upstairs to the third floor two at a time. When I reach the doors of my room, they are open. My heart rams into my ribs as I summon cold magic to my fingertips. Black whirs in my one hand and sputters faintly in the other. With one hand full of power, I shove the door open.

The box on the living room coffee table is empty. Diadem gone.

But there is no one there.

The room has been turned upside down, the desk is half decayed. Picture frames on the wall are securely in place, but the glass on them is scorched. The door to my grandmother's bedroom is open. I rush through, and my heart stops when I find a charred hole through her closet door. Beside it is Dexler, hunched over on the floor, unconscious with a blotch of blood on her head.

Her breathing is shallow. I try to sit her up, but she's too heavy to move. I glare at the ripped-open secret closet, fully exposed, and dash inside.

The room is empty.

It's gone. The *real* diadem is gone. A lump rises in my throat. I can't breathe. What have we done? What have *I* done?

I back away and slam into Jordan.

"We're too late," I mutter, trying to swallow a sob. His head swivels as he paces the bedroom, then living room, searching to make sure there's nothing we missed. He touches Dexler's wrist, then her wound, smelling the blood.

"Get Abby now."

I race downstairs and burst back into the ballroom. Ube has returned, standing near the dessert table with his hands in his pockets. When I spot Abby, I pull her outside and update her on Dexler before racing to her office for supplies. Then back upstairs.

Abby is pale as she rummages through her bag beside Dexler. "How long has she been like this?"

"A half hour at most," Jordan says.

She dribbles an elixir onto Dexler's lips. Then she pats another concoction on her wound. It fades almost instantly, the skin shifting to a healthy color. But she still doesn't wake up.

"Is she going to be okay?" My voice cracks.

"She's out cold," Abby says. "It's too early to tell."

Jordan stands, his jaw clenched, ire darkening his green eyes. He helps move Dexler to my bed before starting for the door. Darkness bleeds from his steps. When he sweeps past me in a blur of shadows, I race behind him.

We reach the ballroom, and Erla sits at a table, stewing, beside a preoccupied Ube. *Yani.* Just as I think her name, I spot her adjusting her dress in a corner all by herself.

"Everyone besides Abby is here. The rat has to be in—" I start, but Jordan pulls the grand doors closed. He shoves magic against them, and with wide, sweeping gestures, a curtain of writhing dark mist like I saw in the Shadow Cells forms over the ballroom doors. I gasp.

He marches to the second set of doors. The music stops. The ballroom is deadly silent as Jordan covers the doors in the magic veil, sealing us all inside.

"No one leaves," he says. "Someone here is a traitor."

FIFTY-EIGHT

Nore

When Nore reached the stables, there was a figure in dark robes waiting for her. She swung out of her saddle, and Yagrin's deep brown eyes emerged from the hood.

"You're alright!" She ran toward him but stopped and cleared her throat, keeping distance between them. Nore had made peace with the physical connection they had. It suited her. She couldn't feel love for him, but she felt *need*. Desperate need to have his brain, hands, and body by her side. He seemed to be tolerating it.

He stuffed his hands in his pockets. "We have to talk."

"So much has happened. I was . . ." *Scared. Panicked.* She'd woken each night since he was gone, thinking of him. "Under the impression you got into some trouble."

"You were worried," he said.

"You were so delayed that it was only logical for me to be concerned." Her face flushed with heat.

"I should have written. I'm sorry."

Last night haunted her. The feeling of living in this prison, of being embroiled in a war she didn't ask to be a part of. She would give anything to forget it all for a moment. His hair brushed his cheek. Their sharp angles sloped to a beautiful jaw and perfect mouth. She strode past him. He grabbed her and pulled her body to his. Warmth rushed through her.

"I did miss you." He ran a thumb along her jaw, and it tugged at her like a tether tied to the deepest parts of her soul. "But we need to talk somewhere private. I have news about the Scroll. And it isn't good."

She grabbed his hand and could feel the thrum of his heart in his fingers. Yagrin was on her side. And he was back by her side. Somehow they would get through this. He watched her holding on to his hand, not letting go.

"I also have news about my brother and the dead." She gestured for him to follow her to her room.

The minute the door to Nore's room closed, their insistence to talk died when he pulled her into his arms and drowned her in his loving affection. They lay in her bed now, arms and legs tangled around each other. She listened to the hum of his chest, like a song she loved but couldn't remember the words to. Yagrin's hand ran through her hair. The tips of his fingers traced circles on her back. She exhaled, noticing how long had passed since they'd been hugged together like this. She pulled herself up and off him.

"Stay," he said, pulling her back to his chest.

She resisted.

"I know the Nore with her heart loves me. Forcing me away won't change how I feel. Let me hold you."

"We have matters to get to." She peeled herself away from him. He deserved so much better than this. He sighed, and they moved to opposite armchairs near the fire.

"What happened?"

"You first," he said.

She swallowed, summoning the horrors she'd seen in the forest to the front of her mind. "No, you, please. I'm still processing."

"The Scroll is not findable. We've been collecting a replica of the original."

Her grip tightened on the chair. *"Impossible."* Her brother was looking for the Scroll, too. He'd done more research and for longer. He would not have missed this.

"I wouldn't tell you this unless I was positively certain." He went on to explain how the Duncan Elder he'd spoken with told him all about how the Scroll pieces had been found centuries ago.

"So Caera was just making a name for her House? She was a fraud?"

"Is it that hard to believe?"

It was like looking out of glasses with the wrong lenses. *Is this what my mother meant? Did she know?*

"We need to break the Pact with the ancestors," Yagrin said. "I have a plan. But first, tell me what I missed while I was gone."

Nore poured herself a kiziloxer and let the bubbles mellow her out. She sat back in the chair by the fire and told Yagrin about Ellery and Adola working together to burn the ancestors' bones to kill their spectral spirit. How they were hurrying to finish before sunrise.

"My cousin?"

"*Your cousin.* Who I told you not to trust!"

His head cocked. "Maybe this works for us? We want the ancestors out of the way. If he kills them all, then we can take your heart back without fear of retaliation from them."

"We'd still have my brother to deal with." She rubbed her temples. "I know Ellery. If he is doing this, he is certain it will get him closer to Headship. Somehow the two connect."

Yagrin didn't speak for several minutes. He stared with deep consternation.

"I don't understand," he finally said. "I've never heard of magic like that."

"Well, somehow Ellery has, and he's training your cousin well."

He crossed his arms.

"I *watched* her help my brother set my ancestors' remains from the grave on fire. Right before she kissed him." She grimaced.

"That House is full of traitors." Yagrin's mouth formed a hard line. He got up. With his back still to her, he said, "I know how we can break the Pact. The dead want to survive, and they think, somehow, access to a heart with toushana will help them. They have yours, but they would be *much* more excited to have a heart with strong toushana." He faced Nore with heavy-lidded eyes.

He wouldn't . . . "Your brother's heart?" *He can be savage, and his rivalry with his brother goes deep.* But this?

"His heart is rotten anyway. That's what power does to people; it corrupts them until it kills them."

Is that what he thinks of me?

"Yagrin, there may be another way—"

"My brother's against us now, Nore. This *is* the way. If the dead will accept, my mind won't be changed."

He wanted to sacrifice his brother's heart to save her. Since Jordan wasn't an Ambrose, it would kill him. Cold skidded across Nore's spine. Was she really on board with this? She racked her brain. The temptation to break the Pact was too great to ignore.

"The dead have their own problems at the moment," she told him. "I'm not sure we can convince them." Even if they could persuade the ancestors, they still had Ellery to deal with.

Nore circled her chin, trying to picture what had happened to the ancestors' bodies once the bones burned. *It was ash.* She hadn't looked inside the grave to be sure. It was hard to make out everything happening in such darkness.

"I need a better look at this magic in the daylight," she said.

She didn't like this plan of killing his family to save her. But weren't they doing the same thing? Ellery had to die if she would ever be safe. Her fists sweat as she and Yagrin hurried out the door.

The sun was fully awake when they rode out to the forest. And they found the grave sites in disarray. Piles of ash and charred bone were scattered. Trees had fallen over, and branches and debris covered the ground. Nore spotted the grave that was dug up the night before. It was partially refilled. How had her brother gotten so close to the estate? And why were the dead helpless against him?

She recited what she knew. "The ancestors' shadow shriveled up and crept back toward the mound until it disappeared."

She squatted beside the grave and stuck her hands in the dirt. "Help me look around in this one."

He moved the dirt around. They were utterly filthy, elbow-deep, feeling for something.

"Any bones left in there?" he asked.

Her hands only grazed rocks and broken sticks. "No." The moment she said it, something cold brushed her fingers. "Wait." She grabbed hold of the gummy substance and pulled. Out came a suit of skin with hollow eyes and rotting flesh.

Yagrin stumbled backward. Nore surveyed the body, more intrigued than shocked. A magic that could kill the corpse's spirit and leave the shell of a person behind. How did the Anatomics work? She had so many questions. Though she didn't covet it, magic could be *fascinating*.

"Jordan. It's just like he described. The Dragunhead—" Yagrin was white as a ghost.

"We should get out of here." She kicked dirt back over the desiccated body and pulled a stiff Yagrin back to Daring. She rode in the front of the saddle, and he hugged her. As they fled back to the house, she asked, "What about the Dragunhead?"

He held her tighter. "He also uses this magic."

Ellery wasn't working alone. She kicked her horse's flank harder, white-knuckling the reins. She needed to think. Their list of enemies only seemed to be growing. And this one terrified her.

FIFTY-NINE

Jordan

I gape at shadows dripping from my fingertips as the veil settles against the wooden doors to the ballroom. Everyone's stares burn my skin. But all I can see is the house where I grew up in a heap of ash.

My father is dead.

And my mother is—

The thought chokes me. My brother is as good as gone. And now Dexler's been caught up in this mess. Worst of all, the life I wanted for Quell is slipping through my hands. Toushana pumps so steadily in my veins, the world's colors dull. The Dragunhead was in Tippets Square that day, watching, delighted because he knew. He *must* be stopped.

"Jordan, what are you doing?" Quell rushes over.

"Someone in this room is working with the Dragunhead. They're cornered now."

"Some of these people we *know* weren't—" she starts, but my voice booms above hers as cold cracks in my chest.

"Maezre Dexler has been attacked, and a precious artifact *full* of the Sphere's proper magic has been stolen from Quell's room." The room gasps. "*No one* is leaving until we find the thief!" The widening eyes speed up the thud of my heart. If they fear, they will cooperate. If they cooperate, we *will* find the traitor. I won't take risks with Quell's life.

"Form a line, shoulder to shoulder. Children, too."

Ube shoves himself between a mother and her son. The liar, backstabber, dead man. I know he's behind this. *Make a memorable example, and no one will forget it.* I can hear my aunt's voice, and cold hums in me. *He should die in the most painful way.* I never trusted him, but I didn't expect him to outsmart me right under my nose. *Because you're weak.* My father's chastising haunts me.

I try to push away the dark thoughts, but there is truth to them. I am weak. I should have known to keep a close eye on him. On everyone. I was too merciful at the start. *Mercy is best used as a weapon.* My aunt's rearing scrapes at my skull, and the toushana billowing around me thickens.

I glare at Ube. Fairness is a perception. A powerful one. We still have to run a successful extraction with these people, and it's important to Quell to smooth things over. Instead of marching right up to him and ripping his head off his neck, I start at the beginning of the line and take my time, approaching the first person, a middle-aged woman in a mint-green dress with silver stitching and a big, fluffy skirt.

"Empty your pockets."

"My gown does not have pockets."

"I thought all dresses have pockets."

"They should, but they do not."

"Strange. Lift your arms."

She does, and her dress bust is fitted to her so tightly, there is no place she could hide a jeweled headband.

"You." I indicate to a girl with thin, long braids beside her. "What is your name?"

"Imalia."

"Imalia, pat her down."

She hesitates but hurries over. What happened to Dexler can't happen to anyone else, especially Quell.

"I didn't steal anything, I swear," the lady says, turning red as fat tears roll down her cheeks. *I believe you*, I want to say.

"Underskirt off. She could be hiding a dozen diadems under there."

People shuffle, muttering under their breath.

"No moving! No speaking!"

"Jordan, *no*," Quell says.

The ballroom is silent. Imalia reaches under the woman's gown and unties her pettiskirt. It falls to her feet. She kicks it away, and I decay it down to ash to be sure there is nothing there. She pulls off the outer layers of her dress, checking each one, until she's in a thin undergown. "Spread your legs. Now pat."

"She doesn't have anything," Imalia says. The woman holds her face, sobbing. I offer her my handkerchief.

"Jordan, stop this, *right now*!"

"Quell, you understand how serious this is. Stand aside."

"*Search Yaniselle.*" She pulls her from the lineup. "Don't harass these people for nothing when we both know who the liar is here!"

"You stupid girl," Yani spits. "Ube was missing for twenty minutes during the ball. He came down the stairs from the third floor, then to Sunrise Corridor."

"Which you only know because *you* snuck out there, too!"

Ube steps out of the line. "I was checking on the extraction lab to make sure everything was okay. What were *you* doing out there?"

"The lab doesn't require you to go to the third floor, liar." Yani tries to wrestle herself from Quell's grip. But she shakes her still.

"Imalia, keep checking down the line." I snatch Ube by the collar, relieved he just made this painful process more efficient.

"Imalia, you will not!" Quell yells. The girl hooks her hands. The dark magic around us grows with my agitation. Shadows spill from Quell's hands as she marches up to me.

"They already feel like prisoners!" I can feel her frustration tangled like a nest inside me, and it feels like my heart being ripped in two.

"The traitor may not be working alone. How clever would the thief be if they hid the diadem on themself? We have to pull out roots *with* the weeds. Or this place is not safe. *You* are not safe. There's no other way now. Don't you see? The *only way* to protect you is to *find the thief*! There's no Scroll to save your life, Quell. I can't"—my voice cracks—"lose another—"

She holds her chest, where she feels the storm raging inside me. "What do you mean?"

"The Scroll pieces were collected centuries ago by someone on their deathbed. They've probably used it, for all we know. It's a lost cause. The history books are a lie. It's *all* a lie."

All eyes in the room are on me. My side throbs so hard it unsteadies me. I hold the spot where it hurts. "*Everyone* is searched. If you're innocent, you have nothing to fear."

When Willam steps forward, my thread of patience breaks.

"*Get back* in line!"

But Willam gestures for Knox to join his side, and she does. Dimara and Kedd follow, along with the twins. "We had nothing to do with this." He circles them up, putting himself between me and them. "We want *no part* in any Order *you're* building."

Quell still holds on to Yani, but glares at me with disappointment I haven't seen on her face in a long time. It threatens to knock my knees from under me. But she is not safe, people are getting hurt, and time is ticking on my life. Someone has to make the hard decisions, even if it's unpopular.

"Leave here and I will hunt you down myself," I tell Willam before releasing Ube and approaching Yani. If Yani's the culprit, which I doubt, Willam's crew have nothing to do with the theft. They hate each other. But if Ube's guilty, as I suspect, he could have gotten his claws into Willam. *Especially* Willam.

I search Yani myself as Quell insists. But she has nothing on her. I finally move back to Ube, and to my great surprise he has nothing on him either. When Imalia and I finish checking the entire line, everyone stares at me, the raging fool. I glare at the ground. *All this and the diadem isn't even here.*

Cold seizes in me.

Worthless. Inept. Useless.

The world is falling apart because it's in my hands.

One of them did this! I ask Yani directly, "What were you doing in the Sunrise Corridor?" I watch for her tells of dishonesty.

"When I left the ballroom, I saw Ube heading that way, so I followed him." She answers without a flinch or touching her hair.

Toushana stalks through me.

End him.

Prove you're not a failure.

"I didn't see anything in his hands," Yani says. "But he probably had it hidden under his clothes or something. And now he's put it somewhere."

"Why were you on the third floor?" I ask him. He looks beyond me, at his sister. "I saw Yani go upstairs, so I followed her. But I lost sight of her and was looking for where she'd gone. I assumed the lab."

"Erla, what do you know?"

His sister joins our interrogation circle.

She tugs at the sleeve of the bright blue dress she's wearing. "I saw them both leave the ballroom. That's all."

"Who left first?"

She hesitates. But her eyes sweep in the direction of her brother.

"He did."

I knew it. That lying snake. Ube shouts something at her in Latin that I miss.

"I will not lie," she says to him, and my mind is made up. *He will die for stealing the Sphere's magic and nearly killing a maezre.* I pull Erla away from the line of guests, out of earshot of her brother. "How savvy are you on the extraction procedure?"

"I've worked side by side with my brother."

"Leave here, go straight to the lab, alone. I will meet you there. You will lead the extraction from now on." I grab my fire dagger and tear through the icy barrier at the door.

She shares a wordless, forlorn look with her brother before departing.

"And me, sir?" Ube asks.

"Just another moment," I tell him before taking Yani aside, dark magic curling inside, nestling beneath my withering ribs. Each day we put this procedure off lessens my chances of surviving.

"You will go to Triveyna and search for the ring stones we need. You have forty-eight hours. Any longer, I'll assume you've betrayed me."

She's not trustworthy in all things, but with this she's desperate to prove herself. I can allow her this errand. We're out of options and low on time.

"Everyone line up at the north door to be taken to your rooms. No one leaves for any reason until the culprit is found."

I shred the veil as the line shuffles to form at the door. Willam shoves past me with his people, hurrying out. I'll have to deal with him later. Quell is with Ube, waiting for me.

"Jordan, I'd like to question him," she says.

"No use. He lied to me. He's a dead man."

Ube breaks out in a sweat. He stares, terrified. "*Okay!* I took it, alright?" His hands fly up in surrender. "I figured you might search us, so I hid it in the lab beneath the supplies. Dexler was there already. I made her tell me where to look."

Quell gasps.

"The Dragunhead told Zecky he wanted that diadem, and I—"

I grab him by the throat. "The Dragunhead's eyes aren't welcome inside these walls." Shadows bite at my fists, begging to rip through my hands. "Ube, by the authority of the *New* Order, I sentence you to die for stealing the world's magic with ill intent. For assaulting an innocent and leaving them to die. And for aiding and abetting the Dragunhead, who is working against the Headmistress of the House you're standing in."

He's as rigid as a fish on a hook. Quell's heart rams in both our chests as she stares, speechless.

"He will sleep in confinement and be executed at sunrise to honor Sola Sfenti. A symbol to all who are watching. Including the Dragunhead."

I lock Ube in the basement, restrained with a cuff harness that keeps his hands pinned to his sides. Then I meet Erla in the lab alone, as I instructed. By the time I arrive, the deadly toushana inside me has settled. She works fusing together a circle of metal with a murky brown stone.

"What are you making?"

"I mentioned to my brother some time ago that we should test the procedure on metal and gems. The mix of the substances is a good model for an ancient relic."

"Yaniselle will return with something soon."

Erla purses her lips.

"Why'd you rat out your brother?"

"I didn't squeal on anyone. I just don't agree with lying. Zecky was very dishonest, and my brother admires that sort of thing. I do not."

"Is that why you don't like Yani?"

She looks up from her work. But she doesn't say anything before returning to what she was doing.

"She is retrieving the stones from Triveyna. If there's something I need to know about Yani or your brother, now is the time to tell me."

"She's had it out for me since we met, trying to get close to my brother. I see right through her. You know everything I know about Yani. I find your choice to trust her risky."

"My options are slim. Another question. What do you know about ring forging?"

"Rings? Like Cultivator rings?"

"Precisely. Yani will be retrieving ring stones, not a relic." With no way to reach Lady Ruby, rings are our best bet. Housing toushana inside rings will make it easier to manage access to it. Once it's in trustworthy hands, it'll be impossible for one person to steal or possess all of it.

"An ancient relic would be much more secure because of how old the magic is." She sets a hand on her hip. "We can try rings. I forged a few with Zecky. But spreading the magic equally doesn't work if the stones are not all the same. And you'll need *dozens*. There's a lot of power inside you."

The list of those I'd give toushana to is short. "When the procedure is done, if I'm—er, uhm, unavailable, give five rings to Quell. Bury the rest securely somewhere."

She nods. "I will do as you said."

Because she is painfully honest, my heart thuds easier. "Also, we won't be extracting all the magic. I want to remain bound to toushana." *If I survive.* "But just enough for a single person."

"You'd like to keep as much as a Darkbearer would have?"

I shift on my feet. "I guess so." If by some twist of luck I survive, I can deal with the Dragunhead. If I die, dark magic dies with me. And while I hate that Quell would lose her magic, the Dragunhead and Darkbearers would lose theirs, too.

She will be safe.

"You need to fly on your own more often," I tell Erla.

She tries to hide a smile.

"Now run trial extractions moving dark magic from one stone to another, increasing the amount of dark magic each time. Use whatever you have. Do it over and over until it doesn't implode. Ideally, none would be lost. No one should get hurt. It needs to be *perfect*. Do it fifty times if you must. We need the procedure ready to go the *minute* Yani returns."

She swallows. "That could take all night."

"You better get started." I find a seat at a table in the corner. Quell won't like me deciding on the rings without her. But time is running out. I try but fail to get more comfortable in the metal chair, thanks to the persistent pain in my side. Once I have found a position that works, I pull out an envelope and paper. My pencil hits the paper, but I'm not sure what to write.

When a tear breaks free, rolling down my face, the words begin to flow.

Dear Mother,
I hope this letter reaches you and that you got away somehow.
I just have been meaning to say that I'm sorry we don't talk much. Father's shadow always loomed like a storm cloud. It was hard to do

anything other than hide from the next boom of thunder. I have failed you as a son. But I'd like to start being a better son now, if you think that's okay. I understand if not.

Please write back and just let me know that you're okay. If there is anything I can do to help you, I want to.

Yours,
"Jordy"

SIXTY

Quell

When Jordan disappears down the basement steps, I watch until he comes back up, without Ube.

He was rash. Maybe I should have pushed harder to stop him or get in the way. But when Ube admitted *stealing* the diadem, hurting Dexler, and knowing what the Dragunhead wanted from Zecky, it was hard to hear much else. Jordan detours to the Sunrise Corridor to meet Erla, and I dash down the stairs. If Jordan sees me challenging him this way, he'll be heartbroken. I'm not sure how much more his heart can take.

But in my gut, I believe there is more to Ube's deception. The relationship between him and his sister is strange. She is a mouse around him. But also bluntly disloyal. The others don't have much to say about him. He was close with Zecky but so quick to switch loyalty and help Jordan. And now he throws his life away to steal the diadem for the Dragunhead? None of this adds up. And if he dies, the truth dies with him.

The hall is dark, but Ube's yelling can be heard from the bottom of the steps. I find him locked inside a utility closet. Weak shadows thrash in my palm when I draw magic to my fist. But it's enough to decay the door open.

Ube gapes in fear. His voice is raspy from yelling. He struggles for words.

"Not here." I drag him down the hall, farther out of earshot of the basement stairs, inside the maezre storage room.

"Why?" he manages.

"That is the first thing you say?"

"I am cursed with a deep need to comprehend."

"I want the truth you plan to take to your grave."

His nostrils flare.

"In exchange for your freedom."

He meets my eyes for the first time since I found him. "You'll let me go?"

I've thought through it a few times. If the Dragunhead is counting on Ube to bring him magic or Jordan, he has failed on both counts. My guess is he will run instead of going back to the Dragunhead empty-handed. Ube on the run doesn't hurt our cause at all. Him dying with secrets is the greater risk.

"I will lead you out of here myself tonight."

"What do you want to know?"

"What is it between you and your sister? Are you protecting her?"

Ube groans. "My sister is complicated. She prides herself on honor. I told her there is no honor in business like ours."

"And what sort of business is that?"

"We sell secrets. Information is our currency."

"Who is *our*?"

"Everyone here from Zecky's neck of the woods. We observe, collecting insight, and sell it to the highest bidder. In your case there is one bidder, and he can pay by guaranteeing us life."

I go cold all over.

The Dragunhead.

"*Except* my sister."

Ube is such a good liar. I can't tell if this is true or if he's saying this to protect her. "So the Dragunhead is *paying you* for secrets on us?" I fold my arms.

"You misunderstand. I didn't know the Dragunhead was interested in hiring us until his messenger told me. I haven't taken it to the group yet. But this is what we do, sell secrets."

"His *messenger*?"

"Yes, she tried framing me, knowing that we were working together. But two can play that game."

"Who?"

"Yaniselle."

I steady myself. "Your people up there would willingly help *a mass murderer*? The Dragunhead is a monster!"

"When you live as we have, it no longer matters who the monster is. It only matters that he doesn't treat us like *we are* one."

I can't form a cohesive sentence; so many thoughts are converging in my head at once. Everyone here was about to be offered a chance to spy on us for the Dragunhead, so Ube says. But *he's* the only one who actually has. He and Yani.

"I need proof of Yaniselle's involvement."

"You said if I told you the truth, that was enough for my freedom."

I close the distance between us, swelling the shadows in my hand. "*I lied.*"

Ube puts distance between us. "I don't have proof. She mentioned it casually as we worked on a trial extraction. She knew who we were and what we do. She asked if I was available to hire. She said she could guarantee our freedom if I'd pass information to her for the Dragunhead. She insisted that betting on you and Jordan was foolish, when the Dragunhead has other Houses behind him *and* an army of Darkbearers."

I choke on nothing. My heart rams harder.

"I asked what information she wanted," he goes on. "And she said to get to know you as best as I could and pass on anything, even the seemingly inconsequential, to her. She had me write notes of your behavior. I'd pass those to her during the day. Once we were locked in our rooms, it grew harder to spy on you. Then when there was news of the ball, she told me to get the diadem from your room and leave it in Sunrise Corridor. Then she turned on me, framing me for the job *she told me* to do!"

"And you didn't say that in the ballroom in front of everyone because?"

"And blow the whistle on my people's knack for spying? That reputation remains our best-kept secret and everyone's most secure source of income. Besides, Jordan wasn't going to believe anything I said. I was a dead man when Yani spoke up."

"And now you've just traded their freedom for yours."

He shrugs. "There is no honor in this business, like I said."

"One last question." It's been needling me since we were locked in the ballroom. Jordan said the Scroll's pieces were found and probably *used* centuries ago. *What does that mean?* "Do you know anything about an Immortality Scroll?"

"A what?"

I repeat myself, and he stares, earnestly bewildered. "Never mind."

"Well, then, let me out. Unless you were lying about that, too?"

"You've failed the Dragunhead. I'm sure he will punish you better than I ever could."

Ube doesn't say a word as I sneak him back upstairs, through the broom closet corridor, and into the Secret Wood. I point west.

"Out here? You want me to just—"

I draw on the shadows sleeping in my bones. *"Now."*

He runs, and I watch until he is a dot in the distance. I was right. Yani is the traitor, but the deception goes deeper than I realized. How much of what Ube said is the full truth? That everyone inside would help our enemy given the chance. That no one believes in the new world being built.

A reckless part of my brain urges me to race after Ube. To escape and hide away. But those days are behind me. So I loosen the tightness in my chest and release my diadem. I run my fingers across it, savoring the spiky parts and smooth jewels. Then I blow out a breath and hurry back inside.

I sleep on the events of the night and rise before the sun.

When Jordan discovers Ube is not in the basement, I feel his rage all the way upstairs. As he interrogates the maezres, I rush to the dorms, find room sixteen: Yaniselle's, and summon the darkness to open her locked door. I need proof of her betrayal to show Jordan. Her room is dark. Her bed is neatly made up, her entire space impeccably tidy.

I pick through a few stacks of books beside her bed. Then I thumb through a journal. This one has worn paper and stained pages. The dates are old. More than a few years. I read a few words, and my stomach curdles—letters between Jordan and Yani, from when he was a Ward and she was interning in Alaska. I toss it aside, my magic slipping out and leaving its leather cover burned to a crisp. *Oops* . . .

I open her closet and pull out a few of her things, holding them against myself, wondering if it would be easier if I were more like her. *She thinks like him.* They're trauma-bonded from what they went through at Hartsboro. I only got a sample of what they endured for *many years*. When I catch a glimpse of myself in a mirror, the regalness of my diadem shines even in the poor lighting.

She is gasoline to his fire. I am sand.

I spot her virtue pin box on her dresser open, a full set of pins. But it's the outside of the box that gives me pause.

It shines.

Its woody, oily stench confirms my suspicion.

This was recently polished.

Half an hour passes. I've turned Yani's room upside down, but there is no evidence she is working with the Dragunhead. I've stripped her bed and overturned her drawers. I did a number on her closet and even shattered her mirror.

It's like when she returns, I'm *hoping* it turns into a fight, a reason for me to kick her out. Or perhaps it's something more sickening: feelings that should be beneath me but that creep up like sudden bile. I shove her things out of the way of the door before opening it, making no attempt to put her room back together. Let her find it. This is my House. *You meddle with my things, I meddle in yours.*

Beside the door, I notice the honing table covering some kind of paneling in the wall. I push it aside and find a trick cabinet, disguised to look like wall. Inside the secret storage are extra pairs of clothes, a few journals, and envelopes banded together. My pulse drums as I thumb through the pages and open the envelopes. But what I find inside makes my heart stop completely.

A series of correspondence with House of Perl.
My eyes race across the first one.

Yani,
Understood. I won't say a word.
But knowing helps us prepare.
I will let the Head know.
—Adola

PS. My aunt is very ill. Keep her in your thoughts.

"What are you doing *here*?" Jordan's voice startles me. The letters fall to the ground from my shaky hands. Ube was telling the truth. It's been Yani, a puppet of House of Perl, who is helping the Dragunhead.

"What are *you* doing here?" I ask, realizing Jordan is standing in Yani's doorway. He looks like he hasn't slept in a month. "Looking for her?"

"I'm looking for *you*. I know where she is. I spent the night watching Erla work. Only to wake up to Ube *gone*! These people could be hiding hi—"

"They're *not*." My heart ticks. "I saw him flee through the Secret Wood. He was too long gone for anyone to catch him." I can't meet his eyes. It isn't a complete lie, but it's hardly the truth. The real factor here is that Yani is behind it all. And he can't see that. She could be bringing the Dragunhead back here, for all we know.

"I stopped in to see Abby." His gaze darts away from mine. "Afterward, I came looking for you."

"How is Dexler?"

"I'm not sure."

"Jordan!" It's Erla, red-eyed from too little sleep. "Quell. Yaniselle is back with the stones."

"She's *back*?" I ask. "Alone?"

Erla furrows her brow but nods.

"Quell, I have to see to this, now. I'm sorry."

"Jordan, she's a *traitor!*" I shout, but he and Erla are already down the hall. Frustrated doesn't begin to describe the emotions rushing through me. The events of the last several hours are like a slow drip in the same spot in my skull. We are so close to doing the extraction, to freeing magic, and yet we are still so far.

Jordan went to see Abby, but doesn't know how Dexler is? I hope she's okay. When she wakes, she can probably help us piece together more of what happened and be sure no one else is involved. I have to be sure. It's not just my life on the line anymore.

I make a beeline for the Healer office and find Abby writing furiously in some kind of folder. She startles, shuffles the papers on her desk, and hops up.

"Are you alright?" she asks.

"I came to see Maezre."

She jabs a thumb backward to a room with a small bed, where Dexler is still unconscious. My heart sinks. "How is it looking?"

"Not good. Usually we'd see signs that she's going to wake up within the first few hours, with the elixir I used. But I'm going to keep trying everything I can."

I hug her. "Thank you for all you're doing." We hold the embrace. "Jordan said he came by."

"Oh, yeah."

I glimpse the papers she tried to cover. Jordan's name is all over them. I skim numbers that don't make sense, hastily written annotated equations all over the page, in the margins, sideways. There is a lot crossed out and underlined in red. My head throbs, trying to make sense of it. Abby breaks the long embrace. I grab the papers from her desk. At the bottom of the page are words that are crystal clear: *probability of survival: none.*

"Oh my goodness." The words fall out of my mouth, and I clamp a palm over my face to catch them. *He's going to die.*

"Quell, I'm so sorry. His wound never truly healed. I told him to tell you." Abby apologizes again, but I don't have words yet for my frustration with her for not warning me. All this time, I've been trying to get magic out of him to save him. When that procedure is most likely to kill him! I turn to go.

"Quell, please," Abby says to my back.

THAT NIGHT, JORDAN doesn't come to my room. I stay in my room, reliving every conversation Jordan and I had. Each time it only riles up my frustration. I dig through my grandmother's library of books, reading up on any- and everything that could be remotely useful. And when I find nothing, I burn through pieces of furniture just to feel good. When I collapse into an armchair, I finally exhale. Daylight outside fades to darkness, and it feels like fading hope that somehow this will all be okay. That the future I want is still possible. That I have to fight for it more before it slips through my hands.

I gather up all the evidence I have on Yani from her room and sort through it again, when a card is slipped under my door.

Dinner.
I want to apologize.
—J

I fold the note. I have to confront him. Tell him everything I know about Ube, Abby, and the procedure. But most importantly, I have to take the diadem with the Sphere's magic away from him and remove him from power before he hurts anyone else.

Including himself.

SIXTY-ONE

Quell

A thousand candles are lit all over the dining room. The sweetest melody greets me, along with an aroma of the most deliciously savory meal. A path of black rose petals on the floor leads me to the opposite end of the grand room, where Jordan sits at a glistening piano, working furiously over the keys. The tune is one I remember from the first time we danced. Memories flood me. I stop and breathe it in. *It was all so new then.* An attraction we couldn't fully understand.

I realize now it was our kindred thirst for freedom.

Then the world fell apart, shattered by our hands. The only thing left to cling to was one another. The hope for what we'd never seen in the world, an understanding of what should be, and a stubborn determination to see it through.

I set down the stack of evidence against Yani on the table and run my fingers along the beading of my gown, trying to remember to breathe. Servants pass, filling the fluted glasses on the table and layering out lavish platters of fruits and cheeses. Jordan plays harder, his long fingers dancing over the keys. I rehearse what I want to say in my head, how firm I will need to be and what will happen if he doesn't listen.

Passing a gilded mirror on the silk-lined walls, I spot my diadem, which shimmers in the dim light, perfectly matching the sparkly studs at my ears, which are a stunning complement to the plunging neck of my black satin gown. I clench my fists at the girl in the mirror.

Not her mother's daughter. Not an heir. Not a runaway. Not someone's puppet.

A writer of her own destiny. A girl who knows her power.

The knot winding in my chest unravels with my breath. I dry my slick hands before touching his shoulder.

The music stops, and the suddenness of the quiet hammers in my chest. He rises to meet me, the green in his eyes bright. His face is clean-shaven, and his tuxedo cuts against his body, flawlessly tailored to him.

"You came." He reaches for me, running the back of his hand gently on my cheek. His fingers curl around my jaw, then they slip behind my head. His touch lingers, and it makes my insides ache. When he pulls me closer to him, his scent sends shivers all over my body.

"It's been so long." I close my eyes, remembering the last time he touched me like this for this long. He snaps his fingers, then scoops my hand into his with the other around my waist. Music fills the air, and he sweeps me into the first step of a dance. His lips bow in a sultry smirk, and I melt into him, sliding with him into each step, twisting to the cadence. The next move makes the room spin as we step and turn, step and turn, step, step and turn.

"You're a natural."

I'm smiling. He smiles, too. An unbridled one, showing most of his teeth. Creases linger around his eyes.

"You should smile more often." I don't think I've ever seen him happier.

He spins me out and in, his chest against my back as I wind my body, dancing against him, before the next count. His breath brushes my neck, and his lips graze my collarbone, sending shivers all over my body. When we face each other again, we lace hands and spin. Holding him so close ignites a tenderness in me that *wants him*. We turn faster as the music speeds up. He winds me around, more insistent with my hips, pulling and pushing them this way and that. I dance to his tempo, following the urging of his touch. Imagining how this dance would feel if this were all that existed between us.

When the music crescendos, he dips me for the finish. His arm is an anchor at my back. His body hovers over the neckline of my gown. His gaze traces my body, then his tongue plays on his lips. When he brings me up, setting me on my feet, I let go of him to shake off the desire to feel him against me.

"Jordan, we need to talk."

He waves away the servers.

"I found letters between Adola and Yani. They've been talking this entire time." I point to the stack tied with a ribbon I set on the table.

"I don't understand."

"I brought it all for you to see. Yani was the ringleader in stealing the diadem, not Ube."

His mouth parts as he approaches the stack of mail cautiously. He picks up several letters, flipping through each. He stops occasionally to read some of the letters. With each passing moment, his scowl deepens. When his narrowed gaze widens, something dark moves across his expression.

"She has been feeding information to the Dragunhead."

He drops the stack on the table and glares. He doesn't speak, and several minutes pass. The servers are turned away. Jordan stews in silence. My heart hammers. When he finally turns to me, the tenderness in his expression has returned.

"I'm sorry for not listening to you about Yani. It was arrogant to think I could keep her in line." He scatters the envelopes on the table before stacking them up and turning his back on the stack. "That could have been *you* instead of Dexler. I've never been so scared in my entire life." He rubs my arms, caressing them. "But I was short with you at the ball. I'm sorry. Can you forgive me?"

"Thank you for that. And yes, I can. But Yani—"

"Please, let me finish." He takes my hands. "Despite the chaos, I need a night where fear doesn't rob us of what we're truly fighting for: each other." The sweetness of his stare does something to my heart. I would like all this chaos behind us, as well.

"Do you think we could try that, tonight? A reset. A moment for us."

The letters on the table taunt me. I've been consumed by everything but the one thing I want to be consumed with—my love and freedom. If that makes me selfish, then maybe I deserve a moment of selfishness. A night of it. Before I ruin it all, taking his power away from him.

He folds down to hover his mouth above mine. "I've prepared for so long to be near you like this, for as long as you like, without fearing our magics will clash. I planned *seven* courses inspired by the most magnificent beaches around the world. One day you will see each of them. Each course has a musical selection. I thought we'd dance for some. But there's a few I'll play for you."

I am dreaming. I must be. "*We* will see them, together."

"Is that a yes? Tonight is ours?"

My chin rises to meet him as if charmed by a song. My thoughts scramble. And all I can think of is how right the world feels when he is near me. How badly I want to pretend this is all there is. We are all there is. And how every time we find ourselves this close, he always pulls away. Tonight, he burns with insistence.

"There's so much we need to discuss," he says. "But when it's just us, everything is very simple. Simple sounds nice for an evening."

I smile. "It does."

He closes the sliver of air between our faces and rubs his lips across mine, deliberately slow. Then he presses our foreheads together. And we exhale, which morphs into a laugh.

"How are you doing this?" I ask.

"I've been feeding my toushana every night. Sometimes all day. For a very long time."

His fingers are bruised. I kiss them. Then I hold his hand to my cheek, savoring the warmth of his confident embrace. The choice to love me burns in every second of his touch.

"I *told* you feeding it would help."

"I had to be sure there is no chance I can hurt you." He says something else, but I hardly hear him, lost in his green eyes. The color of growth, change, hope. I touch his lips, trying to remember precisely what they felt like the last time we kissed. They're softer than I remember. He purses them in the gentlest peck against the pads of my fingers.

My mind whirs with questions. But the thrill on my skin from the dance, the feel of our bodies so close, the tight squeeze of his hand around mine, being this near the person I love, steals every word I was going to say.

"If I save all of magic," he says, "but never live in the moment for myself, I will regret it." He shakes his head. "Regret is not worth its high price. I want this time with you."

Yes, and if I can't have a moment like this, for myself, am I really free?

His mouth touches mine again. His lips spread, opening me up to his kiss. A fire blossoms inside me. The feel of his tongue slipping inside my mouth, exploring, licking, tasting, sends a rush of heat all over my body. And a pang of love in my heart.

"Tell me I'm yours," he whispers, nipping at my ear.

"You're mine. All mine. And I'm yours."

He devours my mouth with a kiss that grows hungrier. The heat rushing through my body pulses, and every part of my skin tingles. Somewhere, someone with a tray rushes out the door. He kisses me again until the dining room and the Chateau and magic and the Order all disappear. Until our breaths mesh in a harmony sweeter than any song we've ever danced to. His love is intoxicating and endless. He holds me so close to him I don't know where he ends and I begin. His touch is gentle yet insistent, stretching each moment of tenderness into a yearning ache, to want more of him, to be closer to him, for this night to never end. He tends my heart like a garden, carefully ripping weeds from my soul. Then he buries me in his love until morning comes.

I WAKE IN my bed alone. The spot where Jordan slept is cold. There is a note and a single rose beside my pillow. *Breakfast.* I check the locked metal box with the real diadem Jordan recovered from the lab. Thankfully, it's still there. I remove it, and hide it in the bottom of my closet. Then I relock the drawer.

That's half of the magic in my possession.
Now for the other half.

I throw a dress over my head and get out the door. Jordan is at the breakfast table, looking bright-eyed, with a plate full of all kinds of food. Pancakes, pastries, stacks of bacon.

"Do you always eat so much?" I greet him with a long, slow kiss. "We still need to discuss things, by the way." My stomach twists, dreading how he is going to take this.

"Ravenous. What can I say? Please eat." He folds and unfolds a copy of *Debs Daily*. His plate, I realize, has hardly been touched.

"How long have you been here?"

"Just arrived. Good timing." He signals for a servant to get me a plate. With it comes a copy of the *Daily*. The front cover image makes my heart stop. A body tied to a balcony at Hartsboro. I blink, staring closer. But the dark hair and eyes are unmistakable.

"It's Yani."

Jordan sips his coffee. "Abby is concerned Dexler may not wake up. Her wounds were intended to be fatal." He is wearing last night's clothes under his morning robe.

I try to swallow but can't.

He did this. Jordan snuck out last night and somehow did this?

He sentenced her to die without telling anyone. Without telling *me*.

I can't breathe.

Bile rises in my throat.

"Justice is not for the faint of heart, Quell." He rises from the table. "The extraction of the toushana and forging of the rings is set for midnight."

"Jordan, I know what Abby told you about the extraction procedure!"

"Then you understand time is of the essence."

"No!" I stand, too. "You will *not* do this. I am removing you as any kind of leader here. I've taken the diadem, and no magic will leave your body until I say so." Toushana bleeds from my hands. "Erla will work with me directly on it now. We will find another way to preserve the Sphere's toushana *and* your life."

Confusion knits his brow.

I don't move, urging my faint magic to swell.

But Jordan doesn't raise a defensive hand in response. He doesn't even look angry. More sad than anything else. "I will not fight you."

"Then you will do what I've said." I ball my fists.

"Quell, preparations are already underway." He raises his shirt. His wound has returned, larger than before. "We ran a trial on me already and got a little of the toushana out. We will do the full procedure tonight. There's no turning back now." He takes my hand and kisses it. "I love you so very much." He turns to leave.

He will die tonight.

To save magic.

And to save me.

SIXTY-TWO

Yagrin

He had to *make* the dead understand.

He'd seen the shadows enough to know where they were looming. But he'd never tried to talk to one. When he and Nore returned to the estate, she pulled every book off her shelf and started jotting down all she knew about her brother, this magic, and the Dragunhead.

He needed to get their Pact plan in place. She hadn't agreed, deeply uncomfortable with it. But she hadn't outright disagreed either. He had to make a choice. And the only way out of this mess that he could see was to offer up his brother as a sacrifice.

Now he just had to convince the dead.

They were notoriously prickly. If his plan to break the Pact went awry, he didn't want them to suspect Nore had anything to do with it. He left Nore in her room and found Isla, who agreed to help.

The entryway that led to the ice garden was vacant of shadows. Instead, they were lurking in the garden, watching the forest, waiting for the trees to quake.

"You're sure about this?" Isla asked.

"Giving them a heart they want *more* than hers is the only way." He pushed the doors open, and they strode into the cold air. He waited and waited for them to notice him. But no sudden shape in the darkness moved.

"Use their language," Isla urged.

He pulled the Latin from the dregs of his memory.

"Loquere mecum."

He may as well have been a mouse shouting in a crowded ballroom. The shadows didn't acknowledge he was even there, still focused on the trees in the distance. He pulled his coat tight around himself and stormed to the middle of the ice garden, right in the thick of where they were. The chill of death cut through his bones as the ancestors moved through him.

"Ego potest auxilium!" He balled his fists.

The shadows shifted at the word *help*. Darkness closed around him. He slammed into a wall of shapeless void, and his body turned to ice. He backed away, trying to unfocus his eyes the way Nore had told him to. He let his vision blur, and the shadows grew crisper, taking the silhouette of human form.

"My native tongue is easier for me. May I speak this way?"

Three letters wrote themselves on a snowy headstone on the ground.

YES

Yagrin's heart leapt. "You want Nore Ambrose to grow toushana."

The shadows didn't move.

"But if our world survives, you could wait a *decade* or more before she can master it."

The dead thrashed around him. More joined them, looming so tall he had to tilt his head back to see them fully.

"I have an offer." Power had corrupted Jordan like it did everyone. He was unsavable. He would self-destruct eventually. At least this let his life amount to something good. But as the words tried to form in Yagrin's mouth, he couldn't get them out. He was committing to steal his brother's heart, which would kill him. He glared at the ground. This would haunt him. Doing this would never be something he could forget.

But I have to.

"I can get you a heart with robust toushana. The Dragunheart has all of the Sphere's magic inside his body. He has a heart *full* of dark magic."

The circle of darkness tightened around him. Yagrin watched the snow, waiting for their answer.

> WHAT DO YOU ASK OF US

His heart thudded faster. "Release Nore's heart from the Pact. Give it back to her."

The darkness watched him intently with hollow pits for eyes.

> WHEN HE DIES

That wasn't his problem. But it was Nore's, which made it his problem. He chose to love her fully, which meant helping see this ancestral House through.

"You can keep the heart even after he dies. It should still possess power. If it doesn't, I'll get you a skilled Darkbearer." He would harvest hearts from every Darkbearer in the world if that's what it took to make Nore whole again.

> SEAL IT IN BLOOD

Yagrin hesitated. The shadows writhed, writing in the snow furiously.

> NOW

Yagrin held out his arm. Darkness grabbed him. Something sharp ran across the inside of his wrist, and warm blood poured from him, dripping in the snow. When it was over, he opened his eyes and the shadows were gone. A dark glove covered in shadowy mist was beside him on the ground. He stuffed it in his pocket. There was no turning back now. He could hardly breathe as he ran inside.

He'd found a way to rescue Nore.

It just meant he had to kill the only other person who'd ever loved him.

He found Nore in her bedroom reading a letter. There were books and papers everywhere, stuck to the windows, covering the fireplace. Large posters were lying over the seats in her room. Her bed was covered. The floor was hardly discernible. She rushed to him, gripping him by the shoulders.

"Necrantomy!"

"Never heard of it."

"But it existed. *It's all here.*" She turned a page, stabbing it with her finger. "This is *ancient* magic!"

"Does it say how it works?"

"That is hardly what matters. *You said* the Immortality Scroll was found ages ago by someone on their deathbed. Why get the Scroll at that point if they're not going to use it?"

"Right. But that would mean . . ." *An immortal exists. Today.*

"Where have you seen a magic so old it is hardly recognizable to us? Magic only talked about in old dusty books? Ancient magic from an *ancient* being?"

"The body at headquarters. And here."

"The common denominator is—"

"The Dragunhead."

"He's immortal! If you think of how Ellery has been able to do all kinds of things, like getting the ancestors to cross thresholds, enter other Houses' estate grounds. He didn't learn that magic here. Someone ancient helping him makes it all make sense. It's the only plausible conclusion." She shoved her hair out of her face. He could feel her panic. And he didn't know how to comfort it. How could they defeat someone who could not die?

"Why would the Dragunhead help Ellery?"

"Maybe he's not *helping Ellery* so much as he's working *against* Quell and Jordan. He wants what they have—the Sphere's magic. And we're on their side."

Are we? "Listen, we need to get rid of the Pact first, then we find a way to get out of here. This isn't our war."

Nore looks past him and says something that shakes him to his core. "I'm not sure I'm ready to just get up and leave. So soon. Can you? Honestly?"

He wanted to say yes, that none of this mattered to him. That he didn't care about helping her lead an ancestral House. That he didn't value what Winkel saw in him. That building a House on principles Nore believed in wasn't one of the most thrilling ideas he'd ever heard. But Yagrin knew how to run. He knew how to shove down feelings and take what he wanted for himself. Could he really do that now?

"What are you saying?" he asked.

"I think there's something here for me, maybe? If I want that, Pact or no Pact, does that mean you would go?" She pulled her hair over her shoulder, braiding it. "You, of course, *could* and *should* if you want to."

"Nore, I'm with you. Whoever you are. Even if that's a Headmistress." The admission fell out of his mouth before he'd thought about what it really meant. How he'd spent his life hating the Order. And now loving her meant being right in the thick of it, trying to make it better. But it was true. He was in this with her, for better or worse.

She cradled his cheek, and he cherished the touch.

"Well, there's also this." She sat back on her bed and handed him the note she was stewing over when he arrived.

Jordan and I and a few others are en route to Dlaminaugh.
We need your help.
—Headmistress Quell Janae Marionne

"This is good news."

She didn't look so sure. But his hope was bright. Perhaps fate was finally on his side.

SIXTY-THREE

Quell

When Jordan leaves breakfast, I race to the healing ward to find Abby. She's in her office soaking a set of stones in a clear liquid.

"Quell? I'm so sorry."

"I don't have time for your too-late apologies now. You should have told me."

"He is the holder of the source of the world's darkest magic!" Abby grabs my arms, nails digging in. "I advised him honestly. I tried to help. What more did you want me to do?"

"I wanted you to risk something to do the right thing, Abby. To not think about where helping him could get you."

"Don't make this about that. I deserve to try to survive this world *you and he* broke. You don't get to take that from me!" she fumes.

Isn't that what we all are doing here? Every person in this House is trying to sort through the chaos and find some ember of hope to cling to. To survive. The clench of my fists loosens. I peel Abby's grip off my arm and squeeze her hand. Being on Jordan's good side was the boon she found at the expense of our friendship. It wasn't fair to expect her to choose between that and survival.

"I hadn't thought about it that way."

Her eyes water. "Do you have any idea how terrifying it's been keeping that secret? Trying to pretend like I knew nothing, so he wouldn't call me disloyal? And my one friend, I never got to see. If I did, it was a passing glance. You were absorbed in something else. And you *never* came to visit me."

I was so consumed with my own survival. She is right.

"And after what Mynick did to me, I felt like I didn't have a friend in the world. Jordan and Dexler checked in on me. No one else." She blotted her face, drying tears. "The silence from you, the *Headmistress,* while reading the headlines was . . ." She hugs around herself.

Hearing my title pokes me like a knife in the ribs. That's what people see when they look at me now. A House. Power. Someone in control of freedoms and fates.

"I'm sorry," she goes on. "This isn't just about me. That's not what I'm saying." She sobs, and I pull her into a hug.

"You needed a friend, too, Abby. I hear you."

She holds on to me so tightly it brings tears to my eyes. *My first friend.* If she feels this way, I can only imagine how Erla and the others feel. When we let go, I eye the time and realize there isn't much of it left.

"Jordan is planning to go through with the extraction."

Her lashes flutter. "He is planning to die?"

"To save me, yes."

"What about the Scroll?" she asks.

I update her on the Scroll. "I need you to call him here for something dire. Perhaps tell him there were some additional tests you need to run, or some epiphany you've had. I'm going to go destroy the lab before he has the chance to use it."

"Then what?"

"I need some kind of sleep elixir. Something that won't hurt him. I'm going to lock him in the basement and seal it with protections so he cannot get out." With him locked away, I can figure out a safer plan to get this magic out of him.

"I don't know about this. He will be furious." She stuffs her hands in her pockets. "Wouldn't it be easier to just leave him to his fate?" Abby's countenance darkens. "You don't need him. You just need the magic inside him."

"Sometimes we have to fight for those we love when they are hurting too much to fight for themselves. I won't abandon him in his most desperate time of need."

She shrugs and turns back to her rocks. "I'll send for him like you asked. Just let me know when."

An unsettled feeling sticks to my ribs.

When midday lunch comes, I spend the time in the halls, watching for Jordan, who appears right as planned. He moves at a fast stride down the corridor, through the foyer, and turns the corner toward the healing ward. I stroll casually, careful to stay out of his line of sight. When he disappears into the Healer office, my heart thuds.

It's now or never.

As I linger in the hall while a handful of people are escorted to their rooms with lunch trays, I spot Erla. She speeds up. I catch up to her.

"Wait up."

She's rigid with fear, eyeing the stragglers in the halls. "I know what you did."

What I'm *about* to do . . .

"My brother."

I swallow my exhale.

"At least I am free of him now." Housemates linger in the corridor, waiting for her.

"Move along," I tell them. "Back to your rooms."

"I should get back to my room, too." Erla pulls away from me and runs off. I clench my fists and race toward the Sunrise Corridor. The long hall of session rooms is empty. I will just have to do this myself. I reach the extraction lab and twist the knob with a fistful of toushana in my free hand.

It's locked.

I burn through the door with my toushana, but the room is dark and empty. Where there were once rows of tables and lines of chairs is just stone floor. The chalk wall that was covered in equations has been wiped clean. Everything for the extraction is gone. I stumble backward and out of the room, checking to make sure I have the right one.

I break into the room next door. Also empty.

The next several are wiped clean, as well.

The world sways.

He knows what I planned, and he beat me to it.

I search the entire estate for over an hour. But find nothing, no indication of where the lab was moved to. I circle back to Abby's office, but the door is open, and her things are disheveled as if she left in a rush. Dexler is still unconscious.

"I wish you could give me advice," I say to her slumbering body. "I'm so sorry this has happened. I hoped . . . It wasn't . . . You didn't deserve this."

Dexler was always so helpful. She was the first maezre to see something in me. She waited here and protected House of Marionne the best way she could, hoping I'd show up. When so many others left, she believed in me. "I'm really sorry. Somehow, I'm going to fix all of this."

I dash out of Abby's office, feeling a bit silly talking to someone who probably can't hear me. And also feeling a bit relieved. I check the third floor for Jordan. Maybe he came to find me. But he is not there either. I am out of breath when I make it to the dormitories. But the entire wing is vacant.

The recently repaired walls have caved in. Blackened, rotting doors have been ripped out of their hinges. I nearly trip over heaps of rubble, trying to check each room to be sure no one's there. My throat is dry as I race back toward the stairs to the ground floor. When I hear a whisper of voices, it sends my pulse racing with foolish hope. The faint sounds lead me through the foyer, past the grand ballroom, past the broom closet, and down the narrow stairs that lead to the basement. The voices disappear.

A shriek rips the air.

I run toward the sound.

There are shouts. Another scream. Something crashes. Someone wails.

Then Jordan's voice shatters the silence.

"*Enough!*" he says again.

I follow his voice to the maezre storage closet where extra enhancer supplies and furniture are kept. When I push against the door, it doesn't budge.

"Jordan! Erla, are you in there?"

The voices quiet. But there is another crashing bang. I pull all the magic I can muster to my hands and shove shadows against the door. It rots beneath my fists, inch by inch. When the hole is wide enough, I force myself through.

The storage room is set up with a table like the extraction lab. A tangle of wires runs between Jordan and several golden rings. The wires' ends are frayed and broken, held in Jordan's fist. He stands, seething, beside the table. But it's what's around him that chills me to the bone.

Everyone is in metal restraining handcuffs, their wrists linked together. Mothers, children. Willam's have been tied to rusted pipe. Knox's arms are in cuffs in her lap, paces away from him. Erla is clamping a restraint on someone else.

"You shouldn't be here!" Jordan says. "I made *every arrangement* to ensure you would not be here."

"Jordan," I manage.

"I caught two of them trying to replace the rings with this mask." He holds up an ornate, polished full-face white mask. "They were going to *steal* the toushana."

"And destroy it," someone shouts between sobs.

"Erla, tell her."

"It is true. I uncovered the treason myself."

"*Ending* all dark magic, including *yours*! You see what I'm fighting against? They will *stay here* like this as long as it takes, until I say!"

Two of them. And yet every person in this house is held against their will. "Jordan, you have to stop this. Because one is guilty doesn't mean they all are." That's what the Order believed about toushana. Fear has turned him into the very thing he's trying to destroy.

Shadows bleed from him. A haze of dark magic hangs in the air like storm clouds. Dimara cowers at Kedd's feet, holding on to his legs.

"I tried to stop them, and then things get hard to remember." He chokes on his words. "I lost control, Quell. And now we're *weeks* behind, if we can even salvage this at all." He shakes the frayed wires. "I have failed you. I have done nothing but fail you over and over again. This is the *last* thing I could do for you. I can't even do this right!" He trembles with rage because it feels safer to him than fear.

"There is only a thread of him left, Quell," Knox says. "It's now or never, Headmistress."

I see Jordan clearer than I ever have. The guilt he wrestles with, the anger he finds comfort in, the darkness urging him to act on his most desperate desires. Desires growing like weeds in a heart full of fear. He is responsible for this mess. No one else can be blamed for his actions. But I can't stop running from the truth either—the future is in my hands.

I have to take control. *And lead.*

"The magic—" he starts.

"It's not the magic, Jordan. Look around. This is all *you*." Force would break him. Maybe love can rebuild him.

His eyes narrow. "How could you say that to me?"

Nothing is more loving than telling him the truth. "This is you fighting for something you never needed to prove. You've never felt good enough to be loved by your father, to be respected by your aunt, to be a person of your own choosing. You were forced to *prove* that you are worthy of their love. You've cut them off, but their voices still whisper in your mind."

His throat bobs. His nostrils flare. But a glaze gleams in his eye.

"And all this time you've been trying to prove to yourself that you deserve my love." I move closer to him, pulling the wires out of his hand. "You already have my love. Not because of your magic or the family you come from or your ability to fix the world's problems or even your ability to save me! You have my love, Jordan, just as you are. On the messy days and the good ones. At the times when you're strong. And the times when you are lost. I love you, Jordan, because of who you are, *not* what you do. You're worthy of love and freedom, simply because *you exist*."

It breaks me that he's never known that kind of love. My own mother had to learn that I need to be seen and loved, toushana and all. Just as I am.

"That's the only kind of love that can silence the constant voices saying you're not good enough."

He shakes his head. "I don't understand." He shoves away, tears forming.

"I know. But I hope by hearing the truth, you can begin to."

He storms out.

SIXTY-FOUR

Jordan

The halls of Chateau Soleil are as silent as death.

What have I done? Memories of the last hour are hazy. But the faces of everyone in the basement with tethered wrists haunt me. Imalia, who helped me search everyone. Kedd. The twins. Mothers cuffed, arms roped with their children. *They weren't in on stealing the magic!* I claw at my scalp. *How did I get here?*

Out. I need out of this place.

My chest aches as if it might burst. I run upstairs, through the foyer to the broom closet, and keep running until I'm outside filling my lungs with the scents of earthy oak and ash. I glare at my hands, unable to move.

I've ruined so many lives.

I've torn families apart, destroyed peace in the name of creating a *better* peace. My gut lurches, and I hunch over, expecting my insides to spill at my feet. All the people I've sentenced to die as a Dragun, and later as a Heart, the safe houses I've raided.

I can still see their faces.

Several deserved justice. But most didn't. Duty blinded me; they all looked the same.

And here I've let fear choke me into the same deception.

My knees hit the ground, tugged down by the weight of my calcified heart. The smell of dirt sends my heart racing. I glance backward, expecting to see Beaulah. Somehow she is the mastermind behind all this, toying with and twisting my mind. The promotions, the recognition, the old pins on my lapel were my pats on the back, the squeeze of a real hug, the *good job* I craved.

I claw at my chest, phantom feelings of pins being stabbed there send goose bumps up my arms. *Second son*, my father'd called me when he took me on my first raid with him. After I proved to him I could make perfect marks and outperform my peers at every turn, only then did he take me under his wing. He gifted me our first hug. He kept me away from my mother as often as he could. *Her love is too soft*, he'd chastise. Tears burn my eyes.

I was only a failure to him, not a son. Until I wasn't.

The problems became mine to fix. My father's legacy was mine to repair. My brother was mine to save. My aunt was mine to keep contained. I've buried those relationships. But their hold on me feels like arms reaching from a grave. *Why would Quell love me any differently? Why would anyone?* More tears come, and I can't fight them anymore. A rush of sorrow drowns my cheeks.

I claw at my hair, squeezing my skull between my hands until it hurts.

Quell has battled the same magic and come out of it controlled.

It's not the toushana.

It's me.

Haunted, angry, resentful *me*.

Quell is right. It is choices, not magic, that makes a person good or bad. My entire life's been built on a lie. This whole Order is a lie. A broken system run by corrupt people who villainize those they want to oppress.

They created enemies to erase their humanity.

Was I not tempted to do the same thing? Fear made me forget the joy of seeing laughter in Stryker's eyes. The affections between Kedd and Dimara. The terror of being thrown into a world without knowing the rules.

In trying to save the girl I love, I destroyed everyone else's hope.

And yet it's hope that I see in Quell's brown eyes. It's hope that made me come to House of Marionne in the first place. Hope made me believe that I could save her. Hope does more good than any one person can.

With hope, we are never truly powerless.

It's hope that sparkles in the black gems of Quell's diadem. Defiant, rebellious hope. I glare again at my bruises. Hope is how the world changes, not by the power in one person's hands.

Who am I to make a new world everyone has to live in? How does that make me any different from the monsters I'm trying to escape?

The truth unsteadies me. I curl up on the ground, my heart heavy.

"Jordan?" Quell crosses the damp ground and kneels beside me. She strokes my hair. The tears come harder, and it feels like a rotted dam finally buckling. She pulls my head into her lap and slips something into my hand. A bag of candy. She plucks a green one and offers it to me. I take it with shaky hands.

I don't have answers.

I don't have plans.

I'm not sure I have a future.

But I can't help but feel like this is where true healing begins. I settle my head against her, letting her hold me. And I cry until there are no tears left.

Then I cry some more.

PART FOUR

SIXTY-FIVE

Quell

It takes every single person in the House with any kind of Shifting magic two full days, sunup to sundown, to repair the damage to the dormitories. Jordan does his part by hand, without rest or magic. In the meantime, the entire private family floor has been fully opened up for anyone. The rooms are furnished with double-stacked beds so that there is plenty of space.

I still have the Sphere's magic to deal with, and I need to figure out the best way to move forward. This is on my shoulders now, but that's my choice. So it feels different.

After Jordan addressed the group, apologizing profusely, I did as well—for not taking the lead sooner. I told everyone they're welcome to stay and help save the House and join it officially, magic or not. Or they can leave. No one will stop them.

Ultimately, people have a choice to make. How do I covet freedom for myself but not fight for it for everyone? I can't anymore. We have *so much* left to do, but if freedom is my legacy, it won't be just for me. Maybe that's why my grandmother did what she did. Maybe that's why my mother serves where she serves: to give others choices they wouldn't otherwise have. I have the power to give everyone here a choice. So I did.

I'd expected most to bolt the minute I undid their cuffs. But only a few left. Everyone was so shaken up and unsure where to go with the

Dragunhead on the loose. There was also a fair amount of relief that Dexler's attacker is out of the house. Many have stayed, deciding to give *me* a chance.

While the House worked on repairs, I spent that time listening to the concerns of those who are still here to better understand how a new Order could serve wider needs that include everyone. It was interesting to hear that some of them have no desire for magic at all. Others are very curious and enjoyed the magic classes Dexler had put together. We spent last night drumming up all kinds of ideas about safe houses. Willam even attended the meeting. Though he sat in the back and just listened, it felt like a step in the right direction. We haven't spoken since everything happened.

My first order of business today is to talk to Willam and Knox about my plans to save magic. I need their help. And their forgiveness.

Jordan has a ticking time clock on his life.

And the Scroll is a dud.

I stroll the hall toward the stairs. If someone on their deathbed got the Immortality Scroll, they used it. And if they used it, they are still alive somewhere. The only way to defeat death is immortality. And if the immortal is findable, maybe their blood would do the trick? A transfusion, perhaps, with Jordan's blood at the same time as we run an extraction?

I rub my clammy hands on my clothes. I can't help but see all the glaring holes and potential problems in my plan. It feels like holding on to a balloon with too much air. I have more questions than answers. But this time at Chateau Soleil has made me realize, we are stronger together. If we can focus on what unites us, we just might survive. For the first time in a while, it feels like magic, *and Jordan*, might actually have a chance.

When I reach the first floor, I spot him. He walks beside me so close our arms brush.

"Ready?" he asks, and I smile tightly.

"How is today?" I ask him, as I have each morning the last couple of days.

"Yellow with some blues." Between repairing the estate, he's been spending time alone, sifting through the wreckage of his past, looking for ways it's still on his back. I've started asking how he is doing instead of assuming. And he's started digging deep for an honest answer, even when it's not pretty. He uses colors to describe his mood. It is easier for him to be vulnerable that way.

"Yellow is good."

He laces his fingers between mine. We walk in silence toward my office, where Willam and Knox are waiting.

"Don't be nervous." He can feel it. "You'll know the right thing to say." He doesn't offer another word of advice. He didn't even ask for the details of my plan when I mentioned this to him yesterday. He only knows that I asked him to be with me when I unveiled it to Knox and Willam. I hold his hand tighter, grateful for his complete trust, which only makes me determined to trust myself more.

"How is your pain level?"

He grimaces. His heart might be repairing, but after the damage he did to the dormitories in a rage, the magic rotting the side of his body has spread to his limbs. When we reach my office door, Jordan squeezes my hand.

"Do you mind if I say something first?"

"Sure."

Willam folds his arms over his chest when Jordan enters the room. I wouldn't blame Willam if he never wanted to talk to Jordan again. I'm surprised he didn't haul out of here the first chance he got. Dimara did. But he, Knox, Kedd, and the twins stayed.

We take our seats across from Willam and Knox.

Jordan jumps right in. "Before anything, I want to apologize to you both, face-to-face. Especially you." He looks right at Willam. "I've put everyone through a lot, but I've put Willam through hell. I won't make an excuse for it. I just hope I'll have the chance to earn your trust again."

Willam pulls at the collar of his shirt, which is unbuttoned, the Darkbearer tattoo mark not hidden anymore. "You're one determined bastard. I'm not sure we'll ever see eye to eye. But you were right, there was a very dangerous traitor among us. I hope your maezre is alright."

"Still unconscious," I say.

"You both have a lot on your shoulders," Willam goes on. "I could have been more understanding of that. I *am* grateful Yaniselle was found out before she hurt anyone else. But the one thing we can agree on, Jordan, is that girl right there." He points at me. "I'm sorry, Quell, again, for not being up front about our Darkbearer allies. I realize this is complicated, and it wasn't right for me to act like it's simple. None of this is simple. I believe you want to set things right. And that's what matters most."

Knox rubs his knee. "We talked, and we want to see it through."

"See *you* through," Willam adds. "If you're steering the ship, we're on board."

Their trust makes a lump rise in my throat, and no amount of swallowing shoves it down.

"Well," I say. "That's a relief, because I need you both. I'm drawing up a declaration. Our House is marching to Dlaminaugh. We need to work more closely with House of Ambrose." They're the ones who understand immortality magic better than anyone. I explain my plan.

"Is a magical artifact still needed? We know a Trader who can procure anything. Her name is Lady Ruby."

Jordan and I share a look.

"We can write to her and ask her to bring what she has to House of Ambrose. She knows us well. She'll do us this favor."

We agree on it. It feels good to be on the same side, fully, for once.

"We're a team," Knox says, reaching across the table to shake my hand. "I was tough on you at the end. But Rhea's daughter came through."

"Quell, call me Quell, please."

She smiles. "What about everyone left here during the march? This place hasn't felt like a home for too long."

"Because the wrong person was leading them," Jordan says. "It's your decision, Quell, but could Knox be left in charge, officially, while we're gone?"

"Exactly what I was thinking. I'll draw up an addendum to the declaration. Knox Molaudi of the West Coast Molaudis, in my absence, you are acting Headmistress and beneficiary of House of Marionne."

SIXTY-SIX

Adola

From Beaulah's bedroom, Yaniselle's body could be seen swaying against the iron railing of the second-floor balconies. It felt intentional. Adola pulled the curtain and returned to her aunt's bedside, where the Healer was tending to her. She didn't see who'd hung her there, but this had her cousin's fingerprints all over it.

The room reeked of sickness. Adola didn't know what death smelled like, but she was fairly sure this was it. Her aunt's Healer removed the cooling cloth from Beaulah's forehead, replacing it with a new one. Adola poured the tea, waiting for the meeting to start. Her aunt couldn't wander very far these days. So she insisted the meetings took place in person at her bed.

When her Healer finished tending her fever, Beaulah Perl rose to sit on the edge of her bed. Adola rushed her walking stick to her, and she thanked her with a stern look. Appreciation only a niece to Beaulah Perl would recognize.

"Take my arm." Adola held it out at her aunt, who slapped it away. Beaulah pulled her robe tighter across her body and smoothed the edges of her hair before carefully making her way from the bed to the sitting lounge near the fire adjacent to her bedroom. Adola followed closely behind.

"My tea," her aunt demanded as the Healer departed.

The others were already in their seats. Ellery Ambrose. The Dragunhead.

"Nice of you to be here, Ellery." She petted his arm. "That Hargrove girl was never right for you."

"I quite agree," he said.

"And, Sal, it is nice of you to come all this way," her aunt said, gesturing for their guests to take their teacups. She was determined to convince everyone that she would survive this sickness. Adola wasn't so sure. Beaulah fell ill shortly after the Sphere broke. Adola brought in every renowned Healer in her House, but none of them recognized what was plaguing her.

Beaulah shooed them all away, certain they were inept. She called on her Healer who had served her since she was born instead. No one had been allowed to tend to her since. Adola was thrust into House duties immediately. More forcefully than she would have wished. She had no love for her aunt, but Headship *would* be hers eventually. She was committed to proving she could be trusted.

"It's no problem. I am sorry to hear about your—" The Dragunhead gestured to the body hanging beyond the window. Beaulah fell into her seat and reached for her tea, which Adola set in her hands carefully. Her aunt drank, exhaled, and waved a flippant hand at the Dragunhead.

"She was a tortured girl, her own worst enemy. I knew she'd hang one day. It was never wise of you to trust her to spy for you."

Ellery hadn't moved. He was always uncomfortable during these meetings. Just then they caught eyes, and he reached for her hand. Adola set her fingers in his. He stroked her skin, and she remembered to smile.

"It sends a strong message," Adola said. "They are onto us." She hadn't felt like sending Yaniselle to betray Jordan under the guise of being kicked out of House of Perl was the *best* plan. Even sending her with Yaniselle's secret thorned rose column tattooed on her wouldn't help. Jordan was too suspicious of a person to fall for that. He and Yaniselle also had a complicated history.

"Sending her after my nephew will either work convincingly or blow up," her aunt had said. She was right about that, at least.

The Dragunhead set his cup down. "Not to worry. Yaniselle got me what I needed to know most. Beyond that, she was a decoy."

Adola sat up. She'd never imagined herself in the middle of a feud over what the magical world would become. But she intended to have her own House in the new world, whatever it took. She was done being in her aunt's shadow. If she'd learned anything from her, it was that to get what she wanted she had to take it.

"Aunt Beaulah," she said. "More tea?"

SIXTY-SEVEN

Nore

Nore climbed the steps to the Caelum. She snaked her way through the library and rapped her fist on Winkel's door. The door parted, revealing the priest in a shockingly bright blue robe. He was chatting with Kimper and Pizor. They adjusted their drab gray line robes as they rose from their seats before excusing themselves with only contemptuous glances in Nore's direction.

"Is everything alright, child?" He let her in.

She had been to Winkel's private quarters countless times. When she was little, sometimes he'd let her hide in there to get away with her mischief a while longer. But that morning, the mirth in Winkel's expression was replaced with a frown.

"I'm sorry for coming without notice." She sat on his kneeler by the fire and a large window overlooking the ice garden. On the ledge of the window was a mug-sized ring of condensation. His hand trembled as he poured her a cup of tea.

"How can I pray for you, my dear?"

"I *want* answers." She sipped the warm drink, and he sat on a bench beside her. She felt bad for snapping at him. "Sorry. You've been watching the forest, too?"

"I pray day and night for whatever is afoot in there."

"Ellery is determined to get rid of the ancestors in case they try to protect me. And the Dragunhead is helping him by *killing* the dead." She watched him for surprise. "Necrantomy."

Winkel straightened his glasses and strode to his shelf. His finger trailed rows of spines. "Hmph. Must have lent it out."

"What is it?"

"*Ancient Studies of Ascension.* Only ancient Marked knew how to use ancient magic techniques. It's been lost to modern magic."

"It hasn't if it's being used by Ellery." Nore's mind raced ahead of her words, rumbling over questions. There was a world of things she didn't understand. Like why the Dragunhead would help Ellery. What could Ellery have promised him? What would someone who can live forever want?

"How do I beat someone with a magic I don't even understand?" Someone who'd changed personas like clothes *for centuries*?

"Mmmm," he muttered. "I suppose it's understanding what this someone *truly* wants. Have you pondered that?"

"I'll take any books you have on Necrantomy." This wasn't helpful. She wanted him to answer her plainly, not in riddles, or give her more questions than she already had. "I should go." She'd hoped he would be less cryptic. She stood to leave, but when she reached the door, Nore said, "Kendall Dorset. Do you know the name?"

"Your cleverness leaves no stone unturned."

Nore let go of the door's handle and faced her old friend, the shock of the last few hours fusing together in her mind impossible conclusions. "Who was he?"

"Kimper and I were told that your mother's suitor *had* to be Kendall Dorset. A fellow we didn't even know. Our votes and review of him were perfunctory."

"*Who* told you that?"

"Priest Pizor. He said the Sovereign had appeared to him and gave him a divine revelation of the name of who should be chosen."

Nore couldn't sit still. The Dragunhead could appear as *anyone* to Priest Pizor. And say whatever he wanted. The pieces fell together.

Kendall Dorset didn't debut from House Ambrose.

He didn't drop out.

Nor was he one of their esteemed dead.

Because Kendall Dorset was one of the Dragunhead's aliases.

Her head hurt. She would bet everything she had to her name.

"Priest Pizor was fooled by a master trickster of many faces," she said.

My father is immortal. And he is helping my brother plot to kill me.

She stormed out the door past a gaping Winkel.

Her mother was going to finally tell her the *full truth*!

NORE FOUND ISLA wandering the halls near her own quarters. When Isla spotted her, she rushed toward her.

"There you are!" Her mother was out of breath. "I've gotten a message from your brother."

Inside Nore's room, she snatched the letter from her mother and tore it open. It was addressed to Isla, not her.

It's not too late.

Nore ripped it in half. "What does it mean?"

Isla scrambled for the confetti floating to the floor. "He wants me to support his claim for Headship, which I will never do. It's you. It's always been you." Nore met her mother's eyes and waited for the snippet of criticism, but it didn't come.

"He is writing to you because you two were close, I assume? He thinks he can turn your loyalty."

"He is my son, Nore. My firstborn."

"And I am your daughter. So excuse my surprise that he'd think you suddenly have a conscience."

Her mother flinched but held her tongue. Nore's gut twisted. "I'm sorry. I shouldn't have said that." She wasn't sure how to relate to her mother anymore. Dealing with her now, considering all the secrets and distance between them, only made matters more confusing.

"It's forgotten," her mother said, but Nore could tell from the way her mother's bottom lip shook that she was deeply hurt.

"I'm sorry, Mother, really."

"Thank you."

"Ellery is in the forest, digging up graves, killing our dead with ancient magic that he *didn't* learn here."

Her mother bit her lip and looked away.

"*You knew.*"

"I feared it the moment I saw something was happening in the forest."

"You feared more than that."

Her mother held her shawl around her as if it were armor. As if this conversation risked shredding her to pieces.

"My father, *our* father, is helping Ellery—the Dragunhead."

"I *did not* know, Nore, for a very long time! He showed up at my door decades ago, and I thought he was hand selected by the priests and confirmed by the House through vote, like the custom. I even grew fond of him. He knew I couldn't love him, but we had an understanding. He was as close as I could get to having someone. I didn't get pregnant right away. It was difficult. But he *stayed*." Her mother's broken heart was evident all over her face.

"He became a maezre under a different name to keep close by. We shared a life. I believed . . ." She sighed. "When I told him I was finally pregnant and it was a boy, he was disappointed. He wanted to make an heir with me, he always said. When you were born, I never saw him again. Nore, I didn't have a heart, and it hurt like hell. I grew angrier year after year. I had my Draguns hunt for him, but he was a ghost. Then I discovered that Kendall was a persona. I *still* feel nauseous about it." She rested a palm on her stomach and turned her back to me. "I kept digging. When I realized it was just one of his many aliases, I spent a decade, most of your childhood, trying to track him down and figure out exactly who he was and how he infiltrated this House." She white-knuckled a seat back near her. "It took *years*, and you were growing so fast. I never found conclusive answers. I feared he might want something from you when you took on your Headship." Her expression darkened. "I won't lie. I wanted to find him and kill him."

She'd never heard her mother talk this way.

"Then his name faded and mention of him or any of the aliases I'd uncovered completely disappeared."

"Mother, he's immortal. Think about it."

Her mother stared blankly. Then her smile faded as Nore's words sank in.

"He's been changing aliases for lifetimes. And now he is coaching Ellery to get rid of the ancestors to get to me. What I need you to tell me is *why*. I need to know everything."

There was no way out of this without blood. Either Ellery died or she did.

"All those years." Her mother smoothed her bangs off her forehead. "Your brother would take trips away. I wonder if he was maintaining some kind of relationship with him behind my back."

"My brother changed bedrooms when he entered induction. Which was his?" Nore was going to search it for any hints of her brother's weaknesses. She had to bring down a duo who felt impenetrable, who had all the advantage and lifetimes of magic on their side.

"It's the fourth suite in the family's private wing. There's a faulty lock on the door. I never had it fixed."

"Stay here." She crossed the room to her door.

"Nore, fight for what you really want."

She stopped, remembering Yagrin's plan to break the Pact. She didn't like his plan, and she was terrified to let herself hope something like that was possible.

"I made a life with someone who wasn't real. That was the beginning of the end for me. I stopped trying to make something beautiful out of my mess." She grabbed Nore's hand, and Nore let her. "Don't be like me. Grow roses in a field of ashes. Dare to get your heart back if you want it."

Nore stared, speechless.

"You are far cleverer than I ever was. If there is a way, I am confident you will find it."

Bang. Brrrrang! Bang.

Nore jumped. The sound came from the estate's grand entrance. Nore rushed out of her mother's room and down the hall as débutants piled in, pulled from their studies by the noise.

Quell Marionne and Jordan Wexton appeared in the foyer of Dlaminaugh Estate.

Jordan looked like death. And Quell was haggard, along with another of those traveling with them. The crowd of Ambrose in the entryway corridor of the estate swelled with débutants gawking at the guests.

"It's him," someone whispered.

Nore elbowed her way through the crowd. She heard her brother's name shouted. Someone stumbled into her as she tried to get to Quell and Jordan. Glass hit the ground and shattered.

"Headmistress, should we lock him up?" someone yelled as she passed. Nore clenched her fists. "If the rumors are true—"

"*Are* the rumors true, Headmistress?" another asked. "Did he steal magic? Is *he* the reason our magic is intermittent?"

The building rocked with voices and people. The walls felt like they were closing in.

She screamed, "Eyes *here*!" She wouldn't live a lie anymore. The deception had to stop, and it could, right now, with her. "I have an announcement you're going to want to hear!" Nore climbed halfway up the stairs for a better view of the foyer teeming with a hundred or more.

"This House has been steeped in deception and secrecy since its inception."

Every voice was silent.

"The Headmistress of this House has a Pact with the dead ancestors.

They get to channel our magic to keep themselves in spirit form. And we get to channel their magic to enhance our House members' born-magic, making our magical intellect sharper than the rest." She wanted many things. But more than anything, she wanted to be *done* living in secret. She held up her hands. "That Pact should have killed me. Because I don't have magic."

A gasp swept across the foyer.

"That is why you never saw me in your classes. That is why I was whisked away to my cottage and on sabbatical. That is why I have hated this place." Her voice broke. "But these last few weeks it has grown on me. We are in crisis, my fellow Ambrosers. And I can get us out of this mess. I know I can. But I need you to trust me *and our guests*."

Stares shifted to Quell, Jordan, and now Yagrin, who'd joined them. He stood beside Nore.

"Ellery is killing our ancestors, which is a threat to all our highly developed magic. And he's trying to kill me to take this House for himself. I have no intention of letting him. If you don't like that, there's the door. But if you turn your back on me now, you are never welcome to return."

At first, no one moved.

Then a few shoved their way through the crowd, muttering to themselves, before storming out into the snow.

"Anyone else?" she asked. She spotted Lauren in the crowd, who pressed a palm with knotted fingers to her heart. Nore felt something strange bite at her lips. A smile. She drew strength from her mother's words, who watched from across the crowd.

The audience parted, allowing their guests through.

"About the other matter. We will need to be careful," Yagrin muttered to her. "My brother is a naturally suspicious person. And nothing gets past Quell. Are you with me?"

"If it's the only way, yes, I am." She was going to get her heart back. Whatever it took.

SIXTY-EIGHT

Quell

The halls of Dlaminaugh reek of death. Dead rove the halls. Most of the walls are the color of cement, and the whole place is frigidly cold. I sit down in a chair in Nore's office as close to the fire as I can, holding the metal box with the diadem of proper magic. Jordan lingers behind me, standing, refusing a seat at the table. Erla is beside me, pulling at the hem of her dress. We wait for some time.

"I hear they are very smart," she says when maezres enter the room in drab gray linen with stoic stares. Isla Ambrose, Nore's mother, is on their heels in a deep blue gown with silver stitching. Her plain diadem arced over her head is ornamented with a single gemstone.

I hold my own fidgety hands still and say, "*You* are smarter." I whisper to Jordan, "Maybe we should have brought some more of our own."

"No second-guessing yourself." He returns to his post just as his brother enters with Nore. The brothers share a hard glare. A wall of ice can be felt between them all across the room. Nore, too, is in a bright blue gown with gold buttons and capped sleeves. A rust sash is sloped across her chest. Nore takes a seat at the head of the long meeting table with Yagrin beside her. Jordan crosses the room, sticking to the perimeter, giving his brother a wide berth. I straighten in my seat as Nore updates everyone and makes formal introductions.

"I've invited our lead maezres and priests. They are some of the brightest magical minds, House loyalties aside, I'm sure we all agree."

"What is the plan here?" One of their maezres jumps right in, addressing Isla. But Nore's mother only has eyes for her daughter. "Will the Sphere be re-created?"

Nore gestures at me.

"The Sphere's proper magic is secure at the moment. It's the other magic that needs to be preserved. Toushana. It will be held in rings." I explain my version of Jordan's plan. Thirty times more rings than he'd originally planned, so we can make sure *many* have access to toushana. I still don't like the idea of dark magic only being given to a finite number of people, but rings are efficient to make, and we are short on time. "If the rings work well enough for the toushana, we may move the proper magic to rings in the future to prevent the vessel it's currently in being stolen. If magic is housed in many places, it can't easily be stolen."

"The *dark* magic?" a different maezre with a silver mask sloped over their face says, their beady blue eyes darting around the table.

"Yes," I go on. "One entrusted to each of the Houses. And a few other new Houses."

"*New* Houses? Toushana in rings? Is this your plan?" The maezre turns to Nore.

"Maezre Ogle, we do not have the Sphere's magic," she says. "They've come to us with it. We can't just—"

"The desire to hold on to dark magic is *deplorable*," a maezre says. "Why not get rid of it?"

I watch Nore carefully, unsure what she thinks of the world to come.

"I don't have any desire for *any* magic," she says. "Does that mean I should get rid of proper magic, too?"

"Toushana has existed just as long," I say. "Long ago, toushana was not dark. It was feared and treated as forbidden by those in power." I brandish a stream of dark mist in the air. "My magic has its uses."

Most backs in the room stiffen. Except Nore's. She smirks as she rolls up her sleeves and a puff of shadows emerge in her fist. I gasp.

"My mother did everything she could to unearth magic in me," Nore says, and her mother's stare hits the ground. "And deposited a seed of this by mistake. I told you, no more secrets. That's the truth."

Eyes move to Isla Ambrose. "It is. The greatest regret of my life."

Ogle is wide-eyed. The others don't speak.

"I have plans to get this out of me by choice," Nore went on. "But these are our only allies." She shifted. "It is illogical to ostracize Quell because men who lived hundreds of years ago were scared of what she could do with her fingers." Nore laughed, breaking the rigid silence. Only Jordan grinned as he leaned against a wall.

"This discussion is over," Nore says.

"So we're not going to come up with a way to get rid of it?" Maezre Ogle asks, apparently hard of hearing.

"Both magics need to exist," the priest says, coming through the door, finally joining us. "They don't need each other to exist. But they are each more potent when the other exists. We have to save toushana, too."

"*I wouldn't* agree to getting rid of it even if she said to," I say to the maezre directly. "This is who I am. You don't have to like it."

Nore and I met eyes. "I like you."

Winkel sits beside her.

"Quell, you have much more experience with toushana than I do, I imagine. So we will follow your lead on how to help secure it safely." Nore eyes the skepticism around the room. "*All of us* will follow your lead. Or you can join my brother outside. Any more on that, Quell?"

"The most pressing matter is that the Sphere's toushana is still inside Jordan."

Winkel winces. "Oh, that sounds awful, young man."

"We'll need to get that out fast and *safely*. Or it will be lost. To do that we need immortal blood," I go on, "which is why we are here. That is your specialty."

Nore pales.

"There's no such thing," Ogle says again, determined, turning a bracelet on her dainty wrist. "Everyone here knows that. The secrets were buried by our inaugural Headmistress and have yet to be found."

"The Scroll—" Nore starts.

"*The Scroll* will *not* be discussed so publicly . . ." Maezre Ogle fumes. "*It is sacred.* Have we forgotten ourselves?"

"Caera Ambrose was a fraud," Nore continues, ignoring her, addressing every other face of shock in the room. "Caera finding the Immortality Scroll was a ruse to build her great name."

"I *cannot!*" Maezre Ogle shoots up from her seat. "First the toushana. Now this! You are outside of your lane, young lady!" Her fists slam the table, and Nore turns to a Dragun.

"See her out. Walk her all the way to my brother in the forest." She clears her throat and steeples her hands.

"As I was saying, *lying* runs in our veins in this House. And I'm frankly *sick of it.*"

Erla sinks into her chair beside me.

"Caera worked tirelessly to produce *replicas* and then planted them in the Houses to give them the aura of authenticity. She wrote diaries to herself, journaling lies upon lies about what she did. She fabricated a scavenger hunt, knowing people would *die* to find her alleged secret. And she did it all to ensure she was revered as the most brilliant Ambroser to ever live. Then she named the House after herself. It's true. Yagrin spoke to a Duncan elder who confirmed the original was written on goatskin. I researched the rest myself."

Winkel shoves his glasses to his nose. "We've suspected as much but could never be sure." He tucks his lip, and his shoulders sink.

Mouths are open all around the table, including mine. But I button it up and bring us back to why we're here. "If we can find this immortal's blood," I say, "the plan is to infuse it into Jordan at the *same time* that we extract toushana."

Erla nods.

"Hmm," a maezre adds. "I'm Maezre Tutom, Nore's governess when she was small. It's a pleasure to meet you, Headmistress Marionne. This fellow has to be strong enough. If he isn't, we can't risk touching him without some kind of mortality plan." They stroke their beard. "This is good. Quite good."

"The blood *is* a sound plan," another adds.

"As brilliant as it sounds," Jordan cuts in, "where are we going to find this immortal?"

"You're in luck." Nore's color returns. "Turns out I know him. Kendall Dorset. My father. The Dragunhead."

I don't believe my ears as Nore tells us about her conversation with Winkel, confirming that her father was—*is*—a man of many faces. Jordan's grip is white-knuckled on the lapel of his coat. Nore slides a list of names across the table toward me.

"More of his aliases my mother found over the years."

I skim the list, flip the page, and there are more. "May I borrow this?"

Nore waves a hand in the air. "How do we lure him here?" She taps her chin as she surveys her maezres.

"Use Quell as bait." Jordan peels himself from the shadows. "He's wanted her since my time in the brotherhood."

"Why?" I ask.

"That, I don't know. But when the Sphere cracked, he told me to go after Beaulah and he'd retrieve *you*. If you offer a meeting with Quell, he will come. Just a suggestion. I'm not in charge here." His brother glances at him, then quickly looks away.

I recall the creepy way the Dragunhead didn't take his eyes off me during our meeting.

"Do it," I say. "Let's tell him that I want to meet."

SIXTY-NINE

Nore

Silence fell over the room. Nore gripped the table. What about Ellery? Her brother, who was encroaching on her position, her life! Quell and Jordan's only concern was the Sphere's magic.

"Before we go any further, my brother is something we need *your* help with."

"The magic inside Jordan is paramount." Quell leaned across the table, tearing herself from the list of my father's names. "We have to get it out of him urgently."

Nore's eye twitched. "I disagree. I've heard your requests. And if we are a team, now you will hear mine."

Quell sat back in her seat.

"My brother is outside these walls murdering our ancestors so he can break in here without being stopped. That is our immediate threat. And our immediate concern."

Quell didn't respond, but Nore could practically hear her thoughts. How was that even of the same stature of an issue as saving the world's magic?

"The walls of this House have become your fortress," she said. "So when it comes to protecting this House, I expect each of you all in."

"That's only fair," Yagrin added.

Jordan's lips thinned.

"You have our support," Quell said. "But do you not see my point about magic?"

"I also want magic safe," Nore said. "My House is relying on me for that. But my brother is the biggest problem at the moment."

"Hardly," Quell said. "What use will Houses be in a world with no magic? We need to divide and conquer."

The clock was ticking, Quell wasn't wrong. This *was* a conundrum. The others stared at her, waiting for her to speak.

"Well?" Yagrin pushed, eyeing his brother, expecting an answer from him. "Are we still on the same team, or are we not?"

Nore's head swam at the question because she knew Yagrin's intentions. But Jordan didn't respond. He wasn't in charge.

"Of course we are," Quell said.

"It sounds like we are outnumbered," Maezre Tutom said.

"How many dead are there?" Yagrin asked. "The brotherhood was a disaster, but we knew how to rally."

Nore's mind noodled. It was never clear to her which dead Ambrosers came back as spirits and which did not. Some of them simply appeared. But one thing was for sure—there were over two thousand graves on their estate, and only a hundred or so had ever wandered the grounds. Much fewer now.

"Respectfully, Headmistress Ambrose, we must focus on protecting our House above all else," Tutom said, and several others nodded.

Quell sat up. "Ellery is *significantly weaker* without the Dragunhead backing him. The numbers don't matter if we cut off the snake's head."

Ellery, the Dragunhead, the Pact, or *magic*.

Which did they prioritize first? Picking one could mean sacrificing another.

Nore had an idea.

She'd made her decision. She gulped down her nerves. "The only sure thing that will bring my brother across the gates of Dlaminaugh is my death. We will announce I've died and my funeral is being held. Along with a coronation for Ellery. We will invite everyone and follow all social protocol. A program, a formal reception, all the things." It was the most convincing plan she could think of. "Quell, write to the Dragunhead and tell him you will be attending and you'd like to meet *before* the ceremony. We will focus our efforts on trapping the Dragunhead—"

"Killing him," Quell says. "Using me as bait."

She nodded. "If you agree."

"It's brilliant."

Nore exhaled. They had a plan. "We will deal with my brother after that. I see the logic in getting rid of the Dragunhead first."

"A mistake!" The shout erupted into chatter.

"Magic could be of use here. We haven't explored those options."

"Well, the girl doesn't have magic. She doesn't think in that way."

"True, very true."

Nore burned with embarrassment. But it was Isla who slapped the table.

"Your Headmistress has spoken," she said. "And she is clever and doesn't need magic."

A jolt of joy fluttered through her vacant chest.

She was. And she didn't. This would show everyone.

As the crowd dispersed, Nore looked for Quell to thank her for showing up and being willing to help. But Quell was flipping through the papers again, concern fusing her brows. Guilt twisted in Nore's stomach at the way Yagrin planned to betray them.

But she set her mind on the Dragunhead.

She had to kill her father. And her brother. Then she'd be free.

SEVENTY

Quell

A bright blue and rust orange flag billows violently at half-mast as we climb the steep steps to the Caelum. With the public notice of Nore Ambrose's death out to *Debs Daily*, our plan is in motion.

"Do you think it'll work?" I ask Jordan.

"That flag will be sweeter than Christmas morning to Ellery Ambrose. He will come."

Riders on horseback dash across the snow toward the edges of the property. Arrangements for Nore's funeral and Ellery's coronation are being set up on the field outside and in the ballroom to take place one after the other.

If the Dragunhead gets inside the gates and their plan *doesn't* work, Jordan and I both will be dead within days. I hand him the letter I wrote to the Dragunhead.

"Still working on the wording."

Jordan reads as we finish the next several hundred steps in silence, my mind whirring about the papers Nore gave me tucked under my arm. The longer I think about it, the more my stomach twists. *All those aliases.* By the time we make it to the top, the estate on the ground is imperceptible. I feel sick, and it has nothing to do with the elevation. *I have to know.*

Jordan and I snake our way to the library and find the study room

Abby was given to make a cloak to paralyze the Dragunhead. She's on the other side of the glass door, drowning in threads and fabric. Beside her is a woman I don't recognize.

"She came," Jordan says. "It's Lady Ruby."

She guides Abby's hand back and forth with a gold-handled brush, dipping its stiff bristles into an iron pot swarming with misty wisps of the paralyzing magic of the Shadow Cell doors. The same magic Jordan used to cover the ballroom doors. Abby paints the magic in careful strokes across the velvety orange cloak before working her magic on the garment to add embellishment detailing, concealing that it's been tampered with.

"I'll get the artifact from her and take it to Erla." Jordan reaches for the door, but I grab his hand.

"Are you alright?" he asks.

I pull the list of names from under my arm and stare at the one that makes me queasy. *Thadius Marqet.* Jordan watches over my shoulder.

"Do you know a Thadius?"

"I know a few Theodores. But not Thadius unless he goes by another name."

My heart pounds so hard it blurs the letters on the page. I see my mother's face. The letters I found in her chest. *Yours, Teddy.* Was it a nickname for Thadius? It could be; it's close. My body hums with cold all over, my toushana agitated. I press back against the wall and close my eyes. *If I'm right, would it even matter? Would it change anything?*

Jordan holds his chest. "Quell, you're worrying me."

"Jordan, I think—" But the words stick in my throat. I've wondered but never gotten clear answers. So I stopped asking so long ago that I've forgotten my mother conceived me with anyone at all. Jordan smooths hair out of my face, and I nestle into his hand.

"I think the Dragunhead is also *my* father."

He sucks in a breath, but has no words. I take the letter back from him and quickly write a new one. One I suspect the Dragunhead won't be able to ignore.

Teddy,
I'll be at the funeral at sunrise to view the body privately.
If you are who I think you are, meet me.
Just us.
—Quell

SEVENTY-ONE

Quell

Dlaminaugh is being pummeled with snow the morning of Nore's funeral. For two days the ancestors' presence has grown around the estate. But the trees in the forest still shake in the middle of the night, which Nore explained means Ellery hasn't given up picking off the ancestors one by one.

Dark gray is the color of mourning at House of Ambrose. And it is everywhere and on everyone. Nore hasn't been seen since the meeting in her office. Letting the entire House in on our secret was too much of a risk. So shortly after the announcement went out, the House went into official mourning.

The last lie my House would ever stand for, she'd called it.

The estate has been scant and silent since. Flowers have been laid all over the grounds. Walls have been graffitied in bright colors in Nore's honor. Nore's maid hasn't eaten in days, inconsolable. And Yagrin has even roamed the halls with Isla, making a good show of their grief.

The night sky glows with the promise of morning over hundreds of chairs arced around a raised dais, where there is a stand for Nore's body to lie. So many have responded to the post in *Debs Daily* requesting permission to attend. At first we considered saying no, but to keep the veneer of honesty, we had to go along with it fully.

"Are you ready?" It's Abby, working with Lady Ruby to add the finishing touches to the cloak so that once the Dragunhead's wrapped in it, it renders him immovable. She looks like she hasn't slept in days. Isla and Erla sit beside a window with a view of the funeral setup outside. Erla inspects the artifact from Ruby, a long dagger with an ornate, curved handle. All is in hand. When Nore's mother isn't wailing or patrolling the halls, she hasn't spoken much. I hand her the metal box with the diadem of the Sphere's proper magic.

"Remember, it stays up here. No matter what."

"Promise me you will do whatever you can to protect her from him."

"He won't touch her."

Erla hands her a tissue.

"Do you have the rings, too?" I ask her.

Erla nods, showing me the pile she forged the last two days, several dozen. "The minute the Dragunhead is paralyzed, we take his body, and Jordan, to the lab for the blood transfusion and extraction. We will try the rings first, as Jordan wants. But we have the dagger as a backup. We are as ready as we can be."

"Very good."

"It will work, Headmistress," Erla says, and I desperately want to believe her. I leave them there, returning to Jordan, who peers outside the doors to the room where shadows loom. The Ambrose dead have taken a liking to us, particularly Jordan, following him wherever we go.

I check my watch. "Take the cloak to her," I tell Abby. "We don't have long before her body is set out at sunrise."

"You've done good," Ruby says, patting Abby on the back. She hugs me, and I squeeze her back, wondering how we actually pulled this off, so many hands on board, on the same team.

The funeral doesn't start until noon. But when the sun crests the horizon, the Dragunhead should be there. The cloak will be lying partly over Nore's body like a mourning blanket, and when he is close enough, she will toss it over him, trapping him in it. Jordan and Yagrin will be waiting to step in and apprehend him in order to take him to the lab. It isn't a perfect plan, but it is the plan we have.

And the first leg of it depends on me.

Yagrin lingers in the shadows of the room, not speaking to anyone. He watches pensively as Abby folds up the cloak and stuffs it in a bag. He and Jordan haven't spoken. And what's even more odd is that until now, anytime we were in the same room, Yagrin would leave.

"What do you make of him?" I jab a thumb back at Yagrin.

"I hurt him," Jordan says. "He's angry with me, rightfully so."

"What did you do?"

"Before they knew the Scroll was a hoax, he and Nore were planning to steal it from under our noses. He wanted to save her."

"Instead of me."

"Yes."

"Can you blame him?"

Jordan sighs. "No, I can't. But I told him if he was lying, I'd gut Nore myself."

"Jordan."

"*I know.* I knew it was wrong the minute I said it. But knowing isn't enough. I need to talk to him."

Abby drops the bag, and it rips. She groans. Jordan and I rush over. We wrangle it into a new bag for her. And once she's all set, she is out the door. The sky outside steadily brightens.

"It's nearly time. I should go."

Jordan takes my black rose corsage and ties it onto my wrist. Then he tosses my House sash over my head. "I'll be a hundred feet away, no more, watching everything. If you need me—"

I kiss his cheek. "I know."

"And remember, he will try to appeal to you in a fatherly way." Jordan strokes my face. "But you're everything already without him. You have never needed him, and you never will." He plants a kiss in the palm of my hand, and I hurry to depart the estate.

Outside, Nore is being laid on top of thousands of blue flowers. Her perfectly made-up face is a picture of her frozen in time. Her hair has been curled, and blue flower buds are sprinkled throughout it. The cloak is folded across her from the waist down. Her hands lie on top of one another on her chest. In her fingers is a single bloom. Abby was supposed to give her some kind of elixir to help her breath become shallow, but Yagrin protested, not trusting anything that would alter her ability to react quickly. So she lies there, trying to not breathe noticeably.

"Leave me," I tell everyone, before scanning the perimeter of the forest. There is no sight of the Dragunhead anywhere.

When I am alone, I whisper to Nore, "You're doing incredibly. You know, there is something that I never got to talk to you about. I probably should have before now. But thank you for welcoming my House here and standing up for unity the way you did." My suspicions about the Dragunhead have me in a knot. "If things come to light today as I suspect, I am even *more* thankful for you. For giving me an opportunity I may have never had. I've always wanted a sister."

Nore's lip twitches, and it makes me smile.

"Do you always talk to dead people?" The Dragunhead's voice sends my heart knocking into my ribs.

I face the man walking toward me with clasped hands. *Showtime.*

"I prefer to talk to people when they're alive. But if the chance escapes me . . ."

His wavy gray hair is loose down his back. He wears a thick leather coat embroidered with each House's sigil. The sleek lines of his face are sharper and more severe than I remember. And he is much taller than I recall. He walks with a stride uncharacteristic of someone of his age. How did I not notice that before?

"Well, I would never want to put you in that position." He joins me on the dais and gazes at Nore. He touches his chest, his mouth turning down.

"You can't. Because you can't die. Isn't that right?"

"Not easily." He moves closer to Nore, and I pray she is holding her breath.

"Was there anything you wanted to say to her? Your daughter."

"Many things, when she was alive. But her mother kept her away."

"That's not what I hear."

His attention moves to me. It's only then I notice a bouquet at his back. He sets it on top of Nore's body, and my insides slosh for her.

"With as much family as you've lost, aren't you grateful for a sister?"

He doesn't know my mother lives. "I wish I'd have known about her years ago." Angering him isn't the goal. I need to position him somehow with his back to Nore. But he stands across the dais from me, staring between Nore and me.

"Thank you for coming," I say, biting back my frustration and all the accusations *and magic* I wish I could hurl at him.

"You don't need to thank me, child. I should thank *you*."

My heart ticks faster.

"This wasn't my plan, Quell. I never wanted to leave you or Nore. You know, I came up with her name."

"Oh?" My throat thickens. I watch Nore, and thankfully she doesn't move. The Dragunhead's body hasn't turned away from her, but his eyes are all on me now.

"It was Noriana. But her mother said that sounded like a disease. So I shortened it. Noriana was my mother's name."

"Thadius's mother?"

"No, Quell. My real mother. Noriana Paru, daughter of Areya Paru, whose name you might have heard."

"Areya Paru is the Mother of Magic."

"That's what they called her for trying to protect her ancestors' legacy. A legacy that she didn't understand and never asked for. I always found her honorable."

Cold writhes in me. "And do you always find yourself that way?" I bite my tongue too late.

"I am sorry, Quell. I am very sorry."

My next thought abandons me, and I manage a feeble "Thank you." I clear my throat. It is small. It is probably a lie. But it is something. And for everything I've been through, my mother's been through, Jordan's been through, an apology is nice. Even a fake one.

"Your mother wouldn't hear a word about your name. It was Raquell. Period." He smiles, and I stare at the ground. He is good at pretending. Practiced at it for centuries. None of his sentiment is real.

"So then, tell me, what should I call you?"

He steeples his hands. "You can call me whatever you like. I was born Yaque Paru, eldest son of Noriana Paru and eldest grandson of Areya Paru. I was born on Daughter's Den Isle and lived there, escaping by pirate ship with the magic my mother managed to save by seeking asylum there. The island was a graveyard when I left. Cut off from the rest of the world, your books call it the—"

"Den of Bones."

"Yes. I have lived through horrors you cannot imagine."

I swallow my sharp retort and instead angle my body away from Nore to face out toward the empty concrete seats, hoping he maneuvers to stand beside me. "It's a beautiful ceremony, don't you think?"

"You are the spitting image of your mother." He stares at my profile, unmoved. "I was deeply sorry to hear about what happened to her."

I can see my mother's face, the real tears in her eyes over cherished lies.

"You should have told her. It's very hard for me to act like you didn't break her heart."

"You don't have to pretend, Quell. Be angry. I am angry at many things I've done in my time. Do you know how many mistakes a person makes in a hundred lifetimes? They will haunt me forever." He pulls a bauble out of his pocket, a gold chain with two dangling hearts. One with an *N* and one with *Q*.

I look away.

"I deserve nothing but your contempt. But can I at least tell you how we got to this point?"

Unable to think of a single reason to not listen, I gesture for him to go on.

"It started as a plan to fix things. Magic was never good or bad. It was its own power with a diversity of uses. Both magics had a role and place, and they exist best *together*. Ever since the secret of magic leaked, greed burned hot in people. Misa rose. The Uppers were established, which came with more regulations about what magic was and who could use it. People and governments alike were consumed by the power magic could give them. I watched it all. Can you imagine the responsibility I felt? Knowing it was *my* grandmother who fled to protect magic. It was her direct ancestor who had found magic in the first place. I had to fix it. I know you've felt that pressure before."

I don't respond. But I also can't move, taking all of this in. He is not who I thought he would be. Much of what he says makes so much sense.

"When Misa fell," he goes on, "people were murdered by the thousands. Families fled into hiding. I helped set up the House system, picking the families who I trusted to have a House in their name. Making good on promises I'd made to their ancestors centuries before. Some Houses were to be instituted right away; others, for the sake of the appearance of democracy, would need to be established in time. But even the House system grew unwieldy. And toushana became more shamed. So I thought of a scheme, I'll be honest, to *force* magic to exist in balance."

I watch him, still unable to move, not believing my ears.

"I remember the glory of ancient magic, the magic my family died for. That power lives in me. And magic is in the blood now, so to pass it on I had to have a child. I decided there would be two. One with a ferocious toushana. And another with brilliant mwertae magic—its ancient name—like the world has never seen. But genetics are not as easily controlled as magic. My first daughter never showed magic." He again looks at Nore, whose lips are now slightly parted.

Breath sticks in my chest.

"And my second," he continues, seeming not to notice, "was caught in a system that wanted to kill her. It took *quite* the scheming to make sure I was selected to be in charge of the brotherhood to oversee things."

"*Many* have died or lived their lives in fear because of your command."

"In the grand scheme of centuries, what are a few hundred? I can save those who matter. And I did. I became Dragunhead to make *sure* you and Nore *lived*."

"*You* want credit for saving me? No, my grandmother and mother did that."

"That is fair. But can't you see? I want what you want, a world where toushana is free."

I meet his eyes, overcome with a feeling I don't know what to do with. "So what do you want now? Because you're working with your son, who tried to kill your daughter."

He sucks in a nasally breath. "Ellery is a complicated boy. Has been since he was born. He would never have killed Nore. He loved her."

"That is not love."

"I won't make excuses, there's been much wrong done. But we are standing on the edge of the future. And I am telling you, daughter, what we can build is greater and better than anything that's ever existed. Will you hear my plan?"

He turns his back to Nore, and my heart skips a beat. But he's still a few paces too far from her for Nore to be able to reach him.

"Go on," I say.

"I know you're fond of my Dragunheart."

"He has a name."

"Jordan. His body can't handle the magic inside him. He is an obstacle for you and for magic. I *tried* to get rid of him. If we put the Sphere's magic all inside me, an immortal, it will not kill me, and it can be forever *safely* possessed. From there we can change the world, do away with the Houses and build new ones that instruct toushana. We gave mwertae magic too much dominance. It's time to flip the scales."

My conversation with Jordan after the horrors in the lab plays like a song in my mind.

"*You* would hold on to all this power? For safekeeping."

"Exactly. No one else can."

"I see."

"It is good, isn't it?" Tiny creases hug his old eyes. Even in this moment, the person sharing these confessions wears a mask. I don't even know what my father really looks like. He spreads his arms as if for a hug, and a reckless urge comes over me, to take something I never had, in case it's as sweet as I always imagined it could be. My toushana flickers in warning. But I embrace my father in a big hug.

So big, he stumbles back a step.

Then another, nearly bumping against the funeral stand.

I hold tightly to him and say, "Someone I admire once told me that the world is changed by inspiring hope in *others*. Not one person having all the power."

Nore rises like a ghost behind him, all fiery red hair and angry eyes. His stare widens as she wraps the cloak around him like jacket. His movements become slower. He groans. I race to help Nore get down from her burial table.

I turn back just as the Dragunhead throws off the cloak.

Nore and I freeze. He shifts the weighty robe to a heap of threads. Fury burns in his feeble eyes.

I stumble backward into the funeral bed. Nore shrieks as he grabs a fistful of her hair.

"*No!*" My heart hammers as I reach for my magic. I hold my palms open, but not a wisp appears.

SEVENTY-TWO

Jordan

I'm shivering, watching from behind a tall headstone as Quell and the Dragunhead talk. The ice garden is quite the distance from the funeral, but the specks against the depthless white backdrop make the funeral easier to see.

Their talk is going much longer than it should. But the Dragunhead is smooth with words. Cold magic pulses in my bones, begging to be used. The bastard stabbed me the last time I saw him. *An immortal.* There are so many things about him that make so much sense. His strange affections for history. He would sometimes have me spend the whole evening reading sections of texts aloud to him from tomes that he said he'd collected. From where, I always wondered.

My brother hasn't moved, leaning against a tree a few paces away from me, watching the scene unfold in the distance.

I should apologize to him now. But I'm not sure where to start.

"This will be over soon," I say to him. "That's some relief, isn't it?"

"Aye," he says without meeting my eyes. There is a hardness in him I've never seen before. And I've seen my brother stonewall Beaulah and our father many times. *Does he know about Father?*

"I wrote Mother," I say. "No word back yet."

He remains silent.

"Yag—"

Someone slips from the edge of the forest near the ice garden graveyard where we are. A few someones. They creep along the edge of the forest, dressed in all black, shadows coiling in their palms. *Darkbearers.* My pulse picks up. Yagrin notices them, too, pointing in that direction. I keep a finger at my lips. They don't see us.

Then a yell shreds the air.

The scene at the funeral has changed. The Dragunhead throws off the cloak. Quell stumbles. And he swipes at Nore, grabbing her by the hair. His arm is around her neck.

"The Darkbearers. Keep them back," I say.

My brother says something, but I'm rushing toward the funeral before I hear him, pulling at the icy death rushing through my veins. Closer, I can see Quell is back on her feet trying to summon magic. I pull at the threads of cold and urge my body into pieces to cloak.

The air takes me.

I reappear beside Quell, shedding my cloak. The Dragunhead cocks his head, taking all of me in.

"This is fortuitous."

Nore breathes heavily, his hand clamped tight over her mouth. Her gray eyes are all anger.

"*Let her go,*" I say.

Quell pulls my arm, shoving me back. My brother appears beside me, roiled with anger. He spews timid shadows in his hands.

"Do as he says," Yagrin says. "Let Nore go."

"Your father screamed as he burned, did you know?" His words chill me to the bone. "Do you want to know what your mother sounded like?"

Yagrin lunges, but I pull him back. He shoves my arm off him, but I hold on to him tighter until he backs away, fuming. He can hate me for the rest of his life, but neither his blood nor Nore's will be spilled here.

"Our parents have nothing to do with Nore," I say. "Let her go."

"What is she to you, Jordan? Why do you pretend to care?"

My brother's heart. "She is another daughter you've damaged. It's all over her face." I've never looked Nore in the eyes, but I've looked into Quell's plenty of times. And it isn't hard to spot the scars of a father who doesn't care. Who treated his children like pawns on a chessboard.

To my surprise, the Dragunhead gazes down his chest at her. "That's not true, Nore. Don't you listen to any of it. I made you with your mother with all kinds of great dreams for you. The irony of my ancestors dying to shepherd magic into this world. And you all would stand here *against me* possessing what's left of it."

Tears stream from Nore as she claws at his hands, scratching and scraping.

"Maybe you love your daughters in your own twisted way," I say. "They are your legacy whether you like it or not."

Quell startles, beside me. She digs her nails into my arm. "*I know what he wants*," she whispers. *"Me, remember?"* But what she does next stops my heart.

"He's right," she says. "He's immortal. The magic is safer in him. That *is* what you want, right? To make magic safe?" Quell moves closer to him, and the toushana pouring out of my body swells. "I'll trade you Nore for magic."

Yagrin and I share a glance, but she doesn't hesitate. The Dragunhead's glare narrows.

"It's the safest plan for magic. I don't like you, but I can't deny that." She pulls the diadem with the Sphere's proper magic out of her dress and sets it on the dais between us and them. "All the Sphere's proper magic now. And the toushana after we extract it from Jordan."

The Dragunhead steps toward the diadem, and my pulse spikes.

"Do something," my brother mutters.

"No," I tell him. *The world isn't mine to fix.* "I just want Nore." *That's mine to fix.* The Dragunhead picks up the diadem and works his magic over it, and the gems on the silver band glow.

"*Quell,*" Nore says. "Don't do it. Yagrin, tell her!"

But my brother is still speechless.

"We have an extraction room set up and ready," Quell says. "We can stream the Sphere's toushana into you directly. But we will transfuse your blood with his so that he survives the procedure. His body isn't strong enough otherwise. And as you know, if he dies, *all* toushana dies."

"He has to turn over Nore first," I say. "Now. You already have half of all magic."

Ambition glints in the Dragunhead's eye. Yagrin stares horrified.

"You and I could be great together, Quell. Born into an ancestral bloodline, bound to toushana, *and* with immortal blood in your genes. You're unique."

That's what she meant. That's what he wants—to put the magic in *her*. It would be stronger and greater because she is already bound to dark magic.

"Show me you can do the right thing by us for a change, and I'll consider it," she says.

The Dragunhead shoves Nore toward us. She lands in Yagrin's arms, and I finally exhale.

SEVENTY-THREE

Yagrin

Nore held on to Yagrin, and the pace of his heart slowed. "Are you alright?"

She trembled but pulled herself upright and dusted her clothes off.

"Quell is a genius," she said, and it was the last thing Yagrin expected to hear. Quell led the Dragunhead toward Dlaminaugh. Jordan trailed behind them. Yagrin hardly recognized his brother.

Nore slowed her pace. "There are Darkbearers in the forest. And Ellery out there."

Yagrin's jaw hardened. He had the one thing he wanted—Nore, back in his arms. All he had to do was break the Pact and kill his brother. The brother who'd just fought to save Nore's life. His hand grazed the shadow glove in his pocket. Now was the perfect time to pull him aside and take his heart. Nore was all Yagrin wanted. He could care less what happened with the Order and magic.

If that was true, why did he feel so ill about it?

Because his brother just saved Nore's life.

"Jordan," he called his brother, who he had thought was as good as dead. Jordan stopped. Yagrin eyed his brother's chest. Nore grabbed his arm. But she didn't need to say a word. Yagrin knew he was staring at someone he'd never met before. His brother was no longer consumed with power, the one he possessed over people because of his last name and title nor the one humming in his veins. He'd set it aside somehow. He'd stopped carrying the world on his shoulders.

Hadn't Yagrin pushed Nore away for a similar reason?

Power corrupts.

But if that were true, why was Nore still alive thanks to his brother? Yagrin's chin hit his chest.

"I can't do it," he muttered. His brother watched him, perplexed.

Nore shook his arm and gasped. "That's it! Yagrin, you don't have to."

"I gave the dead my word." His heart thundered.

"Your word about what?" Jordan asked.

"Nothing. Nothing at all, brother." He looked toward the forest. "Ellery's in the forest where we saw Darkbearers earlier," he said. "I took out a few, but I'm sure there are more. Where am I most helpful?"

Joy gleamed in his brother's green eyes. Yagrin may as well have said, *I love you.*

"I don't know what Quell is doing, but I trust her," he said. "Do what you need to do about Ellery and the Darkbearers. I'll come and help as soon as I can. Nore, I hope you're okay."

"Thank you, Jordan." Nore smiled, and it was a real one.

"I need to speak with Quell." Nore squeezed Yagrin's arm again. She was up to something. He didn't want her to go with him into the forest anyhow. It would be dangerous without magic.

"Send your Draguns," he told her. "Send the dead. Send whatever you have."

Nore kissed him before taking off. Jordan and Yagrin stood in silence.

"You're going to make it," Yagrin told him.

"If I don't, tell Mother—"

"You *will.*"

He slapped his brother on the back affectionately before taking off toward the estate.

⚜

YAGRIN LOITERED IN the ice garden until a swath of dead came, along with three Draguns, two young men and a girl with silvery-streaked dark hair. At first he was curious how Nore had convinced the ancestors, but he realized, as they marched toward the ominous quaking trees, that they shared an enemy.

"What are we looking at, exactly?" the silvery-haired girl asked. He explained what they saw the other night and that he wasn't sure how many Darkbearers there would be, or what Ellery and Adola would throw at them.

"What *are* you sure of?" one of the Draguns asked.

"That if we fail, this House falls."

The blanket of snow made the trek across the estate painfully slow. They didn't speak as they entered the forest. Yagrin's boots were frozen. Ellery's camp was a tent made of stones and draped fabric. A trench of fire had been dug around it, creating one narrow entryway. Light glowed inside the tent. But it was what was around the campsite that raised the hair on Yagrin's arms.

There were bodies everywhere.

Collapsed on the ground, folded over logs, as if they'd died suddenly, just sitting up. Their faces were purpled, mouths frothing. He smelled an overturned cup, and it reeked of something sour. *Poison.*

Commotion in the tent at the center of their camp shook Yagrin.

"I thought you said we are their only enemies," a Dragun asked him.

Yagrin signaled for them to quiet. The Draguns opened their hands, drawing toushana from the air. Yagrin had them form up around the tent, unsure if Ellery or Adola tried to escape, which direction they'd go. The dead cloaked them all in shadow. They were as prepared to confront Adola, Ellery, and however many Darkbearers were in there as they were going to be.

Metal clanged.

Someone grunted.

"Now!" Yagrin screamed, ripping the tent open.

He froze.

"Oh my word," someone said behind him. Yagrin ducked inside, trying to make sense of the horror in front of him.

Beaulah was hunched forward at a table, eyes lolled in her head, foam dripping from her purpled mouth. Her pale skin was tinged with death. Inches from her fingers was an overturned teacup on the table.

Across from her was Ellery, who didn't move either. His glassy eyes were widened in shock. He was dead.

Adola sat in the final seat at the table. She rose and broke the silence.

"Cousin, I hoped Nore would be with you. Please accept this gesture of goodwill from the *new* House of Perl."

SEVENTY-FOUR

Quell

No one in the extraction room breathes as Erla connects the Dragunhead and Jordan with spindly tubes. Light dims outside, and the study lounge turned lab glows with firelight. No one sits on the concrete armchairs or pores over the walls of books. Every person lingers on the perimeter of the room, watching Jordan and the Dragunhead sitting on two tables several feet apart.

"Lie back, please," Erla tells them both.

"Not a chance," the Dragunhead says, double fisting the diadem in his hands.

Ominous shadows lingered over the doorpost when I arrived, fingers of darkness stretching inside the room every few moments. Nore rushed to close the door just as her mother joined her side. They haven't moved since, holding hands.

I have a plan.

But Nore made it better.

The Shadow Cell magic residue Jordan gave Abby wasn't strong enough on the cloak. But it would be stronger streaming *directly* from the source—Jordan. They weren't going to put the Sphere's magic into the Dragunhead. It would still go into the rings as planned.

They were going to saturate his body with enough paralyzing magic to restrain him.

Then Nore was going to steal *his* heart—the heart of an immortal with powerful ancient magic—as an offering to her dead.

We can't kill him.

Making him a prisoner to the dead is our best hope.

With the Pact nullified, they can have his heart and it has no bearing on their House or their magic. It *does* mean Ambrose has to earn their intellect fair and square, but they wouldn't be at the mercy of the dead anymore. It is their best shot.

Jordan lies back, and I lean over to kiss him on the forehead, whispering through gritted teeth, "Shadow Cell magic."

A divot appears between his brows. I haven't had a chance to tell anyone Nore's plan. I squeeze his hand, hoping he gets my meaning.

"I hope you know what you're doing." Winkel watches from the perimeter of the room, hands stuffed in the pockets of his gray robes embroidered with blue flowers along the collar. "Our Headmistress has much faith in you."

Abby turns the handle of Lady Ruby's dagger. Winkel notices. He whispers, "It may not kill him, but in a pinch, it would slow him down. Good thinking."

I join Erla between the tables. Jordan reaches for my hand, and I lace my fingers between his. Cold inside me tugs toward him, but I hold still.

"Are we ready?" Erla asks, sliding the box of rings onto the table beside Jordan.

"Sorry, a slight change." I look at her with a deliberateness that I hope makes what I'm *not* saying clear. "No rings, Erla." I take the box and pretend to set it aside, blocking the Dragunhead's view with my body. Carefully, I pour the rings onto the table beside Jordan, out of sight. "The magic goes directly into him."

Erla grabs her necklace. "What do you mean?"

I glare at her, willing her to understand. "Run wires both ways. His blood will infuse Jordan to keep him from dying. And Jordan's magic will be siphoned into him. *No* rings." I quirk a brow slightly.

"O-oh, alright." She fidgets.

The Dragunhead hops off the table and snatches the now-empty box of rings from the table. He spots the stack hidden beside Jordan and glares at me. I go cold all over, and it's not my magic.

"We have a deal, Quell. *All* the magic, to *me*." He destroys the rings with sharp sparks of darkness like I've never seen. The rings' gold castings melt into puddles on the floor. The stones crack under the pressure of his strange magic. When he's done, the collection of rings we worked so hard to get are all gone.

I glance at the dagger in Abby's hand and swallow. The Dragunhead returns to his table and leans back without fully reclining. He drapes his hands across his body, fingers drumming on stomach.

"Get started."

I blow out a breath and nod for Erla to start. My mind spirals. Black-tinged blood travels through a tube toward Jordan as the magic moves from the Dragunhead's body to him. When it reaches Jordan, his chest expands with a deep inhale. Then his breaths grow longer and deeper. I lift his shirt, watching the bruise on his side. *Unchanged.*

"Jordan, start pushing the magic out of you."

Erla works the tubing around his fingertips. We meet eyes, and he nods imperceptibly.

Toushana laced with haze fills the tube traveling toward the Dragunhead, who sits erect, watching the magic slink closer with skepticism in his stare. Bystanders watch. Winkel grips his robes, shaking his head as if something is terribly wrong. But when the icy Shadow Cell magic connects with the Dragunhead's skin, he inhales. So sharply his head tips back, as if he's taken in a gulp of the freshest breath of air. He lies back on the stone bed with a sublime expression.

I wait, watching, waiting for him to realize.

But he hasn't yet noticed that the sleek, dark magic funneling into him is laced with a paralyzing haze. Jordan's bruise on his side begins to fade, the dark red flesh lightening and filling out around his hollowed ribs.

"It's working."

The Dragunhead grunts. It morphs to a moan. Then he thrashes on the bed, trying to sit up. He claws at the tubes. I throw my body across his, pressing him down to the table.

"Hurry! Help me pin him down."

He groans louder this time, clawing at anything he can reach as Abby and Yagrin hold down his ankles. Isla grabs him by the hair. He howls in pain.

"Jordan, *more* magic. As much as you can!" I anchor my body down across my father, holding on to the underside of his bed.

The Dragunhead grabs my throat. His grip is iron.

"*You!*" His speech slurs, the magic taking hold. I can't breathe. I claw at his wrists. My eyes burn, and my throat begs for air. He squeezes so tight the world darkens. I dig my nails deeper into his wrists, tearing at his skin. If I am dying, I am taking as much of him with me as I can.

Yagrin drives his elbow into the Dragunhead's throat. He wails, his grip on my neck slipping, and I gasp for air. I blink the world back into focus.

Shadow Cell magic still rushes through the tube toward him. When a gush of magic siphons into him, he bucks on the table, trying to fight it.

"Hold him tight!" I choke out, my lungs refilling as I pin down one of his arms. Nore grits her teeth. Isla double-wraps his hair around her arm.

The Dragunhead tries to resist my hold, but his movements grow clunky. After several moments, I can feel his muscles relax beneath me. He exhales and sinks into the table, his arms dangle at his sides, then their swaying grows stiff. Until they stop moving completey. His mouth sags as the last bit of fight goes out of him.

"Now!"

Erla rushes over. She widens the opening of the tube so his blood flows faster into Jordan. Abby dribbles a clear liquid down the Dragunhead's open mouth.

"It's a sleeping draught," she says. "I don't know how long it will work or if it will work at all. But it can't hurt."

Foam bubbles at his lips. We release him. And to my great relief the monster doesn't move. His chest rises shallowly, but the rest of him is as rigid as death. Nore exhales. Then she spits in his face before collapsing in her mother's hug.

"Jordan," I say, noticing his face has nearly drained of all color.

"He doesn't have long," Abby shouts. "This excess toushana needs to go somewhere before it forces its way into his bones."

Erla grabs me. "There are no rings."

I take the dagger from Abby but freeze. All toushana in *one* thing makes it too easy to steal.

It sounds like a thousand voices in the room talking at the same time.

"Quiet!" I can figure this out. I can get us out of this mess. If only I could— Isla shakes Nore by the arm, trying to get her to think of something.

And it hits me.

As long as magic is in one thing or one person, it will be coveted.

The Sphere's magic—the locus of control of *all* magic—has to be in *everyone*.

That's the only way to level the playing field and give everyone a fighting chance. First, we need to distribute the Sphere's toushana. Giving it to everyone in the Order sounds impossible . . .

But Isla Ambrose did it.

And Darragh Marionne used it as a cover story because she knew it was possible. I pace in a circle, tuning out the rising arguments. Winkel is trying to convince Nore to bring Kimper in.

"Isla!" I pull Nore's mother aside, who is still wiping away grief from her cheeks. "I need to know exactly *how* you poisoned Nore by accident. What did you do?"

She sniffles. "I, um, I folded enhancer stones into a dagger that were supposed to awaken magic. I used a dagger because they can hold large amounts of magic. We fold hundreds of enhancers into them. It seemed like the best choice. The enhancers folded in nicely enough. But then I let the blade touch her blood, and I—I knew something was wrong right away. Magic drained from the metal like a sieve into Nore. In seconds, black dripped from her fingers."

"And now, because magic is in the blood," I say, realizing this is the key, "it can pass down genetically." This is how we share the Sphere's magic now *and* keep it alive in all Marked for generations to come. "This is *great* news!"

"What are you thinking?" Erla asks as I hand her the dagger. Jordan's fallen unconscious. The Sphere's toushana is agitated. We need to hurry.

I hand Erla the blade. Nore hovers near the Dragunhead's body, waiting for my signal with a dark glove in hand. Erla cuts an incision into Jordan's side and slides the dagger against his ribs. The blade glows red, then darkens. She holds it there, and I watch as black peels itself off his insides and siphons into the dark silver.

"Is it working?"

But Erla doesn't answer. Her mouth pushes sideways in consternation. Jordan groans. Then his head lolls.

"What's happening!"

"He's tired," Erla says. "Talk to him."

"Stay with me," I tell him. "Can I try?"

She hands me the blade's handle, and I hold it firmly against him, watching his chest rise and fall slower than before. The stream of blood running to his body from the Dragunhead slows as well.

"Jordan, can you hear me? We've done it! The world is not yours to fix, but dammit, this is. *You stay with me! You fight.*" Tears sting my eyes. "*Hold on* with everything you have. You *can't* leave me now. Not when we've nearly won." I press my forehead to his, tears forcing their way down my cheeks. "I can smell saltwater. Can you hear the waves?" I sob against him, my tears dripping onto his face.

His mouth moves.

Then his hands.

"*His bruise*," Erla says. His purpled skin fades like a ship on the horizon. Gradually, after several long minutes, what feels like a lifetime, the layers of rot fade from his ribs, leaving thick, sturdy bones in their place.

Jordan gasps, batting his eyes open.

And I can finally breathe again.

SEVENTY-FIVE

Nore

Yagrin and Nore descended on the ice garden. She held the glass box with her heart in her hand and the shadowy glove with the Dragunhead's heart beneath her coat.

"Why are we here again?"

He didn't know her plan. She'd just dragged him out of there as fast as she could once Jordan was up and talking. She wasn't even sure it would work. The dead were prickly. They'd made a deal with Yagrin for Jordan's heart. Showing up with a different one was a risk.

"Just trust me."

Yagrin's hand slid up her back as they walked. And she couldn't help but lean into the comfort. If this didn't work, this would be the last time she saw him. When you renege on a deal with the dead, the penalty is death.

When they rounded the corner, Nore gasped at the number of dead she found. The amount of shadows had grown tremendously.

Yagrin stuck near her side.

"What exactly happened in that forest?" she asked. "You never said."

He set a hand on her shoulder. "Your brother is dead. I'm sorry."

A strange discomfort nudged her. The brother who she'd loved, the only one who had ever tried to protect her, was gone. And she hadn't even said goodbye. She hadn't even gotten to see his face one more time. Yagrin's touch slid to her hand. She held his hand, realizing she *had* seen her brother before he died. He was lost the minute he turned on her. The brother she loved was long gone and had been for some time.

"Thank you," she told him.

But before Yagrin could respond, Nore pointed in the distance at the snowy landscape. The grounds were covered with overturned holes, dug-up graves every several paces. Had they found a way to raise more dead? Her hands were slick on the glass box when the darkness closed in around Yagrin. She watched as a message appeared on the ground.

YOUVE COME TO FULFILL OUR DEAL

"I have," she said with a lump in her throat. She blew out her fear with an exhale and held out the glass box. "You will give me back my heart as promised. But I don't have the Dragunheart's heart."

Shadows thrashed in a vortex of anger. Darkness encircled Yagrin's wrists, stringing him up in the air. He uttered something. Nore watched her heart to see if it had just stopped because she could not breathe.

"Let him go!"

SEALED IN BLOOD

The agreement was airtight. If he didn't deliver up the heart, his blood, his *life*, was theirs. He was completely at their mercy.

"*Nore*," Yagrin pleaded. "Go, just run!"

She balled her fists. "No! I have something better." She pulled out the Dragunhead's heart, and the dark bloody lump pulsed slowly in the glove.

"You want *powerful* magic? You want a heart you don't have to chase down heir after heir for? A heart that won't ever die?" She held the heart up for their inspection. "The heart of an immortal! With ancient magic that's been dead for centuries."

Abby and the others were filling the Dragunhead with more Shadow Cell magic before burying his body in a concrete tomb under their ice garden. He would be gone forever, but his immortal heart could belong to the dead. It was better than Jordan's heart. And certainly better than hers.

The dead didn't move.

"If you take this, you will *never again* be forced to rely on our Headmistresses to survive. This frees you, too!"

Shadows encroached, inspecting the heart closely. Darkness slid past her, chilling her skin at each spot they grazed. Yagrin still hung captive in the air.

The dead swiped at her fingers.

She pulled the heart back inside her cloak. "Annul the deal you made with him." She held out the glass box with her heart in it to them once again. "Free me and end the Pact with my House *forever*. You will have an immortal heart. But *no* connections or claims to influence in our House."

The dead writhed around her. More than she'd ever seen. She watched the snow for a message, hardly breathing. She waited, clinging to the only thing she had, a gift from the love of her life—hope.

When they dropped Yagrin, he hit the ground with a thud. The jolt sent life through her limbs. She inhaled deeply, watching as they opened the glass box, removed her heart, and crushed the glass box to nothingness. Her breath quickened as she handed over the Dragunhead's heart and took her thumping organ from them.

The dead rose, clearing the ice garden and disappearing into the snowy abyss.

Nore was breathless. She held her heart tight and collapsed against Yagrin. He scooped her up into his arms and rushed her inside.

AINSLEY WAS INSIDE Nore's quarters, finishing up lighting candles everywhere. There were flowers all over the room and tiny chocolates in the shape of a heart. She plowed into Nore with a huge hug, wiping her eyes.

"They explained everything." She sniffed. "I thought you were dead."

Ainsley buried her in a hug again, and Nore hugged her back. When the maid calmed, she smoothed her clothes and finished primping the flowers.

"I don't understand," Nore said.

"Either way, I knew today would be a day of celebration for you," Yagrin said. "I was getting your heart back, whatever it took."

"Well, that took a turn, didn't it?" She smiled. Yagrin set her down gently on the bed as Ainsley finished decorating. Soft light flickered along the dull walls, and it felt like the room was coming to life. The flowers he'd chosen were stunning, in every shade, pinks, purples, yellows, and blues. Nore still held her heart tight to her, blinking over and over, still not sure this was real. But it was there, warm and beating, in her hands. She was free.

"I'm *so* relieved you're alright, Headmistress." Ainsley's clothes were stained, and she looked as if she had stayed awake since Nore saw her last.

"Thank you, Ainsley, for everything."

Her maid smiled, swiping one last tear before tucking Nore's frigid toes under two blankets and leaving.

It's over. It's all over.

"Are you feeling well?" Yagrin asked.

"I think so." Nore tried to put some pep in her tone. But it was the next part she was most scared of. Would she feel like her old self again with her heart back? Yagrin worked at the fire, building its flames. When he finished, he joined her at her bedside. She opened the glove, showing him her heart.

"Is this really happening?" Tears welled in her eyes. And she realized his were watery as well.

"Come back to me," he whispered, urging her heart closer to her chest.

"Would you?" She handed him the glove with her heart, and she knew it had never been in safer hands. Then she pulled her shoulders back, creating space in her chest.

"Ready?"

She inhaled. He drove her heart back in place. Her lungs swelled with air. A flood of memories rushed through her, every heartless moment she and Yagrin had shared the last few weeks. Tears came strong, gushing down her face.

"How do you feel?" Yagrin held her face in both hands, and it rocked her soul. She felt such adoration in his touch. She could feel her heart twinge with that nostalgic ache of love.

She tangled their fingers together. "I'm so sorry I couldn't give you the part of me you deserve most."

"All you can give is what you have each day. Whatever you give is enough." His words tended her soul like a garden starved of sunlight. "You are enough. Heart or no heart. I love you, Nore."

Words rushed through her and sprang out like water from a fountain. "And I love you."

His lips found hers. His kiss was soft and so tender. She opened up to deepen the kiss, and her mind flooded with their happiest memories. He trailed kisses down her jaw, and she felt her love for him awaken with each thump of her heart. He held her tighter, a bubbly feeling buzzing through her chest. It sparkled and felt like a puzzle piece of her soul just slotted into place.

They held each other close, wriggling in the covers around each other, and the waist of her pants slipped down past her hip bone, exposing the hemlock flowers she'd tattooed there. Yagrin studied the mark.

"I couldn't fathom this," she said.

"Oh, how wrong you were." He pressed his lips to her hip, kissing those poisonous flowers, before bringing his affection back to her neck. He nuzzled her there and then gazed back into her eyes. He looked at her as if he could see *through* her. She was fully clothed and yet felt naked, exposed, vulnerable, and safe.

She urged his body back against her pillows and loved on his neck before pressing kisses all over his bare chest. The chest that held a heart *full of hope* for her when she'd had none. He pulled her mouth up, and they kissed until time became a montage of sweet memories and happy tears. Until every nerve in her body prickled like a string on a bow strung too taut.

"I love you. I love you so much." She rested against his chest and let her eyes close, forgetting about everything else. She drifted to sleep free of disguises and lies, free of a life she didn't want.

She fell asleep who she chose to be.

Listening to the thrum of her love's heart.

EPILOGUE

Quell
Three months later

House of Marionne is more magnificent than it's ever been as all manner of guests stream through its doors.

The estate is fully repaired but also reoriented a bit. The rose garden has been replanted. I replaced the garden of black roses with white lilies, which remind me of new beginnings. The Belles and Gents Wings have been expanded to accommodate twice the number of students. And as the grand entrance doors open, welcoming another announced couple, I spot my favorite addition: a new statue. There are two statues on the grounds now. The one my grandmother had made of her mother and sister, and another of just Grandmom in her old age, holding a single rose, the way I remember her.

Violin and piano notes dance on the lively atmosphere as more seats in the ballroom fill.

"Still surprised you didn't get rid of the tradition of a formal ceremony and dance altogether." Jordan lingers beside me, keeping an eye on the guests trailing from the entrance into the grand ballroom, where the ceremony is about to begin. He's in a dapper white tux. There is no sash across him or heart pendant. He does not wear any vestige of the Order at all. And while he is still bound to toushana and would have it no other way, he has washed his hands of any formal role completely.

"No one gets dibs on ceremonies, dances, or formal dinners. We have to keep creating new traditions. There's much work to do. But inclusivity means giving access to old traditions to everyone. That's freedom." I chuckle. "That was the easy decision. I'm still not sure having the inaugural induction for the *new* Order here at Chateau Soliel made the most sense?"

"Determined to spiral about something, are you?"

"Fair. But nothing worries you these days."

"Jealous?" He grins an infectious smile that fills his eyes with amusement. Leaving the Order behind was the best decision he ever made. I wasn't sure where it made the most sense to host our first Induction Ceremony for the new and improved Order, a true—*Nova Misa*—but the other House leaders insisted it was fitting to host it at mine. There are so many new faces it wriggles my stomach with nerves. Jordan ropes his arm onto mine as I wave at a familiar face coming through the doors: Kedd, from Willam's old safe house, with a date on his arm. The twins are with them, much bigger than I remember.

As the foyer crowd thins, we follow them inside. There are flower arrangements everywhere, tables draped in every House color, including black. There are pink-and-gold plates with matching flatware, sparkly dark jewels hanging from branches sprouting out of luscious centerpieces. Silks slope along the ceiling in rippling patterns in every House color. Shimmering chandeliers dangle above a center table that runs the length of the room. I spot Dexler and wrangle her over.

"You've done a beautiful job on this." It took her a week to wake up and nearly a month to fully heal. I notice two others behind her. One in particular that makes my heart squeeze. My mother's arms are open before she reaches me. We hug, and it will never get old. Knox is with them.

"I couldn't have done any of this without their help," Dexler says. "It was a team effort."

Knox smiles. My mother pinches my arm and winks. "Proud of you, ma'am."

A group of débutants trails behind my mother, chattering among themselves with excitement. She brought them with her from their hideaway. Nova Misa won't be a legend or a secret anymore. Now it will be real. Dexler whisks them all away to their seats before I get too mushy-eyed.

At the long head table is a place for the Order's leadership. Drew is in their appointed Headship seat, having their champagne refilled, while Nore, beside them, gushes about something that must be quite funny.

"She looks like she's recovering just fine," I tell Jordan. After the Dragunhead was buried, with Erla's help, Nore underwent a similar extraction procedure to remove the seed of toushana that had begun to grow in her. She was truly free, as she'd always wanted to be. The procedure's success ended up being a great help to my mother as well, who was able to offer it to any in hiding with her who wanted free of the toushana they didn't ask for. Some kept it; others did not. But their hideaway was disassembled, and everyone was invited here today to join the Order properly if they'd like. A Nova Misa for everyone.

"Is Litze here?" Jordan asks, scanning.

"Oh, did I not tell you? Ever since Drew ousted her as Headmistress by popular vote, she's been on sabbatical in Fiji for an indeterminate amount of time."

Jordan rolls his eyes, and I giggle. Former Draguns fill the seats, along with many from Zecky's safe house. I can't imagine they are all here, but whoever wants into Nova Misa will be given the benefit of the doubt and a chance. Everyone gets a clean slate, and a chance to pick their own path. If they choose violence and carnage, they will be dealt with accordingly. But they won't be judged by their past. Knox leads a line of friends bound to dark magic to a row near the front before flagging down Willam to say hello to him. But he sits in the last seat at the farthest end of the table, tying and retying his bow tie.

"You should really help him," I tell Jordan.

"You're right. Poor guy." He heads that way.

The audience chairs are nearly filled, with all eyes on the center of the ballroom at seven raised stands. One for each House. There is a hand-painted sculpted fleur-de-lis I found in my grandmother's study on one stand. An ancient set of Duncan-esque balancing scales on another. A tied bushel of dried yew leaves is in an ancient stone vase from House of Ambrose, a bouquet of the most beautiful red roses with spiky thorns is wrapped with a leather strap courtesy of Adola, an ornately hand-carved and painted mask preserved by Drew Oralia, a hand-carved sun on another, and a golden heart on the last stand.

Dexler gestures for me to join her at the front, and my stomach's nerves never cease to surprise me. This is the first time the Order has ever welcomed anyone who wants magic to take their pick on House *and* type of magic. I look for Erla but realize she's beaten me to the front, decked out in a jade-green dress ornamented with jewels dangling from her ears fit for ancient gods. She's breathtaking.

"Headmistress." She greets me with a hug before handing me a slender box. I peek inside, and there are two daggers there, the one Lady Ruby gave us imbued with dark magic, and the other an ancient leather-handled blade Dexler found in the Chateau's attic.

"You did it!" I asked Erla to move the Sphere's mwertae—proper—magic from the diadem into a dagger as well, to make sure they present equitably to the masses. Neither is favored anymore. Toushana will be as available and as revered as any other kind of magic.

"And you're sure it'll work for people who have already used some born-magic inside them?"

"Being anointed by binding with the Sphere's magic directly is *such* an overwhelming amount of power directly to the heart, it'll reset their magical affinity. If they want to keep training in the strand of mwertae magic they already know, they don't need to be reanointed. But if they want to try a new strand, of either variety, they can plunge the dagger into their heart, and it'll function like a fresh anointing of Sun Dust."

"Saying 'Thank you' doesn't quite seem enough."

"You can forgive me." She winks and hip-bumps me. "For abandoning you."

I purse my lips, pretending to give her a hard time. *Everyone* got to choose their own House. And Erla really loved Dlaminaugh. So that's where she's chosen to stay. They are making her a maezre to head up their Anatomics section.

"You will do well there. My hope is that together we can steer this ship in a better direction."

"We will." She gestures at the table. "Look at our leadership."

I hug her again just as the horn blows, signaling the start of the ceremony, when I realize there are still two chairs empty at the head table. Yagrin enters the ballroom with his cousin Adola on his arm. They hustle to the front, to their respective seats. Adola, Headmistress of House Perl.

And Yagrin, the new Dragunhead.

Of a *new* brotherhood.

I step up on the dais. All eyes are on me. Dexler clears her throat, making her way to the front with a walking stick. She's been on the mend still, but it's a relief to see her awake and up on her feet. When I spot my mother in the crowd, she winks. I search for Jordan and find him leaning on a back wall. He blows me a kiss and taps his watch.

I finally stop rehearsing in my head what I want to say and just start. "Welcome, everyone, to the inaugural induction into Nova Misa, a magical guild of mwertae and toushana!"

The audience erupts in cheers. I look out to the crowd and see there are all manner of people—ancient House families, newer ones, former safe housers, ambitious young Marked ones, older ones, too. And I can't help but feel like *this* is what Sola Sfenti envisioned when he discovered magic. Something special. Something lasting. Something for everyone.

"Before I go any further, I'd like Yagrin Wexton to stand."

He shuffles awkwardly as he stands. Nore beams. I told her my plan, and she loved it to pieces.

"Today you will also have the choice to select admission into the brotherhood. No longer by invite only and with a *brand-new mission.* Yagrin, tell us about it."

His cheeks flush. "I have to admit I never saw this role for myself. But, um, I'm looking forward to leading a *new* brotherhood that, instead of punishing people for how they live, serves to *protect* the rights of all members to pursue magic of their choosing."

The explosion of applause is more raucous than before. Some of Willam's friends stand. It's contagious, and in minutes the room rings with applause. I thank Yagrin, and once everyone quiets, I manage to give my welcome speech and facilitate induction without passing out from nervousness.

Thirty-seven new faces join House of Marionne. Half chose the toushana track, plunging Ruby's dagger into their hearts. The others chose the mwertae track, binding with the ancient House blade. And one ambitious pupil wanted to try both. So we let him. The other Houses picked up a bunch of new débutants for their roster. Willam nabbed several. He gave a spiel about how his House will be smaller, with more individualized attention and focus on empowering people very new to magic. That perked up many in the audience.

By afternoon, the ballroom was full of dancing revelry, and for the first time in my life, I *didn't* want to say yes when Jordan sashayed his way over to me with a quirked brow.

"Come on, one spin around the room?" he pleads with those gorgeous green eyes.

"I cannot move another inch." I kick off my shoes.

"Does that mean *our* sabbatical is officially beginning?" He rubs his hands together, and I'm not sure I've ever seen Jordan Wexton more excited to do literally nothing but lie on a beach.

"My mother said she will stop by."

He nuzzles my neck. "Hopefully she calls first."

"Knox has my instructions. She's in charge. My mother's staying on to help." I shrug. "I think we can tiptoe out of here." The estate rings with celebration as we exit the ballroom. The air is full of laughter. The Audiors we reserved will be playing until sunup.

"We did good, I think."

"*You* did good."

"Sure." We lace fingers, and I turn my back to all of the House business, when Yagrin comes darting through the ballroom doors. "You're heading out?"

"Yes. Try not to break everything we just fixed," I joke. He laughs. Yagrin and Jordan stare awkwardly. This is the first time they've seen each other since everything happened at Dlaminaugh. Jordan and I returned to the Chateau right away.

"How long are you going?" Yagrin asks.

"No idea, really," Jordan says.

"Mom said you *have to* try the street food there."

"I will." Jordan shifts on his feet. Yagrin does, too. Then they tackle each other in a hug that brings joyful tears to my eyes. They hold each other for a long moment. When they break the embrace, Jordan swipes beneath his eye. Yagrin slaps him on the back before retreating inside.

The car waiting for us outside the Chateau is loaded down with our things. I packed a bunch. Way more than I'll need.

"After you, Miss Marionne." Jordan opens the door for me.

"Where to?" the driver asks once we're snuggled up inside.

"Freedom. True freedom."

APPENDIX

THE HOUSES AND THEIR HISTORIES

MEMENTO SUMPTUS

HOUSE OF PERL

Est. 1822
At Hartsboro Estate
Territory: East and Northeast

Hartsboro Estate, located in Connecticut, was originally the operating Headquarters of the Order's governing body: the Upper Cabinet. In 1822, on the heel of the Sorting Years, to support the development of the Order's growing member numbers, Upper established a formalized magic-studying system using a boarding school model. Members would continue in the débutante tradition, which had been in practice since the onset of the Industrial Revolution, but be organized into Houses and territories. Houses would be overseen by a Headmistress.

    The Upper Cabinet relocated its Headquarters and commissioned its first House: House of Perl, naming Beatrice Perl inaugural Headmistress. At the time, Beatrice had been serving in the Cabinet. Before agreeing to sign on, she insisted that the seat of the House pass down in family lineage by the matriarch. Upper agreed, and so it remains. The House of Perl sigil is a cracked column.

SUPRA ALIOS

HOUSE OF MARIONNE

Est. 1874
At Chateau Soleil
Territory: Southern

House of Marionne was the second established House of the Order as their numbers swelled, with more and more showing a propensity for magic. The origins of the philosophies that shaped House of Marionne are rooted in the Era of Indulgence.

After the fall of Yaäuper Rea Universitas, the Silent Years followed. Formal magical education had come to a screeching halt as it was forced to shift to underground. It is said generations of magical people lost their magic because of sparse access to training, study, and development, until a lowly but studious Order member, Loken Delosu, was sought out by King George I of England. He was courting Loken's affections, as he'd heard rumors his family dabbled in sun magic. George was in a long-standing war with the French and wanted any edge he could get. Around that same time, King Louis XIV, the "Sun King," heard of George's interest in Loken and sent his own parties to sway Loken. Louis, being a man of abundance, showered gifts and hospitality at the feet of Loken and his family, his friends, anyone he knew, in exchange for one thing—his company.

King Louis XIV was incredibly ambitious and eventually pressed Loken directly to know more about magic, but Loken refused. He held to the age-old tenet that magic should be kept far away from government. Louis beheaded him. The Order was divided on how to feel about the French and English years of courtship. But the years dabbling in French culture had left its mark evident in House of Marionne's architecture, culture, traditions, and art. The Upper Cabinet commissioned Claudette Marionne as inaugural Headmistress. The House of Marionne sigil is a fleur-de-lis.

COGITARE DE PRETIO

HOUSE OF DUNCAN

Est. 1875
At Wigonshire Estate
Territory: West and Midwest*

House of Duncan was established on the heels of House of Marionne at the urging of Upper Cabinet members who were rumored to favor House of Perl's Dysiian influences. The House was intended to be a replica in culture and architecture of House of Perl but located in Colorado. The estate's inaugural Headmistress was Maisie Duncan. In 1938, an explosion in the Midwest killed thousands of Unmarked. The news reported that the accident was the result of an industrial explosion. However, House of Duncan, whose new Headmistress was experimenting with using toushana to mine gold, was behind the tragedy. The dark magic she'd been illegally using spiraled out of control, and twenty-three hundred barrels of kor elixir leaked into an oil shipment being transported west. The result was catastrophic. The Upper Cabinet shut down the House immediately and required each member within its territories to reapply. Most were denied on grounds of distrust. The then Headmistress, Beil Duncan, was publicly beheaded, a rare but symbolically vicious act at the time. The House of Duncan sigil was a scale and darkened sun.

*The Midwest territory, formerly under House of Duncan, was initially moved to House of Ambrose. In later years the Midwest was split, its northern side under Ambrose territory and its southern side under Oralia.

INTELLECTUS SECAT ACUTISSIMUM

HOUSE OF AMBROSE

Est. 1877
At Dlaminaugh Estate
Territory: Northwest and parts of the Midwest

House of Ambrose, nestled in the tallest peaks of central Idaho, was the fourth established House of the Order. Its inaugural Headmistress was Caera Ambrose, a well-known member of the Order who had built her reputation on leading efforts to push the bounds of understood magic. Her views were seen as outlandish, but she received the votes needed from the Upper Cabinet. Caera's ancestors were immigrants to America with a strained and hostile history with Europeans. Thus, Dlaminaugh Estate was erected as a neo-Gothic replica of Yaäuper Rea Universitas and commissioned to be the first House in the Order that defined itself as distinctly separate from European influence. Caera desired to usher forward a generation of débutants who would be known for their supreme intellect, not ostentatious shows of wealth. The House of Ambrose sigil is three yew leaves intertwined.

UTI VEL AMITTERE

HOUSE OF ORALIA

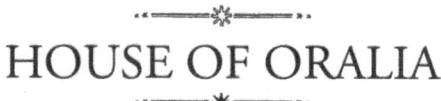

Est. 1942
At Begonia Terrace
Territory: West and parts of the Midwest

House of Oralia was the fifth and final established House, located in northern California. Donya Oralia was its inaugural Headmistress. Her grandmother had been a candidate for Uppership but was ultimately passed over because of her progressive views on women's rights at the time. In 1942, House of Oralia was commissioned by a slim majority vote, as the world was engrossed in World War II. They are known for using magic as a means of artistic expression and enjoyment, believing magic serves the wielder and not the other way around. The House of Oralia sigil is two smudged dollops of paint.

THE DRAGUN BROTHERHOOD

Est. Late nineteenth century
Headquarters: Wexton MidCenter Hotel

Dysiis was a student of Yaäuper Rea Universitas who believed that to understand the full breadth of magic's capacity to be a positive influence, one had to understand the full intricacies of its darker parts. He studied toushana until he died. His studies were stored in the university library, despite much concern at the time that they could inflame if they fell into the wrong hands. Several decades later, a faction grew among magic pupils who were fascinated by Dysiis's teachings. Dysiisians took his teachings further, believing there was a place for the destructive magic in their world. Since so little was understood about the dark, powerful magic, the faculty at Yaäuper Rea Universitas forbade the study. Groups continued to meet about toushana in secret, and for a century, Darkbearers, a rebel group of toushana-users, used the destructive magic to terrorize villages, amass their own power, and infiltrate the highest levels of Church and State. This era is known as the Second Coming, referring to the Age of Vultures returned. It persisted until a group of Yaäuper Rea alumni banded together (referring to themselves as "Sunbringers") to bring Darkbearers to justice. Sunbringers used toushana, but only as needed to apprehend Darkbearers.

They found burning the rebellious dark-magic users was the only way to ensure they and their toxic magic were dead, earning them the nickname Draguns.

When the city of Misa fell, the Order began building the House system. The next century was called the Sorting Years, when safe houses were illicitly erected to harbor toushana-users who'd fled Misa. The Upper Cabinet recruited descendants of Sunbringers, or "Draguns," to serve in an official capacity as a security, protection, and intelligence force: the brotherhood. In the early years, Houses were allowed to nominate débutants for the brotherhood before it shifted to by invitation only. Some Draguns can trace their lineage to original Sunbringers.

The brotherhood underwent significant shifts in leadership shortly after the death of the Headmistress and rise of a new Headmistress of House of Marionne. All former Draguns were disbanded and a new order was established to focus Dragun work on protecting Order members' right to explore and practice both branches of magic: mwertae and toushana.

LEXICON

BINDING—the process of joining the enhanced magic, now held within the dagger's blade, with the magic user by plunging the magical dagger into the user's heart.

COTILLION—a formal ball at which débutants are presented for membership into the Order, a ceremony that includes completing Third Rite in front of an audience of members and publicly agreeing to the membership oath.

DARKBEARER—a group of magical persons in the thirteenth century who bound to toushana.

DRAGUN—a nickname for a Sunbringer, a uniquely skilled member of the Order trained to hunt and eradicate threats from the Order, primarily those with forbidden magic.

DRAGUN BROTHERHOOD—the community of Draguns across Houses, which collectively makes up the law enforcement and security force of the Order.

DRAGUNHEAD—the senior member of the Dragun brotherhood, a rank equal to the Headmistresses in authority, but with a separate and autonomous jurisdiction over all Draguns.

DRAGUNHEART—the senior understudy to the Dragunhead, a rank with second-in-command authority over all Draguns.

ELECTUS—a neophyte débutant who has not yet completed First Rite.

EMERGING—the manifestation of one's magic as either a jeweled mask across the top half of the face or a diadem arced above the head, proving one's magic is strong enough to be molded and used. Each person's magic is unique, and how it manifests will vary according to the magical heritage, skills, and talents of the magic user.

ESSENCE—the translucent aroma temporarily left behind where a magical person dies.

FIRST RITE—emerging a diadem from one's head or a mask on one's face.

HEADMISTRESS—the lady in charge of a magical training school.

HONING—the process of refining a dagger by forging it with gems to enhance its magical effectiveness.

MARKED—a person with a demonstrated capacity for proper magic use.

PRIMUS—a débutant who has passed First Rite and is actively working on Second Rite.

SECOND RITE—honing a dagger by folding specified enhancers into a blade to infuse one's own magic with added power.

SECUNDUS—a seasoned débutant who has passed Second Rite and is actively working on Third Rite.

SIGIL—an inscribed or painted symbol that represents a particular House and its set of values.

THE SPHERE—a magically encased orb that houses a connection between ancient magic and all magical people.

THE UPPER CABINET—established in the early eighteenth century, the Upper Cabinet was the original governing body of the Prestigious Order of Highest Mysteries, consisting of twelve male members.

THIRD RITE—binding with one's magic by plunging a fully honed dagger into one's heart in front of an audience of members at a Cotillion ceremony.

TOUSHANA—a forbidden, destructive magic.

UNMARKED—a person without magic.

ACKNOWLEDGMENTS

I just finished writing the end of this trilogy and am staring at the final page in disbelief. Bringing a world of characters to an end is no easy task, especially when you've lived with them for six years. I've written so many more thousands of words of these characters' lives than ever made it to the page. I can't believe it's done! *Or is it?* Ha! There are so many more stories I'd love to tell in this universe. But sometimes the best thing you can do for a story is give it time to breathe. So we will call this the end of the series for now, and we will see what the future brings.

This series would not have been possible if it weren't for *so* many who dragged me across each finish line. First, I'm so grateful to God for the gift of storytelling that's such a part of who I am and who I was created to be. I am so blessed to be able to call this "hobby" a full-time gig. What a dream. I also could not finish a single story without the generous support of my husband, who single-handedly holds the house together when I need to disappear into the writing/editing black hole. Thank you for handling the overly stinky litter box, for mastering a spaghetti recipe the kids prefer even over mine, for being my driver, for keeping me from getting abducted from a random airport, for keeping me punctual (ish), and for going along with all my wild ideas. Oh, and agreeing to get chickens! Thank you, beloved, for all that you are and everything you are becoming. You inspire me.

My three (not so little) little buddies—Mariah, Daniel, and Sarah Grace—thank you for the deep sighs and teenager-y (these are new!) eye rolls when I tell you, "I can't, I'm on deadline." I cherish how much you covet every single second you can spend with me and your dad. I love that you guys are family-time junkies! I am so, so grateful for your endless patience and understanding when I missed evenings of laughter, game nights, vacation shenanigans, unforgettable sports games, and so many other seemingly tiny moments. Keep giving me a hard time. Keep reminding me of what's most important. I love you each to the moon and back.

Jodi Reamer, you are the best.

Full stop.

Thank you for coming into my life right when I needed you and creating space for me to envision a life for my family that was inconceivable. Thank you for middle-of-the-night emails, for always listening when I need an ear, for fighting for me like no one else can, for always telling me the truth, and for pushing me to believe in myself even more. And thank you for introducing me to the wonderful powerhouse publishing team at Penguin Young Readers.

Ruta, you are such a gift to work with. Your fierce advocacy for things you're passionate about is contagious, and I feel very lucky to have you in my corner. Thank you for caring as deeply as you do. Thank you to Jen L and Jen K, who are constantly cheerleading and saying yes to all my out-of-the-box ideas! Thank you to the incredible marketing and publicity teams. Felicity, *my dearest Shannon*, Tracy—designer extraordinaire, James! Kaitlin and Jaleesa, I appreciate the support, so much. Special thanks to the sales team for how hard you work to help this book reach its readers. I couldn't have dreamed of a more ideal match to launch this series into the stratosphere.

Kassie, thank you for your big goals and dreams for this series, and for my work overall. I am so lucky to have you. Thank you to countless others who have had their hands on this series who I've never gotten to meet. I appreciate every single minute of your time. So much goes into getting books out, and I take none of it for granted.

My work could never have made it to my editor's desk if it weren't for a few people who kept my fingers moving over the keyboard over the years. Emily Golden, the peas to my carrots, the strawberry jam to my peanut butter, literally half of my writing brain, I love you so big! Thank you for enduring the pace of my publishing life right alongside me. Thank you for letting "the curse" upend your life, too, ha ha! I couldn't imagine doing life the way we do with anyone else. This book, this series, would not exist without you.

Thank you to the other biggest believer in this series—Ali Hazelwood, who attacked me in a New York elevator with her love and support. Who lets me drag her all over the country to shout about these characters. And who keeps a drawer of clothes for me that I recklessly leave when I stay over. Your kind heart is rare in this world, sweet friend. I adore you.

Thank you to my sweet Ronni for *Sims* and Zoom dates. For being in Manhattan the minute I needed you on tour. Your friendship got me through the pandemic, and we're still going strong. You make my days brighter. ☺

Thanks to every writer and friend who encouraged me along the way. Especially Del S and Andonnia, who are always willing to read at the drop of a hat! Diana, you too! I'll never understand how you all read so fast. Thank you to Lindsay, the love guru. Thank you, Julie Lochridge. Your artistry has been one of the unforgettable highlights of publishing this series. Thank you, Denean, my sister, who walks with me each day. Thank you to Jennifer, whose idea about skulls and crowns sparked a fury of inspiration in me for this world.

Thank you to every author who took time to blurb and boost this series, those who showed up for tour events, made time in their schedules, welcomed me into a genre of YA fiction I am so new to. I appreciate you more than you know. Sabaa, my sweet friend, thank you for always holding me up. Victoria, your kindness has been so refreshing. Adam S, Alex A, Nicola, Stephanie G, Rachel G, Adalyn G, Kerri, Jordan G, Shelby M, Brigid K, Alex B, Marissa M, Jason J, Jumata, Tricia L, Jennifer Lynn—you all have been so supportive, and it means the world to me. I am inspired by your success. Blue Willow Bookshop, thank you for rooting for me always! Cathy and Cherry-Pie-Baking Jen—I love you oodles!

There are a bazillion more people I could thank. The list is truly endless. For those whose names I couldn't fit here, please know that every single like, comment, share, preorder, word-of-mouth mention, et cetera—*all of it*—means the world to me.

But my biggest thank-you goes to you, reader. Without your support through *three books*, WOW, I wouldn't have been able to bring this series to shelves. Thank you so much for following Quell, Jordan, Nore, and the fan fave—*Yagrin*—this far! I hope you have found something in this story that tends your heart.

You are worthy, your magic is special, and you are lovable *just as you are*.